OREGON
WEDDINGS

OREGON WEDDINGS

THREE-IN-ONE COLLECTION

KATHLEEN E. KOVACH

BARBOUR
PUBLISHING

Cover design: Kirk DouPonce, DogEared Design

Published by Barbour Publishing, Inc., P.O. Box 719, Uhrichsville, Ohio 44683, www.barbourbooks.com

Our mission is to publish and distribute inspirational products offering exceptional value and biblical encouragement to the masses.

ecpa Member of the
Evangelical Christian
Publishers Association

Printed in the United States of America.

Dear Readers,

I enjoyed writing about southern Oregon. Although I've never lived there, I have family who reside in and love the area. It was in visiting them that I first experienced it. I have been to all of the places in this book. . .several times. Ashland and its creativity, the coast and it's wild nature, the phenomenon called Crater Lake—I've loved it all and am so honored to place my characters in these settings.

My desire is that you see Oregon as another character as you read—that you will feel her breath, hear her heartbeat, and fall in love with her as I have. I will visit her often, and I hope after reading this book, that if you're not already captivated, you will sojourn into her borders and explore every facet of what makes her unique.

The three stories within these pages, while showcasing a beautiful location, also venture within the human spirit. In *God Gave the Song*, Skye Randall and Ruthanne Fairfax learn how to forgive others through the help of a melodious alpaca. In *Crossroads Bay*, Meranda Drake seeks a family treasure while Paul Godfrey seeks her heart. And in *Fine, Feathered Friend*, Glenys Bernard is an actress afraid of birds who enlists the help of a bird trainer afraid of actresses.

In all three stories, God is the main character leading the players through their own paths that lead to righteousness. Forgiveness, yielding, and trust are the themes explored in these fictional lives, but my prayer is that you, the readers, will glean some nugget, some truth you can hold onto when faced with your own journeys.

As we step into these pages together, I pray you experience the Lord's nearness as fully as I did while writing these stories.

GOD GAVE
THE SONG

Dedication

I dedicate this book to my husband, Jim, who makes my heart hum every day.

I would also like to acknowledge the people who helped me research this story. To Stargazer Ranch in Loveland, Colorado, and owners Cynthia Fronk and John Heise, my extreme gratitude for walking me around your ranch, introducing me to your alpacas, and sharing your love of these unique creatures. And to the many people I met at the State of Jefferson Alpaca Show in Medford, Oregon, especially Gabrielle Menn, Janet Hedley, and Richard Smith.

I'd also like to thank my sister, Shari Warren, my mother, Ruth Keal, and my brother-in-law, Neil Warren, for setting aside their busy lives and becoming tour guides for a couple of weeks.

And finally, my critique partners who keep me grounded. To JOY Writers and ACFW Crit2, I thank all of you for going the extra mile and teaching me how to make it all work.

Chapter 1

Ruthanne stood over Hannie in the hospital bed, wincing as the older woman rasped out another bone-jarring cough. Her employer and friend was still young at sixty-six, but her health had declined since the hospital admitted her a few days prior. It was only pneumonia. People—strong, faith-filled people like Hannie—recovered every day from that illness.

Why did she ask for her lawyer?

Hannie's nephew, Paul, entered with Vaughn Stanton. Paul gently slipped his hand into the once-strong palm that even now looked oddly ready to pitch hay. "Auntie, we're all here."

Hannie opened her eyes and removed the oxygen mask, keeping it near. Vaughn removed a small digital recorder from his pocket and turned it on.

With a thin voice that sounded like sandpaper on wet wood, Hannie spoke. "I have a son, and I want you to find him."

∽

A month later

Skye stood in the doorway, mere feet from his mother in the hospital bed. The *shush-poc* of the respirator accused him, as if it knew what he was thinking.

He should go to her, hold her hand. Let her know he was near. Pray for her. But who was he kidding? He wouldn't even have come if the lawyer hadn't been so insistent. Truthfully the only reason he agreed was to ask the woman one simple question.

Why?

"Excuse me."

Skye turned toward the male voice behind him.

"Do you know my aunt?"

"I'm her. . .son." Skye shook off the spiders of anxiety clinging to his flesh due to his mother's nearness and reached for the man's outstretched hand. "Skye Randall."

"Paul Godfrey, her nephew. Her lawyer told me he'd contacted you yesterday. Thank you for coming so soon."

Skye searched the younger man for a family resemblance. Paul's dark hair matched his own, but Paul's eyes were a deep brown while Skye's were blue.

"We're not related, are we?" Skye felt disjointed, like a puzzle not yet completed.

"Not by blood, no."

9

The stab of regret surprised Skye.

He glanced at the paper placard outside the door with his mother's name. HANNAH GODFREY. She must have married this man's uncle. He wanted to ask if his mother had other children but thought better of it. Would the answer be too much for him to bear?

Skye jerked his head toward the bed. "When can I talk to her?"

Paul looked toward the floor. "They didn't tell you her condition when you came in?"

"No. Mr. Stanton gave me the room number, so I found it on my own."

"Oh man." Paul's gaze darted down the corridor. "The doctor should be here soon. That's why I'm here." He rubbed the back of his neck. "You should know though. She's in a coma."

The four simple words carried the weight of a sucker punch.

The man moved to the side of the bed and lifted her hand. His fond gaze directed toward his aunt spoke volumes to Skye. "Aunt Hannie has a tendency to overdo, to the point of exhaustion sometimes. Add to that her visits to children's hospitals, nursing homes, prisons—she ended up contracting a virus that turned into pneumonia. But then it took a nasty turn."

The doctor entered, interrupting the list of saintly duties this woman had supposedly performed. Skye forced a brief smile to his lips as Paul introduced the doctor to him.

Dr. Harris lifted the chart at the end of the bed and made some notations. "Your mother has ARDS, Acute Respiratory Distress Syndrome. What this means is that the pneumonia is now in the tissue surrounding her lungs. This takes more time to heal since it's impossible to get medicine there. To make her more comfortable during the process, we chose to put her into a drug-induced coma this morning."

"Then she's not going to die?" Skye's words spilled out in an emotionless query. However, when Paul's head snapped up, he regretted being so blunt. *Sorry, Lord.*

The doctor placed his dark hand on Hannie's white wrist and inspected her fingers. "Ah, color is coming back." He gently laid her hand down and regarded Skye. "I'm not going to lie to you. This is a very serious illness. The survival rate is about 60 percent, but that's better than the 30 percent it's been in the past. We're more aware of the disease now, and we have better equipment." He patted Skye's shoulder on the way out. "Don't worry, we'll do everything we can to keep her in the right percentile."

Paul walked out behind him, shaking his head and muttering, "A 40 percent death rate."

What was he? A glass-is-half-empty kind of guy?

Skye tagged on to the end of the procession, not eager to be left alone with the stranger in the bed. Coma. He hadn't expected that. He'd wanted to get answers from the woman who turned her back on him, and now all he had was more questions. And a bit of guilt. This Paul guy really seemed to care about her, yet the woman he described was nothing like the one Skye had known. How was he supposed to reconcile the two?

Conviction slowly seeped into his soul. He hadn't communicated with God since the lawyer called him. He didn't want to pray about the situation. He only wanted to hear his mother's story. But things were getting complicated, so he managed to wring out three words: "God, be near."

They entered a waiting area with putty-colored faux leather couches and armchairs. A television droned on in the corner, with the morning news turned so low it was barely audible. Large, frameless paintings of flowers hung on each wall. The cheery yellows, greens, and reds only served to agitate Skye further, and he clenched and unclenched the car keys in his hand, making them jangle.

As they sat, Paul seemed to have trouble making eye contact. "This must be awkward for you."

"You have no idea."

"I'm sure Aunt Hannie regrets losing you."

Skye thrust himself from the chair. "She didn't lose me. She. . ."

. . .left me.

It took all his restraint not to throw his keys at the television. How much did this man know?

After an uncomfortable moment, Paul said, "Did he mention her property?"

"He said he wanted to meet with me tomorrow regarding it. What? Does she own a small plot of land?" He didn't care about his mother's property. With his mother in a coma, there could be no closure. For either of them.

Why on earth am I still here?

Paul's eyes flashed. "She owns a ranch."

Skye's interest perked up. "A ranch?" Thoughts of bronco busting evoked a happy memory from his childhood.

Paul's cell phone rang, and he excused himself to answer it. Skye heard Paul's voice in the corridor as it raised in a heated conversation, but he couldn't make out the words.

When Paul returned, he was still gripping his cell phone.

"This is Ruthanne, Aunt Hannie's assistant. She's been calling every hour to check on her status. She's wondering if you'd like to come out to see the ranch before your meeting tomorrow. It's just south of Oakley. Are you free the rest of the day?"

With his emotions going up and down like the parachute ride at the county fair, Skye wasn't sure how to answer. On one hand he didn't want to have anything to do with his mother. On the other the thought of visiting a working ranch intrigued him. Dare he step into her world? Who had this woman become after all these years?

With a shrug, he slammed his hands into his pockets. "Sure, why not?"

Paul nodded. "Great. Would you like to see her again before we go?"

The ride plummeted once more. "No."

"Do you mind if I do?"

He hesitated just a moment. "No, of course not." The daily lunch odor wafted from a cart rattling down the corridor and assaulted his nose. Beef broth. His stomach lurched. "I'll meet you in the parking lot and follow you out."

Paul disappeared down the corridor and into the room. Skye rattled his keys all the way to his car.

⊗

Ruthanne replaced her phone in her pocket and leaned back against the paddock. She closed her eyes as the humming of the animals and the scent of fresh hay calmed her soul. Lavender from the garden had the same effect.

She needed that sense of serenity right now. Paul hadn't been happy with her suggestion to bring Hannie's son over, but it felt like the right thing to do.

Something woolly brushed her shoulder, and she opened her eyes. She'd just received an alpaca nudge, a reminder that she should be forking the hay instead of inhaling it. You'd think since they grazed all morning that they wouldn't be so testy in the afternoon.

She stroked the alpaca's long russet-colored neck and looked around at the other teddy bear faces surrounding her. They all depended on her now.

As she scooped hay into the first manger, she assured the gathering alpacas that their mommy would be home soon.

Hannie.

Like a mother to her, too. And now Ruthanne could do nothing to save her.

Except pray. She did that a lot lately. Especially since this morning, when she received the call that Hannie would be placed in an induced coma.

She gazed across the green pastureland toward Oregon's Siskiyou Mountains. The verse in Psalms about lifting your eyes to the hills came into her mind, and she drew strength as she recognized the Creator of those hills.

With a prayer on her lips, a strident chorus of outraged alpacas drew her away from her meditation. Harriet, a bossy female who insisted on first dibs at mealtime, had pushed her dapple gray and black body through the group and now lay on the feeding trough so no one else could eat. Ruthanne tried to coax her off but backed away just in time to miss a blast of hay and spit from the alpaca's mouth.

"Okay! Have it your way!" Wheelbarrow in hand, she moved on to the next feeding area. "Sorry, gang, she'll be full soon. Then it'll be your turn."

A roan-colored mother alpaca named Cinnamon chortled from another enclosure, cushing with her legs folded beneath her. She looked like a puffy beanbag pillow with a neck. Her cria romped nearby, playing a game of "let's bounce off Mommy." Baby Payton ran to the farthest side of the pen, turned, and with long, spindly legs loped at full speed toward Cinnamon, landing in her soft fleece and springing off her in a double roll.

Ruthanne welcomed the comedian's antics. She entered the pen and patted his sandy brown neck. "Laughter is good medicine. I should have named you Isaac."

She forked hay into their trough and moved on to her own alpaca, Lirit. Snowy white—and just as pure of heart. Lirit had a special language all her own. Her humming signaled a contented soul and often soothed Ruthanne's emotions. Hannie had given Lirit to Ruthanne as a cria at an especially tough time in her life, and the two bonded instantly.

Movement on the main road caught her eye. She pulled off her work gloves as she walked between the barn and house and sidestepped the muddy prelandscaped yard to meet them in front. Soon two cars pulled into the circular gravel drive. Paul's blue hybrid whirred in first. The second was a trendy charcoal gray SUV, one the owner would probably never take off-roading. No doubt a gas-guzzler, too.

Ever since Hannie's bombshell, she had puzzled over the mystery surrounding the son. *How did they become estranged? How does he feel about his mother? Does he truly care about her, or will he prove to be a vulture, circling above a victim?*

She shook her head. Not every man was like Brian.

A tall man dressed in business casual—blue khakis and a gray polo shirt—followed Paul up the steps to the porch. By his stormy countenance, he was clearly unhappy. She looked closely to see if he resembled Hannie. Not in the hair. His was dark with a slight wave. The tiny bits of silver told her he was probably in his midforties. Hannie's short crop was blond and straight, although streaked with gray. But as he drew near, she gasped. Those were Hannie's eyes, curious and taking in the surroundings. Looking into his clear blue irises made her wonder if those black clouds circling his head had a silver lining.

Paul greeted her, but his usual cheerful demeanor seemed just as morose as that of their visitor. She felt bad for Paul. With both of his parents gone, Hannie had become a mother to him. His mother's bout with lung cancer no doubt colored his faith now that Hannie suffered from a lung ailment.

She held out her hand. "Hi, I'm Ruthanne Fairfax." She noted the smooth warmth of his hand. He obviously didn't work on a ranch.

A small grin played on his face. "Forgive me, but I thought you would be older."

She flipped her auburn farm-girl braids. Why hadn't she taken more time on her appearance this morning? "The name often fools people. I'm named after my grandmother."

His gaze roved over the house and surrounding land. Ruthanne puffed with pride. "It's something, isn't it?"

"It's beautiful. My. . .mother. . .owns all of this?"

How long ago had this man withdrawn from Hannie's life? "Twenty acres. She and her husband had the house built to their specifications. He worked with the architect, and she made sure her flair was evident."

As they moved inside, Paul asked, "What do you do for a living, Skye?"

"I'm a real estate broker."

Ruthanne spoke over her shoulder. "Then you should be very interested in the construction of this house."

"I noticed the large oak door. That was custom, wasn't it?"

"The whole house is custom built." She nodded toward the sweeping staircase that spilled into the large foyer. "Hand-carved pedestals. There are three bedrooms on the second level, but Hannie's room is on the main level, at the bottom of the stairs." She pointed to the closed door next to the banister.

"That was their original office," Paul interjected. "When Uncle David was diagnosed with multiple sclerosis, they knew he wouldn't be able to navigate the stairs. The office is now a small room off the kitchen. Which is where I'm headed. Ruthanne can show you the rest of the place."

Ruthanne frowned at Paul's retreating figure. There was nothing pressing in the office.

They moved into the two-story great room, and she nodded toward the massive stone fireplace to the right. "This would be the focal point of the room, but—"

"But"—he finished her thought—"the double french doors are what capture the eye."

Ruthanne was impressed. He seemed to know his stuff. "Yes, the hill behind us is framed in their glass, creating living art. Hannie and David named it Singing Mountain, the same name as our ranch. The locals adopted the name and eventually made it official."

He nodded his approval as he wandered around the room.

Ruthanne pointed upward. "Hannie made sure nothing but natural products were used. Those are real wood beams on the ceiling, not Styrofoam." Then down. "And instead of a plastic product on the floor, she insisted on slate."

"This isn't what I expected."

"What did you expect? Something larger?"

"No. Something more—this sounds strange—psychedelic."

"Ah." Now she understood. "Your mother was a hippie."

"Yes."

She chuckled. "She still is but in a mature, healthy way. Let's see, did she have long blond hair, granny glasses, and flower power?"

If she expected a pleasant reaction from him, she was mistaken. He gave a slight nod, but his nose turned up as if he'd just caught an unpleasant odor; then he turned away and walked toward the french doors. She found herself whiffing the air. Only the cheerful aromas of lilac and forsythia floated in to greet her.

They stepped through the french doors to the redwood back deck where he could view the entire alpaca herd spread out before him. He seized the rail with one hand and pointed with the other. "What are those?"

"Our alpacas."

His face puckered. He watched them grazing, seemingly disappointed with what he saw, yet too fascinated to look away. His slouched posture made her think of a child forced to endure the family vacation.

Under a frown, his eyes searched the grounds. "Aren't there any cows—or horses?"

What was wrong with this guy? Most people found alpacas charming. Perhaps her first instinct had been right, and he was a con artist after Hannie's property. A cattle or horse ranch might be easier to sell.

"No, just alpacas." With a wave, she said, "Oh, we do have some Angora rabbits."

He turned and glared at her. "Rabbits."

Suddenly feeling like a reprimanded child, she pointed weakly to the henhouse attached to the far side of the barn. "And chickens."

He shook his head just a fraction. "Alpacas, rabbits, and chickens."

Was that a snort? How dare he mock something into which Hannie and David had poured heart and soul.

Before she realized it, she placed her hand on her hip and gave him an indignant glare.

"I'm sorry. I expected. . ." His shoulders sagged. "This is all so surreal to me."

Ruthanne suddenly wished she knew more about this man's history. When had he and his mother become estranged? Why hadn't Hannie told her about him? And the question Ruthanne would rather not explore: What about the past had Hannie felt necessary to keep hidden?

Chapter 2

"Hannie, I met your son." Ruthanne sat by the bedside, saddened that her friend couldn't open her eyes and engage in her animated way. How could such a vibrant woman have been struck down so quickly? It certainly made her think of her own mortality.

She ran her fingers through Hannie's short hair, trying to fluff it the way she always wore it. "Why didn't you tell me about Skye? When he walked into your house yesterday, he acted as if he didn't know you. How long has it been since you've seen him?"

At least three years. That's how long she'd known Hannie, and he'd never visited. Something must have happened. She tried not to judge, but knowing her friend's sweetness and Skye's surliness, he must have been the one to pull away.

"He wasn't there long. I thought he'd want to go into the yard and meet the alpacas up close, but he said he had an appointment." She went on to talk about the alpacas. How they seemed a bit off their feed without her there.

Except Lirit.

How she knew she belonged to Ruthanne was a mystery. Throughout this ordeal, Ruthanne often sat with Lirit long into the evening. Just the thought of her gentle hum calmed Ruthanne's spirit.

She prayed for that same heart song, a physical gauge to know she was in God's will. Tears welled in her eyes. "I know I've thanked you, Hannie, for taking me in and loving me."

And saving my sanity.

Brian had nearly destroyed her. He never made her heart sing. In those days, seeking God's will was foreign to her.

She flicked a tear off her face and smiled at Hannie. "You sure found a good man though. What was it? Sixteen years of marital bliss before David died? I'll bet you couldn't stop your heart song if you wanted to."

With closed eyes, Ruthanne spoke to God. "Lord, I want a man like David to share my life with. Please send me someone who will make my heart sing." She squeezed Hannie's hand, as if the woman had been praying with her. "Okay now, you have to get well. As my future matron of honor, I can't have you lying around all day."

Paul entered the room, and Ruthanne felt a burn on her cheeks. Had he heard her very private prayer? He avoided looking her in the eye, but he gave no indication when he drew her into the corridor. He offered his usual kiss on her temple and added a gentle squeeze to her shoulder as he led her to the waiting room.

Ruthanne stopped in the middle of the empty room and looked at her friend. His eyes had lost their twinkle. "I'm praying, Paul."

"I know. So am I. But we need to get a grip on reality here."

She shook her head. "Reality is Jesus, and He can heal her."

"Like He healed my mother?"

"It's not the same thing."

Paul rubbed his neck. "I know. Aunt Hannie doesn't have lung cancer."

"I'm sorry about your mother," Ruthanne said. She tried to be sensitive, but Paul grappled with the faith issue in several areas of his life.

He drew her into a hug, but she fisted her arms at her side, stiffening at his touch. Against his shoulder, she asked, "Do you have faith?"

"You know I do, but you also know that faith in God means trusting Him no matter what the circumstances. I've never seen her this sick. What if God chooses to take her home?"

She pulled away to look him in the eyes. "Stop that! She's not a doddering old woman."

Ruthanne grabbed her ears to still the buzzing and sank onto a sofa. The colorless beige cushions reflected the gloom she felt in her heart. She grieved Paul's lack of faith more than Hannie's illness.

Changing the subject, she promised herself to continue to pray for the man until he got it. "Paul. . ." Ruthanne fidgeted with the smooth piping on the couch. "Did you know about Skye?"

He sat next to her and leaned his elbows onto his knees. "No."

"You were young when Hannie married your uncle. You don't remember them talking about him at all?"

He shook his head. "If they mentioned him, I was never aware. After I moved in years later, I'm sure no one mentioned him."

Ruthanne tapped her lip. No mention of an adult child? What had happened to their relationship?

❧

The next day Skye entered the square two-story building to meet Paul and Ruthanne at the lawyer's office. Paul stood just inside the foyer, ending a call on his cell phone.

Skye shook his hand as Paul slipped the phone into his front pocket. "That was Ruthanne. She'll be here in a minute."

They entered through a frosted glass door where a receptionist greeted them. "Please have a seat until your third party arrives. Then you can go in." She pointed to two leather chairs flanking an oak table.

After an awkward silence, Skye started the conversation. "So, you've known my mother how long?" He winced. Even to his own ears, his question sounded like interrogation.

Paul didn't seem fazed. "She married my uncle when I was twelve. I have very few memories of him without her."

Lucky you.

The receptionist spoke into her phone with heated tones. Skye shifted his eyes toward her. "Thank you. I'll expect you this afternoon."

She hung up and addressed Skye, who just realized he'd been staring at her. She pointed toward the ceiling with a pen. "Sorry about the canned music. The speaker's been cutting in and out." She used the pen to air loop her ear. "It's been driving me crazy!"

Music? He hadn't noticed it. Turning back to Paul, he pressed with one more question. "And what about you? Has she been supportive of you all these years?"

Paul's eyebrows shot upward, lines creasing his forehead. "As much as I have been of her." His voice held a defensive edge. "Now *I* have a question."

With a nod, Skye accepted the challenge in his statement.

"Why didn't I know about you?"

Skye ground his teeth. "That's something only my mother can tell you."

Ruthanne entered the room, ending the standoff.

The receptionist stood and led them to a conference room painted in earth tones of green and brown. They each took seats, Paul and Ruthanne on one side and Skye on the other.

A man entered, carrying a folder, and introduced himself to Skye as Vaughn Stanton. The young lawyer looked barely old enough to have passed the bar. Skye shook his hand but must have looked skeptical. "I'm not the Stanton in the partnership. That would be Dad." He pointed to a photo on the wall of three men—Hurst, Hurst, and the elder Stanton. "But someday. . ."

Skye caught Ruthanne's expression in the polished walnut veneer tabletop. Her eyes showed strain. In the brief time he'd known her, Skye had concluded that she was an old soul in a thirty-something's body.

"It's a pleasure to meet you, Mr. Randall," Vaughn Stanton began as he took his seat at the head of the table. "I've known your mother for several years." He glanced at Paul and raised a questioning eyebrow.

"Go ahead," Paul said. "He might find it interesting to hear how you met Aunt Hannie."

"I don't normally let my clients know this tidbit about my past, but since you're related to the woman who changed my life. . ." He reached out for the folder he had brought into the room. "I was a troubled teen and did community service at your mother's ranch. I fell in love with the animals—and with Hannie. She helped turn me around."

The more the man talked, the more Skye wanted to bolt.

When Skye didn't respond, Vaughn fidgeted with the folder. "Yes, well. . .let's get down to business. When Hannie became ill, I think it frightened her. Perhaps it had to do with losing her husband a few years ago, but for whatever reason, she left clear instructions on what to do if she were incapacitated, even briefly." He brushed each of them with an empathetic gaze. "I'd say a coma qualifies. It is her request, in the event she can't run the ranch, that you, Skye, are made aware of her wishes. Her intention is that you get to know the business."

Skye leaned forward. "Why?"

"Because she wants you to inherit the ranch."

He gripped the arms of the chair. He'd always wanted to own acreage. But could he accept it this way—from this woman? "Assuming I want the ranch, how am I supposed to learn the business? I have a job in Medford."

"This part isn't going to be easy then. You must stay at the ranch for a minimum of thirty days."

With a force that propelled his chair backward, Skye stood. "Physically?" He stabbed the table with his finger. "On the property?"

The lawyer nodded. "Day and night. It's her wish that you experience the full effect of ownership."

Skye sank back into the chair, the wheels in his brain turning.

"Obviously you'll need a coach." Vaughn nodded toward Ruthanne. "This is where you come in. Hannie has asked that you show Skye around, involve him in the workings of the ranch, and perform business as usual. I'm assuming that Hannie doesn't want any interruption, and she knows you'll need help running it."

Ruthanne nodded. "We have a part-time employee who is out of town at the moment. Paul does what he can, but he has a job. We have events coming up, and I know she doesn't want me to cancel." She chewed her lower lip, no doubt weighing the pros and cons of inviting a stranger to the ranch. Her gaze darted to him, then to her hands clutching each other on the table. She closed her eyes briefly. Was she praying? Finally she drew a breath. "I can definitely use the help."

Skye also sent up a quick prayer. But his analytical mind still had questions. "And what if I refuse? What happens to the ranch then?"

Vaughn closed the file and folded his hands. "In the event of Hannie's death"—Ruthanne squirmed—"which won't be for a long time, but she wants us to think about it now, the ranch will be sold, with 10 percent going to charity and the rest split between Paul and Ruthanne."

Ruthanne turned to look at Paul. Skye suddenly felt like the third wheel. They didn't need him to keep the ranch going—they could hire someone—and if he walked away from the whole thing, they'd come out ahead. Why would Ruthanne even help him learn the business?

Vaughn continued. "And if you accept, please understand that you must continue the workings of the ranch for five years unless it becomes a burden to keep it. If that happens, she asks that you discuss the future of the ranch with Paul and Ruthanne before selling."

This was too weighty a matter for Skye to make a snap decision. "When do you need to know?"

"Take all the time you need, but remember, Ruthanne could use your help now. You could fulfill the one month, and then when"—he glanced at Ruthanne—"or rather, *if* the time comes, you can make the decision to take over for five years."

Skye left, promising to give his answer within the week.

◯

Skye returned to his home in Medford with a half day to be productive, but he decided instead to take the afternoon off to pray. Changing out of his business attire, he got sloppy with cutoff jeans and a T-shirt.

In the backyard, Ruddy greeted him with a wet kiss. He ruffled the big red dog's ears and looked deep into his brown eyes. "What do you think, boy? They don't know about you. Would everything be called off if I brought my brute?" An Irish setter/Great Dane mix, Ruddy's size alone had caused the neighbors to cross the street, until they got to know him. Ruddy grabbed his Frisbee and frisked about the backyard to entice his master to play. Skye took pity on the dog and tossed the disk around while he talked to God.

At first he laid his feelings out, knowing his Father already understood. "Why would she do this, Lord? Why would she stay out of my life all these years and then offer me her ranch? Her alpaca ranch! Is it a guilt offering?" He decided if that were the case, she must feel horrible for what she'd done to him.

"And what about her nephew and assistant? She embraced them as her family. Why doesn't she just give them the ranch? Why drag me into the middle?"

At one point during his increasingly heated conversation with God, he threw the disk too hard—his attempt at casting his cares, which were heavy—and it landed in the maple tree. The freshly budded leaves grasped it as if capturing their first souvenir of the season. Ruddy whined as he attempted to climb up the trunk, his toy just out of reach.

"Sorry, boy." Skye grabbed a lawn rake and stabbed at the disk until it fell at Ruddy's feet. The grateful dog scooped it up and pranced away, not willing to let his master have the toy again so soon. A game of keep-away ensued, but when Skye tired long before the dog did, he left Ruddy to chew on a rawhide bone while he went inside to chew some more on his own problem.

He sat for a long time, feeling the slight breeze on his face as it drifted in from the open living room window. The normally calming sound of rustling leaves did nothing to relieve his stress. Every argument he could think of bombarded his practical side, and he had just decided to refuse the offer and never think of Hannah again when the phone rang. He looked at the caller ID and answered. "Hi, Mom."

"Hi, honey. How'd it go today? I've been so curious."

Skye laid his Bible aside and silently thanked God for the woman who had chosen him. "Sorry. I came home to pray and think about their offer."

"Offer?"

After relating the crazy thing asked of him, his mom, in an attempt to make things easier, took away his one excuse. "If you need to be there for thirty days, I'm sure it won't be a problem with your dad. You've pulled in more than your quota this year. You deserve a vacation."

Skye gritted his teeth. Why couldn't he work at a regular brokerage house, with a hard taskmaster and a whip? No, he had to go into the family business where TRUST AND OBEY was more than just a phrase on the plaque over the door.

Mom must have sensed his hesitation. "Perhaps you need prayer."

No, I need a ticket out of town.

"Lord, You know how hard this is for my boy. Please give him direction and wisdom, but moreover, Lord, please give him compassion. Only You know what's going on in his heart, and I pray You give him the strength to make this life-changing decision. In Jesus' name. Amen."

Skye's throat tightened through the prayer as conviction squeezed him, but he managed to croak, "Thanks, Mom. You're the best."

"Now while you make this decision. . ."

He smiled. Mom might pray for direction, but no matter how old he became, she'd always keep her hand in shaping his character.

". . .remember that Hannah is a person, too. She deserves prayers as much as anyone else. I hope you've been lifting her before the Lord."

He hadn't.

Mom went on. "Your dad and I have been praying for this woman ever since we adopted you. Now it's time for you to forgive."

He tried to tell Mom what she wanted to hear, but his clenched jaw prevented it. The subject mercifully moved to more mundane things, but the words *"it's time for you to forgive"* continued to ping around in his brain.

When he hung up, he called Vaughn Stanton.

Chapter 3

On Monday morning Ruthanne stood with Paul on the front porch as Skye pulled into the drive.

Lord, are You sure about this?

Emotions roiled within her as the tires crunched the gravel then stopped. By agreeing to Hannie's wishes, Ruthanne felt as though she were already losing her friend.

She descended the wooden steps, planning to help Skye unload, but before she reached the bottom, a furry red monster came bounding out of the SUV. It rushed at her like a linebacker ready to tackle.

"What is that thing?" She flung the words over her shoulder as she hustled back up the stairs, hoping to hide behind Paul. But her protector had retreated behind the screen door, where she quickly joined him.

"Ruddy! Come here! Bad dog!" Skye called out, taming the wild creature into submission. It slunk back to him with tail tucked under and long ears drooping. "Sit." Skye pointed to the ground where the animal dutifully sat with a huff.

Skye looked up at Ruthanne. "Sorry. You said on the phone that I could bring him."

Ruthanne willed her heart to stop tharumping. "You said he was big, but I didn't realize how big." She cut a sharp glance at Paul.

"What?" Paul motioned with his head toward the animal. "You ran, too."

Skye tapped his hip, and the horse/dog stood. He then paced at his master's side, his long legs like California redwoods.

She watched with a wary eye as the two ascended the stairs. "What did you call him?"

"Ruddy, for his ruddy complexion. Isn't he a handsome dog?" Skye ruffled the hip-high red head without bending over, causing the ears to whip about in a furry frenzy.

She joined man and dog on the porch, brave now that the beast appeared tame. Ruthanne wasn't short by any means, but this monster's warm breath near her midsection made her feel like a Lilliputian. And he was Gulliver!

Skye stroked the dog's neck. "He's really very gentle. Go ahead and pet him."

She reached out and tapped Ruddy gingerly on the forehead then brought her hand back, dripping with slobber. "My, what a long tongue you have!"

Skye laughed. "The better to kiss you with, my dear." He wiggled a swarthy brow as he handed her his handkerchief, then he pointed to a corner of the porch where he directed Ruddy to sit and stay.

Ruthanne wiped her fingers and handed back the handkerchief. Her stomach fluttered at his teasing. Or was that mild flirting? With her dry hand, she combed her fingers through her braid-free hair, grateful she'd taken time to style it that morning. Maybe she'd be able to endure the coming month after all.

Skye followed Ruthanne into his mother's home.

Lord, are You sure about this?

He imagined himself walking into a large, gaping mouth where his past would consume his present and belch out who knew what of his future.

"Your room is up here." Ruthanne started up the stairs, her patchwork wrap-around skirt dusting the steps. On her feet were the ugliest brown shoes he'd ever seen on a woman. She wore a cream-colored knit cardigan to finish the odd ensemble.

Paul followed, carrying the shaving kit and garment bag, casting dubious looks at Ruddy when he reached the top. Skye brought up the rear, keeping Ruddy in check, knowing his dog would much rather beat everybody to the second floor.

As he placed his foot on the bottom step, he glanced toward his mother's closed bedroom door. He had expected to have some issues living in his mother's house, so his uneasiness near her personal space was no surprise. He hurried up the stairs to join the others.

Ruthanne had disappeared into a room, and Paul, now free of the items he'd carried up, excused himself. "I'll make lunch while you get settled." He skirted around Ruddy on his way back down.

As Skye entered the room to join Ruthanne, he asked, "Is Paul here all the time? If so, he'd better get used to my dog, or this is going to be one long month for him."

Her fond smile and glance toward the door told him she had feelings for Paul. Just what kind of feelings were they? "Paul lives just a few miles from here, in town."

"So, what's his role, besides being the heir apparent until I came along?"

"When David's MS prevented him from doing the office work, Paul stepped in and took over that role. This put him near the kitchen, so he also became our personal chef to be sure we were all well fed. His real love has always been cooking. It's in his blood. His grandmother owns a restaurant on the coast. He's a chef at the Pine Creek Inn. Have you ever eaten there?"

"No." And if she really wanted to know, he rarely lingered in Oakley because of its strong nonconformist influence. The farther he could get from anything resembling the hippie lifestyle, the better.

He walked over to a large bay window with a blue-cushioned seat. "This is a nice room. Is yours as big as this?"

"This was Paul's room. He moved in with Hannie and David while he was going to college. His mom had recently died, and David needed help, so it all worked out."

Ruddy proceeded to sniff every object in the room while Skye and Ruthanne stepped through a sliding glass door and onto an upper redwood deck.

"I live in that mobile home on the edge of the property. It was Hannie and David's while they built the house. I've been there for three years, and it's just the right size for me, although Hannie has been trying to get me to move in here." She picked at a thread on the bottom of her shirt. "I'm considering it for when she comes home. She'll probably need help getting around."

She took a big breath and leaned on the deck railing. "Occasionally you will have to come out to investigate things. If you hear the alpacas become agitated, it could be a predator or stray dog in the area."

Skye gazed out on the pleasant ranch scene from the deck, his eyes roving from the barn to the paddocks and out to the pasture where some of the animals munched the grass.

Ruthanne also looked at the panorama but with proud eyes. "Hannie *will* come home to this."

This was the second time Ruthanne had mentioned Skye's mother coming home. He recalled the doctor's assurance that they would try to keep his mother in the surviving percentile. But then he also remembered Paul's defeated slump. Her odds weren't that great with just over half a chance to survive. "How can you be so sure that's going to happen?"

Ruthanne grimaced and seized the rail. "I have faith."

Was she a believer? He had to know. "In Jesus?"

Her eyes misted. "Absolutely. And in Hannie."

She turned to him. "What about you?"

"I have faith in Jesus." He'd lost faith in his mother.

He walked back into his room to give Ruthanne a private moment. "Ruddy! Off!" Grateful he'd given his dog a bath just yesterday, Skye nevertheless brushed the window seat cushion where Ruddy had claimed his spot. The dog obeyed, but Skye knew this would be an ongoing battle. He whipped out his handkerchief and rubbed the nose prints off the window.

Ruthanne came through the door, hugging her body with one arm and wiping at her cheeks with the other.

He changed the subject. "Do alpaca ranches pay that well?" He couldn't imagine how alpaca breeding could garnish enough income for such a palace.

"It does very well, but David had the means to be able to afford most of this before he married Hannie."

My mother's a gold digger, too?

Ruthanne walked out of the room. "If you need anything else, please let me know. I'll leave you to unpack, then we can have lunch."

She disappeared before he could say thank you. Was she still emotional over his mother, or did she feel as awkward about the situation as he did?

⟨✑⟩

As Ruthanne left Skye, she wanted to think the best of him. Had he asked about the income because he was considering keeping the ranch? Or was he calculating its worth for when he sold it? *Please, Lord, no.* She wanted to like Skye for Hannie's sake.

During lunch she had to struggle to keep from laughing at Paul. With Ruddy sprawled in one corner of the kitchen, Paul sat where he could watch him, keeping his back to the wall.

When they were through, Paul showed Skye the room off the kitchen. Ruthanne could hear him while she cleared the table. "This is our business office. I've been cataloging Aunt Hannie's weavings for Internet sales."

Ruthanne filled the dishwasher while thinking of the Internet portion of the business. Paul had been such an asset since his uncle's death, and the online sales were his idea. She was grateful he took an active part, because she had enough to do just to keep the ranch running.

Perhaps it was good that Hannie had requested Skye be contacted.

He came back into the kitchen, pointing his thumb over his shoulder. "Are there enough books on alpacas in there? Or do you need to stock up on some more?"

She smiled. "When you realize Hannie and David started from scratch, not knowing a thing about alpacas, it's no wonder they own every book on the subject. Did you see the bookshelf that contained craft books?"

"You could start a library. Does my mother make all the crafts?"

"Most. She's the artist. Her weavings tell a story. You can see them throughout the house, but most are downstairs in the shop. I've made some things, too, but they're not the same quality." She dried her hands on a towel. "You ready to try your dog outside?"

"Are you sure?" Skye glanced at Ruddy.

No, she wasn't sure. "We have to test him around the alpacas sooner or later. He was so well behaved during lunch—let's try him on the deck at first. Do this slowly. Maybe tomorrow I can put the alpacas in the barn and introduce him to each one separately."

"Okay." Skye tapped his hip. "Let's go, Ruddy."

The dog rose from his prone position in the corner of the kitchen and took his place beside Skye.

With a mischievous tone, she called out to Paul, who had holed himself up in the office. "Would you like to come with us?"

His muffled voice drifted to them. "Depends. Where is the black demon?"

"In the far pasture."

After a pause, he called out again. "That's okay. I have stuff to do here."

She chuckled as she led Skye down the stairs off the deck. "He's referring to Gabriel." She pointed to the magnificent alpaca standing alone at the far fence. Long, pitch-black dreadlocks flowed from his back, and he held his head high, as if he knew they were admiring him. Framed by the rising mountain behind him, the view would have made a perfect postcard. "For reasons known only to God, Gabriel has waged war on Paul. He grunts and spits whenever he comes near."

They stopped on the back deck and allowed Ruddy a view of the alpacas. Skye remained alert as his dog spotted them. His tail and legs went stiff, and he began to *wuff* softly.

"Easy, boy. It's okay—they belong here." Skye patted the dog's head.

Ruddy sat but continued to whine. Ruthanne breathed a sigh of relief—but too soon. Apparently it was too much for the dog. He let out an earsplitting howl as he bounded down the steps toward the pasture.

"Ruddy! Heel! Heel! Come here!" Skye sprinted after the dog but couldn't catch up to him.

Ruthanne brought up the rear, hiking her skirt to her knees, intent on protecting her animals. In horror she watched Ruddy sail over the fence. Gabriel advanced.

"Skye, get him away from Gabriel!"

Ruddy ran and barked as if trying to rally a group to play softball, but Gabriel clearly didn't want to play. He charged, stopped short of running the canine over, and spit.

Ruthanne winced. Green slime on a red dog was not at all festive. Ruddy got the message. He pivoted, jumped back over the fence with the finesse of a hurdler, and headed for the deck. A giggle rose in her throat. Ruddy stood trembling on the deck, and Skye loped up the steps two at a time, scolding the dog all the way.

Paul came out onto the deck, laughing so hard tears had come to his eyes. "See? I told you he was a black demon!"

<hr/>

Skye felt the heat rise out of his collar. Ruddy had never done this sort of thing before. But then again, he'd never seen anything as strange as an alpaca.

"I'm so sorry. I don't know what got into him."

Ruthanne joined him on the deck and dabbed at her perspiring lip with the back of her hand. "No harm done," she wheezed. "I doubt he'll mess with the males anymore. I think we've all learned a lesson."

Together they managed to get Ruddy back down the steps. Skye hosed the vile-smelling slime off his dog, despite Ruddy's quivering throughout the process and casting side-glances toward Gabriel. When Skye turned off the water, Ruddy shook off the excess and loped back to the deck.

"I'll tie him up there."

Ruthanne placed her hand on his arm before he could leave to get Ruddy's leash. "Wait. Look at him."

Ruddy sat in the farthest corner he could find away from the alpacas. A wet sewer rat wouldn't have looked more pitiful.

"I don't think he's going anywhere." Ruthanne giggled.

Skye slid his hands into his back pockets. "I think you're right. What a chicken."

"Go easy on him. He's just had a traumatic experience. Maybe it was a good thing. Look who's just made a new friend." Paul knelt next to the dog, offering him what looked like a leftover piece of veal cutlet from lunch. "I think they've found common ground."

If this continued, he knew he'd have a spoiled dog on his hands. But the pampering was all worthwhile if he didn't have to tether him every time Paul was around.

They walked to the paddocks. He was surprised that they didn't smell that bad. Kind of like hay. Even the droppings seemed to be all neat and tidy in one community pile.

Ruthanne must have noticed him looking at them. "Alpacas are fairly clean animals. They all go in one place, which is great for you."

"I'll be shoveling that," he stated.

"Yep."

She led him through the paddocks attached to two sides of the barn. The paddocks each had access into the barn and were really one large pen with movable fences. "We keep things portable so we can either segregate or bring everybody together. It's also easier going from one paddock to the other when we don't have to go into the barn to get to each stall."

He liked the system and could see how it would make life easier than walking from the paddock clear around to one central door.

Ruthanne entered a pen where four babies romped near their mothers. "Little ones are called crias, and the moms are dams." A mother and baby were fenced away from the rest. "This is our newborn that came into the world yesterday. We've named her Princess."

The fawn-colored infant looked like a lamb with short, curly fleece and an extremely long neck. She stood with steady, capable legs but never strayed from her mother.

"She sure seems strong." A grin tugged at Skye's lips.

"They get their strength fast. We were keeping her from the other babies until we were sure she could hold her own. She seems to be doing fine, so why don't we try putting them together?"

She untied the fences, and the other mothers and young ones swarmed the newborn. Mom alpaca did her best to keep everyone at a respectable distance by getting between her baby and the well-wishers.

"See these three male crias rushing up to see what the fuss is all about?"

Skye could imagine the three boys as human, tumbling all over each other and trying to engage the smaller children in a game of roughhouse. The new baby hid behind her mother.

Ruthanne continued her tour. "Alpacas are easy and fun animals to work with. Occasionally one needs special attention, so we play vet when we have to."

One curious mother grunted as she eyed Skye with black, nearly pool-ball-sized eyes. She came up to him, apparently just to get a better view, because she shied away when he reached out to touch her.

"Alpacas don't like to be touched on their heads, but it's okay to stroke their necks or backs." Ruthanne handed him a peanut. "Give this to her, and she'll be your best friend."

He did so and was surprised at the stiff hair on her chin. It looked soft but had a slight prick to it. Pliant lips scooped the peanut into the alpaca's mouth.

They moved through the pen with the mama following now, hoping for another peanut.

Ruthanne continued on, introducing each animal as if it were part of the family. "We breed both suris and huacayas here."

"Wa-*who*-ahs?"

"Huacayas." She regarded him as if he were a toddler learning how to talk. "Repeat after me. Hwa. . .ki. . .ah."

As she pronounced the word, he found watching her naturally rosy lips enjoyable. He continued saying the word wrong until she gave up.

"You'll get it eventually," she huffed.

She pointed to a chocolate brown animal. "This is Hershey. You can tell she's a suri by the dreadlocks. Her sire is Gabriel."

"I can see that these animals are in the camel family by the way they sit."

"Yes, llamas and alpacas are in the camelid family. When they sit on their legs like that, it's called cushing."

Hershey rose from her folded position and joined them. Skye reached out to touch the strands of dense wool flowing from the animal's body. After the coarse chin hair, he found it much softer than it looked. "Is her mother brown?"

"No, believe it or not, her mother is white. No one knows why they throw their color the way they do. We were only mildly surprised when black and white equaled brown. In fact, alpacas are bred in twenty-two official colors."

"Impressive."

"The huacayas look like teddy bears." She came to a white animal that rose from the ground to greet her. They nuzzled each other's faces. "This is Lirit. She's mine. . .or I'm hers." She shrugged. "We belong to each other."

He reached out to touch Lirit's fuzzy fleece but stopped short. The intelligence in her huge black eyes unnerved him. With a small snort, she shied away from his touch and trotted to the far corner of the pen.

Ruthanne frowned. "That's odd. She's usually friendly with strangers. Well, alpacas often remind me of cats in their behaviors"—she waggled a finger in Lirit's direction— "*and* in their independent natures."

They moved on. "This is the boys' hangout. These five are fully grown but still teenagers." Two of the males seemed engaged in a power game, pushing at each other, the long necks dueling like flexible, fuzzy swords.

"What are they fighting about?" Skye winced as the brown one nipped at the cream-colored alpaca's left flank.

Ruthanne didn't seem concerned. "They love to roughhouse, seeing who has hair on his chest. The dark one is Winston, and the light one is Chester. They were born only six weeks apart and got along when they were younger, but now they're establishing the pecking order. Chester is bigger, so I imagine he'll win. We trim their teeth regularly so no one draws blood."

This little tussle actually pleased Skye. He was afraid these animals were as frail as they looked.

Ruthanne spread her arms wide. "This is it—Singing Mountain Ranch."

"I have to admit, it's impressive." Skye found himself looking forward to working on the ranch, even if there weren't cows or horses.

On their way back to the house, Skye asked, "How did you start working with alpacas?"

Ruthanne took a deep breath. "I'm so blessed to be working here. I met Hannie at a craft fair. My husband and I had recently moved here from California."

Husband?

He noticed her enthusiasm over the animals didn't translate when talking about her husband. The spark left her eyes.

She continued. "We'd been living in a small apartment in Oakley—barely making it. Brian was an artist but didn't make much money. Hannie and I clicked. Our booths were located next to each other, and the alpaca there took to me right away. After I confided in her, she consulted David, whose MS had magnified, and he agreed to let us stay in the mobile home on their property if Brian and I would help out." She pointed to the far end of the pasture.

"I haven't met your husband. Is he traveling on the fair circuit?"

The spark returned, but it flashed hot. "No. He's. . . I'm a widow."

"I'm sorry."

She turned her moss green eyes to him, eyes almost as big as those of the alpacas she loved. "Don't be."

Without further explanation she moved on with her shoulders squared, apparently ready for a fight. Subject closed.

They walked into the herdsire paddock. "These guys are our prize sires, dads to most of the animals here."

He glanced out toward the pasture at the majestic black that bested his dog. "Why isn't Gabriel with the other sires?"

"He's an import from South America. Down there, they don't allow the interaction like we do here. He never developed social skills and likely won't. We've just gotten him to the point where he'll let us near, except Paul, of course. Where he's from, humans treat them like animals."

Skye laughed. "I hate to tell you this. . ."

"I know." She giggled, and he found the sound as relaxing as the wind chimes on the deck. "They are all my family."

"Especially. . .what did you call her?"

"Lirit. Hannie gave her to me after my husband left."

Left?

Did they have more than his mother in common? Had Ruthanne been abandoned, too?

Chapter 4

N ot even a week from the time he first learned about his mother, Skye awoke in her house to the discordant *buzz* of his travel alarm. Through blurry vision from a short night's sleep, he saw the numbers: 7:00. He groaned.

Ruddy's snore rumbled from his doggy cushion at the foot of the bed. Skye reached for his Zane Grey paperback book on the nightstand and tossed it at the animal, hitting his right flank. Ruddy merely lifted his head, snorted, and lay back down again.

"Oh no you don't. We're in this together." He stood and slapped his thigh.

Ruddy dragged himself to all fours slowly, acting more like an old man than the teenager he was.

The pair went downstairs to the kitchen, where Skye found a covered plate and a note on the counter. The note read "Skye, Paul made these orange and cranberry bagels. Cream cheese in the fridge. Help yourself and then come on out to the barn. —R"

Ruthanne had told him yesterday that she normally started her day with a light breakfast while she read her Bible. Then by eight o'clock, she would start her chores. He thought that sounded like a good idea.

He released Ruddy outside, and the dog cast a wary eye toward the far pasture where he'd had his altercation with Gabriel. It wasn't long before he loped back up to the house. Skye knew Ruddy wouldn't stray as long as he was near. However, in lieu of keeping the dog sequestered in the bedroom where he could do some damage, Skye would have to figure out a way to keep him in the yard if he'd be gone for any length of time.

After breakfast and a distracted devotion—it was hard to focus on God while sitting in his mother's kitchen—he changed out of the sweatpants and T-shirt he wore to sleep in. Leaving Ruddy on the deck, huddled into his safety spot by the door, he rubbed the soft, red head. "Sissy."

He sought out Ruthanne, who met him in the first stall. Two braids lay stiffly on either side of her head, and she wore a blue oversized man's flannel shirt that drooped to the knees of her faded jeans. These she had stuffed into unattractive green rubber boots. He had to admit she actually looked cute, like a little girl wearing her daddy's clothes.

After greeting him, she handed him a gallon-sized plastic milk container with the spout cut off for scooping and showed him where the grain was located. "We feed them vitamin-fortified grain in the morning then hay about midday and in the evening."

As they entered each stall, alpacas swarmed them like curious hummingbirds.

Fuzzy faces inspected Skye for food, but finding none, they concentrated their attention on Ruthanne.

"I'm very popular this time of day." She grinned.

"I can see that." Skye soon had his turn in the next stall. It seemed they didn't care who brought the food. Their favorite person was whoever made up the wait-staff for that day.

When they finished, she pointed at his feet. "I hope those aren't good shoes."

"No, they're new, but I bought them for here." He wiggled his toes in the leather work boots, already feeling like a ranch owner. "I thought of buying cowboy boots, but since there are no cows or horses, I thought these would be more appropriate."

She accepted his good-natured teasing by handing him a rake and a shovel, effectively deflating his romantic dreams of owning a real ranch. "Here, we'll start with this. Grab that wheelbarrow over there, and I'll show you how to harvest beans."

"Beans?"

She leaned close. "Alpaca poop."

He tossed the garden tools into the wheelbarrow with a clatter and grabbed the rough wooden handles. He then followed her to the corner of the stall where the pellet-sized "beans" lay in a tidy nest of hay. "Seriously? You call them beans?"

He loved her laughter. It was genuine and came so easily. "Believe it or not, that's the acceptable term in our circle."

Skye rolled his eyes, hoping to elicit another giggle from her. She didn't disappoint him.

Once his wheelbarrow was full of beans, she showed him the compost pile where he could dump all of it.

"Nothing's wasted, huh?"

"Nothing." She said it with conviction. Apparently she'd become as much of a tree hugger as his mother had. "We clean the stalls and paddocks in the morning and then again in the evening. This makes it more pleasant not only for us but also for the animals. Alpacas like to be clean."

They finished, and Ruthanne looked at her watch.

"Think you can gather eggs while I start breakfast?"

Even though he'd never been alone with a live chicken, he didn't think it would be hard. However, after she left, he found an overprotective hen who squawked and flapped until he feared she'd hurt herself. He needn't have feared her frailty, though. Her hard beak left peck marks on his hands as he removed her eggs, leaving him to wonder why she thought she had laid them there in the first place.

He took the eggs back to the house in a feminine wicker basket with a red gingham bow attached to the handle, muttering under his breath. "A real man brands cattle and breaks horses. Beans. Eggs. Fluffy bunnies. Bah!"

When he entered the kitchen, Ruthanne stood at the counter slicing oranges. She'd shed the man's shirt, revealing a clean pink T-shirt. He thought she'd suspended the Bohemian look to work outside, but when she turned, he saw the left waist of the shirt had been tie-dyed yellow and green. Blue socks, a solid color, covered her feet.

She padded over to him and took the basket. "Take your boots off outside, please."

"Oh! Sorry."

"That's okay. There's a bench near the door, and you can just shove your shoes under it."

When he returned, she grinned at him. "I hope you like omelets." She stood, whipping the eggs in a bowl with a fork, the shells tossed into a small bucket on the counter. No doubt a compost pile somewhere awaited the scraps. "I'm always famished by midmorning."

His stomach growled. "If I get omelets every day, I won't mind the chicken abuse."

She snickered. "Guess I'll have to show you how to extract eggs without ruffling feathers."

Skye rubbed his sore hands. "That would be nice."

After breakfast Ruthanne pulled on the ugly boots but left the man's shirt behind, entreating him to follow her. "I'd like you to help me exercise the animals."

He looked out at the acre-wide pasture as they passed the barn. "Don't they get enough exercise running around out there?"

On the far side of the barn, they walked to a round, fenced-in area with short wooden obstacles laid out strategically.

"This course is mostly for our show animals. It helps them get used to maneuvering through doors or other things they'll encounter away from the ranch. This is also an opportunity to teach them to be haltered and work with a lead." She pointed to what looked like flat debris near the far fence. "That bit of roofing is where we walk all our alpacas who are skittish about the scales they get weighed on. With the various objects we have here and the roofing, it teaches them not to be frightened when they encounter something strange under their feet."

Wouldn't horses be easier?

They entered a paddock where a gray-fringed alpaca eyed them warily. Ruthanne approached him despite his grunts to warn her away. "This is Silver Bullet."

"I like the name. The Lone Ranger only used bullets made of valued silver to show his desire to value life and only shoot to maim."

"You know some strange trivia, Skye Randall." She shook her head.

"Don't get me started on Roy Rogers."

"Don't worry." She held up her hand. "I won't."

During the course of the next hour, Skye learned how to put a halter on Silver

Bullet and how to exercise him by walking him over and through the obstacles.

Ruthanne sat on the fence while Skye put Silver through his paces. "Are you feeling comfortable with him yet?"

"Who are you talking to, Silver or me?" Even though the alpaca was smaller than a horse, Skye felt the power in his long neck.

"Both, I guess." Her intriguing laughter floated on the still air. "One last obstacle and you can bring Silver over here. I need to tell you about what's happening on Friday."

Silver stepped over a block without fighting for control and allowed Skye to lead him to Ruthanne. She hopped off the fence and patted Silver's neck, praising him for a job well done.

"Hey, what about me?" Skye feigned hurt feelings.

Ruthanne reached up to touch his neck but pulled her hand back. "You, too." Her cheeks glowed an attractive pink.

What would her hand feel like? Calloused and rough or as gentle as her alpacas?

"Anyway." She cleared her throat and opened the gate to release Silver into the pasture. "The ranch is hosting a field trip for the area schoolchildren. They arrive throughout the day in buses. We give them a tour then hold a little craft time with them in the large room off the gift shop."

Skye clenched the gate, the cool metal quickly warming from his sweaty palm. "Wait a minute. All day you've been saying 'we' when it's actually been me doing all the work."

"That won't be the case on Friday." She laughed. "Usually I do the tour and Hannie does the craft segment while showing them how she weaves on her loom. They make their own little weavings that turn out like lopsided coasters. But it teaches them how to work with alpaca fiber."

Did she honestly think he could teach them how to weave? "I'm not qualified for either job."

Ruthanne waved her hand. "Don't worry. I'll do both, and the teachers know how to do the craft, so they can supervise that. Paul will feed the kids, something he looks forward to every year. I'll just need you to move things along and make the animals behave. After this week is over, you'll be fairly comfortable with them."

Throughout the week her words proved correct. Skye found he could halter even the most obstinate creature and lead it through its paces without difficulty.

As the buses approached on Friday morning, he prayed he would be as comfortable around the children.

"Sorry, boy," he said to Ruddy, who strained against the chain attached to a spike in the yard. "This was the best I could come up with. I don't want you scaring the kids. Maybe I'll let you play with them after they get used to you."

Ruddy's sharp whine nearly made Skye change his mind. But then he turned the corner of the house. Excited children spilled out of the vehicles, scurrying like ants from a crushed hill. His dog would only add chaos to chaos, he feared. Teachers and parent volunteers managed to corral them, and somehow Skye and Ruthanne filtered them out to the pasture for their tour.

Ruthanne had chosen the more docile alpacas to interact with the group. Even so, their guttural grunts sounded a warning as the intruders gathered on the far side of the fence. Soon most of the alpacas greeted the children, their necks stretched toward them in curiosity, as if they'd never seen a human that short before. Once the two sides were comfortable with each other, Ruthanne opened a gate and allowed the group in for their up close and personal tour.

Skye marveled at Ruthanne's stamina as she led several groups through the premises at intervals. *Her ugly earthy shoes must support her feet pretty well.* She'd opted for jeans with a beautiful woven belt. Turquoise beads threaded on strings hung off the belt and hit her hips when she walked. Her gauzy tunic top made her look as young as some of the sixth graders.

Even though the tour was the same Ruthanne had given Skye, he learned so much more because the children thought to ask questions he'd never dreamed of.

"Why don't they have pupils in their eyeballs?"

"They have them," Ruthanne answered. "But because their eyes are so dark, you can't see them."

"Why do some of them look like my shaggy dog and others look like my Chia Pet?"

Ruthanne pulled one of the alpacas near. "This shaggy dog is a suri. Her hair has no crimp and grows down from her body in pencil-like dreadlocks." She dug into the coat and let the children see what she was talking about. Then she wrapped her arms around the neck of another alpaca. "This Chia Pet is a huacaya. Her fiber does have crimp so it springs from her body. It's fuzzier and very soft." Again everybody felt deep into the coat and watched how the layers bounced out.

One little boy recoiled. "Ew. It's just like my sister's hair!"

"Speaking of hair. . ." Ruthanne reached to her own head and pulled a strand out. "I want everyone to grab a hair. . .from your own heads, please."

Giggles and then yelps of pain followed.

"Now compare it to the alpaca hair."

Skye, feeling like one of the kids, dug into the wool and compared his hair with the alpacas. The silkiness of the alpaca hair reminded him of a cat.

"Hair is measured in microns. The thinner the hair, the lower the micron."

One boy raised his hand. "What's a micron?"

"It's a type of measurement, like inches or yards. But a micron is very tiny."

His teacher addressed the group. "We'll go back to class and learn about microns so you can understand what Miss Ruthanne is talking about." She smiled at Ruthanne, who looked relieved at not having to go into great detail.

"The human hair measures around sixty to one hundred microns," Ruthanne continued. "Alpaca hair measures sixteen to thirty microns. Plus, its hollow core makes it smooth and light."

She let this sink in before continuing. "Your grandpa's socks made from sheep's wool are much heavier and itchier than alpaca socks."

At one point during Ruthanne's talk about why alpacas hum, one nine-year-old girl held up her hand. "I like to hum when I'm happy. Do they hum when they're happy?"

"Some do, some don't," Ruthanne answered. "They have a unique language that includes grunts for distress or gentle humming as they talk to each other. Even though they love kids, you probably heard them when you walked up. Can you make that same sound?"

They all tried, most sounding like little pigs.

Ruthanne continued. "There is one special alpaca that loves everybody and seems to hum when she's happy." She sifted through the alpacas. "This is Lirit. Her name means 'lyrical' in Hebrew. The owner of the ranch, Hannie Godfrey, takes Lirit to nursing homes, orphanages, and prisons. Lirit helps people learn to love again. Hannie gave her to me at a very special time when I needed a good friend. Have you ever talked to a pet about your problems?"

While the children chattered about their own pets, a mother chaperone pulled Ruthanne aside. Skye, who stood nearby, made a point to listen when he heard his mother's name mentioned. "Hannie visited my father at Northwoods Senior Center a few months ago." The woman suddenly had tears in her eyes. "She brought Lirit. He always had a soft spot for animals. For the first time in his life, Dad allowed someone—Hannie—to tell him about God. He accepted Christ as his Savior that day. The next week he passed away."

Both women were in tears now, but they quickly swiped them away before the children saw them.

This was the first Skye had heard that his mother had become a Christian. But had she really? She'd used that line before to get some quick cash from an innocent pastor, with five-year-old Skye by her side to make her look respectable.

What game was she playing this time?

Ruthanne's lilting voice brought him back to the present. "Listen. Lirit loves all of you. Hear her hum?"

Skye was standing back a ways, apparently too far to hear Lirit. Then again, he never remembered hearing the alpaca hum. He'd been working on the ranch for a week, and all he got from sweet Lirit was attitude.

The children moved on to the classroom where crafts and Paul's snacks awaited them. Skye lingered near the alpaca. "So, what is it about me that you don't like, girl?" He offered her a peanut, one of many he kept in his pocket. She regarded him as if he'd lost his mind, turned her back, flattened her ears, and effectively ignored him.

"I don't get it," he muttered as he joined the rest of the group.

As the last bus pulled away, Ruthanne stood in the driveway and waved. She couldn't wait to sit on the back deck and put her feet up. She loved children, but she'd never hosted so many classes by herself before.

She had just eased herself down on a deck chair when Skye showed up with a tray of punch-filled glasses and a plate of small sandwiches.

"Thanks. These aren't the whipped peanut butter and jelly bean ones that Paul made for the kids, are they?" She carefully lifted the top half of the croissant, fully expecting to see a purple piece of candy nestled inside. "He gets imaginative around holidays, and jelly beans are his favorite Easter candy."

"No, these are chicken salad. He said you'd like it." Skye plopped into the chair next to her.

Ruthanne took a healthy bite, savoring the mixture of walnuts and sweet dried cranberries. She hadn't realized how hungry she'd become.

Once her unfed stomach stopped grousing, she noticed Skye's haggard face. "You look as tired as I feel. Thank you for filling in the gap. I never realized how hard this would be without Hannie."

He tilted his mouth as if he were going to say something but must have changed his mind.

Trying to fill the ensuing silence, Ruthanne found herself babbling. "I love children. They're so curious, and the whole world is before them, waiting to be discovered. What about you? Do you like kids?"

"Sure. If I ever have one of my own, I'll protect him and always make him feel special."

Nothing particularly odd about that statement, but the haunted look in his eyes disturbed Ruthanne. It passed quickly, though, so she continued the train of thought. "Have you ever been married, Skye?"

"Nope, never found one who would put up with me."

She found that hard to believe. After watching his work ethic and his gentle-manly ways, she suspected he had some mighty high standards of his own. "If I get married again, I'd love to have a boy and a girl. One of each."

Paul stepped through the door from the kitchen and plopped onto a deck chair. After preparing the snacks, serving them, and playing with the kids, he'd worked as hard as they had. He continued their conversation. "Two kids sounds great. A child for each lap. No one fighting over who gets to sit by the window in the car."

Skye smiled for the first time since they'd begun talking about children. "You two have obviously never grown up in a big family."

"And you have?" Ruthanne leaned forward. Maybe she'd finally get some of her questions answered.

"I'm the oldest of five kids."

"But. . ." Ruthanne glanced at Paul, who simply blinked back at her. "Hannie never mentioned having children. Then again, she never talked much about her life before marrying David."

"No, she wouldn't have done that, would she?" Skye thrust himself from his chair and stood at the deck railing with his back to them. His shoulders tensed like two cement blocks on either side of his spine. When he turned around, he seemed to be willing himself to relax. "I was adopted. My family consists of two awesome Christian parents and four sisters. The others are my parents' natural offspring, but they always treated me like blood."

She moved to stand next to him and leaned on the railing. Reaching out to touch his arm, she tentatively asked, "How old were you when you were adopted?"

"Thirteen."

That answered why she hadn't seen him around. And from Hannie's testimony, she guessed someone had removed him from the home due to drug abuse. However, that didn't answer why Hannie never told her, or even Paul, about him. Only Hannie could satisfy that question.

Chapter 5

"It's been a week. How do you feel about the ranch?" Ruthanne asked Skye during breakfast on Monday.

With everything he needed to do, his days flew by. It surprised him that he only had three weeks left. "It's not as hard as I thought it would be. I'll admit, I'm having fun."

"Even without bronco busting and cattle branding?"

"Okay, I thought alpaca ranching would be lame. . . ."

"And?" Her eyes twinkled, making him glad he'd shared his disappointment with her.

"And that no real man should be caught dead shoveling their, er, beans."

"Wait until one of them gives birth. If you can survive that, you will be a real alpaca rancher."

He shuddered at the thought. "I remember you showing me the pregnant ones. How many did you say are due in the next three weeks?"

"Only four of them."

Skye groaned. *Any way they could all be overdue, Lord?*

"Relax, a couple of them have a habit of waiting a month then surprising us when we least expect it. And they do most of the work." Ruthanne rose and took her plate to the sink. "Would you like to see your mother today? I thought I'd go this afternoon."

Nearly every day she asked if he'd go with her to the hospital, and he always came up with excuses.

"Actually I need to drive into Medford today. Check out my house, make sure the plants haven't died."

She turned with the dish towel wrapped around her hands. "Would you mind if I tagged along? I can see Hannie this evening. I need to get some supplies for the craft fair next weekend. Mundane stuff, like PVC pipe and plastic crates."

"Sure, if you don't mind being gone the whole day. My parents have invited me out to lunch."

"Oh." She waved the towel then turned to wipe the counter dry. "I don't want to intrude."

Intrusive was the last thing Ruthanne could be. Her gentle spirit had often calmed his soul this past week as his emotions churned like a thunderstorm. He smiled. "I would love to have you come and meet my folks."

Ruthanne replaced the towel on its wooden rack by the sink, leaned on the counter, and drew lazy circles on the granite finish. "I don't know. . . ."

Seeing her hesitation, he decided to seal the deal. "You'd be doing me a favor. I'm bombarded with questions whenever I talk to my mom on the phone. She's curious about the alpacas, and it would be great if she could talk to the expert."

The finger circling stopped, and she gently tapped the counter. "Okay. If you're sure they won't mind."

Skye whipped out his cell phone. After briefly apprising his mom of the change in plans, he hung up and smiled. "She can hardly wait."

❧

After her chores Ruthanne cleaned up to prepare for her day with Skye. He wanted to leave at 11:00, but at 10:55 she was still standing in front of her closet without a clue of what to wear.

She was going to put on jeans and her favorite peasant blouse to visit Hannie, but now that seemed frumpy. Finally she grabbed a robin's egg blue top and a mid-calf-length broom skirt with a peacock-feather pattern. The spring day had started to warm nicely, so she opted for her green ballet-type slippers.

As she assessed herself in the mirror, she felt silly. Why should she worry about what to wear the first time she met Skye's mom? Even so, she brushed out her braids and fluffed her hair so it fell past her shoulders, adding vintage chandelier earrings. Before walking out of her bathroom, her hand hesitated over her sparse makeup bag. She opened it slowly, feeling as though someone else was guiding her hand. Repeating to herself *Silly, silly, silly,* she dusted her face with translucent powder to dull the freckles and swiped on the pearl pink lipstick she'd bought last year for an event honoring Hannie. With a last check in the mirror, she left her trailer and walked the gravel path between the pastures.

When she entered the back door, she called for Skye. He was on the front porch, waiting for her.

"I'm sorry." She fingered her skirt, suddenly self-conscious. "I felt I needed to change if we were going out to lunch."

Skye took in her appearance, coolly appraising her. No compliment for her efforts?

"No problem. You're right on time." She followed him to his car, wondering about his mood swing.

❧

Skye glanced at the woman sitting next to him. Why did she have to wear *that*? He'd become used to Ruthanne's hippie clothing while at her house, but she was about to visit *his* world. The last thing he wanted to do was infest it with anything that resembled his birth mother.

When they arrived at the restaurant, Skye opened his car door, but Ruthanne flipped the visor and checked her makeup in the vanity mirror—something Skye had never seen her do before. In fact, he'd never seen her in makeup. She looked fine without it.

As Skye accompanied Ruthanne inside, buttery garlic smells swirled around them. "This is my favorite Italian restaurant." His stomach growled, punctuating his comment. The hostess led them to the table where his parents waited, and they both rose to hug him.

"Mom, Dad, this is Ruthanne Fairfax."

His dad held out his hand and pumped Ruthanne's arm. Mom drew her into a hug. Over Ruthanne's shoulder she mouthed the words, "She's cute," to which Skye mouthed back, "Don't even think about it."

Feminine, young adult arms wrapped around his waist.

Without looking back, he said, "And this would be my baby sister, Robyn."

"Hey, big bro!"

She unwound her arms and curtsied. "You're Ruthanne. Pleased to meet you. I'll be your waitress this afternoon."

As they scooted into the booth, she took their drink orders then disappeared less enthusiastically than she had appeared.

"Our little actress," Mom explained. "Waitressing pays her bills, but she's getting a performing arts degree at the university."

"The campus in Oakley?" Ruthanne picked up her napkin and removed the utensils before placing it in her lap. "Has she been to the Shakespeare Festival?"

"Frequently." Dad rolled his eyes.

Mom playfully slapped his shoulder. "Acting runs in my family. My brother is a producer in Hollywood." She waved her hands. "But I want to know about the ranch."

Most people bombarded Mom when she confessed about the thespian half of her family, but today, as Skye had predicted, Mom had plenty of her own questions.

"I'm fascinated with the process of taking the wool and turning it into those colorful yarns I see in the craft stores."

"And boy, it is a process, too." Ruthanne laughed. "A long one. Hannie used to do all of the carding and dyeing herself, but now she sends the fiber out to be done. There are people who specialize in just that. Then we get it back, and she spins it into those yarns you see. This weekend we're participating in a craft fair in Oakley. Please come out if you can. I'll be doing demonstrations all day of how we go from the animal to the finished product."

"Oh, I'd love that. I hope you're selling some things made from your own alpacas."

"Absolutely. That's part of the fun."

Skye and his dad glanced at each other and smiled. Mom loved crafty things but only had the patience to learn scrapbooking.

By the time the main course arrived, Ruthanne had invited his parents to the ranch for a tour. They settled on a date, contingent on Hannie's health.

"Skye." His mother finally acknowledged his presence. "We have a favor to ask."

"I knew it." He smacked the table. "You've been plying me with food to soften me up." He gave an exaggerated sigh. "What is it?"

"Since your house is empty, we were wondering if the Maxwells could use it while they're here." She turned to Ruthanne. "Ted and Kellie Maxwell are missionaries with our church. Our house is already full with another family passing through, but the Maxwells have a new baby, and it would be nice if they could get away from the chaos."

"No problem." He included Ruthanne in the conversation. "I went to school with Ted, so it's not like they're strangers. I'll have to be sure the house is ready for company, though, if that's okay with you."

"That's fine. We don't have to get back to feed the animals until this evening."

While Mom and Ruthanne continued their animated talk about crafts, Dad turned to Skye. "I'm worried about your sister's car. I don't think it has long to live."

"Well, she wanted that cute little sports car." He laughed. "And whatever Robyn wants, Robyn gets." He explained for Ruthanne. "When she turned twenty-one, she bought her own car, but it's a lemon. We worry about her every time she drives the thing." He spoke to his dad again. "I'll take a look at it this weekend. I suspect it's something in the transmission."

"Excuse me." Ruthanne looked at him with wide eyes. "I didn't know you were a mechanic. Why didn't you tell me?"

He leaned on his forearm, draping the napkin from his fingers. "Because you'd probably have me fixing your old tractor. You've got me doing everything else."

After a bite of lasagna, he was going to share the story about harvesting alpaca beans, but his mom interrupted with a question to Ruthanne. "How is Hannah? Do you think she'll pull through?"

Skye would rather talk about alpaca beans.

Ruthanne swirled her pasta with her fork. "I'm praying she does. The coma is medically induced to help her lungs heal, but the doctor says her recovery afterward could take some time."

Mom reached for Ruthanne's hand. "We've been praying, too, dear."

Ruthanne muttered a thank-you while Mom slid her gaze toward Skye. Did he see accusation there, as if he were supposed to agree to be praying, too? It left as quickly as it had come, but he knew he'd just been reprimanded.

∽

As they entered Skye's house, a charming redbrick bungalow, Ruthanne glanced around with interest. What little she saw from the living room told her volumes about the man who had invaded her sanctuary a week ago.

For a male domain it was surprisingly neat. He probably cleaned up knowing he'd be gone for a month, but still. No suspicious dog hair lay in the baseboard crevice, no fingerprints on the television set; the nap of the rug suggested regular vacuuming. Did he hire someone to clean for him? Or maybe his mom had taken the opportunity while he was gone.

"Make yourself at home." He tossed his keys onto a shelf near the door.

"Would you like a drink? I have soda." He pointed toward the kitchen.

"No thank you. I'm stuffed from lunch." She wandered farther into the room, taking in the decor. The Wild West seemed to be the theme. A painting of cowboys sitting around a glowing campfire created a peaceful tone for the room. A striking bronze statue of a horse rearing up on its hindquarters adorned the coffee table.

After watering the plants, an assortment of philodendrons and other easy-to-care-for foliage, he slipped into a hallway. "I just want to check the spare bedroom."

For what? It must look like the rest of the house.

A small fireplace, made of the same brick as the exterior, drew her. Atop the dark wood mantel, pictures of Skye's family sat in strategic clusters. The people in them smiled, waved, and struck silly poses in photos taken in all seasons. His sisters all looked like his mother, strawberry blondish hair of various hues and hazel eyes. Skye was definitely the standout with his dark features and blue eyes.

They all seemed happy.

"There's a photo album in the cabinet by the fireplace." Skye startled her as he moved through with an armful of sheets, blankets, and pillows.

"Is there anything I can do to help?"

"No, that's okay. All I have to do is make the bed."

No doubt. The missionaries couldn't have it cleaner if they moved into a five-star hotel.

She pulled out the photo album, an artfully done scrapbook covered in a brown material simulating leather, put together by a loving hand.

After settling herself on the couch, she opened the book to a page titled OUR FIRST CHOSEN, showing pictures of Skye and his new family. The teen's face held a haunted, almost wary look under his shy grin.

She turned the page. Fourteen-year-old Skye with a birthday cake in front of him. The candles' glow on his scowling face broke her heart. She breathed a prayer of thanks that God had put him with such loving people.

As she flipped through the book, she noticed his demeanor change. Tentative smiles began to appear as he held up a baseball award then broader grins during camping trips, Christmas mornings, and. . . What was this? Skye in a choir? What kind of a voice did he have? He must have gotten his talent from Hannie, whose beautiful solo voice ministered during many a Sunday morning.

She grinned as an impish thought formed in her mind. Skye needed to come to church with her next Sunday so he could meet Hannie's friends. . .and so Ruthanne could hear him sing.

"Okay, I'm ready." He popped into the living room, interrupting Ruthanne's scheming.

She closed the album and put it away. "You have a beautiful family."

His face softened. "Yes. God is good."

"All the time." And would he recognize that God had been good to Hannie as well?

On the way to his car, Ruthanne took in the surrounding neighborhood then glanced back at the house. "This is a lovely home. Do you have someone come in to help you keep it up? Or does your mom make you toe the line?" Curious minds and all that.

He chuckled as he shut her door. When he entered the driver's side, he glanced at her, still smiling. "My mom is a great influencer but no. I had to learn to be neat while in the foster system." The grin on his face vanished as the subject moved from his mom, whom he clearly loved, to the foster homes. "Some places were good, the parents fair. But others. . ."

Ruthanne put her hand on his arm. "That's okay. I can hear it in your voice."

He started the ignition. "When I joined my forever family—"

"Forever family?" She quirked her brow.

His chuckle came back. "That's what my folks call it. Silly, I know."

"Not at all. I'm sure it made you feel secure to know that they loved you enough to keep you forever."

He didn't answer, but his serene smile told her more than words ever could.

"Anyway, I'm the neatest of the bunch." He waited at a busy cross street for the light to change. "My sisters don't know what it's like to be walloped for leaving a toy on the floor. I wanted to be sure I stayed with this family, so I did all I could to make Mom and Dad happy."

"Hannie is the neatest person I know. Maybe you got it from her genes."

His face clouded over as it often did when she spoke of her friend. She vowed to press on in the coming days, hoping to weave stories of Hannie's goodness and to fill in the tapestry of her life for this man who had missed the good parts.

"So, where do you have to go?"

She jumped at his abrupt change of subject. Opening her purse, she quickly drew out the list of craft-supply stores. "I have a handful of stores on my list."

They visited each store, with Ruthanne faithfully sticking to her budget. When they were through, they headed for the interstate, stopping at a red light near a little park.

Not wanting this one-on-one time with Skye to end, Ruthanne turned to him. "I can't believe that huge lunch has worn off already. Would you like to get a hot dog and eat it in the park? It's such a beautiful day."

He pulled away from the intersection slowly while eyeing the park then nearly floored it. "No. I have to be getting back."

To what? The animals weren't due for feeding for another hour. What got him so agitated? Had she said something wrong? No. Something else triggered this reaction. She looked back at the empty park, searching for answers, but whatever disturbed him was no longer there.

Chapter 6

Every Sunday morning Ruthanne fed and watered the animals by herself. Skye's church met earlier than hers, and because he had to travel a half hour to get there, she'd agreed to split the day's duties, she taking the morning and he the evening.

Once she'd finished her chores, she stood in her own kitchen, sipping green tea and looking out toward the main house. A light was on in the kitchen. Perhaps Skye was fixing his breakfast. Who was this man? Good-natured one moment then ready to box with the world the next. Was he there to honor his commitment to a mother he barely knew? Or was he assessing the property at close range with plans to sell it the moment Hannie was no longer in the picture?

She stood for a good five minutes arguing with herself before finally deciding to go over there. All week she had tried to gain courage to ask Skye to church. Why did she hesitate? Could it have been the ride home from Medford and the strained silence that nearly deafened her? And the ensuing storm clouds in Skye's demeanor the entire week?

Carrying her mug and a plate of cinnamon muffins Paul had made, she tentatively opened Hannie's back door—halfway hoping Skye had already left the kitchen. But no such luck. He sat at the table eating scrambled eggs, drinking coffee, and reading the Sunday comics. She heard his soft chuckle and hoped they'd put him in a better mood.

"Mind if I join you?" She held out the plate, almost as a peace offering. Ruddy rose from the corner of the kitchen to greet her and tried to act as taste tester. She held the plate high, although she doubted that could have deterred the big dog.

"Ruddy, go lay down." Skye deflated all hope, and Ruddy returned to his corner but watched the floor for any errant morsels. "Sorry about that. Have a seat." He motioned to a chair. At least he didn't bite her head off. That was an improvement over yesterday. She eased herself into the chair across from him. He returned to his paper where a one-dimensional Garfield the cat grinned back at her from the paper.

"What have you got planned today?"

"My church starts"—he lowered the newspaper long enough to check his watch—"in an hour. After that I don't know."

Ruthanne took a deep breath. "Would you like to go to church with me this morning?"

This made him lower the paper and stare at her. One would have thought she had asked him to rob a bank. "No obligation, of course," she quickly clarified.

"I just thought you might like to visit Hannie's church. See where she worships."

She hopped up to refill his coffee cup and to give him time to think about his answer.

When she sat back down, he'd lowered the paper, but he had a death grip on it. His sky blue eyes grew dark. But then they narrowed. "I'll go to see where *you* worship."

She accepted the challenge. "Fine. Your car or mine?"

His lips twitched as if he enjoyed the game. "Mine."

She held out her hand. "Deal."

As his hand squeezed around hers, pleasant tingles shot up her arm. She pulled away too quickly, bumping his coffee cup.

"Ow!" She swept away the hot liquid that had spilled onto her wrist.

"Are you hurt?" Skye popped out of the chair and had her at the kitchen sink in nearly the same motion. He gently rinsed her hand off in cold water. "Let me look at that."

Ruthanne watched this man—this caring individual, of whom only moments before she had thought the worst—inspect her burn with a tenderness that touched her soul. What guided his ever-changing emotions?

◦◦◦◦

"I don't think it's bad." Skye inspected the burn, marveling at the softness of Ruthanne's fingers in spite of her rough work at the ranch. Reluctant to let her go, he slipped the dish towel from its bar and dabbed around the reddened skin to keep the water from dripping on the floor.

"It wasn't that hot. I think I reacted before I felt it." She slid her arm away and took the towel from his fingers to finish the drying.

Man, she smelled good. They had worked in close quarters in the stalls before, but with the alpaca scent, he never caught how her hair smelled like flowers. Gone was the makeup she'd applied the other day. Good. She didn't need it to cover her natural beauty.

When he realized he was still only a few inches away from her and staring like an adolescent with a crush, he moved back to the table with a dishrag. "What time is church then?" He concentrated on wiping up the small puddle.

"Eleven o'clock." He looked back at her. She regarded him with her head tilted, as if she were trying to figure him out. Well, good luck with that. He hadn't figured himself out since meeting her. One minute she angered him by speaking about his mother, and the next he was falling all over himself trying to please her.

She left to finish getting ready for church while he cleaned his breakfast dishes and then took Ruddy outside. After a quick game of keep-away with a teeth-perforated disk, he clicked the long leash attached to the spike in the ground onto Ruddy's collar. "I hate to do this to you, but you can't be trusted inside." As he walked away, Ruddy raised on his hind legs, straining against the chain, looking like a roan-colored stallion. "Hey, buddy. Go easy, will ya?" Skye checked the spike to be sure it was secure. He had brought Ruddy's doghouse over and placed it under the back deck out of the weather. "You'll be fine. I'll be home soon."

He noticed Ruthanne in Lirit's paddock. The two nuzzled noses, and Ruthanne petted the alpaca's neck while murmuring to her. What kind of girl talk did they share?

∞

"I don't know, Lirit. I can't figure him out. At times it's as if he's only doing this through some odd sense of obligation. At others he seems so eager to learn."

Lirit flattened her ears and emoted a disgusted grunt that made her lips flap.

"Why don't you like him?" Ruthanne had heard of animals with a special sense toward humans. Did Lirit know something about Skye that he hadn't revealed to Ruthanne? Was he the land-grabbing monster she had painted earlier?

But he was a Christian. And he took care of her coffee-drenched hand. And he smelled so good. It was all she could do to keep from leaning in and taking a big whiff as he tended her wrist. Something woodsy. Not what you'd expect a business-man to wear. And certainly not what Paul wore. Sometimes he was so drenched in cologne she could hardly breathe. She remembered Hannie admonishing him once. She railed on him for ten minutes about how his cologne probably killed hundreds of animals in the testing phase. Then she moved on to what the chemicals were doing to his body. Hannie never wore perfume. Nothing with chemicals ever touched her skin.

And yet she still ended up in the hospital.

"I'm ready." Skye's voice from the side of the house startled her. With one last pat to Lirit's neck, she tugged the strap of her woven purse tighter to her shoulder and joined him.

∞

As they made their way to the garage, Skye saw Ruthanne dart a shy glance toward him. He had to resist the urge to put his arm around her.

"You look nice." He meant it this time. Even though her pink skirt had a strong gypsy influence with the billowy top, it didn't scream hippie like her other choice of clothing.

"You, too. But you don't need to wear a tie."

He glanced down at the tie his mother had given him for his fortieth birthday. The color of his eyes. He didn't know what came over him when he chose to wear the tie that morning. He never wore one to his own church. "You want me to take it off?" He started to loosen the knot.

"No. It looks good." A blush dusted her cheeks. Yep, that's why he'd chosen the tie.

They reached his car parked in the drive. He opened her door for her, but before she slipped inside, she grabbed the door frame. "Skye, Paul is taking me to see Hannie right after church. They did a tracheal intubation on her yesterday."

"I know. He called to tell me."

47

"I'm anxious to see her without her face obstructed. Although I'm not sure I can handle a tube in her throat." Her large eyes searched his. "Would you join us?"

He agreed, sensing that she was asking for herself this time. But an excuse hovered just inside his lips, ready to rescue him.

Fifteen minutes later Ruthanne instructed him to pull into the parking lot of Faith Community Church, a small building probably built in the 1960s. The roof slanted in a long slope, and the windows were in a geometric pattern.

Just inside the small foyer, Paul stood talking to a woman. About food, of course.

The ample middle-aged woman clung to Paul's elbow. "I didn't expect you to take on the whole party. I'll bring the teas though."

"That's good, because I know food, but tea is a woman's domain."

The henlike woman reached out for Ruthanne, and Skye trailed behind her. "What a gem you have found in this man. I hope you plan on keeping him."

Ruthanne's half grin didn't suggest a woman in love.

Paul stepped in. "Hey, Ruthie and I are just good friends." He draped his arm over her shoulders.

Good friends? All Skye had witnessed since moving in was Paul's attention toward Ruthanne. He told himself to keep his distance until he assessed the playing field more thoroughly.

The woman finished her conversation with Paul and bustled into the sanctuary.

Paul noticed Skye and shook his hand. "Hey, glad you could make it. Ruthanne called me to say you were coming." He looked down at her. "I notified the girls."

Her hand flew to her open mouth. "You didn't!"

Skye looked at Ruthanne and then at Paul. "The girls?"

Ruthanne's gaze darted around the foyer as she placed her hand on Skye's arm. "Four of Hannie's friends. They are remarkable artisans and have sort of formed a club with Hannie as their leader."

"What? Like the Ya-Ya Crafthood?"

"Something like that. They're all about the same age and—"

"There he is!"

Skye turned at the sound of a woman fast approaching him, her sandaled feet slapping the tiled floor. Short burgundy hair adorned her head, and she seemed weighted down with the turquoise jewelry around her neck and on each finger. Three other women trailed after her like naturally graying tails on a brightly colored kite.

Oh great! Granola-fueled earth mothers.

Ruthanne tried to step between Skye and the women, but they sailed past her.

"Look at his eyes. Just like his mother's." Skye felt like a museum piece as they scrutinized him. He wished he'd had a corded rope surrounding him to keep them from touching.

Each woman had been a hippie in her day. He could tell by their natural-fiber clothing, the long, uncut hair of the trailing three, and the telltale wrinkles around their mouths from drawing on too many homemade marijuana cigarettes.

He wanted to hurl. Any one of them could have been in the commune when he was little.

Ruthanne made the introductions. "Skye, this is Lark, Daisy, Saffron, and Agnes."

Agnes?

She must have tried to break out of the stereotype. Agnes had led the pack. She slipped her long, bony fingers around his bicep. "We're all praying for Hannie. She's one special lady."

"So I've heard." His brusque response convicted him, and he softened when he saw how deeply these women loved his mother. He covered her hand at his elbow. "Thank you."

Through a shimmer of tears, Lark glanced toward the open door of the sanctuary. "The music has started. Please, if you need anything, let us know."

Skye nodded, and the four flower children left him the same way they had arrived. Nonconformists. They all looked alike, so what was the point? But these women had good hearts, and they obviously loved the Lord.

Ruthanne drew him into the sanctuary. Only then did he hear the music. As they made their way to the chairs, she leaned toward him to speak. "I'm sorry about Hannie's friends. Paul shouldn't have told them you were coming."

He glanced to Paul, who was clapping and singing on the other side of Ruthanne. "It's okay. That's why I'm here, right? To learn about my mother?"

Ruthanne offered a sad smile but didn't say anything. She briefly squeezed his arm. From that moment on, Skye had a hard time concentrating on the service.

⊂≥

During the praise music Skye never opened his mouth. Now how was Ruthanne supposed to compare his voice to Hannie's if he didn't cooperate?

The music finished, leaving her feeling in a less than worshipful mood. She had concentrated too much on Skye and not enough on the Lord. But when the pastor announced prayer time, Ruthanne began to feel the gentle pull of the Holy Spirit.

"We have so many needs in our body today," the pastor spoke. "Let's turn to our neighbors and take a moment to pray for each other."

People began whispering their requests to each other, the soft voices like a straw broom whisking away debris. Paul turned to Ruthanne. Normally she relished their prayer time together. But today she whispered that she wanted to pray with Skye. He tipped his head slightly in resigned agreement and instead of joining her turned to the person on his right.

She took Skye's hand, and his eyes widened in surprise. "Please pray for Hannie with me."

He winced as if Hannie's name had become a hot poker. But he allowed her to take the other hand, and standing there together, they bowed their heads. Ruthanne uttered a heartfelt prayer, one she'd prayed often since Hannie's illness. But then she prayed for Skye.

"Lord, I pray for peace for Skye. This hasn't been easy for him. I can't imagine the emotions he's had to deal with since learning about his mother. He may someday have some decisions to make—" Her throat caught. Silently she prayed she wouldn't cry. Those decisions could affect her adversely, but she didn't want this to be a selfish prayer. "Tough decisions that I trust You'll guide him through. Above all, I pray You help him to smile more. . . ." She let the last request trail off, realizing she was about to say, *as that would be an indication that You're working in his life.* But she didn't know him well enough to be so bold.

When she looked up at the end of her prayer, he was gazing at her. No storm clouds in those eyes. They seemed brighter, as if unshed tears purified their color.

"Thank you." He pressed her hand to his chest. How long they stood there together, she had no way of knowing. But eventually the pastor's voice pulled her back.

<hr/>

Skye tore his gaze from Ruthanne and noticed Paul glancing toward them, his eyes darting to their clasped hands. He reluctantly let go. Did Paul think their behavior inappropriate, or did he indeed have feelings for Ruthanne?

Skye only knew that after his mother's friends had assaulted him, he had decided he would make yet another excuse to avoid seeing his mother. But an incredible strength surged through him as Ruthanne prayed.

As long as she was there, he could enter that hospital room.

Chapter 7

S kye's shoes squeaked on the freshly buffed floor as he followed Ruthanne and Paul down the corridor. The closer he came to his mother's room, the more he wanted out. Ruthanne glanced over her shoulder and smiled at him.

He took a deep breath. He could do this. As long as she continued to gift him with that sweet smile, he would be strong.

They entered the room, and the other two walked to either side of the bed. Skye hung back, his shoulders pressed into the doorjamb—one foot in, one foot out. So much for staying strong.

His mother lay in exactly the same position as the first time he'd seen her. But she looked different with the respirator mask off. Even with her face exposed, she was still not the mother he remembered.

Ruthanne leaned down and spoke softly. "Hannie, we're here." She took a comb from her purse and began grooming the woman. "Honestly, Hannie, you don't move an inch, yet your hair is always mussed when I come in."

Paul followed suit. "Hey, Auntie. Brought you a tofu burger."

Ruthanne looked at him in surprise. "Now what would you do if she woke up and wanted it?"

"I'd go make her one." Paul began rubbing the frail arms and legs. He spoke to Skye. "This helps keep the circulation going."

Skye nodded. The lump in his throat refused to budge. Watching these two dote on his mother stirred an emotion Skye never thought he'd have: jealousy. It rose up from his bowels, clinging to every nerve ending on the way up. This was *his* mother, a woman he barely knew yet she'd made room for two strangers in her life. No, more than that. She'd made room for an entire community.

A voice in his head, clearly not God's but impossible to silence, challenged his thoughts like a bully on a playground. *Look at these two people. She loved them far more than she ever loved you.* Skye squeezed his fists into his eyes to shut out the scene before him. *You were worthless. Just something that needed to be fed.* His heart bled from a tangible wound as the bully struck his final blow. *She never loved you. You were a tumor that she couldn't wait to get rid of after your father died.*

He bounded out of the hospital room, nearly spilling a metal meal cart, his chest about to implode. Hot tears burned his eyes like acid.

Somehow he managed to navigate the halls out to the parking lot. Good thing Paul had chosen to take his own car to the hospital after church. Ruthanne had a way home.

A mist fell that chilled him to the core. He climbed into his car and shot an angry glance upward through the windshield toward the sky—his namesake. The hippie name once sickened him. His mother often told him the sky was his father, and he had his eyes. Whenever he was in trouble, he should look up. Father Sky would solve his problems.

Skye ground the gears and tore out of the parking lot. Down the road, a traffic light suddenly turned yellow. He skidded to a stop. Only then did he realize he'd been going twenty miles over the speed limit.

Gray clouds hung heavy behind the red traffic light. Another voice entered his swirling thoughts—that of the woman who raised him. His spiritual anchor, Mom. *It's okay to look to the sky, but remember, you'll only get your answers from the One who created it.* He clenched the steering wheel. The other voice drowned out that reason. *If your mother lived so close, why didn't she try to find you earlier? What made her do it now? Guilt? The fear of dying?* With one foot on the clutch, he revved the engine until the light turned green. When it changed, his foot bore down on the gas pedal.

Just out of Oakley, the two-lane highway opened before him, and he took the curves like a Grand Prix veteran. His accuser's voice clung to the back bumper. *What game is she playing now? If she got her life together, why didn't she find you when you grew up? What does she want from you?* Skye couldn't go fast enough to shake it. A couple of miles later he swerved onto the road leading to the ranch.

Mom had told him: *Remember that Hannah is a person, too. She deserves prayers as much as anyone else. I hope you've been lifting her before the Lord.*

Conflicting memories sparred within. He sped past the few homes dotting the valley. The ranch suddenly came into view, his preoccupation nearly causing him to sail on past.

Then—

A flash of red fur.

He fought the steering wheel as he veered left.

Slick mud marked for landscaping.

The barn.

Wood cracked and splintered.

The car finally stopped in an SUV-sized hole. The air bag, a rough, powdery marshmallow, punched his face and slammed his head into the headrest. An acrid smell assaulted his nose.

Disoriented, he opened the door and slid out. A sharp pain jabbed in the arch of his right foot. He stumbled, twisting his ankle, and fell to the cement floor on his left shoulder. Agony sliced through his body.

He lay there on his back, praying the whole thing had just been a nasty dream. He rolled away from the car, but—

Knifing pain.

Blessed darkness.

Squawking chickens brought him back—probably only moments later—encircling him in a feathered frenzy. From his supine position, he could see long-haired rabbits springing among the poultry.

What had he done?

"Skye!"

Ruthanne's voice. Outside. She must not have been far behind him. He tried to get up, but his arm wouldn't work. Her voice grew nearer. He wished he could crawl away. Disappear. Never be seen again.

"Skye?" She was in the barn, but he didn't call out to her. His own voice accused him. *Stupid!* He closed his eyes.

Her trembling hands gently inspected his face and chest. "Oh no. Skye! Please, God, no!"

"Go away."

The hands lifted off him. "What?"

"I'm an idiot and don't deserve any medical attention."

Tender hands touched his cheeks. He opened his eyes, fearing what he'd see there. Ruthanne's face showed nothing but concern. A siren sounded in the distance, and he groaned. His car's emergency system must have alerted the paramedics when his air bag went off. He squeezed his eyes shut again.

"Skye!" She grabbed him by his shirt. "Stay with me." Was she going to slap him?

"I'm not unconscious. Just embarrassed."

He opened his eyes again to see her kneeling, elbows akimbo as she leaned her hands on her hips. "What happened?"

"I guess I was going too fast when I pulled in the drive, and something red came out of nowhere." His breath caught in his throat. "It was Ruddy!"

Her sad eyes frightened him. "Yes, it was Ruddy."

He tried to sit up again, but she pressed him back down. "He's okay. You must have clipped him though. He's favoring his back leg. When we pulled up, we saw him slinking toward the front porch. He's probably trying to escape punishment."

"I've got to find him." He tried to sit up, but the pain caused a buzzing in his ears.

She placed her hand on his chest. "Paul ran to catch him before he could take off. He'll be fine. We'll have our vet look at him."

"Now."

"Soon. First we need to get you to the hospital."

Not the hospital! He didn't want to go back there where it all started.

He had no choice. The rescue unit arrived and loaded him into the ambulance.

⟨⟨⟩⟩

"I'm glad we left the hospital not long after him. He must have just landed in the barn when we got there." Ruthanne paced the emergency waiting room while Paul sat in a chair. She rubbed her arms and muttered, more to herself than to Paul.

"Why did he run? What is it about Hannie that scares him?"

Paul shook his head. "Not a clue. Have you asked him?"

She stopped pacing and looked at him. "It's not really my business, is it?"

"It might be now. He's caused a mess out at your place, all because of this thing with Aunt Hannie."

Ruthanne sank into the chair beside Paul. "You're her nephew. Why don't you talk to Skye? You *are* family."

Paul frowned. "I don't think he'd tell me. We're not exactly friends."

"You're probably right. All we can do is pray." Ruthanne sighed and looked at the clock. Skye had only been in there a half hour.

The glass door opened, and Skye's parents rushed in. Mrs. Randall's face was full of concern. She spotted Ruthanne and nearly ran into her arms.

"He's okay." Ruthanne could barely get the words out as the woman squeezed her neck like a boa constrictor. "Just banged up a little."

Mrs. Randall relaxed. "I know, but a mother imagines all kinds of things. Thank you for calling us." She pressed a tissue to her chest with one hand and held her husband's hand with the other.

Paul stood, and Ruthanne made the introductions.

"I'm sure he'll be out soon." Ruthanne pulled Mrs. Randall to a black plastic chair and sat down beside her.

Mrs. Randall drew a deep breath. As the color returned to her face, she turned to Paul. "How long have you known Skye's birth mother?"

"She married my uncle when I was twelve. We all love her."

Ruthanne noticed the older woman's lips pinch into two cranberry lines. Was this as hard on her as it was on Skye? What did she know about Hannie's early life?

Before she lost her nerve, Ruthanne posed the question she wished she could ask Skye. "Do you know what happened to Skye when he lived with Hannie?"

His parents cast sidelong glances at each other. Mrs. Randall answered. "Not all of it. Only what has come out gradually."

"Do you know why Hannie put him up for adoption?"

They both shifted in their seats. Her questions were having an uncomfortable effect on them.

"Did he tell you she did that?"

Mr. Randall's question took her aback. They acted as if there were another alternative. "Well, no. He hasn't said anything about his mother."

Skye's dad leaned forward with his elbows on his knees, pinning Ruthanne with a firm yet compassionate gaze. "We're not at liberty to discuss Skye's affairs since he hasn't given us permission for that. I'm sure, if you continue your friendship with him, much will come to light."

"We have prayed together often for his birth mother," Mrs. Randall said. "I'm pleased that she found such loving people to finally settle down with."

Finally? Ruthanne felt an odd, queasy feeling in the pit of her stomach. Her husband had been a rover. He never "finally" settled anywhere. Had Hannie been like Brian at one time? Could that have been why she held such empathy for him?

Hannie, what kind of a mother were you?

Just then Skye hobbled into the room, with his left arm in a large sling and a crutch under the other. Abrasions across the bridge of his nose indicated where the air bag had made contact. He was lucky nothing had been broken.

His mother gasped and rushed toward him.

"I'm fine." His words had no effect as she began inspecting him for further wounds. "They gave me a tetanus shot because I stepped on a nail sticking out of a board when I got out of my car. The nail caused me to sprain my ankle. Not bad but the doctor said it will be sore for a week or two. But because of the sudden pain from my ankle, I fell onto my shoulder. It's dislocated." He smiled weakly at his mother. "No other injuries, I promise."

"I'm sure you're sore all over just from the impact."

"Yeah. There is that."

His father touched his good shoulder. "We'll take you to our house since the missionaries are in yours."

"No." Skye looked past his father at Ruthanne. "I have an obligation and now a mess to clean up. I'll stay at the ranch."

Ruthanne had mixed feelings about that. The more she became acquainted with the man, the more she liked being with him. However, what could he do to help now? "Skye, you can go home and heal then continue your thirty days."

By the set of his jaw, she could tell he'd made up his mind.

"Fine." She raised her hands in resignation. "I'll take you home."

In her car he asked about Ruddy.

"Paul left him with my vet before coming to the hospital. I'm sure he's okay."

He stared out the passenger-side window. "Let's swing by there."

"Skye—"

"Please." He turned his gaze on her. She knew the pain she saw there was greater than his physical discomfort.

"Okay." She took the next left instead of going straight.

At the veterinarian's office Ruddy sat in a large cage, whining and wagging his tail so hard it beat a rhythm on the plastic sides.

Skye shuffled to the cage and gingerly knelt down. "I'm sorry, buddy. I didn't see you until it was too late." He looked up at Ruthanne. "He must have been frightened by the thunder. That's the only reason he would have escaped his collar and run around to the front of the house."

Poor Ruddy had a cast on his right back leg. Ironic, since his master had his right foot bandaged.

The pair made quite a sight as Ruthanne loaded them both into her small car. Ruddy filled the backseat, where he licked the back of Skye's neck.

Ruthanne had to laugh. "Looks like there are no hard feelings."

Skye managed to reach behind his head to pet the dog. "Either that or he's trying to get on my good side so I won't punish him for leaving the backyard."

When they pulled into the driveway, Ruthanne forced herself not to cry. The tow truck had come for Skye's car, and the gaping hole in the barn was bigger than she'd thought.

"Ruthanne, I'm so sorry. My insurance will pay for the damage, and I'll do what I can to make it as good as new."

She opened the driver's side door. "We'll talk about it later. Right now let's get you and your dog inside and comfortable."

Chapter 8

Ruthanne felt compassion for Skye as he tried to help Ruddy into the house. She didn't know which one hobbled the worst. As she opened the door, the delicious aroma of succulent beef stew greeted her. She rushed through the house and found Paul in the kitchen, a wooden spoon in his hand. A warm feeling settled into her weary bones. "You didn't have to do this, you know."

Paul looked up and grinned. "I was going to take you out to dinner tonight but figured this would work out better. I had the stew in the freezer."

She walked over to him and stood on tiptoes to place a kiss on his temple. "Thank you."

When she turned, Skye and Ruddy were in the doorway. Skye seemed to avoid eye contact. "I'm not hungry. I think I'll go to my room."

Ruthanne scurried to his side. "Let me help you up the stairs."

"The stairs." He drooped his head. With a glance at the crutch under his right arm and the sling holding his left shoulder, Ruthanne knew he was calculating just how he was going to maneuver the staircase.

"Uh-oh. The handrail is on the wrong side, isn't it?"

Paul had stopped stirring the stew and was now slicing artisan bread into hearty slices. "I could carry you, old man." Was he serious or not? Ruthanne couldn't tell.

"No thank you," Skye nearly growled at him.

Ruthanne took the crutch and slipped under Skye's arm then guided him to the sofa in the living room. When his leg was propped and a pillow supported his arm, she handed him the television remote. Ruddy settled on the floor near his master, and Ruthanne promised him a special doggy treat for his faithfulness.

With hands on her hips, she looked at Skye. "Now, you will rest here, and when supper is ready, I'll bring it out to you."

Skye started to protest, but Ruthanne held up her hand. "I've spoken my piece." Then she turned and headed back to the kitchen.

❧

"I've spoken my piece." Skye chuckled under his breath as he watched her retreating figure. She sure looked cute trying to tell him what to do.

But then he remembered walking in and seeing her kiss Paul.

Skye mentally kicked himself. What was he doing, falling for someone who already had a great guy? And worse, someone who was dedicated to the woman who ruined his childhood?

Frustrated by his mixed emotions, he turned on the television and found a Seattle Mariners baseball game.

⤫

While Paul prepared their dinner, Ruthanne slipped out to tend the animals. When she was through, she leaned against Lirit's paddock, placing her foot on the bottom rail. The two nuzzled noses while Ruthanne stroked the long neck, praying, "Lord, I don't know why You've brought that man here. He's been nothing but trouble. And now he's put a hole in the barn."

Tom, their part-time handyman, was due back tomorrow—and not a moment too soon. Skye said he'd fix everything, but it was a mystery as to how he would manage that feat.

After a good-night hug for Lirit, Ruthanne went back into the house where Paul had joined Skye. The two rivals now cheered for the same team. Paul had brought out Skye's supper and was just finishing his own. Ruddy had a bowl on the floor, licked spotless.

She moved into their line of vision since neither had acknowledged her presence. With her arms folded, she looked at both of them. "You could have waited."

Skye slurped the last of the gravy from his spoon. "Couldn't. It smelled too good."

It did smell good. She offered to bring Skye seconds and filled her own bowl.

When the game ended, Ruthanne walked Paul to the front porch where she thanked him once more for the stew. "You're always there for me. What a great friend you are."

Paul's eyes dimmed. "Friend?"

Ruthanne kissed his cheek. "A wonderful friend. You were there when Brian left me. And when word came that he'd died, you walked me through it, gave advice, prayed. And you keep taking care of me."

There was a time when they dated briefly that she wanted to love Paul. However, eventually she had known he could only be a brother to her.

A slight breeze blew a tuft of hair over his forehead, and she reached up to move it back. "Go home, Paul. I'll see you tomorrow."

He nodded, offering a tiny smile, then slipped his hands into his pockets and whistled while he strolled to his car.

Ruthanne shook her head. Until the day he found his true love, he would keep trying.

She went back inside to find Skye fighting sleep. Kneeling down next to him, she spoke barely above a whisper. "Do you need anything? A pain pill?"

"No, I just took one, and that's why I'm groggy." He grinned at her as he sank further into his pillow. "Thanks for putting up with me. I promise I'll make it up to you."

"We'll talk about that later. I know you don't want to try the stairs. Would you like to sleep in Hannie's room tonight? There are fresh sheets on the bed."

His eyes widened, and a look of terror replaced the silly drug-induced smile. "No! I can't go in there."

Can't?

"Okay, you can sleep on the couch tonight." He relaxed, and she watched him fall asleep. As much as she loved Hannie, she couldn't push aside the fact that her son was afraid of her.

She moved a stray wisp of hair from his forehead the same way she had with Paul. But different feelings stirred within her. Protectiveness, yes. She wanted to fix whatever bothered him. But something else, too. She closed her eyes to remember how their day had started. Yes. Those feelings were there when they'd prayed together at church.

His arm felt cool, so she rose and found a blanket. He didn't even stir as she gently laid it over him. Emotions played ping-pong in her heart. Was this man her enemy? Or would he turn out to be the one to heal her heart after Brian had torn it to shreds?

She left before the temptation to kiss his lips grew too strong.

Early the next day, Ruthanne rose to feed the animals. When she entered the barn to retrieve the wheelbarrow, she noticed Skye struggling with it. The crutch lay on the ground, and his left arm had escaped the sling. But what alarmed her was that he had somehow managed to load the large feed bag. He made a pitiful picture with his injured foot barely touching the ground and his bad shoulder drooped to reduce the stress.

"Oh for goodness' sake," she muttered as she ran to help him. "What do you think you're doing?" With a light push, she nudged him out of the way and grabbed the handles of the wheelbarrow.

"My chores."

"The alpacas will starve before you get this over to them. How did you manage to load a forty-pound bag?"

"I tipped the wheelbarrow on its side, knelt down so I wouldn't put pressure on my foot, then scooped the bag into it with my good arm."

"I'm impressed by your ingenuity, but you didn't plan the rest of the execution very well, did you?"

He stroked his chin. "Guess it's back to the drawing board, huh?" He grinned, and Ruthanne suddenly remembered how she had almost kissed those lips just the night before.

"I'll make you a deal." She began wheeling out the door. "Let me feed the animals until you can maneuver better. We'll find light duty for you until you heal."

He hesitated as if he were about to argue. But after regarding the crutch still on the ground, he sighed. "You're right." He hopped the few feet to pick it up then slowly gimped his way out of the barn. "Sorry."

"Skye."

He turned back to look at her.

Ruthanne placed her hands on her hips. "If you keep asking for forgiveness, I may have to rescind it."

If it were possible for sad eyes to twinkle, his did. "Yes, Boss Lady."

Ruthanne finished feeding and watering the alpacas. In the process she checked on the pregnant females, watching for any change in their behavior.

When she finished, she heard pounding coming from the barn. Skye stood at the workbench, making a new door for the rabbit pen.

"Where did you get the wood?" She inspected it and found he'd done a decent job.

"I took a board from inside the wall that I smashed through. I was gathering all the debris and saw some boards that could be trimmed and used for other things."

"Nothing's wasted?" She tilted her head, trying to get a good view of his face.

"Nothing." He smiled back.

"What happened here?" a male voice bellowed from outside.

Ruthanne looked toward the source. "Tom's back."

Skye watched a large shadow form just outside the hole in the barn. He imagined a hefty, snarling wrestler ready to tear him apart for creating such a mess. "Who's Tom?"

"Our handyman."

A knot formed in Skye's throat. If that shadow were any indication of the guy's size, he was really in for it.

Ruthanne cupped her mouth. "We're in here, Tom."

Snitch.

The man stepped through the jagged cavity rather than using the door. Although not the monster Skye had imagined, Tom was still tall but portly and seemed to be somewhere in his sixties. He wore jeans, a Western-style plaid shirt, and sported a receding rusty gray hairline and a long ponytail.

Ruthanne gave him a brief hug. "How was Colorado?"

Tom couldn't seem to take his eyes off the hole. "It was fine." He dragged his gaze toward Ruthanne. Skye stood behind her, where Tom noticed him for the first time. "Who's this?"

"I'm sorry. Where are my manners?" Ruthanne pointed toward Skye. "This is Skye Randall, Hannie's son. You know she asked for him when she became ill."

"Yes, I knew." Tom's demeanor changed, and he peered into Skye's eyes as if trying to see what was inside his head.

"And this is Tom," Ruthanne finished the introduction. "A dear friend and the best all-around fixer-upper in southern Oregon. He's just been to Colorado for his daughter's wedding."

Skye held out his hand and felt the raw power in Tom's meaty grip.

"I didn't want to leave with Hannie so sick, but Ruthanne insisted."

"Hannie would have insisted." She patted his arm and filled him in on Hannie's condition.

"Now what happened here?" Tom pointed to the gash in the barn.

"I happened here." Skye swallowed the lame excuse that leaped to his lips.

"Excuse me?"

"I drove my car into the wall."

If Tom's shadow seemed fierce, the man himself suddenly embodied the wrestler of Skye's imagination. "Were you drinking, boy?"

Skye jumped to attention. "No, sir. It had been raining, and I hit a slick patch when I swerved to avoid my dog."

"I saw the tracks in my landscaping. I was going to get to it when I got back." The way Tom glared at him, with one eye nearly shut, reminded Skye of someone. But he couldn't remember who.

Tom turned his gaze to Ruthanne. "He telling the truth?"

She nodded. "I've never seen Skye drink. He's a Christian."

The wrestler suddenly turned into a large teddy bear. "That's great!"

Was that a tear in the man's eye? What was wrong with this guy?

Tom grabbed Skye's hand and pulled him into a one-armed hug.

Skye extracted himself and tried to bring the conversation to the more practical matter at hand. "I plan to fix this mess I made."

Tom looked at Skye's shoulder then at the crutch under his arm. "How you going to do that?"

"I don't know. But I'm not the kind of person who runs from my responsibilities." Not like his mother.

Tom nodded as if approving that statement. "We'll fix it together."

Now Skye nodded his approval. "I'd like that."

❧

That night Skye's ankle, although still extremely sore, felt well enough for him to navigate the stairs. Ruddy followed him up, limping on his own bum leg.

After a long, hot shower with the water running on his aching arm, Skye slipped into bed. Normally at peak condition, he found dealing with a sling and crutch more tiring than mucking out paddocks.

In his sleep he dreamed of a party, and judging by the size of the people, he was a child. Loud music played, the kind that hurt your ears no matter how loud it was. He wandered through the crowd of people, and none of them knew he was there. He might just as well be a stray dog. He wanted Mommy but couldn't find her. Suddenly strong hands grabbed him, and he heard a scream. A woman's scream.

Skye woke up startled, thankful the dream was over. But then he heard the scream again. He sat straight up as Ruddy barked softly from his bed on the floor. Then several women screamed.

He shot out of bed despite his injuries, pulled on his jeans, and tore open the balcony door. Forgetting about his crutch, he launched down the deck steps, favoring his sore ankle. The partial moon above illuminated Ruthanne in the back pasture. She held a rifle to her shoulder with something sighted through the scope. Limping out to her, he called her name so she wouldn't shoot him. She never even twitched. What was the woman doing with a rifle? Was that her screaming? Where were the other women he heard?

"Are you okay?" His labored breathing caused sharp pains in his shoulder.

The rifle continued to track something out in the darkness. She trailed it through the scope. "I'm fine. Why do you ask?"

"Why do I ask?" He grabbed the rifle barrel and lowered it. She glared at him with annoyance. "I heard a woman scream. I thought it was you until I heard several."

Her eyes turned back to the darkness. "Ooh! There he is." She lifted the gun again. *Pop!* "Missed him."

"Is it a wolf?" Skye squinted, thinking he saw something canine darting around in the brush.

"No, just the neighbor's dog. He has a habit of stalking our alpacas, and I haven't been able to convince his owners."

"Are you trying to kill him?" Skye couldn't believe that Ruthanne would harm an animal. But then again, she was mighty fierce when it came to her alpacas.

"I got you now. . . ." Her voice had dropped to a whisper. *Pop!*

The large black lab yelped and ran away with a luminescent yellow splotch on its side.

Skye grabbed the rifle to inspect it. "A paint gun?"

"I thought if I could tag him somehow, I'd have evidence that it was him. Tomorrow I'll go over there and explain why their dog is in Technicolor now."

Was it the stress of dredging up the past? Or the pain in his body? Or maybe the fact that he was falling for this wild, wonderful woman? Skye didn't know. But waves of laughter poured from him, and he sank to the hard ground holding his left arm.

She flopped down to join him, her infectious giggle only making things worse.

"So what was the screaming about?" he finally managed to ask.

"Oh." She wiped her eyes. "That's how alpacas sound when they're frightened."

"No kidding?"

"No kidding."

This only got them started again. When the laughter finally died down, Skye said, "You do realize we're on the ground in the middle of the night and laughing like fools."

Another giggle struggled to escape her throat. "Oh really? I hadn't noticed." The giggle bubbled out of her, and Skye realized he'd have to be the strong one. Her week had been just as hard as his emotionally. And judging by her near hysterical laughter, she obviously needed some good REM sleep.

He nudged her shoulder. "Come on, Deadeye. You look great, but I need my beauty rest." When he realized he had no crutch to help him stand, he looked at her helplessly.

"Allow me." Ruthanne stood, reached out her hand, and hauled him to his feet.

They were now only inches from each other, still holding each other's hands. The moon overhead cast a velvet glow over her beautiful face, which was upturned and, oh, so inviting.

"Deadeye, eh?" She tilted her head. "What does that mean?"

He pulled her even closer, pleased that she hadn't let go of him either.

"In old Westerns, that was always the guy who never missed a shot."

Her mouth twitched. "I think I'd rather be called Calamity Jane. At least it sounds more feminine."

"Calamity it is then." And he leaned down and kissed her.

Chapter 9

The next morning Ruthanne shook her head. "What is he doing now?"

Skye acted like he didn't still have his arm in a sling or a crutch under his arm. Ruthanne found him in the pasture with the four-wheeled wagon and a shovel. At least he'd given up on using the wheelbarrow.

"You are absolutely the most stubborn patient I've ever seen."

"The least I can do until Tom gets here is clean up poop." With his jaw jutted forward and lips pressed into a determined line, he struggled one-handed with the shovel. He slipped the blade underneath the communal pile, trying not to get too many beans so he could lift and toss them into the wagon. Even so, some of the beans escaped on the ride to the wagon and rolled down the short hill. Every time he lifted the shovel, he'd lose some beans. Three young male alpacas found the skittering-beans game a delight and chased them down the hill, kicking at them and inspecting the marble-sized balls with floppy lips.

"Skye."

"What?"

"Let me do that."

"No."

"You're going to hurt yourself."

He stabbed the shovel into the ground and leaned his wrist on the handle. "I will not be the first man in history to have an alpaca poop-shoveling injury. How would I explain *that* to my insurance company?" Bent on finishing the job, he continued the awkward chore.

If a man could be attractive doing this menial job—with a handicap—Skye pulled it off to perfection. She thought about the kiss they'd shared the night before. Actually she hadn't stopped thinking about the kiss. Such a tender man shouldn't have to face the emotional pain he always seemed to carry.

A God-inspired thought entered her head. Knowing he wasn't ready to talk about Hannie, Ruthanne decided to slay two Goliath-sized problems with one stone. She let him struggle a few moments more until she could tell by the luster of sweat above his upper lip that he was nearly done.

"Skye, I've been thinking about the craft fair." She launched her plan. "Without Hannie to organize, I'm thinking of pulling out." She paused to gauge his emotions. "But we've already paid the fee."

Money seemed to light a spark. "And they won't refund it?"

"Not at this late date." She tried to look as forlorn as she could without tipping her hand.

"What needs to be done?"

"Hannie had planned to sell some of her weavings. A small paddock will be set up for a couple of alpacas, too. Paul will be there, but I'll need an extra person to man the cash register while I do the demonstration."

"I can do that."

She had no doubt he would agree to helping at the fair. But her next request required a move from God. "Great. Would you like to help me choose some weavings to put on display? They're all in the shop in the walk-out basement." He had never been in the shop, avoiding it with one excuse or another. She watched storm clouds form in his sky blue eyes, signaling yet another refusal. She'd hoped by presenting the request in a way that would help her out of a predicament, he'd overcome whatever was keeping him from getting near his mother.

Her sneaky approach seemed to work. He finally agreed, weak and somewhat breathless. "Okay."

He allowed her to finish shoveling the pile. As she reached for the wagon handle, he brushed her aside. "I can pull it."

"How?"

"See this rope?" He grasped a rope tied to the handle.

"I saw it, but I don't know why it's there."

He tied the other end around his waist and, leaning on his crutch, held out his arm in a half ta-da pose.

"You are determined, aren't you?" Ruthanne shook her head as they walked together. "Sick but determined."

Once they deposited the contents of their wagon onto the compost pile, they headed back to the house. In the cool shadow under the deck, Ruthanne unlocked the door to the shop, realizing it had been too long since she'd been in there.

With a flick of the light switch, colors, textures, and patterns greeted her like old friends. "I apologize for the mustiness. Maybe I should open this place up every day."

Skye stuck his head in the door, as if he weren't sure what evil might await him inside the room. Finally he walked to a wall displaying several hangings. "My mother did all of these?"

Ruthanne nodded. "She spins the yarn then creates these beautiful masterpieces."

His eyes darted over the rest of the artwork in the room. "How lucrative is this business?"

"You'd be surprised what the Internet brings in." She held up a palm-sized alpaca. "These toys were made by the people she visits. It's great therapy, and 100 percent profit goes into her ministry fund. Among the people represented in this bin alone, more than half accepted Christ while working on these toys."

He raised an eyebrow, but a small grin played on his face. "Impressive." He inspected the fuzzy toy then put it back in the bin.

After a quick glance around the room, Ruthanne spotted where she wanted to start.

⬯

Skye prayed for strength as Ruthanne walked over to a wall where a weaving the size of a small throw rug hung. His mother had touched every piece of art in there. Other than her bedroom, this was her most personal space in the house.

"This is my favorite." Ruthanne glowed with pride as she pointed out the striking two-foot by three-foot woven cloth featuring a butterfly. "This one isn't for sale. She made it for me, and I keep it here to showcase for our visitors. Notice how she contrasted the dark with the light—black background but vibrant shades of orange and yellow for the large monarch in the middle."

Ruthanne stroked a wing with the back of her finger. "This is me." Then she indicated the dark background. "And this is where I was when I first met Hannie. See the leaves that the butterfly is sitting on?"

He looked closer. The two green leaves were in reality two hands holding the butterfly in their palm.

"Hannie told me this is God. I also like to think of the two hands as Hannie and David. God used these two people to lift me up and give me wings."

Ruthanne's eyes shimmered with unshed tears. He caressed her shoulder, longing to draw her into an embrace again. But he sensed a holy moment and decided to let her talk.

"I met Brian while I was in college. He was a street artist. I asked him why he wasn't an art major, and he said school wasn't for him. That should have been my first clue. He had no problem holding odd jobs and living hand to mouth. But we just clicked, you know? We saw each other off and on for a few years despite my parents' objections. I admit, his looks drew me in. He was a beautiful man. . .on the outside. I never saw the inside until after we were married. He was very talented but had no ambition. We hit the craft-show circuit shortly after our wedding day. Tore my mother's heart out. I had romanticized what it would be like on the road, the people we'd meet and the adventures we'd share. Nothing she could say would change my mind. But after a couple of years on the road, I was ready to settle down and start a family."

She frowned at the darkness of the background as if she could see her life playing there. "We eventually made our way to Oregon. I loved it here and insisted we find a more permanent place to live. Up until then we were basically homeless, living in a camping trailer and mooching off other crafters we met along the way. Finally, after four years of marriage, I found a small but cute apartment in Oakley and told Brian that I was through with traveling. I agreed to find a solid job so he could continue to pursue his art, but if he wanted to travel the circuit, he could do it without me."

Skye hated to see her relive the painful memory. Her down-turned mouth told him that it probably went downhill from there for her and Brian.

"He had always been a drinker, but when I challenged him, it only got worse. He spent my paychecks faster than I could pay the bills. We lived like that for about three years, then one day I gathered all the paintings he'd ever done and signed up for the Oakley craft fair. It was there I met Hannie and David. I fell in love with both of them, and before I realized it, I had told them my whole sob story."

Her finger moved to the leaf hands on the weaving. A tiny smile broke through her past like a ray of sunshine. "Hannie and David prayed with me at the fair. Christ entered my heart right then and there. They invited Brian and me to live in the mobile home on their property as long as we worked for them. I took to the animals right away, and Brian became a handyman, although he wasn't very handy with anything but a paintbrush. I thought surely in this beautiful setting he'd find inspiration for his paintings. That this would turn him around. But I was wrong."

The smile dimmed. "After six months, Brian left. I never heard from him again." She looked up at Skye. Her mouth drew into a thin line. "I learned a few months later that he had died in an accident—DUI."

So Skye's hunch had been correct. Abandonment had left an ugly scar on Ruthanne that nearly matched his own. He took his turn to caress the butterfly, longing to touch this part of her life. "And you stayed here."

"Yes. I guess I proved my worth."

An awkward silence passed between them. Skye sensed that Ruthanne had not planned to launch into her life story.

She glanced around the room, as if remembering why they were there. She swept her hand around the room. "Many of the others also tell a story." She spent the next half hour explaining why Hannie added certain elements to her art. A twig with tender leaves signified the sprout of new life. A piece of oak was stability.

One hanging drew Skye in. It was of the mountains in the fall, with red, yellow, and orange dotting the hillside. Three evergreen trees stood in the foreground—one tall and lush, one brown and dry, seemingly stricken with disease, and one in the middle, also healthy but shorter. He knew beyond any doubt that this represented his birth family, the diseased tree obviously his father. The sky above was a vibrant blue with a swirl of clouds in the corner. When he looked closer, he noticed a cross in the clouds. Perhaps his mother had finally dropped the notion that the sky could solve their problems.

Ruthanne broke into his musing. "Do you ever remember Hannie as being artistic?"

"No, unless you could consider braiding a dandelion chain as artistic. I do remember her singing though. She did that a lot."

"I have a tape of Hannie singing special music at church. It was over ten years ago, but she still has a beautiful voice. Would you like to hear it sometime?"

Hear his mother's voice? Was he ready for that? He hated to hesitate too long at the simple question. "Uh. . .sure."

"Great, I'll get it to you after we're done here."

Great.

⤜⤛

That evening after Ruthanne retired to her mobile home, Skye sat on the carpet in the living room, flipping the cassette tape over and over in his hands. At eye-level with the stereo system on the oak entertainment center, the glowing blue lights from the components stared at him as if wondering what he was waiting for.

Good question.

In the couple of weeks that he'd been on the ranch, he'd learned that his mother had become a Christian and that she had a heart for prisoners, orphans, and substance-abuse patients. She opened her business to the community so they could see the animals up close, and she rescued people like Ruthanne and Tom.

He tapped the cassette on his palm. His mother had become a saint, for crying out loud.

Yet he still had questions. Why did she leave him? Had she been in trouble? That wouldn't have surprised him. But then through the years, she got her life together yet never made contact until now. *Why?*

The word continued to echo in his thoughts. He knew he could never accept all he'd learned about her until that question was answered.

He looked over at Ruddy, sitting on his haunches, tongue dangling, soulful brown eyes staring at him.

"What are you looking at?"

Ruddy slurped his large tongue over his own nose.

"Should I play this? Hear the voice of the woman I've hated all these years?"

Ruddy slid his long front legs to the floor and put his head between his paws.

"You're settling in to hear some music, aren't you?" Skye looked at the plastic case in his hands. "Fine." He opened it and dropped the cassette into the little door. With a push, it clicked into place. His finger hovered over the PLAY button for an eternity before he finally pressed it.

A woman's voice drifted from the speakers—an a cappella version of "I Wonder as I Wander." Although more mature than he remembered, her voice swept him back to his childhood. Sweet moments when she'd sung him to sleep. Or times when just the two of them would take walks and she'd hum whatever tune was popular.

A rough memory surfaced. A time when everyone in the commune had gathered together. His father had died a month before, but Skye didn't miss him. His dad never played with him, just criticized him a lot. They were in a small smoke-filled room. One of many in the house they shared. His mother pulled out her guitar and began to sing. Some silly song of which she botched the words. That always happened when she smoked those little cigarettes. He joined in to help her remember the words.

Someone kicked him in the back. One of the men told him to shut up, that he was ruining the song. Skye looked at his mother. She did nothing—just kept on singing.

His back hurt where the man kicked him. His heart hurt because his mother didn't care. He hated her for that. From that moment on, it seemed she started caring less for Skye and more for where her next fix would come from.

The music from the stereo began squawking. "Oh great!" Skye punched the EJECT button. "I've broken the machine." He pulled out several inches of tape that had wound around one of the heads. He twirled the tiny plastic wheel in the cassette, trying to wind the tape back in but gave up when he saw how damaged it was. "Now I have to tell Ruthanne I ruined her copy." He spoke to Ruddy, whose head had popped up and tilted during the noise. "I'm going to bed."

At the word "bed," Ruddy rose and limped toward the stairs.

Skye muttered to himself as he followed. "I've broken the barn, my dog, and now Ruthanne's tape." His shoulder and ankle ached from the day's chores. Using his crutch, he set the rubber tip on the step, but Ruddy brushed past him, knocking him off his support. He stumbled and fell against his mother's bedroom door. The knob came in contact with his hand as he balanced himself, but he pulled back sharply.

He clenched his jaw. Some doors should remain shut.

Chapter 10

They all arrived at City Park by seven o'clock in the morning. Ruthanne smiled as she stood in their usual prime spot, located under a spreading maple tree, near the beautiful Oakley Creek.

Before unloading, Ruthanne gathered her team of men in a prayer circle where they all held hands. Together they gave thanks for the weather. They also prayed for Hannie's ministry, that her art pieces would touch those who needed it. Skye prayed a hearty prayer for the two alpacas, that they would remain calm and enjoy the attention they would receive. She squeezed his hand to let him know how grateful she was for that prayer, and when he squeezed back, she had to force herself to concentrate on his words. His palm, even with the newly formed calluses, felt comforting and safe as his thumb stroked her finger in an intimate gesture. Her other hand gripped Paul's. Just as strong, just as comforting, but evoking no feelings other than the warmth of friendship.

They set up quickly after that, placing Lirit and Shellie, a golden suri with gorgeous Shirley Temple locks, into the portable pen. Walls made of fabric and PVC pipe became the outdoor gallery for the weavings, and Ruthanne decorated with ribbons and straw flowers she had bought in Medford.

She brought out the cash drawer from her car and set Skye up at a table with a pad of receipts and a credit card machine. She indicated one of the folding chairs they'd brought. "Have a seat. Holler for Paul or me if you need help with the bigger items."

"Yes, Boss Lady."

She rolled her eyes, thoroughly enjoying his mock reverence.

"Paul, I know you usually do the selling, but if you can help me field questions about the alpacas, I'd appreciate it."

Paul nodded but muttered, "He'd better not mess anything up."

"Well, Skye can't answer alpaca questions very well, can he?" Honestly, men and their egos!

"I'll be back after I feed the animals." Tom excused himself and wandered through the trickle of people who had come out early for the fair.

Ruthanne settled herself behind Hannie's spinning wheel, which thankfully survived the ride in Skye's rented SUV. Before long she had Lirit's carded, washed, and dyed fiber twisting through her fingers. This brought several curious onlookers.

Skye's parents dropped by briefly, his mom excited to see the alpacas up close.

During a lull, Ruthanne decided to stand and stretch. She moved near Skye to check the sales receipts and perhaps catch any errors before Paul did. She needn't have worried though. "You're doing a great job at pushing the merchandise." She grinned as she shuffled the thin papers through her fingers.

"The alpaca toys are an easy sell."

"You've managed to sell some of the larger items, too. We're very grateful to have you here in Hannie's absence."

"Then I guess I made the right decision to do my thirty days sooner rather than later." He reached out and caught her wrist, drawing her near.

"A decision that I praise God for every day." Her heart dipped as she realized their time was growing shorter. "But I'm afraid it will be over much too soon."

"I may move back home, but it needn't be over." He gave her wrist a shake. "I'm just getting to know Calamity."

And Calamity loved getting to know the man behind that midnight kiss.

"Ruthanne." Paul's voice shattered the moment. "If you're not too busy, we have a question over here. *Do you mind?*"

Reluctantly Ruthanne snatched her hand away. Perhaps she shouldn't show open affection for Skye in Paul's presence, but that might be the only way to get through to him. As she moved to Paul's side, she felt Skye's gaze following her.

A middle-aged couple stood near the pen. After Paul introduced them, he took on a friendlier tone, but she sensed tension under his words. "They would like to know the difference between a suri and huacaya alpaca."

She shook her head, perplexed. Paul knew this, but she answered anyway. While she explained the crimping of the different fibers, Paul stood unusually close to her, even for him. As the visitors continued to ask questions, his arm encircled her waist. She once thought of this as one of his touchy-feely actions with no real meaning. But today it had tons of meaning.

Once the man and woman left, Ruthanne extricated herself from his grasp and looked at him. "What was that all about? You didn't need me."

He glanced toward Skye, who was ringing up a small weaving. Paul jammed his hands into his pockets. "Just a little off with our roles switched."

Ruthanne returned to her spinning but couldn't ignore the green-eyed monster that had suddenly inhabited Paul. She should talk with him, explain her feelings for Skye honestly. How many more words would it take to get him to understand? Her frustration translated to the foot pump, and the next ball of fiber thinned in record time.

After a few minutes of therapeutic spinning, familiar squeals came from across the lawn.

"Oh no," Skye mumbled. "The Ya-Yas have multiplied." He stood as Hannie's entire craft group, consisting of the four from church plus two others, surrounded the area and took him captive. He darted glances about the small booth, apparently looking for an escape route.

"See, doesn't he look like Hannie?" Agnes spoke to the two who hadn't yet met Skye.

Saffron, an ADHD sufferer long before it was invented, allowed her attention to drift before the introductions. "Oh look, they brought the alpacas." She floated away from the pack, her green kerchief blouse billowing like a sail. Agnes, Lark, and Daisy followed Saffron after their brief greetings to Skye, Ruthanne, and Paul.

"Skye, this is Quail and Emerald Dawn," Ruthanne said.

As she made the introductions, he used the table as a buffer between them, as if the women carried germs and he feared infection.

Oh, Skye. Why can't you open up to learn more about Hannie?

❦

Skye harrumphed under his breath. *Ancient hippies.* Lark, Daisy, Saffron, Quail, Emerald Dawn. They had probably forgotten their real names ages ago, except for Agnes, who could have benefited from a flowery name.

Emerald Dawn flipped her long silver-dusted braid over her shoulder. "How's Hannie?"

Ruthanne fielded this question. "I'm. . .confident she'll come out of this as feisty as ever." She stumbled slightly over the word "confident." Was she trying to convince herself as much as the two remaining women?

Quail, who had sold out and used chemicals to dye her hair plum, turned to Skye. "We've wanted to meet you for some time. Hannie is very proud of you."

Emerald Dawn nudged her. A frown creased her already-leathered forehead, and she shook her head.

Confusion swirled around Skye. "How long have you two known about me?"

"Oh, a few years," Quail stammered.

"And my mother has known where I've been all this time?"

Emerald Dawn broke in. "We've known Hannie since her BC days. Before Christ. She was quite despondent in those early years and confessed that she'd had a son, but he was with another family. That wasn't so unusual in our circle of friends.

"But to answer your question: Yes, your mother has known about you. You won a football award in high school. She saw it in the paper. If it hadn't been a color picture, she might not have noticed. But your eyes, and then your name, convinced her that you were her child."

"Well then" —Skye pressed his fists into the table — "maybe you can tell me why she didn't contact me sooner." Anger clawed up his spine.

Ruthanne placed her hand on his arm. "Skye."

He shrugged her off. "No, really. I need to understand this. If she knew where I lived all this time—" He pounded the table and glared at the two hippies, who stood hugging each other.

Skye continued to glower at them, not giving relief. Finally Emerald Dawn let go of her friend and faced him. "I'm sorry, Skye. We don't know. Maybe it was too painful."

He moved around the table and confronted them. "Painful? When she could have done something about it? No, the real pain is knowing your mother doesn't want you anymore, the lost hope that she'll show up and take you home, waking up every morning and wondering what you did wrong. Pain is when the one person you love. . .leaves you."

Turning away from the earth mothers, he spotted Tom talking to a neighboring vendor. Jumping at the opportunity to distance himself, he grabbed his keys from his pocket and threw them onto the table. They landed with a sharp clatter. Ruthanne hugged her arms and gazed at him with tears in her eyes, but he was too angry to care.

"Tom can take over for me. I'm going for a walk. If I'm not back when you leave, feel free to load my car." Grinding his teeth, he stormed past Paul.

The park had grown thick with fair visitors, and maneuvering through the crowds soon frustrated him. Artsy, nouveau hippies in their fruit-dyed clothes and hemp belts only reminded him of the commune. He walked past a booth selling incense and nearly gagged. That stuff never covered the sickeningly sweet smell of marijuana. Not when twenty people were smoking it.

Memories battered his brain, accompanied by the sitar sound track of a Ravi Shankar tune. Times when his mother was too stoned to realize he hadn't eaten that day. Times when her friends treated him more like a stray dog than a child. Times when all he wanted was a good-night kiss, but Mommy was too busy in another room kissing somebody else.

But Skye had learned so much about his mother in the past few weeks. Why did he allow these voices to take over his good sense? She had obviously changed, so he should embrace that fact and move on. But the emotional scars ran too deep.

He finally found a secluded spot along the river where he could sit and think. He sank to a flat boulder and wrapped his good arm over his head, but it was no use. He couldn't shut out the noise when it came from within.

The happy bubbling of the narrow river flowing at his feet only mocked him. A scattered pile of rocks became his arsenal as he lobbed one after another into the water. Some skipped several times upstream, and others, bombs, aimed at Skye's wandering thoughts as they skittered around like dragonflies. He sat for a long time wallowing in self-pity, but he didn't care. He deserved this moment.

All that time his mother had known where he was. He rocked as his heart broke all over again. *Why?* The question screamed so loud he feared his head would split. Finally he uttered a selfish prayer that she'd recover just so he could ask her that one question.

Somehow opening communication with God helped, and he began to pray with a better attitude. With his knees drawn to his chin and his head bowed, he whispered, "Lord, I'm so tired of feeling this way. How can I accept that my mother has changed? Did she have a good reason for staying away from me? Please, I need to know what she's been thinking all these years."

The strain of a street violin drifted into his small sanctuary. A glance at his watch told him the fair would be winding down soon. Time to go back and help pack up.

⊂≋⊃

Ruthanne looked at her watch for the tenth time. Would Skye return before they had to leave?

His outburst had caused feelings that she thought she had conquered. Brian had a temper, and even though he never resorted to physical violence, he often frightened her. Skye had already proved that he was nothing like Brian. Still, she hadn't considered praying for him until twenty minutes ago.

She finally decided she ought to go look for him.

"No, Ruthie. Let him sort this out himself." Paul wrapped his fingers around her elbow, gentle yet sending a message. Had wings of jealousy sent that message? She hoped not.

"I agree, Ruthanne." Tom had already taken the alpacas to the trailer and was dismantling the paddock. "Sometimes a man just needs to be alone."

She glared at them. "A woman would have called five of her best friends by now." When the men turned vacant gazes toward her, she knew she'd lost them with her feminine logic.

Exasperated with the male mind, Ruthanne handed Paul the SUV keys. "Would you please take the spinning wheel to Skye's car? I'll start removing the exhibition pieces and load them in the box."

He wrapped his hand around the keys. "Sure. We did okay today, didn't we?"

"More than okay." The nearly empty booth was a testament to the fact. "Hannie would be proud." She searched the path where Skye had disappeared.

"Why, Paul?" She turned back to Paul, not able to contain her searing question. "Why would Hannie put Skye up for adoption and then not contact him when she settled down?"

"A lot of people do that, Ruthie. Children are adopted out but are seldom contacted by their birth parents."

"But this is Hannie we're talking about. She got her life back on track, married David, and started a business. Why didn't she include her son?"

"She must have her reasons. Do you trust her?"

"Of course I do." But did she?

He thumbed a stray hair from her brow. "Then I'm sure all will come to light." Ruthanne felt her lip quiver. "If she lives."

Paul shook her shoulders. "Hey, where's that faith you've been preaching?"

She didn't know, but the more she learned about Skye, the more she questioned Hannie.

Paul lifted the spinning wheel, leaving her to her thoughts. This was the second time Skye had run out on her. Thankfully she had his keys so he couldn't trash her barn again. She pulled the tablecloth off and folded it while puzzling through her problem. *Yes, he's hurting.* But was running a habit of his? Once again she concluded: He wasn't like her husband.

"Am I too late?"

Ruthanne jumped at Skye's voice behind her. "No, we just started tearing down." She wanted to thrust herself into his good arm, but he walked past her and surveyed the work in progress.

Ruthanne sidled next to him. "Are you all right?"

He turned his face to her, a pained expression answering the question. "I will be. Now what do you want me to do?"

Skye seemed to have pulled himself together, but Ruthanne worried about him anyway. He had been hurt deeply, and it pained her that the one person she loved more than life itself had been the cause.

Chapter 11

On Monday morning Ruthanne sipped green tea and stood at the office window watching Skye water the animals. Paul was going over receipts from the craft fair at the desk.

"Skye did pretty well." Ruthanne's respect swelled for the man she had first thought of as an interloper.

"Yeah, before he freaked out on us." Paul placed the receipts in a metal file box and closed the lid. "He really pushed the toys. Now we can deposit a hefty profit into the ministry fund. I've got to admit, I'm surprised at how enthusiastically he's jumped into his role here."

"I think his accident played a big role in that." A giggle bubbled up Ruthanne's throat. "It must be a God thing."

Paul looked at her like she'd lost her mind.

She went on. "Think about it. Before that he was just going through the motions. After the accident he must have felt so much remorse that he dug in and started taking what we do here seriously." She looked back out the window at Skye favoring his arm. "Since his injury is still tender and he can't lift anything heavy for a while, I think we should have him learn what you do."

When she looked back at Paul, his brow had creased into a frown and his shoulders slumped as he leaned his chin into his hand. He looked like someone had stolen his prized spinach tortellini recipe.

"What's wrong?"

Paul glanced up at her. "So he's replacing my job, too?"

"*Too?*"

What new words could she come up with to remind him they'd never be a couple?

"I'm merely suggesting he learn this side of the business. No one is replacing anybody." She stood behind him and placed her hand on his shoulder. He pulled away with a jerk and stood. "I'm going to see Aunt Hannie. I'll be back tomorrow." Rubbing his neck, he walked out.

The phone shrilled, causing her to jump. The caller ID showed that it was from a friend at animal control.

Although still in shock from Paul's hasty departure, she answered. "Hi, Fred."

After some small talk and an update on Hannie, Fred got to the point of his call. "We confiscated an abused alpaca a few days ago, and the vet has cleared him to leave. I was wondering if you had room for one more."

Ruthanne didn't hesitate. "Of course. Have the owners been charged?"

"You betcha. For neglect. There were several animals on the property—dogs, cats, chickens—all malnourished. We've found homes for the ones that survived, all but the alpaca."

Her heart cried. "I'll come get him today."

"Thanks."

She hung up, seething with righteous indignation. Anyone who neglected another living thing should be hanged.

Even if it's Hannie?

She squeezed her eyes shut. No, her biggest supporter could not have neglected Skye. Yet the more she learned about him, the more she could see the possibility. She thought back to the orphanages they had visited together. Those always seemed hardest for Hannie. She'd leave in tears and be useless the rest of the day. It was all beginning to make sense.

Later that afternoon, Ruthanne invited Skye to go along to pick up the alpaca. They followed Fred through the white-tiled corridor where several different kinds of animals rested in wire cages. Out the back door, where the larger animals convalesced, the tiny huacaya alpaca stood in a corner of a small-penned area. His grunts of distress tore at Ruthanne's heart.

When she saw the little guy, barely five months old and a mere skeleton under matted light rose gray fiber, her anger burned anew. "I hope they throw the book at them," she muttered as Skye knelt in front of him. He stroked the alpaca's neck, and Ruthanne marveled at the bond forming right before her eyes.

He crooned soft words. "It's okay—you're safe now. No one can hurt you any longer."

A shiver crept through Ruthanne as she realized someone may have said those very words to Skye once.

Ruthanne carried the cria to the car. Skye slipped into the passenger seat and held out his good arm. Pride warmed her heart as she watched this ever-changing man snuggle the alpaca in his lap. The cria immediately laid his head on Skye's shoulder. "He already trusts you."

"Yeah, well, we're cut from the same cloth."

Ruthanne prayed silently for this man who had apparently known neglect. She also prayed for herself, that her view of Hannie wouldn't be colored by what might eventually be revealed.

❦

The tiny alpaca shivered in Skye's arms for the first few miles then relaxed. Skye thought of his heavenly Father. How He had held him through the rough times. He couldn't feel God's arms at first, but as Skye's faith and trust grew, so did his sense of security.

When they arrived home, Tom's truck sat in the driveway, loaded down with lumber for the barn. They had been fixing the damage slowly the past week, tearing out the splintered boards and hauling off debris, and were now poised to rebuild the wall. Tom, however, must have been off doing other chores while he waited on Skye.

Ruthanne threw the gearshift into PARK then walked around to help Skye with the cria. He reluctantly released him into her care.

The alpaca twisted and groaned in Ruthanne's arms as Skye slid out of the car. She tried soothing words, but there was no response. "Okay! My, what a fuss." When Skye was on his feet again, she gave the alpaca back, placing it in his good arm and helping him balance with the injured one against the shoulder sling.

The alpaca settled down immediately, prompting Skye's protective instincts. "I'll carry him in from here. He can't weigh more than twenty-five pounds."

"Half the weight he should be. But he'll grow under your care." She grinned at him. "Looks like you're Papa now."

They entered the cria's new stall where Skye set him down. When Ruthanne handed him a prepared bottle, he felt grateful that he could do more.

"Hold the bottle here"—she indicated a few feet off the ground—"to simulate the mother's undercarriage." Skye delighted in seeing the cria, tentative at first, eventually attack the bottle. He laughed as new feelings of protection and provision surged through him. "I guess I'm Mama, too."

"I guess you are." Ruthanne laughed.

When the bottle was empty, Skye lowered himself to the floor and leaned against the wall. The cria curled up into a small ball, snuggled against Skye, and fell asleep.

Ruthanne stood near them. "After he's rested and gotten used to his surroundings, I'll introduce him to Hershey. She's a wonderful mom, so maybe she'll adopt him."

Skye buried his fingers in the soft alpaca wool, wanting to continue to offer comfort even though the animal slept. Ruthanne knelt in front of him, her green eyes crinkling in approval. Skye grinned back at her. It felt great to do something right for a change.

"So," she said while gently stroking the alpaca's thin neck. "What are you going to name him?"

"Me?"

"Of course. He's yours now."

He's mine. Skye remembered the first time he owned a pet. Skye's adoption was final, and the puppy was his gift to welcome him to the family. He'd owned other animals afterward, but this one had remained special because it meant a family had accepted him. It was their way of saying, *You aren't going anywhere, buddy, and we're going to make your stay here permanent.*

That's how he felt with this alpaca. Like Lirit for Ruthanne, this new charge would make his stay, or at least his ties to the ranch, permanent. He decided to give him the same name he gave the puppy.

"Destry."

Ruthanne cocked an eyebrow. "Interesting name."

He laughed at her perplexed expression. "Destry was a character that Audie Murphy played in an old Western. He was this small cowboy who did big things."

She nodded her approval. "And with your guidance, I'm sure the same is in store for our little Destry."

"Our little Destry." He liked the sound of that.

Ruthanne left. About a half hour later, Skye heard hammering. He began to feel guilty for sitting around while Tom worked on the barn, so he quietly extricated himself from Destry's side.

The two men worked on the wall for a couple of hours before it started to get dark. Despite the long ponytail, a reminder that this man was an ex-hippie, he liked Tom. They seemed to be in harmony on many different levels.

Especially their love of the Lord.

They got to talking about their conversions while Tom inspected a board for straightness.

Tom started. "Hannie and David found me at the prison."

"Were you a guard?"

"Nope. An inmate."

Skye's brows shot up. "Really?"

Tom set the board's end on the ground and leaned on it like a staff. "In those days, I stole from convenience stores for drug money."

Skye swallowed hard. Did it have to be for drugs?

"I connected with David, and he promised to give me a job if I cleaned myself up. The day before, I had been contemplating where I could meet my supplier when I got out." He placed the board on two sawhorses.

"What was it that David said that made you turn your life around?" Skye breathed in the fresh pine smell from the wood and steadied the board while Tom sawed through it, still awed that someone so similar to his mother had changed his life so drastically.

Tom stopped sawing. "It wasn't so much his words. I'd heard it all before and rejected it. But the alpaca they brought. . . When that animal looked at me with such trust as I fed it a peanut, I realized there was so much more to life than getting high." He pushed the saw through the board once more and stopped. "And I asked myself, 'How many other wonders are out there that I'm too fuzzy to see?' I knelt right there in the rec room and accepted Jesus as my Savior. And when I got out, David gave me that job and an ultimatum to stay clean or he'd boot me out."

"What a great testimony."

"Oh, I'm not saying it was easy. But without God, I'd never have been able to break free." He swept away the sawdust and walked to where he would nail up the board. "What about you, son? How long have you known the Lord?"

Skye never felt easy talking about his past. But something about this man drew it out of him. "I lived with my birth parents in a commune when I was little. My dad died, and my mother. . ." He wanted to say his mother couldn't wait to get rid of him, but this was Hannie. Tom had idolized her along with everyone else in her world. He decided to leave that part out. "I ended up in the foster system. Shuffled around like an unwanted gift. Then a Christian couple adopted me. They led me to the Lord with their love and patience."

Tom searched through the nail box with a meaty finger. "Not an easy task, I assume."

Skye chuckled. "You could say that."

The last board went up, and Tom declared the job finished except for the paint.

Skye wasn't ready to end the fellowship though. He clasped Tom's shoulder. "I just brought home a new addition to my family. Would you like to see him?"

Tom nodded and followed Skye to the barn.

When they walked into the stall, Tom grinned. "Well, look at that."

Destry had found a new playmate, a black suri that stood only a half head taller.

Ruthanne stood in the corner, a smug look on her face. "I told you Hershey would make a great mom. And now Destry has a brother."

"Destry?" Tom's shocked expression surprised Skye.

"Yes, after my favorite cowboy."

Tom knelt to pat the alpaca on his neck. "Audie Murphy."

"You like old Westerns?"

Tom cleared his throat and rubbed his nose. "Sure do. Maybe we'll rent one sometime."

They watched the two adoptive brothers romp, affording Skye an opportunity to ponder this strange man. Going to prison for drugs? Still, he had turned his life around and become a Christian.

But isn't that what Skye's mother did? Why could he accept that a stranger could reform but his mother could not?

He ground his teeth. Because it wasn't just the drugs. There was the other little question that needed answering. What he wanted to ask her that first day in the hospital. *Why? Why did you leave me?*

Chapter 12

"Remind me why we're doing this?" Skye tackled the unpleasant job. How had he gotten roped into this one?

"Alpacas need to be sheared," Ruthanne answered like a patient teacher. "That's how we get the fiber for the products like those we sold at the craft fair a week ago."

"No, the other thing." Sweat tickled his temple, and he wiped it away with his sleeve.

Ruthanne sighed. "Singing Mountain Ranch hosts Shearing Day for all the area ranchers because we have the most acreage to work in. We all contribute money to hire professional shearers so it gets done faster."

"That's not what I mean."

"Oh. You mean, why are we stuffing mushrooms?"

"Yeah." Skye crinkled his nose. This was definitely not his forte. At first he thought the worst thing was cleaning the slippery bulbs. But even his hen-pecked egg gathering was preferable to holding the caps still while he shoved a mixture of cream cheese and chopped vegetables into them. "Why can't we serve hot dogs and hamburgers like every other American?"

"We are, but Paul has to show off. I think he's outdone himself this time though. There's enough food here to feed not only the workers but the animals, too."

"How can he afford this?" Another mushroom cap slipped from his fingers, and a glob of cream cheese landed in his palm. "Where is he anyway?" Skye glanced around the kitchen while rinsing his hand in the sink. "At home putting the finishing touches on the fatted calf?"

"Relax. He'll be right back. He got an important phone call and needed to meet some people. He's on the verge of starting his own catering business. At affairs like ours, he asks for donations, and if the money is short, he writes that off as advertising. His goal is to get his food in front of people so they'll ask him to their next event."

"Oh, so we're the guinea pigs."

"Exactly."

Their easy banter warmed Skye. Despite the unpalatable task of the day—he hated fungi—he enjoyed being with Ruthanne and hearing her laughter.

She wiped her hands on a towel and slid the cookie sheet of filled mushrooms into the refrigerator. "Once we're done with the food, can you help me sort out the vaccinations? I give the animals their shots on Shearing Day since the alpacas are already contained. It helps to have all the syringes prepared per their weight and tagged with their names so I don't have to worry about getting the right dosages at the last moment."

"Smart." Skye nodded.

He had been working on the ranch for almost four weeks and learned something new every day. Tomorrow would be the much-anticipated Shearing Day, and he looked forward to seeing the process. Even though his shoulder still ached, he was determined to pull his weight.

Around eight o'clock the next morning, two men, one younger and one older, arrived with their shearing equipment. Skye showed them where to set up in the barn.

"Is this a family business?" Skye asked while they laid out their shearing supplies, the long-toothed razors resembling torture devices more than barbering tools.

"Dad here started it after being raised on a sheep ranch." The younger, thirty-ish man referred to his older counterpart.

"Yep," the older man answered. They both had sandy brown hair, but the senior's had faded, with infiltrating strands of gray. "I found out I liked shearin' 'em more than watchin' 'em."

"Dad's the master shearer in the area, and anyone who needs to get a coat off an animal calls him."

Activity outside the barn door caught Skye's attention. The area ranchers were arriving. "By the looks of that crowd out there, you must be doing pretty well."

"Not bad. We serve all of Oregon and northern California. Hey, could you grab one of those tarps there and spread it out? The fleece falls on it as we shear so it's easier to drag away and bag." The father-son team excused themselves to retrieve more supplies from their trailer.

After struggling to open the tarp with one arm, he removed the sling and gingerly tested it for movement. The numbness was gone. Maybe if he was careful and only used his left arm to help steady the larger stuff—

"What do you think you're doing, mister?" Ruthanne rushed to his side.

"I'm fine." He gently slapped her hands away from the sling that now dangled from his neck.

"You're not fine. The doctor said you'd need to keep this on for a full month."

He captured her wrist as she tried to stuff his arm back into the sling. "Ruthanne."

She turned a worried gaze up to him while leaning into his arm to keep it from lowering.

"I'll be careful."

"But—"

"I'm going to do this. If I feel pain, I'll put it back on."

"Promise?"

He released her wrist and held up two fingers for the pact. "Alpaca Apprentice honor."

She grinned then seemed to notice her other arm was hugging his body. When she started to move away, he caught her and pulled her tighter.

"I do like you worrying about me though." He kissed her forehead. "Makes me feel all tingly."

"That's your injury, silly."

"No it's not." He kissed her nose.

"Are you going to stand there and argue—"

He kissed her mouth. The protective arms that had surrounded him now slipped up to his neck.

"Um. . .excuse us." The two shearers stood behind Ruthanne with laughter in their eyes.

"Oh! Sorry." Ruthanne blushed as she broke away to help, leaving Skye wanting more of her kisses but also leaving him annoyed that she could so easily grab the heavy object they struggled with while he could not.

"What is that?" Skye watched as they set up a large six-foot by four-foot board attached to a swivel mechanism and legs. He had compared the various clippers to torture devices, but this thing looked absolutely gruesome.

"The tipping table." Ruthanne pressed her hip against the vertical board. "The alpaca is placed here." Then the two men flipped a bar in the back, tilting the table and lifting Ruthanne so she now lay on top. From her side, she waved in the air. "And voilà! Minimal stress to the animal, and it saves the shearers' backs."

"Cool." Skye looked forward to seeing it used.

The neighboring ranchers trickled in during the next hour, parking their trailers around back. Tom and Skye helped the visitors move their animals into empty stalls. This seemed a good day for the ranchers to check out the other herds. On a couple of occasions throughout the morning, Skye overheard conversations as people bartered their herd sires—a strapping male for another's flawless female. Any offspring of Gabriel's were looked at carefully, and approving nods seemed to please Ruthanne, who bustled around making sure everyone felt welcome and knew what they were doing.

By midmorning, portable corral panels set up an aisle leading into the barn. Several teams formed quickly and began their duties on the assembly line.

Ruthanne gave Skye his instructions. "Follow each animal through the process so you can get a feel of how it's done. I don't mind you stopping to help, but if I see you with so much as a nail clipper in your left hand, I'll send you to the pasture to harvest beans. Got it?" The hand on her hip negated the smile on her lips. Skye had no doubt she'd follow through on her threat.

"Yes, Boss Lady!" He snapped a smart salute and did an about-face, marching off to his designated station.

A visiting white and black dappled huacaya named Oreo was the first customer. She minced her way, clearly uncertain of her handler's intentions as he led her to the first station. Skye stood alongside the team that picked larger pieces of debris off the coats. He reached in and grabbed leaves, chunks of dirt, and pieces of hay off the fuzzy coat. Another customer waited, so he and the two other volunteers picked up the pace.

He followed Oreo down the aisle to the next station. The roar of two Shop-Vacs didn't help Oreo's nervous condition, but the women wielding them did so with deft movements as they vacuumed any remaining rubbish out of the fleece.

"Why not just rinse them off?" Skye raised his voice, competing against the noise. When he got his haircut, the barber always did it wet.

"Because their coats would be too heavy for the shearers," one of the women answered. "Some people still do it that way, but then the animal has to either be blown dry or sent back out to pasture to dry off. If they roll out there, the whole procedure has to be done all over again. We've found this method cuts down the preparation significantly."

By now the assembly line had filled. Two alpacas were in the grooming aisle, and a third now waited its turn. Skye rushed into the barn and joined Ruthanne just in time to see Oreo tipped into her lying position. She seemed only minimally distressed, groaning softly.

"See?" Ruthanne pointed to the table. "It would be so much harder to force her to lie down on the ground. She would get upset and wouldn't lie still."

Skye laughed as the two men quickly finished one side and flipped the alpaca to her other side before she knew what they were doing. "So I guess *torture* is not the word of the day."

"No." She giggled with him. "The real torture comes the next day when you try to get out of bed."

The plastic tarp he had laid out earlier caught the thick blanket of wool from Oreo's back and sides. Some teenage boys and girls pulled the tarp away while others replaced it. The shearers then shaved the neck and upper legs of the animal.

"They're shearing the seconds now," Ruthanne said. "That is less desirable hair, shorter and coarser. After the skirting process, it can be used in batting for quilts or for hand spinning. It won't be as soft as the first cut."

"I had no idea it was such a science."

"Oh, I haven't even touched on DNA matches and special breeding to obtain the choicest fiber."

Skye put his hands over his ears. "Stop. I'm on overload already."

"And just wait until we get into the dyes."

"Hey, what's this over here?" He put a stop to the lecture by tugging her to another station in the spacious barn.

Six women sat around a four-foot by six-foot framed metal screen, balancing it on their knees.

"This is the skirting table. They already have the first batch of fleece on there, cut side down."

The women pulled at the fleece blanket to loosen the fibers then vigorously shook the screen. Underneath, a shower of debris particles and hair fell out of the bottom. Strong, experienced hands searched through the fleece, pinching and pulling.

"What are they finding in there? Wasn't the vacuuming enough?"

"There are always burrs, stubborn bits of hay, and grain stuck in the fiber deep down."

As they found the debris, they tossed it to the floor. When they were finished, more volunteers stuffed the fleece into a clear plastic bag.

"They will tag the bags with the owner's name, and these kids here"—she indicated some older children waiting on the floor—"will drag them to a corner of the barn. When the animals are finished, the ranchers can pick up their bags and go home."

"So." Skye glanced around at the clockworklike activity. "Every person who brings their animals pitches in." He liked that kind of teamwork. It spoke to his sense of organization.

The volunteers on floor patrol swept away a large chunk of hair and tossed it into the trash. "Whatever happened to 'nothing wasted'?"

Ruthanne wrinkled her nose. "This is hair that can't be salvaged. It's not only very coarse but the litter inside is impossible to get out. It's just easier to toss it."

When Oreo was done, they released her down another aisle, where she bounded out to pasture.

Ruthanne left him for a little while to do her part on the assembly line. He continued to ask questions and help haul bags, and he even took a turn at the skirting table.

An hour later Ruthanne grabbed his arm. "Come on. This is the best part of the whole day."

His stomach growled, and he looked at his watch. "Lunch?" Where had the morning gone?

"No, something better."

They headed out to the pasture where the sheared alpacas frolicked after their release. Several skinny, alien-looking creatures rolled in the dust, their long skeletal necks writhing in pure joy. He laughed at the ones standing to the side, looking indignant at the atrocities they had just endured. With their body coats gone, their heads looked huge, as if the spindly necks would never be able to hold them up.

Some of the teenagers had the fun job of sprinkling down the newly shorn with a hose.

"They don't look too traumatized." He laughed along with the crowd who had gathered to watch. It seemed many of the workers decided to take their breaks at that moment. The alpacas romped in the droplets, relishing the feel of the water on their skin.

"I think the end more than justifies the means." Ruthanne dodged a stream of water that flew off the head of a dancing alpaca.

"It must feel good to get all that fur off their bodies." He felt the warmth of the day seeping through his shirt. "Especially as we go into the summer months."

"There are days in the winter when I wish I had their thick coats, but I can't imagine keeping it all year long. Some ranchers prefer not to shear the pregnant animals. But since we hire professionals, we go ahead."

His stomach growled again, and this time it did not go unnoticed.

Ruthanne laughed as she looked at her watch. "It's time."

"Really? We can eat?"

"Let me check with Paul in the kitchen, but I'm sure he'll be prompt."

Together they made the break announcement, which made them very popular. Before eating, Ruthanne called all those gathered for the blessing. As she prayed, Skye raised his face to the warm sun—neither too hot nor too cold, with cotton clouds filtering the sun's rays.

Thank You, Lord, for this beautiful day, for Ruthanne and her patience, and yes. . . even for the circumstances that have led me here. I trust You to finish what You've started. Remembering his unsettled business with his mother, he offered a disclaimer. *I know I say all this while I'm happy. Please remind me of this prayer if things don't go my way. Amen.*

He shook off the foreboding feeling that God had something more for him to learn, something that had nothing to do with alpaca shearing, something that he didn't want to face.

Paul had set up tables under the back deck in the shade. A wicker basket perched on a corner to gather money for the food. Hungry volunteers swarmed as if the doors had just opened on a Harry & David's buy-one-get-one-free sale. Some took their food up to the deck, and others sat under the trees scattered around the property.

Along with a hot dog and hamburger, Skye filled his plate with food he couldn't identify. Had he heard the word *canapé* at the table? He tasted salmon, cream cheese, and dill. And what were those odd little lettuce wraps filled with spicy ground beef, coleslaw, and green onions? He deliberately avoided the stuffed mushrooms. Even if he liked fungi, too many of those puppies had ended up on the floor when he was cleaning them. He settled under a maple tree in the north pasture, his arm a little sore from the day's activities. Several teenage girls invaded his spot. They chattered like the birds in the maple tree outside his bedroom window, reminding him of his youngest sister, Robyn.

Ruthanne eventually joined them. "Whenever you girls are done, Francie could use your help in the barn."

They all jumped up at once, and the giggling gaggle of girls disappeared back into the barn.

"Sorry about that. You probably didn't need all that energy when you were trying to rest."

"That's okay. They entertained me." He chuckled while scrutinizing a lettuce thing.

"Not a gourmet connoisseur?" Her eyes, green as the pasture grass, crinkled as she smiled.

"Um. . .think I'll get another hot dog."

He glanced toward the house where Paul moved about with trays of food to replenish his emptying table. But when he returned the look, Skye suddenly felt uncomfortable. He still wasn't clear on a few things.

"Other than his strange sense of picnic fare, Paul seems to be a great guy."

Her eyes sparkled—not what Skye wanted. "Oh, he's been my best friend ever since I moved to the ranch." *"Friend." Noted.* "No one could ask for a better pal." *"Pal." Even better.* "When Brian left, Paul helped pick up the pieces. He became my rock." *"Rock." That's a step in the wrong direction.*

He had shared only two kisses with Ruthanne, the first that night of the screaming alpaca scare. Had the moon been to blame for their slip into romanticism? Probably. That and the fact that Ruthanne was intoxicated with victory. That poor paint-splattered mutt never stood a chance. He chuckled at the memory.

"What?" She frowned at him.

"What do you mean, 'What'?" He feigned innocence.

"You're laughing. Let me in on the joke."

"I was just thinking of the other night when you graffitied the neighbor's dog."

She blushed crimson as if she'd been the one shot with a paint gun. He guessed she was thinking of the moon as well. Or perhaps their latest kiss just hours earlier in the barn. "Oh, I never told you. It worked. I called them the next day to see if they noticed."

"And?"

"Of course they did. A black dog with neon yellow splotches? I confessed, offered to pay the groomer to get him clean, and told them if I saw him over here again, I'd use buckshot."

"That's my Calamity."

He decided to plunge into the real reason he started this conversation. "So, back to Paul. Just how good of a *friend* is he?" His gaze held hers so there could be no doubt as to why he asked that question.

She swallowed.

"Ruthie!" Paul called from the deck. "Where are the small paper plates you said you had?"

"I'll be right there!" She turned to Skye. "I'm sorry, I have to help him." She sprang up and ran to the house.

Had she deliberately ignored his question?

For the rest of the afternoon, Skye and Ruthanne were never together long enough for even a short, intimate conversation. His question continued to hang in the air like a neighbor's unreturned wave.

Yet she continued to glance at him with—dare he think?—flirtatious looks that made him wish the day would go faster so he could kiss her again.

During an afternoon break, Paul laid out several desserts provided by the visiting ranchers. The little paper plates sat in stacks. Had he really needed help finding them?

Skye ended up near the barn in an exchange of funny alpaca stories with several ranchers. But he could see the back of the house where he had a ringside seat to the Paul and Ruthanne Show. They stood behind the dessert table, acting as host and hostess. Paul would say something funny—Ruthanne would laugh. He'd bump her shoulder playfully—she'd slap his. It all looked very much like a brother-and-sister act. At least on her part. But he feared that Paul was more serious. Skye had never been particularly intuitive, but the man's eyes kept darting in his direction.

That pained Skye in a small way. He scratched his chin. How was he going to date Ruthanne without hurting Paul?

⟡

Every year during Shearing Day, Ruthanne felt in her element as she cohosted with Hannie. But this year, besides the fact that Hannie wasn't there, things had changed. And that change stood a few yards away by the paddocks, watching her with those clear blue eyes.

She'd thought of their first kiss often. And today her heart hadn't stopped humming since he kissed her in the barn.

However, her practical self warred within her. She'd been a widow only three years. Was she ready for a boyfriend?

Another thing to consider was Hannie, who had so wanted to see Ruthanne and her nephew together. The poor dear had played Cupid so many times that Ruthanne feared she'd run out of arrows.

But wouldn't Hannie be just as pleased if Ruthanne got together with her son? And *there* was the elephant in the room.

Hannie and Skye had no mother-son relationship. Skye clearly held animosity toward his mother. In light of that, how could Ruthanne and Skye have a healthy intimacy?

So many questions, which was why she couldn't answer him right away. She tossed up a quick prayer for guidance and tagged on a small request.

If Skye isn't for me, would You please silence this silly humming?

Chapter 13

As a tradition, one of the area ranchers always thought of fun things to do to wind down from Shearing Day. This year for the group, he booked a cruise with Rogue River Hellgate Jetboat Excursions for the next Sunday afternoon.

Skye had heard of the cruise but never had the opportunity to go. It sounded like fun, with high speeds on the water and a meal downriver.

The morning of the cruise Skye once again visited Ruthanne's church and found it only mildly annoying when people talked about his mother. Perhaps he was becoming numb to all the Hannie praise.

Afterward Skye found Ruthanne and Paul in the foyer, deep in discussion.

"I wish you'd reconsider, Paul." She looked at him with concern in her eyes.

"Reconsider what?" Skye nudged his way into the conversation.

Paul rubbed the back of his neck. "I'm not going on the cruise."

"Why not? It won't be the same without you."

"Well, I have to work, and—"

"Didn't you tell me you don't work on Sunday mornings?"

"Yes. . .but. . .I've got tons of work to do at the ranch."

"You worked hard enough yesterday." Skye waved away that thought. "Today you should reward yourself."

Ruthanne had been unusually quiet during this exchange, and he placed his hand on her back. "Talk to him." Her warmth radiated to his hand, and Skye suddenly wondered why he was trying to convince Paul to go.

"I've tried talking to him, but he doesn't like the—"

"The fuss," Paul interrupted her. "I don't like all the fuss. Why celebrate something that's your job to begin with?"

"Okay then." Skye shrugged. "We'll miss you."

He started to walk away, and when a frowning Ruthanne followed under his arm, slipping her hand around his waist, he could barely hear Paul for his heart thumping hard in his chest.

"Wait!" Paul joined them. "You're right. I should enjoy myself after working so hard yesterday."

Ruthanne cocked an eyebrow. "Then you're going?"

"Yes." He cast a glance at her arm around Skye. "I think I'd better."

About sixty people who had been involved in the shearing gathered in Grants Pass later that afternoon. The forecast promised a sunny and warm day, but the smart Oregonians brought their Windbreakers, just in case. Skye allowed Ruthanne to pull him down the dock while Paul dragged behind.

"Come on, pokey." Ruthanne grabbed Paul's arm and placed herself between the two men.

The entire group fit into the boat as they sat on the blue benches. Each bench sat six people, and Skye found himself on the end. "I wonder how wet I'll get." He looked over the edge at the dark, swirling river water.

Their tour guide, who piloted from a taller platform at the back of the boat, told everyone to hang on. He took off in a swirling pin curl that caused a centrifugal force with the five people on the bench. They all slid like beads on an abacus, squishing Ruthanne into Skye's hip. Yep. He was going to like this excursion.

"Better than an amusement park!" Ruthanne's eyes danced.

Skye placed his arm on the back of her seat and cocked his head as he regarded her. "I didn't know you were a daredevil."

She whispered into his ear. "How do you think I got the name *Calamity*?"

The boat took off and drove his laughter back into his throat. Wind blew past his face, taking with it all his cares.

Ruthanne squealed as if she were on a roller coaster. He delighted in that sound as much as her soft giggles. She cast a concerned glance at Paul, though, who white-knuckled the seat in front of him, his mouth a straight slash across his face—and was that terror in his eyes?

Soon the boat slowed down. After the applause, the guide said, "That was a little taste of what we'll experience later on."

During a more leisurely pace, the guide pointed out some stunning nature: an eagle soaring overhead with a fish grasped in its claws, a deer and her fawn getting a drink, osprey landing amid the white bell-like flowers of a shedding madrone.

Eventually the shore began to close in on them. "We're about to go through the infamous Hellgate Canyon." The tour guide eased back the throttle, and the boat floated toward an ever-narrowing passage that sliced a gash through layers of stone. "If you've ever seen the movie *Rooster Cogburn* with John Wayne, this is where he escaped the bad guys on the river raft."

Skye loved that Western. He joined the rest on board as they nodded, recalling that scene.

As they glided through the canyon, appropriately named Hellgate, Skye tipped his head back. Two craggy walls towered above them, revealing a narrow slit of daylight at the top. He swallowed hard. Nothing like a dose of nature's grandeur to restore a man's humility. In the shadows, he thought about God. His love had eroded the hard places in his heart. Hard places that could have eventually opened a gate to destruction. Even as a child he had resisted that love, but it slowly carved a path, reshaping him into the adult he eventually became.

The short gorge finally opened as they made their way through to the other side of the hill, and the pilot sped away, eliciting cheers from the passengers.

Skye cast a glance over at Paul, who had not only seized the chair in front of him but had added extra comfort by wrapping his arm around Ruthanne's right elbow. Skye looked at her fingers to see if they were turning blue. "You okay there, bud?"

"Yeah." Paul's shaky reply suggested anything but. "Just wondering how those rocks stayed glued to the mountainside."

Ruthanne patted his hand. "Have faith."

He seemed to get the message and rode the rest of the way untethered to her.

Finally they reached their destination.

"As you get out of the boat," the guide explained, "the OK Corral is a good stretch of the legs uphill. You can choose to walk the short incline or take the free limo that will be waiting for you."

Skye chuckled when he saw the "limo" was a John Deere tractor pulling a flat, open trailer with seats. Ruthanne wanted the whole experience, so she bounded toward the tractor.

On the ride up the hill, her face lit up as she took in the surroundings. "This place is so beautiful. The river. The evergreen trees. The manicured lawn. Who would have thought an old homestead would have a lawn?" When the large mountain-lodge-looking structure came into view, she could barely contain herself. "That's not a homestead. It's too grand."

Skye loved her enthusiasm. He'd never seen this side of her, and he suspected this was the true Ruthanne, before his mother's illness caused the worry shadows on her face.

The group congregated under a large covered patio held up by honed logs. Wooden handmade chairs pressed against long tables draped with red-checkered tablecloths. Shiny white dishes and clear glasses finished the display. This all lent a homey yet elegant feel to their dining experience.

"When I heard we were eating at an old settlement, I pictured a backyard barbecue and paper plates." Skye gazed around in awe.

"Rustic yet elegant." Ruthanne nodded in agreement.

Aromas straight from Grandma's kitchen filtered to the outside dining room, and Skye chose their seats quickly, eager to get started. Soon the food arrived family style in bowls and on platters. Everyone passed the delicious barbecued ribs, fried chicken, corn bread, and biscuits, and began visiting in one collective noise. Except Paul. Apparently he was still upset from the boat ride. He picked at his food and criticized every little thing.

"Too much pepper."

"Dressing's too thin."

At one point, Skye feared that Paul might storm the kitchen to teach the chef how to cook.

Ruthanne tried to make up for Paul's rudeness by placating him. "What's in this honey-mustard dressing, Paul? There's a mystery ingredient I can't identify."

Dessert included Apple Brown Betty, which Skye and Ruthanne discovered they both loved.

"I like it, too," Paul interrupted them. He stood and pitched his napkin to the table. "A lot!" Then he stormed away.

Ruthanne turned a shocked gaze at Skye. "What was that all about?"

"I don't know." But he suspected. Paul's performance throughout the day suggested a jealous alter ego lurking behind the mild-mannered chef.

After dessert they were encouraged to stretch their legs and check out the terrain. The boat would be leaving in an hour. Skye had eaten so much he feared he'd waddle. He excused himself to use the facilities, and when he returned, both Ruthanne and Paul had disappeared. He chatted with the other guests for a while, but he worried that Paul might be swaying Ruthanne to choose between them. Either that or she had pulled him aside like a disobedient child to verbally punish him for his behavior.

He chose to believe that last train of thought and patiently waited for them to rejoin the group.

⊂⊃

Ruthanne stomped along the gravel path trailing the river. When she finally cooled down enough to talk, she turned and confronted him. "What was all that about during dinner?"

He opened his mouth to speak, but nothing came out. She assumed he was about to give an unconvincing excuse. Finally he shoved his hands into the pockets of his jacket and looked out at the river. "Is it truly only a friendship you want from me?" The quiet question thundered in her ears.

"Paul. . ." She reached out for his arm. "We tried dating. Remember? It didn't work out."

"You said you weren't ready so soon after becoming a widow." His gaze searched her face. "It's been three years, Ruthie."

"I know, but—"

"But you'll never be serious about me."

She pondered a pile of rocks along the path. "No. I don't feel—"

"You don't feel for me the way you do Skye."

She jerked her gaze back to him. "I was going to say I don't feel worthy of your attention. I know you've had feelings for me, and I selfishly allowed them because I needed to feel loved after Brian left. You were safe."

He snorted. "That's not what a guy in love wants to hear."

"Really, Paul? Love? If you loved me, you wouldn't have waited this long to tell me so. In fact, if it weren't for Skye's attention, you might have let this go on for another three years."

He picked at a piney knob on a nearby tree. "Maybe I needed you, too. My love for Aunt Hannie must have spilled over, and I really liked taking care of you both." He grinned. "Neither of you can cook."

"That's true." She laughed, grateful their little tiff was ending. "We might have starved if it weren't for you."

They stood in silence for a moment. Ruthanne imagined the smoothly flowing river carrying away any misunderstandings between them.

"*Do* you love me, Paul?"

"I don't know." An errant twig springing from the tree suffered abuse as Paul twisted it unmercifully. "I guess you were safe for me, too."

Ruthanne turned from the river to give him her full attention. "How so?"

"When you moved in with my aunt and uncle, remember how we clicked?"

"Of course. I could always talk to you."

Paul, who had decimated the twig, now turned his attention on a small, leafy plant, loosening its roots with his toe. He turned his gaze toward her. "I figured we'd continue on forever."

"Forever is fine for a friendship. But if there is a commitment with no love, forever can drag agonizingly slow. Believe me. I know."

After a moment of silence, Paul spoke softly. "I want you as a friend, Ruthanne."

She allowed his words to shower over her. "Me, too. I don't want to lose you just because I'm interested in someone else." She touched his arm. "But I need to be free to pursue other romantic interests. If Skye isn't the one, there will be others. Can you handle that?"

Paul slouched lazily against the tree, his grin drawing out the Paul she had come to love—or rather, *like* in an intense, brotherly way. "Hey, can *you* handle it if *I* meet someone else?"

"I'll do you one better. I'll start praying for someone who will make your heart sing."

As they started back down a path leading to the boat, Ruthanne told him about her gauge for knowing God's will.

"I like Skye, believe it or not." Paul picked his way through the light brush, clearing a path for her to walk. "It could have been worse. I could have lost you to Gerald from church."

She wrinkled her nose. "Gerald? That skinny kid who had a crush on me?"

He tossed over his shoulder, "Pimples and all!"

❦

Skye glanced at his watch—again. He'd already wandered down to the boat but was prepared to launch a full manhunt if his two companions failed to show up. With only ten minutes to spare before the boat took off without them, Paul and Ruthanne stepped out of the woods and walked toward him. He'd half expected Paul to be dragging behind like a puppy that had just had its nose smacked. But instead his easy smile remained in place. Ruthanne grabbed his shoulders from behind and said something into his ear, then glanced toward Skye. Paul nodded, waved at him, and boarded the boat.

Skye joined Ruthanne, and they strolled downriver, being careful not to stray too far. Her silence created a lasso that squeezed his gut. Was she about to break up with him before they even began?

She finally stopped and turned to face him. The sun had begun its descent and glittered on the roving current like diamonds on a necklace. "I never answered your question."

He racked his brain to remember what he'd asked. "What question?"

"The other day you asked how good a friend Paul was." Her smile held him hostage as she paused. "The answer is, a very good friend."

His heart sank. She was about to defend her feelings for Paul. But then she said, "And *only* a friend."

Her green eyes sparkled, emeralds rivaling the diamonds in the river. When she took a step toward him, all his questions fell away and clattered to the forest floor. He wrapped his arms around her waist and thoroughly kissed the lips that had just freed him to love her.

⌘

Paul hopped into his car when they returned to the ranch. Instead of kissing Ruthanne's temple before she got out of the car, he chucked her chin and called her "pal." Skye guessed that was a result of their talk earlier. Then he waved to Skye as he pulled out.

Skye slipped his hand into Ruthanne's while they strolled toward the paddocks to check on the animals. Her answering gaze created a love rhythm as his heart beat against his chest. Dusk began to deepen into evening, creating a feathery haze in the pasture and into the mountain's crevices.

"How was the cruise?" Tom's voice came from the barn.

Ruthanne jumped and slipped away from Skye. "What are you still doing here?"

"You had some lightbulbs out in the yard, so I replaced them after the feeding."

"Thanks. I kept meaning to tell you about them."

"You should have come with us," Skye said.

"I've already been on that cruise. Speedboats freak me out, and I don't need that kind of abuse." Since big Tom could admit that so freely, Skye decided he'd cut Paul some slack.

After Tom left them standing by Lirit's pen, Skye drew Ruthanne into his arms and tasted her lips once more. She returned his love with silent promises, but when they parted, she seemed pensive.

"What's wrong?" He hoped she was only tired from the full day of recreation.

She smiled up at him, placing another brief kiss on his mouth. "Nothing. I'm thinking about my talk with Paul."

He released her. "You're thinking about Paul while kissing me?"

"No, silly." She beat his chest with all the fury of a kitten at play. "Well, not exactly. I told him I didn't feel a future with him was in God's will. Then I told him how I gauged that. I think you should know, too."

As she explained Lirit's hum of contentment, Skye looked with wonder at the supposedly dumb beast that helped Ruthanne listen to her own heart. The alpaca, having heard her name, pushed against the gate to be near her owner.

"You know"—Skye motioned with his eyes toward their subject—"I've never heard Lirit hum when she's content, only when she's stressing like the other animals." He rubbed his chin. "In fact, she never seems content around me. Like she's mad at me or something."

Ruthanne stroked Lirit's neck. "That's absurd. She's the gentlest alpaca on the ranch."

"Whatever." He jerked his chin toward the beast. "When it's just her and me, she either spits or sulks in a corner."

Ruthanne cocked her head and looked Lirit in the eye. "Maybe she senses our attraction to each other."

Skye pondered that statement for a moment. He wasn't sure he believed Lirit was jealous, but she seemed to get some kind of vibe from him. *God's will.* Could she sense his bitterness toward his mother?

With their chores finished, Skye kissed Ruthanne good night then walked back to the house.

Straight to his mother's bedroom door.

Chapter 14

Skye grasped the doorknob and slowly turned it. He almost expected beaded curtains on the windows and the stale-sweet odor of incense-saturated fabric to assault his nose. But this room reflected the taste of the rest of the house. Handcrafted wooden furniture and soft colors of various earth hues in the bedspread and drapes shocked him more than the psychedelic colors his mother used to love.

Her guitar sat perched in an old wooden rocker near the bed, nestled artfully among the soft billows of a knitted afghan. He picked it up and sat on the edge of the bed, manipulating his fingers into the one chord she'd taught him. Was it an A? The *plunk* of his fingertips against the three strings sounded just as childlike as when he was young.

Setting the guitar aside, he remembered how his mother always kept a peach-scented talc pouch in the tiny compartment inside the case. He loved that smell. Sometimes he'd ask her to play just so she would take the pouch out, dry her fingers with it, and hand it to him to hold. He found the case behind the rocker, laid it on the bed, and opened it. The scent wafted toward him, which immediately threw his mind into memories. The gold felt interior was still in good condition, and the tiny compartment that held guitar picks and small items still had the ribbon sewn on to open it. He grasped it and flipped the lid up, knowing the pouch of talc would be inside. It was, lying on top of a photograph.

His fingers tightened into a fist before he relaxed them enough to pick up the photo for a better look. His young mother smiled into the camera, her long blond hair in motion as if a small breeze had decided to play with the fine strands. Unexpected emotion rose up within him, like a parched flower receiving a long-needed watering. He had loved this woman so much. He knew the little boy with her was himself. What was he, about seven years old? He wore a blue cowboy hat and sat astride one of six horses tied to a central hub. This looked like the pony rides at the county fair.

Skye had to wring out his brain to extract the memory. His dad wasn't in the picture, so was he behind the camera? No, he didn't come with them that day. A tight knot grabbed Skye's stomach. They had gone to the fair without his dad, and when they returned, they found he had died of an overdose. That hadn't bothered Skye as much as his mother's hysterical reaction. No wonder he had chosen to forget that day.

But now it came flooding in. They were going to attend the fair as a family, but that morning his dad refused to go, choosing instead to stay with his friends and their funny pipes. Mom was furious. She didn't know how to drive and had no way to get there. Then a man from the commune offered to take them. Skye liked this man better than he ever liked his dad. He often sat with Skye when his parents were away or incapacitated. He bought him that hat.

Suddenly tired, Skye curled up on the bed, the photo pressed to his chest. With his mother's guitar on the rocker the last thing he saw before closing his eyes, he spent the night dreaming of the good times.

⬲

Ruthanne's humming heart woke her before her alarm had a chance. Both Skye and Paul now knew about her gauge for God's will. Her confession made it seem all the more valid. With fresh excitement she looked forward to seeing Skye.

Even so, she decided to drop by Lirit's pen for some girl talk before going into the main house.

"Last night I prayed that God would work things out between Skye and Hannie," she confided as Lirit munched hay. "It was a selfish prayer, I admit. I want to pursue our relationship free of guilt and anxiety. Peace settled in my heart. I just know that all will be well. Hannie will wake up, and she and Skye will talk. They'll set their differences aside, and we can all move forward."

She expected the low droning hum that came so easily to Lirit, but instead her ears flattened and an ugly snort rippled her mouth, spewing wet bits of hay.

"Really, Lirit. Why don't you like him? You know I'd never let a man come between us." She reached out to pet the woolly neck, but Lirit sidestepped out of reach. Ruthanne pulled her hand back and pressed it to her chest. "Do you know something I don't?"

A chill settled in her heart, snuffing out the peace she'd felt last night.

As she entered the main house, dark and empty, an unbidden thought caused her heart to lurch. Where was Skye? Had he left her, just like Brian did? She rebuked that notion, demanding that it not rule over her anymore. She was tired of fearing the worst from men and from Skye in particular. He was not Brian and had proved himself many times over.

She flicked the light switch on in the kitchen, and it illuminated a handwritten note on the table.

"R, I'm sorry to bail on you today. My sister called early this morning. Her car broke down on her way to school, and she called me in a panic. Women! Ha-ha (sorry). Anyway, I need to tow her home, and then I have to fix this thing once and for all. I hope to be back later for the evening feeding, but I'll call you if I get tied up. Love, S."

Disappointment washed over her, then she chided herself for acting like a fifteen-year-old with a crush. However, that didn't stop her from reading his bold handwriting again and focusing on the end of his note—*"Love, S."*

With a spring in her step and the memory of his tender kisses, she headed out

97

to the barn to start the round of feeding. A love song bubbled up from her heart, and she found herself whistling it while tossing chicken feed out to the gathering brood.

"You sound happy."

"Hi, Tom. It's a beautiful day." She tried to act as nonchalant as possible but knew her burning cheeks gave her away.

He glanced around. "Where's your counterpart?"

"A small family emergency—car trouble."

Tom's face fell, and he looked as disappointed as she had felt earlier. "We were going to finish the barn."

"Give me an hour, and I'll help you."

He winked. "You're on."

She breezed through the feeding while Tom hauled water to the troughs, then they worked together preparing to paint the entire barn wall.

"Why can't we just paint over the damaged part?" Ruthanne stirred red paint in the five-gallon bucket, looking dubiously at the other three Tom had left in a corner. "This seems like so much."

"We can't just paint the new part of the barn because it won't match. The whole wall has to be painted for continuity, and if the rest of the barn doesn't look right, we'll have to paint the whole thing."

Ruthanne winced. "What is this costing us?"

"Nothing. Skye's insurance is paying for all the repairs." Tom hauled out the ladder. "So, you didn't tell me last night. What did you think of the cruise? Did you have fun?"

Ruthanne hesitated. Paul was no fun at first. But the memory of Skye's soft lips on hers was quite enjoyable.

"Well? You did go, didn't you?"

"What? Yes." Daydreaming on the job. And—oh swell!—now she had a red paint splotch on her shoe. "I had a great time."

Tom stopped halfway up the ladder and grinned. "What aren't you telling me? Maybe I should rephrase. Did you have fun with Skye?"

"Am I that transparent?" Or had Tom seen their hand-holding last night?

He wrapped his arm around a rung and scratched his nose. "Girlie, other than Hannie or her nephew, I probably know you better than anyone. I may be dumb, but I got eyes." He pointed with two fingers at his eyeballs. "And these peepers tell me you've got feelings for the new guy."

She had no words. He'd summed it up concisely, so she merely nodded.

Tom took another step up and chuckled. "Then you'd better brush up on your Old West trivia."

⌘

"Okay, if you won't junk this thing, I will," Skye mumbled from under the hood of Robyn's cute but failing sports car.

"You taught me to be frugal, big bro." She leaned over the fender to peer at the partially dismantled engine. "And besides, I don't get paid enough to buy a new car."

He turned to look at her. His gorgeous youngest sister had been working hard to pay off her student loans. Skye was proud of her, but enough was enough.

After wiping his hands on an oily rag, he pointed to the engine and pretended to shoot it. "That's what they did in the Old West when their horses couldn't take another step." He palmed his chest over his heart. "It's the humane way."

Robyn flipped her strawberry-colored ponytail and jabbed her finger into his chest. "Are you telling me you can't fix it?"

He started loading up his tools. "Get out the shovel, and bury the old girl." He pinched her chin, purposely leaving a dark smudge. "Go wash your face. I'll drive you to work."

He felt lighter than he had for years. For the first time, he started to feel the puzzle pieces of his life come together. Now if he could only talk to his birth mother. After all the great things he'd heard about her, she must have had a good reason for not contacting him sooner, and he prayed he'd get the chance to ask her about it.

The radio in his parents' garage was blasting contemporary Christian music. As he put the tools away, he barely heard his cell phone ring. It was Paul.

"I just spoke to the doctor. He plans to bring Aunt Hannie out of the coma this afternoon. Her lungs are healing nicely, so he feels it's time."

"How long will it take?" Skye glanced at his watch. "I have to get my sister to school and then go back to the ranch to change."

"Take your time getting here. The doc said after they're out of the coma it usually takes awhile for the patient to wake up naturally."

Skye promised to get there as soon as he could and prompted Robyn to hurry up.

He arrived back at the ranch within an hour. Ruthanne had already left for the hospital. Between fixing Robyn's car and rushing back to the ranch, Skye had missed lunch. He opened the refrigerator, but the contents morphed into a vision of his mother lying comatose in the hospital bed. Would he finally get to talk to her? The coolness from the refrigerator suddenly chilled him clear through. How she answered his *why* question could impact his budding romance with Ruthanne. His appetite gone, he squeezed his eyes shut and leaned on the still-open door. "Please, God. Give me strength."

Without grabbing a thing to eat, he headed out. When he arrived at the hospital, nausea swirled in his empty stomach. He reprimanded himself for allowing his nerves to dictate his common sense.

Ruthanne greeted him in the visitors' lounge then stepped into his embrace. "I'm so glad you're here." She wrapped her arms around his neck. He drew strength from her touch, grateful that God had brought her into his life, if only for the moment when he talked to his mother for the first time.

Paul sat in the corner, his legs and arms crossed while he watched a news channel on the small television hanging in the corner.

Dr. Harris entered and sat down with the three of them. His white coat contrasted sharply with his African-American skin. He spoke with professionalism, but his eyes held compassion. "We've stopped the drug therapy, and tests indicate that she's out of the coma. It's all up to her now. Her lungs are strong, so I'm confident she'll pull through all of this."

A voice from the speaker overhead paged his name, and he stood. "Are there any more questions?"

Ruthanne motioned with her hand. "Can we sit with her so she's not alone when she wakes up?"

"Certainly. I think that's a great idea."

Panic rose in Skye's throat. Could he sit in her room for that long? Mentally pulling himself up by his bootstraps, he decided to be strong.

But as they all walked to the room, the little boy inside him tried to dig in his heels, making Skye's size elevens feel like lead.

Chapter 15

As always, Ruthanne felt drawn to Hannie's side by their invisible bond. Paul followed closely, but Skye tagged behind by several yards. She knew he had never made it all the way into the room, usually choosing to hang out at the doorjamb, but today she decided to help him.

When he showed up at the door, she held out her hand. Warmth spread through her as he stepped inside and joined her. She did notice, however, that he had trouble looking at Hannie.

She squeezed his palm and gazed up at him. "What is it? Talk to me."

"It's hard to envision this woman as the young mom I remember."

Ruthanne caught Paul's glance across the bed. She was sure they wondered the same thing: Would they find out what happened?

When Skye didn't volunteer the information, Ruthanne took a deep breath as she tested their new bond. "Would you like to talk about it?"

He stepped away from the bed but this time didn't flee out the door. He lowered himself into one of the three chairs a nurse had graciously maneuvered into the tiny space. "Let me talk to her first." He balled his fists and pressed them into the arm of the chair. "I'd like to tell you everything, but I'd rather do it with grace, and right now I don't feel that."

She lowered herself into the chair next to him. "I understand. Whenever you're ready." *Please, God, make him ready soon.*

Paul still stood by the bed, fidgeting with the sheet, tucking it neatly around his aunt. Then he stroked her hand. Ruthanne praised God for this compassionate man.

Lord, bring someone into Paul's life who will laugh at his wit, lean on his strength, and love him beyond anything he could imagine.

She tried to picture the girl God would send to Paul. Petite, feminine, an appreciator of gourmet food. She would laugh at all his jokes, love all his quirks, and be a gentle helpmate.

It was almost as if she were penning a want ad. Would God send a sweet Mary Poppins as a result? Ruthanne tried to suppress a giggle.

With a cocked eyebrow, Paul regarded her. She felt grateful he hadn't heard her silly prayer.

He looked back at Hannie. "She looks different somehow. As if before she wasn't really in there, but now she is. Yet she hasn't moved."

Ruthanne nodded. "I see it, too." In fact it looked as if she would awaken at any moment.

But she didn't. Afternoon gave way to evening, and soon they were turning on lights in the darkening room.

Skye glanced at his watch and sat up straight. "Should I go feed the animals?"

"No," Ruthanne answered. "Tom said he'd take care of things while we were gone."

His stomach rumbled, and Ruthanne turned to him. "When did you eat last?"

His blue eyes widened. "Was it that obvious?"

Paul lounged with his leg over the arm of his chair on the far side of the bed. "Hey, I heard it from here."

Ruthanne leaned forward. "Okay, executive-decision time. Why don't you two go get some dinner and bring something back for me?"

"I have a better idea." Paul motioned toward the door. "Why don't you two go have dinner? I ate a late lunch while waiting for you both to come to the hospital."

Ruthanne believed the excuse but also knew this was Paul's way of saying he took their conversation during the cruise seriously. He was willing to be just friends, and his offer was his way of blessing her relationship with Skye. "Okay but we'll consider this the first watch since it seems we'll be sitting with her through the night."

Skye reached for her hand, sending a thrill through her at his touch. "I'll take the second watch so Ruthanne can get some rest." He stood and pulled her to her feet. "If you drag the waiting room chairs out there together to make a bed, they're probably a step down from crippling."

Ruthanne laughed. "Don't try writing publicity copy." She glanced at Paul. "Sounds like a plan. We'll bring you back dinner though."

"Whatever. That's fine."

As a tribute to his selflessness, she tossed up one last request on his behalf. *And have this Mary Poppins want to spoil him thoroughly.*

❧

The hospital cafeteria had already closed, so Skye and Ruthanne found a small café nearby. He enjoyed the small talk, carefully sidestepping any conversation about his mother. He wanted to tell Ruthanne everything but felt the temper of that conversation hinged on what he would learn from the stranger in the hospital bed. If his mother could explain her actions thirty-eight years ago in a way that made sense, then he could speak about it with Ruthanne in a civil—yes, even celebratory—manner. But if the conversation went horribly wrong, he would have no good words to say and would probably alienate Ruthanne. She, along with the rest of the world, had placed his mother on a pedestal. Ruthanne would probably fight to keep her there.

Once the meal was over, they ordered takeout for Paul and headed back to the hospital where Skye took the next watch.

The night nurse came in and felt for his mother's pulse, looked at readouts on the machine, and changed a bag hanging on a pole. She glanced at him then back to what she was doing. "Are you the son?"

"Yes."

"Well, I'm sure she'll be happy to see you when she wakes up."

He nodded, but he wasn't so sure. Now that he was facing an evening alone with her, the enemy had been barraging him again with lies that made sense. *You're worthless. Your own mother tried to get rid of you.* He pulled his pocket Bible out, and the voice sizzled away, like a hot fire doused with cool water.

The nurse spoke again. "I'll bring you a pillow and blanket."

"Thank you."

For most of his shift he flipped through his Bible, reading about vulnerable men who became mighty in the Lord. Joseph, David, Gideon, all with real problems in their lives, some bigger than the giant Goliath. Some as intense as questioning faith. God never let them down, and their strength of character became their legacy.

He closed his eyes. *Lord, I confess that my faith is small right now. The pain is so real. How can my mother make everything right again? Gideon tested You with a fleece. Dry when there was dew on the ground then again wet if no dew was present. I, also, lay a fleece before You. If, when my mother awakes, she indicates no joy at my presence, doesn't reach out for me, I'll walk away and continue my life as before. Amen.*

Oddly peace eluded him after that prayer.

As night swallowed the little room and the nurses began speaking in hushed voices at their station near the door, the words in Skye's Bible blurred then disappeared one by one. He awoke, startled as the book hit the floor. When he retrieved it and stood to stretch, he glanced over at the bed. Instead of a sleeping form, he saw his mother's blue eyes trained on him. Eyes that he had at one time longed to see again but then had haunted his dreams until only a few years ago.

He blinked back stinging tears. Tucking the Bible into his breast pocket, he shifted to stand by the bed. The eyes followed him. "It's me." His voice cracked. "It's me, Skye."

She didn't smile. She didn't reach out. She only stared. Remembering his prayer, the seven-year-old within wanted to reach out and shake her. Knowing that would do no good, he tore out of the room as the accusing voice in his head cackled with delight.

⌘

A sharp pain in her neck woke Ruthanne. Skye had used the word *crippling* when referring to the chairs in the waiting room. He was right. Her gaze sought out Paul in the dim room, sleeping like a newborn cria. He could have at least looked uncomfortable for her sake.

A window faced east where a crimson sliver of light peeked between the slats of the vinyl blinds. She glanced at her watch in alarm then hopped out of the improvised bed as fast as her twisted body would let her. She'd missed her shift.

Where was Skye? Had he fallen asleep? When she reached the room, she peered in. Only Hannie, lying in the same position she'd left her in last night.

With a hand on her hip, she tried to convince herself that Skye had just lost track of time. He probably took a break and hadn't made it back to the waiting room. She glanced both ways down the corridor. No Skye, but a nurse approached her sporting a friendly smile. "Mrs. Godfrey woke up about five hours ago."

"She did?" Ruthanne glanced at the sleeping form, selfishly wishing she'd been the one on watch. "Was Skye with her?"

"Her son? Yes, but only for a moment." She entered the room to check Hannie's pulse. "He let us know at the nurses' station, then he left."

"He left?" Ruthanne rubbed her aching neck. "Where?"

The nurse continued her routine attention to Hannie, apparently too busy to see Ruthanne's confusion. "I don't know. He did ask one of the other nurses to wake you. But then we had an emergency with another patient down the hall. I guess in our busyness no one came to get you."

"No, they didn't." She walked over to Hannie. "She's asleep again?"

"Yes, she'll do that for a little while, wake and sleep. With each interval she'll become more aware." She smiled. "You'd think she'd have rested enough, but for some reason that's not the case."

As the nurse left, she offered her a cup of coffee or tea, which Ruthanne refused.

Her stomach roiled. Why did Skye leave—again? Did Hannie somehow upset him? He seemed on edge last night, but after he agreed to stay with Hannie for several hours, Ruthanne thought he was okay.

The man sure had a habit of taking off. After what her husband had put her through, she certainly didn't need that again.

Remembering the real reason she was there, she put her anger on hold. With one last check on Hannie, Ruthanne noticed something different. A single salty tear track from the corner of her eye to the pillow.

Paul entered yawning, looking like a child with his mussed hair and crumpled clothes. "They just told me Aunt Hannie woke up." He went to Hannie's side but didn't take her hand like he'd always done before. "Is she asleep again?"

"Yes, but the nurse said she'll wake up again and with each time stay awake longer."

After she filled him in on Skye, he asked, "Did you try to call his cell?"

She hadn't thought of that. How could Paul be so logical when he first woke up? "No. I'll do that now." She pulled her phone out of her purse and called but only got his voice mail. After leaving a brief message, her irritation with Skye gave way to alarm. "I hope he's okay."

"Look." Paul sank into the chair and raked his fingers through the dark tangles on his head. "He's a grown man and a dedicated Christian. I'm sure it was very hard for him to see his mom for the first time after so many years. Give him time. He's probably off praying by himself."

Ruthanne nodded, wishing Skye would include her in his pain.

Even while Skye fled back to the ranch, he wondered what he was doing. It was as if something had taken possession of him and he was powerless to stop it.

Thirty days was apparently not enough time to get to know his mother through her friends. Everything he had learned about her dissolved when she woke up and never even smiled. He expected some kind of warmth but only got that same listless stare he remembered when she was high.

He pulled into the ranch drive and stalked toward the house. As of today his obligation was over. He had planned to pack later, but now he threw everything into his suitcase and went outside to retrieve his dog.

Tom was in the far paddock feeding the alpacas. He hadn't seen Skye, and that was okay. It would only lead to more talk about his mother.

He loaded Ruddy into the SUV and sped out of there, anxious to put some distance between him and his past. The paradox, however, was that Ruthanne held his future.

He couldn't think of that right now. Too much baggage lay between them, and he knew he must address it before he could offer her the kind of love she deserved.

Then why, he asked himself, was he running?

He didn't know. He also didn't understand why, instead of getting off the interstate to go home, he found himself plowing ahead, not knowing where he might land.

After passing Medford, he tried to envision his troubles flying out the open windows. He turned on the radio to silence the voice of reason telling him to turn back, but static poured out.

With a flat palm, he smacked the steering wheel. "Great! A wire must have come loose." He slapped the dash, trying to jar it back into place.

Alone with his thoughts, he found himself jealous of carefree Ruddy leaning out the window, the breeze whipping his tongue to his right cheek.

As Skye's adrenaline finally dissipated, he realized he'd driven halfway to Eugene. The car nearly exited itself off the highway, and it was only then that he realized his destination.

Before long, the River Bend Cabins came into view. He had often spent time there with his family for fishing and rafting trips. Yes, this would be a great place to get his thoughts in order. Perhaps if he immersed himself in the positive memories, he could better handle the crazy turn his life had taken the past thirty days.

Since it was the end of the off-season, he had no trouble renting a cabin. After a quick trip to a tiny market up the road, he had enough provisions to last a week, plus a fishing pole and flies. By nightfall he and Ruddy had dined on hot dogs and potato chips and he'd wet his fishing line in the Umpqua River that ran only a few yards from his door.

"I'm sorry to drag you out here, Mrs. Randall, but I'm so worried about Skye."

"Please, call me Cynthia. And it was my choice to come to you."

"Thank you." Ruthanne nodded and blinked back tears.

Ruthanne's concern for Skye heightened when she'd gone home briefly yesterday and noticed that all his things were gone. The familiar panic came rushing in. Brian had left the same way. She called Mrs. Randall, who graciously agreed to meet her at the hospital.

The two women found a quiet corner in the waiting room.

"How is Hannah?"

"She's in and out but can't move yet because her muscles have atrophied. Even a smile is impossible right now. But they'll launch into therapy soon."

"I'd like to see her before I leave. I've never met her, of course."

"The Hannie I know would be very pleased." Of course there was that other Hannie who still mystified Ruthanne. "But first I'd like to talk about Skye." Another person who mystified her. "Does he have a habit of running? I want to understand him, but these disappearing acts are beyond me." Her voice cracked.

Cynthia pulled a tissue from her purse and handed it to Ruthanne. "When he first came to us, he wandered away whenever the mood struck him. I think after living in a commune he had been used to coming and going as he pleased."

Ruthanne, who had been dabbing her eyes, jerked her head up from the tissue. "Skye lived in a commune?"

Cynthia sat back in the chair and crossed her legs. She seemed to be thinking—or possibly praying—about her next words. "Skye and his mother have put you through a lot this past month. I feel you have a right to know some things." She took a deep breath. "Yes, from what he could tell us, that's what we gathered. Skye's parents were hippies, and they lived with several other people. Skye's father wanted little to do with him, but Hannie did love her son. . .as much as she was capable of. He talks of her singing to him and taking him places. But what confused him as a young child was how she could completely ignore him at times. This happened, of course, when she was taking drugs."

Ruthanne squeezed her eyes shut. Brian's addiction to alcohol had eventually led in the same direction. She never wanted to deal with that again. Knowing now what a dangerous situation Skye had been in, she felt a new compassion for him. "Was he abused?"

Cynthia frowned. "He only has one mark in the center of his back. It looks like someone put out a cigarette there."

Ruthanne gulped back her revulsion. She'd never seen Skye with his shirt off, even when the day grew warm and sweat stains were evident.

"As Skye opened up, we learned that some of the men mistreated him. Hannie protected him when she could, but other times. . ."

"She was incapacitated."

"That's what we assume, especially after Skye's father died."

"Were there other children in the commune?"

"He talked about younger children, so he must have been the first to be born in their group. I don't know what happened to the others, but I've prayed they found their ways into good homes."

"So. . ." Ruthanne tried to recap what she'd just learned so her brain could catch up. "He is prone to wandering when distressed, but he won't hurt himself and he'll come back." *He'll come back.*

Cynthia nodded, the peaceful look on her face indicative of the trust she'd placed in her son.

She leaned forward and wrapped her warm hands around Ruthanne's own. Without asking permission, she closed her eyes and launched into a heartfelt prayer that brought the tears back to Ruthanne's eyes.

"Father God, please speak to Skye wherever he is. His soul is hurting, but I know You've brought his mother back into his life for healing. Speak to his heart. Help him forgive." She then prayed for Hannie and lastly for Ruthanne to be at peace and to trust God.

When Ruthanne looked up, she saw a mist of tears in the other woman's eyes. This was a mother who ached because her son ached.

The cheerful strains of the song "Blue Skies" drifted from Cynthia's purse. "That's Skye." She flashed a proud mom smile. "It's our special song." When she answered her cell phone, Ruthanne marveled at her grace. "Hi, honey. Long time no see. Do you have something to tell me?"

By her half of the conversation, Ruthanne surmised that Skye was okay.

"You're where?. . . Oh, that's a beautiful place!. . . Caught anything?" There was a longer pause. "Yes, I'm at the hospital visiting with her right now. . . . Okay, I'll tell her. . . . Love you, too. Bye."

She slipped the phone back into her purse. "He's fine. There's a little place halfway between here and Eugene where he can pray and reflect."

"And fish, I assume."

Again the invigorating laugh put Ruthanne at ease. "Never underestimate the power of a good fishing hole. I have faith that he will get through this. . .and come back to you."

Ruthanne's cheeks grew warm. "Me?"

Without explaining she went on. "He wanted me to tell you not to worry and to thank you for all you've done for him."

"What have I done?"

"He didn't tell me."

Chapter 16

The small Bible felt heavy in Skye's denim shirt pocket. As he sat on a boulder near the river, he confessed that he'd done more fishing than praying in the last few days. His pole now lay beside him, the line still dry. He'd broken away from his reality to be alone with the Lord, and now he had to make good on that promise.

Ruddy had chased a squirrel under a boulder, and the rodent chattered at him from an escape hatch on the other side. Skye attempted to ignore the squabble as he prayed. "Lord, You know what I've been through. Up until my adoption, I had a lousy childhood. And I had pretty much gotten past that when my mother drew me back into her life. Why have You done this to me?"

The rushing river nearly hypnotized him as he gazed at the rocks dancing deep below the surface. But the movement was only an illusion.

Had his life been an illusion? From the time he settled into his adoptive family to the time his mother sought him out, he realized now he'd been living a double life. Outwardly all was well. He loved his parents and sisters. He did well in school and gladly followed his dad into the family business. And yet he harbored a deep, dark secret. He hated his birth mother. And as each year passed with no contact from her, that current of hate dug itself deeper and deeper into the silt until not even a ripple disturbed his smoothly flowing life.

He picked up a flat stone and hurled it into the water, not even attempting to make it skip. It sank into the hidden currents, and his mind landed there, too—to the dark ugliness he had hidden so well. While others were praising him for being such a good boy, he knew he wasn't.

And he hated himself for it. So many times he asked God to forgive him for his dark thoughts, but he never felt peace.

He finally pulled the Bible from his pocket and started to thumb through it. At first nothing he read applied to him. He'd never been one to open his Bible and stab a finger at random pages, but that's what he did now, flipping through book after book, chapter after chapter, in hopes that a verse would bold and magnify itself on the page.

And then it happened. The page flipped to a passage in Mark where his eyes caught the word "forgive" used twice in one sentence. *"And when you stand praying, if you hold anything against anyone, forgive him, so that your Father in heaven may forgive you your sins."*

He must have read that before.

He read it again with the surrounding verses. They talked about mountain-moving faith—if you don't doubt, it will be given to you.

At that moment, he knew forgiveness eluded him not only because of his deep-seated rage against his mother but because he doubted God could ever forgive him for his hypocrisy.

He grabbed another rock. Could forgiveness be as easy as releasing a stone into the river? The hard, cold object weighted his hand as his fingers wrapped around it. He closed his eyes, and in words foreign to his own ears, he said, "I forgive my mother." Then he skipped the stone. It skimmed the water once before disappearing.

With another rock he prayed, "I forgive my mother for not standing up for me when others abused me." The released rock skimmed twice.

"I forgive my mother for neglecting me." The third rock skimmed several times.

He continued this ritual until every issue but one had been satisfied. He felt lighter, but the one question still burned deep in his heart.

Why?

The invisible nudging at his back was as tangible as the last stone in his hand. He gripped it tightly, not willing to release it.

"I can't, Lord. I can't stop wondering why she left me. I can't stop. . .hating her for leaving me!"

"If you hold anything against anyone, forgive him, so that your Father in heaven may forgive you your sins."

Knowing he'd never realize true freedom until he threw that last rock, he squared his shoulders and pitched it with all his might. "I forgive my mother for. . . for leaving me."

The stone skipped seven times over the ripples, a new record for Skye.

An overwhelming sense of release lifted his heavy heart as the burden he had carried for so many years skipped away with the stone. He heard a bird warbling a tune, and the joyful sound orchestrated the music bubbling in his soul. Refreshing tears filled his eyes as he looked to the sky.

"Thank You, Lord."

Before leaving that day, he gathered several more rocks as an altar, commemorating the day he released his anger into the river.

❧

"Look at you." Ruthanne walked into Hannie's new hospital room, happy to see her surrounded by a cheerier motif than the cold, white ICU room she'd been in for the past two months. A swirled mauve and blue pattern on the wall facing her bed seemed to encourage the patient to gain strength. With the ventilator removed, the tube in her throat no longer hindered her.

Hannie's eyes lit up, cheering Ruthanne's heart. She still couldn't lift her arms, but her smile had returned. Ruthanne grasped her hand, praying for the day her fingers would squeeze back.

"Daughter." Her raspy speech shocked Ruthanne. The tube must have irritated her throat.

"Hey." Ruthanne blinked back tears. "You're going to make me cry. It's an honor to be considered your daughter."

"Oh no, not that again." Paul sauntered in, his hands in his pockets. "Hi, Auntie." He took his position on the other side of the bed and began massaging her hand. "It's been nonstop waterworks around here ever since you woke up."

"It has not." Ruthanne wanted to throw something at him, but everything within reach was either too heavy or screwed to the floor. She had just started eyeing one of Hannie's dozens of potted plants lined on the windowsill when she noticed Paul shifting uncomfortably.

Hannie seemed to be signaling Paul with her eyes. He glanced at Ruthanne, and she instantly knew Hannie was asking how their relationship was going. The poor woman was still playing matchmaker.

Both Ruthanne and Paul dropped their gazes to the floor. When Ruthanne looked back at her, a frown had creased Hannie's forehead.

In a retreat maneuver, Ruthanne told her how the craft fair went and about the new crias that had been born in the last month. She was gearing up to tell her how Skye had done on the ranch when the subject himself showed up at the door.

One foot in and one foot out.

Ruthanne raised her hand to him, and he walked boldly into the room.

≈

Ruthanne's hand felt cool in Skye's palm, but her grip left a clear message: *You're not going to run again, buster.* When he smiled at her and squeezed back, she relaxed considerably.

He praised God. Gone was the child who had internally kicked and screamed whenever he crossed the threshold. In his place was a man determined to keep that mountain moved.

His mother watched the exchange then smiled. A small smile but definitely more than the expression on her face a few days ago. Expecting his anger to rise at the memory, Skye exhaled a relieved breath when it didn't, thanking God for silencing the voice in his head.

Letting go of Ruthanne's hand, he knew he could do the next thing by himself. He reached for his mother's hand and held it in both of his own.

She swallowed hard. "Skye." Her scratchy voice seemed to irritate her. Skye leaned down where she could whisper in his ear. "Forgive me."

All Skye ever wanted was to know *why*. However, new God-inspired words slipped from his lips. "I forgive you."

Somewhere behind him, he heard Ruthanne sniffle. Paul, who'd been standing on the other side, almost in protective mode, released Hannie's other hand and backed away.

110

Skye gazed into his mother's tear-brimmed eyes, blue like his own, then bent down and kissed her cheek.

∽

Ruthanne snatched several tissues from the box by Hannie's bed. Just as she was about to blow her nose, she heard a large honk that sounded like a goose had been released into the hallway. Tom stood at the door, wiping his red nose with a handkerchief. His eyes shone bright.

Hannie's eyes trained on him. They seemed to draw him near, and he took the side of the bed that Paul had just vacated. Ruthanne glanced around the room. Paul had disappeared.

She was about to slip out also when Skye captured her hand. Wondering if he needed her strength, she joined him. But once she made the connection with him, she sensed he didn't need her but wanted to include her. She had to still her singing heart so she could hear the conversation taking place.

Tom was explaining Hannie's medical condition to Skye. ". . .and with her in the coma so long, her muscles have forgotten how to work."

Skye glanced at Hannie. "So that's why you didn't react to me that first night." He closed his eyes and drew in a sharp breath. "I'm an idiot."

"The doc says she'll have to go through tons of therapy, but she will get all her faculties back."

In answer Skye raised Hannie's hand and kissed it. Ruthanne remembered what his adoptive mother had said about his childhood and breathed a quick prayer of thanks that he had apparently found peace while away.

Hannie's eyes turned sorrowful. "The park."

Ruthanne felt Skye stiffen. Hannie frowned, touched the bandage at her throat, then looked at Tom. With more force than she'd had a moment ago, she said, "Tell him."

Tom shifted his feet. He clearly did not want to be the one having this conversation. "I'm sure you remember the commune. Do you remember losing your dad? The way he died?"

Skye nodded.

"Well, after that, Hannie fell apart completely."

Questions darted in Ruthanne's mind. How did Tom know these things? Had Hannie opened up to him? Why hadn't she told her? She tamped down the confusing jealousy, realizing there was more at stake in the small room than her feelings.

Tom continued. "She could barely control her drug habit when he was alive, but afterward. . .it was a wonder that she didn't die, too." He rubbed his nose, as if he felt uncomfortable speaking for someone else. "I don't know what she was thinking, but she got it in her head to take you with her when she met her supplier. There was a park nearby, and she told you to play on the swings until she came back."

"But she didn't."

111

Skye squeezed Ruthanne's fingers, and she fought not to cry out.

"No. She forgot where she put you." Tom paused, letting that sink in for a moment. "By the time she was cognitive enough to remember, she learned on a news report that you had already been found by the police."

"It was best," Hannie rasped.

Skye shook his head. "No, a child belongs with his mother."

For the first time, Hannie shook her head ever so slightly. "They would have killed you."

Ruthanne gasped. What horrors had this woman and her child been forced to endure? She suspected Skye's adoptive mom hadn't told her everything about the commune full of drugged men who abused Skye. Perhaps she didn't know it all herself.

"Hannie." Ruthanne ran her fingers through her friend's hair. "Why didn't you tell me?"

Hannie squeezed her eyes shut. "Ashamed."

Tom spoke to Skye again. "She was in pain for a long time over her decision not to find you. I'd like to tell you that she buckled down and beat her addiction, just so she could get you back. But it only got worse. It was four long years before she came out of it."

Hannie's sorrow-filled eyes suddenly gleamed. "God did it."

Tom glanced down at her with affection. "Yes. God grabbed hold of her and wouldn't let go. Right, Hannie? A street missionary gave her a Bible, and she pored over it while in detox. It took a lot of strength on her part, but eventually she never had to go back."

"After she became sober," Skye asked, "why didn't she come for me?" He glanced at Hannie. "I found out that you've known where I was all this time."

Tears trickled down her cheeks. Skye took a tissue and dabbed awkwardly at them.

Tom continued for her. "It took her awhile to get back on her feet. She married David, and by the time she was at the place to bring you back into her life, you were doing very well. You'd landed with people who loved you. Why mess with that?"

Skye folded himself into the armchair. "Wow."

"I know." Tom nodded. "It's a lot to take in."

Ruthanne couldn't be still any longer. "Tom, how do you know all this?"

He drew in a big breath. "I lived in the commune with Hannie and Skye."

Skye suddenly stood and searched Tom's face.

"When Hannie and her new husband found me in prison," Tom continued, "she swore me to secrecy. She'd begun a new life, and her friends didn't need to know what she'd done."

"Did David know?" Ruthanne asked. Skye was trembling next to her.

"Yes. She filled him in on everything." Tom rubbed his nose and took on a sheepish look. He lifted his hand and wiggled his fingers in a tiny wave directed at Skye. "Hi, little Destry."

Chapter 17

You were the nice man in the commune?"

"Guilty." Tom raised his hand.

Ruthanne watched Skye turn from an adult to a child of seven. His feet seemed to move of their own volition. He rounded the end of the bed and met Tom on the other side where the two embraced.

"You made my life bearable." Skye's emotion-filled voice sounded muffled against the larger man's shoulder.

Tom patted his back, blinking away his own tears. "You needed a dad. I needed someone to care for. It just worked out."

When they finally parted, Ruthanne sensed a deep scar had been healed within Skye.

The two reminisced for a few minutes, mostly Tom filling in the blanks of Skye's memory. Then, after another hug that included slaps on their backs, Skye sat on the side of the bed, his left leg in half-Indian style, as close to Hannie as possible. He draped his arm lazily over one knee and filled her in on his life.

Ruthanne drank in the scene before her, the scar in her own heart beginning to soften.

As Hannie gazed with contentment at her son, it was evident how much stress she'd been under. With it gone, she looked beautiful from within.

After snatching another couple of tissues, Ruthanne signaled Tom with her eyebrows, silently asking if they should leave. He nodded and wiped his own nose with his handkerchief. They both left without disturbing the reunion.

They entered the waiting area and sat down. A brief glance told her that Paul was nowhere around. Now that Skye had taken on his rightful role as Hannie's son, had Paul felt unneeded in the room?

She glanced at Tom as a comfortable silence stretched between them.

"So. . ." Tom scratched the side of his nose. "Now you know. I guess we can praise God even in her illness. If she hadn't gotten sick, she may never have had the courage to seek Skye out."

"And none of this would have come to light." Ruthanne massaged her temples. "Poor Hannie. So many years of grief yet knowing she'd made the right decision."

"Well, the right decision would have been not to put her child in that position in the first place. But I'm the last person to judge on that score."

Sensing his need for comfort, she reached out to touch his hand. "I've always been proud of you, Tom."

113

"Thanks, girlie." His eyes glistened. He glanced at his watch. "I better scoot. I've got some work to do at an old house across town. Think I'll tell the ol' girl good-bye before I leave."

Alone now, Ruthanne searched for Paul. She found him in the hospital lobby, sitting by the coffee kiosk. He had relaxed into a café chair, one leg crossed over the other. His hand rested on a round, white metal table and clutched the cardboard sleeve of a tall paper cup. His easygoing posture didn't fool her though. She could see the sadness in his eyes.

When he saw her coming, he quickly replaced the pensive look with a grin. "Hi, Ruthie. Coffee?"

The pungent aroma and a quick check of her stomach told her she couldn't handle anything stronger than tea. Her emotions had bounced her around worse than the river ride. She ordered green tea with a splash of lemon and sat at the table.

"You okay?" She tilted her head and prayed he'd share his feelings.

"Sure." He tapped the bottom of the cup on the table. "Just a lot to take in."

This corner of the hospital was quiet. Paul and Ruthanne talked together in relative privacy about how Hannie's illness had flushed out the pain in her life and brought her son back to her.

"Can you see that God was in it all, Paul?" She searched his face. When he finally dragged his gaze from the cup to her eyes, something different glimmered there.

"I can now. I'm sorry I couldn't have had more faith for you."

She grabbed his forearm. "Not for me. For you. You've been taking care of me—and Hannie—for too long. It's time you considered yourself." She stopped and then spoke her next words carefully. "I'll ask it again. Are *you* okay?"

He pressed his lips together and stared at his coffee. Finally a small grin bloomed on his face. "Yeah, I'm okay. I can see where all this played out for a reason. God knew what He was doing when He allowed Aunt Hannie to get sick. Even though I knew about the drug abuse, it was still hard listening to what her life was like before she met my uncle. But if she hadn't gone through it, she may never have developed the empathy she needed for her ministry."

"And what about your own mother? I'm sure this has dredged up some bad memories for you."

He took a sip of coffee and paused before answering. "I still have questions. But I'm learning that God is God, and He has a reason for everything He allows."

Skye came around the corner, and Paul greeted him with a broad smile. "Come join us. I was just getting ready to talk about you."

"Well then," Skye said as he perused the menu on the wall. "I'm glad I showed up." He ordered a cup of black coffee then pulled up an empty chair from the other table. "Tom is with my mother, so I thought I'd give them some private time." He sat and sipped carefully from the plastic lid. "So, I was about to be your topic of conversation?"

Paul leaned forward. "Ruthanne suggested the other day that she'd like you to learn the management side of the business. I know your time is up at the ranch, but if you still want to help, I can teach you to take over my duties."

Skye turned a warm blue gaze toward Ruthanne that made her toes curl. "I'd love to help out whenever I can on the ranch, and the computer work would be right up my alley."

Through the contented fog that had wrapped around her, Ruthanne finally realized what Paul was saying. Her heart cracked in two pieces. "You're not leaving, are you, Paul?"

"My grandmother called yesterday." Paul twirled the bottom of the empty cup on the table. "She says she's tired of keeping the restaurant going without my grandfather. Since he died a couple years ago, she's kept their dream going but realizes now that without him she'd rather move on."

Ruthanne swallowed. "Your grandmother lives in Crossroads Bay. That's on the coast."

"Same state. Only half a day away."

She ignored his flippant humor. "You're going to go and take over for her, aren't you?"

"Yes." He nodded. "I think I am." His eyes danced. "In fact, now that I've voiced it out loud, I'm kinda getting excited about it."

"Hey." Skye leaned forward in his chair. "Won't it be easier to start a catering business from your own restaurant?"

"That's what I'm thinking." Paul also leaned forward, and Ruthanne suddenly felt excluded. "It's already an established restaurant with a full staff. It couldn't be more perfect, really."

"Excuse me." Ruthanne had to be the voice of reason. Both men looked at her as if they'd just realized she was in the room. "What about the clientele you've already built up? And the investors you met with a week ago?"

"I got their call after my grandmother's. It's a no-go." Paul shook his head. "I think God is closing this door, knowing my grandmother needs me. Opening a window and all that."

Why did he have to take a leap of faith now? All this time she'd been trying to teach him this lesson, and he had to learn it when it would break her heart.

He stood and threw his cup away. "My grandmother gave me a couple of months to move down there." He shook Skye's hand. "Welcome aboard. Just let me know when you'd like to start." Then he slipped his hands into his pockets and whistled a tune as he left the hospital.

Ruthanne, suddenly aware that she was alone with Skye for the first time in several days, met his intense gaze. He cocked his head. "I'd say you look like you've just lost your best friend, but that wouldn't be funny right now, would it?"

"No." She sighed. "But maybe it's for the best. He sure looked excited, didn't he?"

"It's a good thing."

She nodded, feeling better as she began to see how Paul would benefit from this change.

"And now"—he brushed her thumb with his forefinger—"I want you to know what happened to me when I left a few days ago."

"Okay." He could tell her anything he wanted as long as he touched her like that.

"I prayed a foolish prayer the night I sat with my mother. I asked God for her to acknowledge me in some way. A happy grin, a glimmer in her eyes. . .something. When she just stared at me with no emotion at all, I had to leave. I was in so much pain." He lowered his voice as a customer came up to order an espresso. When he left, Skye recounted his time at the cabin.

"This morning I sat at the river, pouring my heart out to God. I started throwing rocks in the water and found with each effort I could release my anger." He rubbed his arm. He must have tossed quite a few issues into the river.

She smiled. "In the room it wasn't hard to tell that you'd found peace."

"I did, and to commemorate it, I made a rock altar on the riverbank." He pulled her hands up to his chin, and she thought he might kiss her fingers. "I want that peace for you, Ruthanne."

Even though his words thrilled her, they also caused a small pain in her chest. He was asking her to forgive Brian. She closed her eyes, not ready to commit fully to that. When she opened them again, he was still looking at her. As if to finalize his argument, he placed his next words on the table between them. "While searching the scriptures, particularly Mark 11:25, I learned that I couldn't ask God to forgive me until I had forgiven my mother."

In her silence, he released her hands. "I'm going to sit with my moth—my mom awhile longer." He stood and reached out to her. "Are you coming?"

❧

That evening as Ruthanne watered the alpacas, she thought about Skye's rock altar. Her garden hose could hardly compare to Skye's river, but the gentle lapping into the troughs, mixed with satiated alpaca noises, brought his words to mind.

She, too, needed to leave her burden on her Rock, Jesus Christ. For too many years she let her disappointing marriage color her decisions. The pain of knowing Brian never loved her and tossed her aside like one of his used painting rags still dug at her heart. But Skye had helped her to trust again, even though he tended to disappear. Knowing this was his coping mechanism—and that it was never permanent—helped to stretch her faith.

As was her custom, she visited Lirit last so she could linger with her into the evening. They nuzzled noses, and Ruthanne looked into the large perceptive eyes.

"I no longer want to hate Brian, Lirit. I'll never have the opportunity that Skye and Hannie had. I'll never be able to sit with him and hear how sorry he is or unburden myself of my own shortcomings during our marriage." Her voice caught as a small sob crept up her throat. "The past is over, and it's up to me to forgive."

Lirit's gentle hum reminded Ruthanne what it meant to be in God's will. She closed her eyes and placed her pain and disappointments on her Rock.

When she looked up, she saw Skye ambling toward the paddocks. A thrill shot through her. Was this confirmation or just a coincidence that he would be the first person she saw after releasing her anger?

~

Skye's lightened heart floated from his chest to hover around Ruthanne. Even in her dyed hemp "hippie" clothes, she never looked more beautiful.

He'd been so enraptured with her that he barely noticed the attention Lirit had decided to give him. But when he got to the gate, Lirit thrust her shaggy head into his vision and searched him with her pool-ball eyes.

Skye smiled at the gatekeeper and stroked her neck. "It's okay now, Lirit. With God's intervention, I'm worthy of her now."

Lirit blinked her long eyelashes, and even though her expression never changed, Skye knew she smiled. The alpaca pranced to a corner of the paddock and dropped to her knees, cushing in her contentment.

When he looked back at Ruthanne in the paddock, he noticed that his heart had not come back. It was waiting near her for his thoughts to catch up.

But unfinished business remained between them. He opened the gate and joined her. "I came over to tell you how sorry I am."

"For what?"

"For skipping out like that. It was rude to leave you worrying. I never wanted to hurt you."

"I'll admit that I was confused, but you didn't hurt me." She touched his arm. "Brian hurt me and made it difficult for me to trust another man. But you showed me what a real man is supposed to be."

He shook his head, not daring to believe her words. "As messed up as I was? I don't think I'm a great role model."

She placed her hands on her hips. "Listen to me. God used you to bring me to forgiveness." After the brief scolding, she reached up to entwine her arms around his neck, her gentle strength taking his breath away. "I'm at peace now."

He could see it. She no longer spat out Brian's name as if it were a disgusting bug caught in her throat.

"Well then, little lady." He suddenly felt playful as he adjusted his imaginary hat. "Think you can use another cowboy on your ranch?"

She tipped her head, teasing him with that delicious twinkle in her eyes. "That would be great if we had cows."

He reached around her waist and pulled her close. "I'll herd alpacas, chickens, and rabbits, just to be near you."

In the shadow of the giant sentinel, Singing Mountain, their lips met as she answered with a kiss. Above the joyful beating of his heart, he heard humming.

And if he could hear Lirit, he knew he was in God's will.

Epilogue

Ruthanne looked out the french doors in the great room toward the north pasture where a small gathering of wedding guests awaited her arrival. They had chosen that part of the property for the grove of maple trees. It took on its role as wedding chapel without the benefit of ribbons, cut flowers, or candlesticks. Ruthanne reveled in the fact that God had painted her sanctuary with vivid purple lilacs and golden yellow forsythias. Their scents floated through the open french doors, reminding her of the day Skye had arrived at the ranch a year ago.

Her gaze drifted out the doors and to the guests. Her mother had just been seated. Up until a few months ago, they hadn't talked since she'd left with Brian. But once God healed her abandoned heart, she called her mom to start the healing process there. Hannie and Skye had inspired her.

Skye.

She imagined Tom, as his best man, giving him a pep talk in her mobile home. Tom had promised to keep an eye on Skye. "Wouldn't want him to run."

Ruthanne smiled to herself, unworried. Skye had promised never to run again.

She glanced around the large room. Hannie had surprised them at the wedding rehearsal, announcing that her present to the couple would be her house.

"It's way too big for me," she'd said, "and I've always loved that little mobile home. The house was a dream for David and me to share together. Now I rattle around in there by myself. I know he'd be pleased if you filled it with children."

Ruthanne's heart swelled with the thought of raising Skye's children in this beautiful place.

From the kitchen, she could hear Paul grumbling about something. She glanced at the clock above the fireplace. "It's almost time to walk," she called to him.

He mumbled then strode into the room.

"Are there problems with the food?" She laughed at his disheveled hair, knowing he had run his hand through it in frustration.

"No, the catering is going great. I just stepped into the office to see how Skye is doing with the inventory."

"Paul, it's been nearly a year since you've looked at that stuff. Do you have to do that today? Now?"

"I'm sorry, but I couldn't help myself. Skye has a different approach than I do. His logging system looks more like a real estate spreadsheet than a log of Hannie's creativity."

"Well, he knows more about houses than he does merchandise."

Paul finger combed his dark hair and adjusted his tie. "He's abbreviated every item. I don't know if AWS is alpaca wool socks or angora walking stick."

Ruthanne frowned. "Do we have an angora walking stick?"

"No. But that's not the point."

"Ah. He's messing with your system."

He stabbed the air. "That's the point."

The clock chimed two times. She glanced outside again, and soon Skye took his place next to their pastor. Even from this distance, he looked incredible in his white tuxedo and lavender shirt, a color she'd picked to make his blue eyes even more vibrant.

Paul held out his arm. "You ready?" She'd been married before, so she didn't feel the need for her father to give her away. But since she knew Paul would be hovering near the kitchen until the last moment, she asked if he'd at least walk with her to the back of the guests.

"I'm more than ready." She took his arm. "Thank you for coming back from the coast to cater and to escort me."

"You'd do the same for me." He stopped short, apparently realizing what he'd just said. "Except for the catering part. . .and the escorting part."

She squeezed his elbow. "I know what you mean. . .and yes, I would."

They walked together until they reached their destination, then he kissed her temple before taking his seat.

As Ruthanne prepared herself to lope—well, that's what she wanted to do—to glide down the grass-carpeted aisle, she was grateful she'd chosen a midlength dress, blue to match Skye's eyes. A traditional train would have come away with grass stains. She wanted an all-natural wedding, and it surprised her that Skye agreed.

Her feet pinched in the wedge sandals she'd chosen in lieu of high heels. She knew spikes would sink in the grass, and the wedge, the salesgirl told her, would look more fashionable than a normal sandal. But she longed for her rubber boots. She should have painted them white.

Hannie turned in her chair in the first row and beamed a huge grin. Ruthanne praised God for providing a mother-in-law she already loved.

The bridesmaid she had chosen made her laugh. Lirit wore a halter that was a piece of work in itself, with blue- and lilac-colored ribbons woven into a fluttering cascade that hung to her knobby knees. Tom had already led her down the aisle to the delight of all those watching.

Music swelled from the string quartet. To her immense surprise, rather than the soloist they'd lined up, Skye himself began to sing to her. Since forgiving his mother, Skye sang often. She'd hear him crooning to the alpacas while feeding them, or she would catch him humming in the office. Now his rich baritone voice assured her in melodious rhythm that God had created their union and nothing would be able to tear it asunder. The song drew her like a bee to a succulent flower until she found her place at his side.

He held out his hand to her. "Hello, my beautiful Calamity." His blue gaze warmed her until all she could think about was getting on with the ceremony to hasten the kiss.

But then her left toe started cramping. She tried to slip off the sandals discreetly, but Skye noticed, particularly when she lost two inches in the process.

He glanced down at her feet. "Comfortable?"

She grinned up at him. "I'm very comfortable, thank you, now that I'm with you." With a squeeze of his hand, they turned to the pastor.

The ceremony was brief, and finally Ruthanne kissed the man to whom she'd just pledged her life. As they stood in their forever moment, she smiled.

Was that Lirit. . .or was her heart singing?

Author's Note

Often authors are asked where they received inspiration for their story lines. The answers are as varied as the stories themselves. I'd like to share with you how this story came to be.

One day I was surfing the channels on television instead of writing. . .but we won't go there. . .when I found a show about people looking for lost family. A man in his forties had hired someone to look for his mother. She had been a drug addict, but obviously had other mental issues. She had kept her daughter, doting on her and denying his existence. I don't remember all the details, but I do remember his reaction. This was a near middle-aged man who turned into a child upon seeing his mother for the first time. It tugged at my heart enough to spark the idea laid out within these pages.

My character, Skye, is a man of God, but there is still one thing that keeps him immature. He hasn't forgiven his mother. Forgiveness is a biggie in the Bible. The lack of forgiveness causes stumbling blocks that we can't even see. Mark 11:25 couldn't put it plainer: "And when you stand praying, if you hold anything against anyone, forgive him, so that your Father in heaven may forgive you your sins."

I didn't start out writing a book about forgiveness. I usually get a spark of an idea and then let God take it from there. I pray if you identify with the issues within this story that you will release those rocks into the river and trust the Rock of your soul, Jesus, to lift that burden away.

CROSSROADS BAY

Dedication

I dedicate this book to my treasure, Jim.

I would also like to thank my sister, mother, and brother-in-law for willingly becoming tour guides and sharing their love of Oregon with me. Special acknowledgments go to my critique partners and to my readers, Angie Scohy and Gloria Clover. Also to those who helped me research that of which this landlubber knew nothing: Genevra Bonati, who knows boats, and Bonnie Doran and Peter Lyddon, who know diving.

Chapter 1

Meranda Drake stood on her boat docked at the Crossroads Bay Marina and saluted the lighthouse on the hill as she'd done every morning since the accident.

"Big day, Pop." She addressed the tall structure while hugging her arms. "I'm taking a whale-watching tour out on the boat this morning. It's a twenty-fifth wedding anniversary party. Remember how you loved those?"

Her dad, the romantic who had lived for adventure.

And that adventure had taken his life a year ago tomorrow. On her birthday. Thirty-one candles had melted down to pitiful, multicolored pools of wax. She closed her eyes and swallowed the fatherless void that lodged in her throat, not ready to think about the events that led to that day. Instead, through sheer will, happier times began to surface, slowly, like bubbles from a sea turtle. She could almost hear him singing to her—"My Bonnie lies over the ocean. . ."—and hear him call her *Bonnie-girl*. She may have been a tomboy, but she was a daddy's girl. "Thank you for teaching me the trade, for sharing everything you knew about sailing." Yes, seawater had run through Pop's veins, and now Meranda felt the brine flowing through hers as well.

She glanced at her watch. The catering crew was due in a few minutes. She needed to perform her last-minute checks before taking the boat out. Her deckhand would arrive shortly. Ethan, the young college kid she'd hired after Pop died, knew boats like most people knew their phone numbers. He also interacted well with the passengers, which meant Meranda didn't have to.

She ducked her head to go below, but *arrgh. . .arrgh. . .* sounded from her duffel bag. She pulled out her cell phone and answered it, silencing the pirate ringtone. "Drake here."

"Must you answer like a guy?"

"Hi, sis." As she talked, she wandered to the side of the boat and leaned on the rail. "Good thing you caught me before I set sail. What's up?"

"First of all, your name is Meranda, not *Drake*." Rose lowered her voice like a man.

"Did you call to harass me?"

"No. I'm sorry. I just wanted to be sure you're coming this evening."

Blast! She forgot. "Of course! I have it all worked out." *Let's see. The tour ends at four o'clock, quick shower. . .*

"I know this isn't your thing, but you have to be here. Mom is already driving me nuts."

"You shouldn't let her do that, Rose. It's your wedding. Do what you want."

"I wish I could just take to the sea like you when she rattles my nerves." She paused. "Please don't bail on me."

"I was going to research the coins more tonight. Check out the interlibrary loan since I've exhausted ours."

"The coins? Still? When are you going to give up on that myth?"

"It's not a myth. Pop believed in them."

The silence on the other end screamed, *Pop was a fool.*

Instead, Rose mercifully dropped the subject and got back to her present angst. "You know Mom. It's not my wedding anymore. It's turning into an event where I don't even have to show up. I need you tonight for backup."

"Is Steven's mother going to be there, too?"

Meranda heard a long drawn-out breath with a slight sob on the end. "Yes."

"Then I can't in good conscience let the sharks have you. I'll be your buffer."

"Thank you!"

"I'll come, make some lame suggestions. Everyone will roll their eyes and look at me like they've never seen a tomboy before."

"You're the brother I never had, Mer. And I'm proud to call you sis."

They said good-bye after more profuse thanks from Rose. Meranda glanced back at the lighthouse. "That was Rose, Pop." The lighthouse stood straight, twinkling its one eye. "Your middle child is getting married. I don't know if he's right for her. Sure wish you were here to advise her. All Mom sees is good money. You know how she is."

The light blinked once more, then stopped, the sensor sleeping now that the sun had pursued the last of night's shadow toward the western horizon.

"She's talkin' to herself again." The voice came from a neighboring boat.

Meranda frowned. *And you're as boneheaded as a backward blowfish.* Perhaps she should keep her phone to her ear while talking to the lighthouse. On a day as still as today, her voice drifted too easily to the other boats docked nearby.

"Loony as her old man." An answering voice from a different boat.

Meranda looked at the lighthouse and whispered, "We'll show 'em, Pop. We'll prove you weren't crazy."

"Hello on the boat," a female voice lilted from the dock. "We're the caterers. Permission to come aboard?"

Meranda raised her eyebrow. Good etiquette. She liked that. She waved at the young woman in black pants and white shirt who boarded with gazelle-like movements. "I'm Jessie Kingston, Paul Godfrey's assistant." She motioned toward the dock. A dark-haired man dressed the same as Jessie tipped his head toward her, then disappeared inside a white van with Tapas Mediterranean Delights in black script painted on the side. "Where would you like us to set up?"

Meranda showed her the dining cabin, then led her to the galley. "Have you ever catered on a boat before?"

"No, but my dad owns one. So I'm quite comfortable."

"Kingston. Are you related to Phil Kingston?"

Jessie smiled. "My dad."

"No wonder you look familiar. Your dad was with mine when. . ." Looking into Jessie's hazel eyes, very much like her father's, caused a lump to form in Meranda's throat.

"Yes. Dad was on that last dive with your father. He tried to save him."

After an awkward silence, Meranda asked, "So, the last time I saw you was about ten years ago? That first meeting when my father started gathering his salvage crew. Your hair was long then. No wonder I didn't recognize you right away."

They wandered to the galley while they talked. "That sounds about right. I was sixteen. After I graduated from high school I went out of state to college, then to Paris to study the culinary arts."

"Wow, I'm impressed."

"When I came back, Paul Godfrey was looking for a sous chef, and I got the job. Then when our client said they wanted us to cater on a boat, I thought of you. I had heard you'd continued your father's business."

"Thank you. I'll try to reciprocate if I hear of anyone needing a caterer."

Meranda showed Jessie around the galley, then excused herself. "I need to test the generator before we sail. Do you need help here first?"

Jessie glanced around. "No, I think we've got it. It will be a simple setup."

"Okay, holler if you need me."

She left Jessie, trying to imagine the bubbly teen she'd met. She now sported a brown boy cut that looked easy to manage in a stiff wind. Meranda's fingers tugged the scarf on her own head—the only thing keeping her unruly curls from whipping her face. But Pop loved her long red hair, said she looked like a wild and free lady pirate.

Soon the anniversary party arrived, and from topside Meranda watched Ethan help them board. The couple looked to be in their late forties, his hair dusted lightly with gray, hers a short brown flip. Another man carrying a Bible followed, probably the minister to help them renew their vows. Behind them were a dozen men, women, and a couple of older teenaged girls. Daughters, perhaps?

Just before they weighed anchor, the caterer boarded, having let his assistant do most of the setup inside.

Meranda stood on the bridge and took the helm, her heart rushing forward in the open air, creating its own wake. She never felt more alive than when the water slapped the boat as she cut her way through it.

The morning fog burned away to reveal gentle waters. Most spring days, the Oregon coast lay blanketed in haze, the occasional squall the only disturbance.

They reached the spot where she'd seen a pod of whales the day before. She cut the engines and called down to Ethan to inform the passengers to keep their eyes open.

Below were her private quarters where a tiny room held a table with two chairs on either side. A window above the table provided light and a chance for her to sit, have a cup of coffee, and keep watch of the changing Oregon weather.

Her laptop called to her, but she knew she couldn't log on to research the coins this far out at sea. Her phone card only reached about a mile off the coast.

She shuffled through the papers she'd printed previously, but held little hope. The elusive coins foiled her at every turn.

Besides the gentle lapping ocean against the wooden hull, she heard the drone of the minister near the bow. Let the renewing of the vows commence. And she heard gagging aft. She wrinkled her nose and went to the stern to investigate.

⋙

"Make it stop. . . . Dear God. . .make it stop." Paul Godfrey draped his body over the hull praying someone would end his misery and push him into the Pacific Ocean.

No career was worth this. No amount of money would ever prompt him to accept a catering job on a boat again. No grandmother, despite the rock-hard determination in her diminutive body, could ever again make him do something he knew he'd regret.

His stomach gurgled again, and he clamped his lips together. Who was he kidding? He had about as much chance of resisting his grandmother's will as he did controlling the upheaval in his abdomen.

His *abuelita* hadn't really retired from the restaurant business. She'd just found a new lackey.

"You okay there, Mr. Godfrey?"

A gentle hand pressed his back. He discreetly wiped his mouth with his handkerchief and turned to look into the most beautiful eyes he'd ever seen. Stormy gray, the color of the churning sea. He glanced over the side at the gentle rhythmic swell of the water that mocked him. Well, it *should* have been churning by the way he felt.

"Um, yeah." He ordered his body to straighten and slipped the handkerchief into his pocket, trying to look as if his guts weren't floating away on the tide. "Just enjoying the view." Or rather, concentrating on the Crossroads Bay lighthouse on shore to the east. It was the only solid thing in his line of vision.

She narrowed those striking eyes and handed him a paper cup of water. "Landlubber, eh?"

"Severely."

"Take anything?"

"Seasick medicine makes me comatose." The last time he ventured on the water was to make sure his girlfriend didn't end up in the arms of another man. A group was going on a jetboat excursion on the Rogue River. Despite his sacrifice, he ended up losing her anyway. But he later felt at peace. God had other plans for his life.

"Come with me." The captain walked away, a vision in tall black boots, blue form-fitting trousers, and a billowy blouse. Her russet hair escaped the black scarf

128

tied around her head. Yes. God had other plans. And right now being available seemed like a good idea.

Laughter floated on the air from the anniversary party at the front of the boat. All seemed to enjoy his food and were unaffected by the fact that every plank beneath their feet was rocking to the waves. Granted, even the slightest movement on the water turned Paul into a nauseated mess. He drew in a deep breath, but when the fish-laced salt air invaded his nasal passages, he felt the familiar reflex in his jaw glands signaling another episode. He swallowed convulsively to keep it at bay and concentrated on the captain's striking figure as she walked away. Mercifully, the nausea ebbed back to where it had originated. New plan. Keep eyes on the tall, beautiful skipper.

She turned and quirked her brow. "Coming? Or would you rather your customers see you upchucking? I don't nurse every seasick landlubber who dares to come aboard my ship."

He snapped to attention, resisting the urge to salute, and willed his feet to follow her. She led him below deck, where he feared his condition would worsen.

"Sit." She motioned to a chair at the small table strewn with maps and other papers. He obeyed, and she sat across from him. "Hold your hands out, wrists up."

"Are you going to scuttle me?"

"You scuttle a ship, not a wrist." As her lashes lifted, he noticed a faint green hue in her irises that had not been there before. Intriguing. Perhaps the seaweed green walls surrounding them had something to do with it.

She took both of her thumbs and placed them on his veins where they formed a *V*. As she applied gentle pressure, he felt the nausea recede.

"Thanks. I'm feeling better. An old sea captain's remedy?"

"No, I think they used ale for most every complaint."

"Ah. The drunker the sailor, the less he feels."

She offered a half smile and those gray green eyes actually twinkled. "Something like that."

The papers under his arms drew his attention. They looked like printouts from the Internet. Some with pictures of old coins, others with maps, still others with drawings of old ships with sails.

She must have noticed him looking at them because she let his wrists go and started straightening them up. "That should help you for a moment."

"Only a moment?"

Excusing herself, she stood and walked out, then returned a few seconds later with a can of lemon-lime soda. "This will help, too. It's not ale, though. Sorry."

"That's okay. I'm not a drinker." He popped open the tab and sipped, allowing the sweet bubbles to soothe his stomach. "Thanks." He waited for her to sit across from him at the table, then made eye contact again. "I'm Paul, by the way."

"Meranda Drake." She grinned and held out her hand.

Her grip felt as solid as the woman herself, contrasting the gentle pressure she'd just applied to his wrists. In his line of work he often met frilly females wanting to either gain an advantage over their rich friends or prove their social status. Not that he minded. They were his bread and butter. This woman, however, clearly danced to her own tune. And he suspected that tune came from a hornpipe.

Excited voices above drew his attention. The room suddenly dipped to the right. He gripped the chair. "What's happening?"

Her gaze darted up the short steps leading to the deck. "They must have seen a whale spout and all rushed starboard to look at it. You want to join them?"

He wrapped one foot around the leg of the chair. "No thank you. I've seen spouts from shore. I prefer it that way."

She frowned. "Why did you take this job then?"

The question challenged his professional integrity. "My catering business comes before my personal needs." *Plus Abuelita made me.*

A knock sounded from the stairs, and Jessie ducked her head into the opening. "Excuse me," she said as her eyes adjusted to the dimmer light. "Is Paul in here? Oh, there you are." She grimaced. "You don't look so good."

"I'm fine, Jessie. What do you need?"

"The couple wants you to make an appearance so they can thank you personally for the food."

Paul groaned.

"Uh, do you want me to say you can't make it right now?" Jessie's face fell.

"I'm coming. Just give me a moment."

Jessie looked from Paul to Meranda, lingering on the captain for just an instant. "Okay." She disappeared back through the rectangular opening.

He turned back to Meranda. "Just out of cooking school."

She nodded, but he could tell she wasn't interested.

"I think I can do this." He pushed himself from the chair.

She cocked an eyebrow. "Are you sure?"

His knees wobbled but held his weight. "We'll soon see." He gingerly crept up the stairs into the bright sunlight. Before allowing his gaze to drift toward the bobbing horizon, he closed his eyes and felt the sun's rays on his face. He thanked God for the beautiful day. It could have been a wet, miserable voyage. But God smiled down and delivered. Now, if He could just freeze the ocean so the boat would stop rocking. . .

⌘

Meranda shook her head. Seasick passengers were nothing new, but she'd never invited one to her cabin before. What was wrong with her? Was she getting soft?

She turned her attention to the papers on the table. *Now, where are you?* She rifled through the printouts as she tried to unravel clues. Her fingers lit on a printed sheet of the coins. This clue was her first in believing they were real. The round silver pendant on a chain around her neck held the same image as one side of the coins: two pillars that looked like rooks on a chessboard with ocean waves between them, as if someone had captured a photo on a stormy day from shore. But unfortunately that had also been the last clue she had unearthed. Looking for sixteenth-century gold coins in several countries and oceans and time periods was worse than looking for buried treasure. No *X* marked the spot.

A retching sound interrupted her thoughts. *Not again.*

She raced up the steps to see Paul hanging over the side of the boat. He turned his head when he noticed her. "They said they liked the salmon puffs."

Chapter 2

Once they docked and the guests departed, Meranda left Ethan to swab down the deck and lock up. She helped the caterers load the van since Paul had to stop every few minutes and moan. The poor guy had nothing left in his stomach.

Before they drove away, Meranda grasped the edge of the rolled-down van window. "You're sure you're okay?" Paul's gray face reminded her of a winter sky.

"I'm fine. Jessie will get me home."

She waved to them as they left the parking lot and stepped into her pickup. In a few minutes, her modest bungalow came into view. It had been her father's before he married Mom. Afterward he'd use it as a retreat during the rough stages of their marriage. Meranda moved into it a few years ago—also to get away from Mom.

It sat on a hillside with a view of the ocean off the deck. And best of all, three-quarters of the tall, white stucco lighthouse could be seen to the south, reaching over the trees as if it were craning its neck to look for Meranda.

After her shower she slipped into her land clothes: khaki slacks, pale blue striped, tailored shirt over a blue tank top, and brown oxfords. She towel-dried her hair on the deck, waiting for the sensor in the lighthouse to awaken and signal a safe harbor. As soon as it winked at her, she waved, then left for Mom's house.

She arrived at the family mansion, actually an upper middle-class Victorian. Nothing but the best for her mother. It had been a fun place for her and her sisters to grow up, with plenty of room for hide-and-seek and wooden floors to slide on in their socks. But now as she looked at the facade, she sensed sadness. The bickering under its roof had long silenced, but it still echoed within its walls.

Her pickup looked out of place among the BMWs and other status cars in the driveway. It seemed everyone else had arrived, which meant Rose would have her head.

Inside she hung up her jacket and walked past the parlor where baby sis, twenty-four-year-old Julianne, sat surrounded by the other bridesmaids, their frilly hairdos flopping in excitement. Julianne looked up with her sparkling eyes. "Hi, Mer! We're looking through brides magazines searching for the perfect design for our dresses. I hope you don't mind looking like a girl for a day."

Please, harpoon me now.

In the dining room, noisy seagulls fought for attention over one lone pigeon, Rose. She broke away from Mom, her mother-in-law-to-be, and Aunt Vera and swooped onto Meranda, grabbing her in a hug. "I'm so glad you're here. My anchor in the storm."

"Well, that's excessive, isn't it?" Meranda patted her sister's back, then squirmed out of the clinging arms.

Rose looked behind her at the three older women, screeching at each other. Meanwhile, the puffins were peeping away in the parlor.

Or maybe not so excessive. It appeared Meranda had her work cut out for her.

Mom looked up from the table and dragged her into the fray without even a hello. "We need to discuss colors. It will all make sense once we get the colors down." She wielded a quilt's worth of swatches.

"I need a decision on the church," Mrs. St. James, Rose's soon-to-be mother-in-law, interrupted. "If we choose ours, there are certain colors that simply will not go."

"Then the same can be said about the flowers," Aunt Vera wailed. Uncle Rex owned a florist shop, which automatically made his wife an expert.

Meranda took her captain's stance in the entry between the dining room and the parlor. With feet apart, back straight, and two fingers in her mouth, she blew a shrill whistle, gaining everyone's wide-eyed, open-mouthed attention.

With her hands on her hips, she spoke to Rose hovering behind her. "What do you want to attack first?"

"Colors." Rose's voice held a resigned tone, as if giving her mother first shot irked her. "In my mind it makes more sense to pick them first."

"Fine. Jules!" Julianne whipped her curls as she turned to look at her from the parlor. "Would you four mind keeping it down so we can think in here? Aunt Vera, we'll get to you soon. Mrs. St. James. . ." Meranda paused to see if the groom's mother would correct her, giving permission to use her first name. She didn't. "Mrs. St. James, please help yourself to some coffee, and we'll discuss the church in a little while."

The fiftyish woman, whose pronounced nose and floppy skin on her throat gave her a pelican look, huffed into the kitchen.

"Okay, enough of this nonsense." Mom grabbed Meranda's arm and hauled her to a chair. "Here's our problem." Mom reached for a pink swatch. "This is the primary color you want to go with, correct?"

Rose nodded.

"It's pink!" Meranda's throat constricted. She would not wear a pink dress. Not even for family.

"It's rose." Her sister pushed out her lower lip. Seriously? At her age? "And it's my favorite color. I want that for my maid of honor."

Mom held the pink swatch under Meranda's chin and fluffed her hair so it lay on top. "See? She looks hideous."

"Thanks, Mom."

"You know what I mean. It's not you—it's the color. There is so much red in your hair." She stroked Meranda's head and slid a lock through her fingers. "So much like your father's." Sadness crept into her eyes. It must have been tough for her mother to plan her daughter's wedding a year after losing her ex-husband, no matter how much they had fought. But she apparently stuffed that emotion away as she barked at Rose. "Do you see what I mean?"

"Yes." Rose raised her hands in frustration. "Maybe we can compromise. What if we do some kind of cape or collar in green?" She slid a green swatch over the pink one still under Meranda's chin.

Meranda looked down. "I'll look like a strawberry."

This set Rose into a fit of hysterical laughter. Mom soon joined her, and before long the whole wedding party engaged in a giggling mass of released pressure.

"Let's table this." Rose wiped her eyes. "Maybe if we look at the design we'll get a better idea of how to dress our strawberry."

Meranda groaned. It was going to be a long night.

⌘

Finally alone, Paul sank onto his leather sofa with a cup of ginger tea to settle his stomach. Jessie had dropped him off, offering to take the equipment back to the restaurant. Grateful, he let her go before requesting she not tell his grandmother about his seasickness. Abuelita would no doubt call and make it all about the restaurant. Then again, perhaps she would take him seriously the next time he declined a job on a boat.

Every time he thought of the day, his stomach cramped. But when he thought of Meranda Drake, and those amazing eyes, he felt tons better. So he concentrated on the fascinating woman clad in an outfit suspiciously similar to what the pirates wore in that movie he saw last summer.

He wished he weren't so shy. Something about the woman appealed to him in a frightening way. Far from his last love interest, Ruthanne, who had married his stepcousin, Meranda didn't seem the least bit interested in being feminine. But she exuded it in a very Maureen O'Hara sort of way. He chuckled. Like that movie he saw the other night, *Sinbad the Sailor*. He stroked an imaginary beard. Could he ever be as dashing as Douglas Fairbanks Jr.?

He sipped the tea and burned his tongue as his home phone rang. Setting the cup aside, he answered. "Hello."

"Pablo."

"*Hola*, Abuelita."

"Jessie tells me you are ill. The crab was not bad, was it? We do not need a lawsuit." Yep. His little Spanish grandma made it all about the restaurant.

"I'm fine, just a little seasick. I'll eat a few crackers before I go to bed, and I'll be good as new tomorrow."

"I will be at the restaurant early in case you don't make it. You are catering a brunch, *sí*?"

"Yes, but you don't have to do that. I'll be there."

"You are fixing my *magdalena* recipe, *sí*?"

"Yes, Abuelita. I will do the cakes justice."

"I will come and help."

Paul wished he could tell her to retire already. That had been the bargain. That's why he had made the decision to move back home. His cousin Albert had agreed to comanage the restaurant while Paul set up his catering business out of the kitchen. Both men were frustrated with their grandmother. But how could they kick her out of the restaurant she and Grandpa had built from scratch?

They hung up, Paul not convincing her that he could handle the brunch by himself. He lifted the now-cooled ginger tea and sipped it. The way his stomach felt, he wondered if he'd picked up a flu bug.

He reached for his Bible. The thought of turning on the television occurred to him, but he hoped he could glean something from scripture on how to handle an old woman.

His cell phone rang, halting his hand. He dragged himself from the chair and trudged to the small round table where he always deposited his keys and phone when he walked into the house.

"Hello, Paul Godfrey speaking."

"Is this Paul the caterer?"

He knew that voice. "Yes."

"Hi. This is Meranda Drake. You were on my boat today?"

"Yes, Miss Drake. An experience I'll not soon forget." He rubbed his stomach and lounged back down on the couch.

She offered a hearty laugh, and strangely it didn't offend him in the least. "I hope you're feeling better."

"Much." *Now.*

"I'm helping my sister plan her wedding, and talk turned to the caterer. Our mother's usual one got deported last month. France. Apparently it was quite upsetting."

"I can imagine. Two questions though. Will it be on a boat?"

Again, that laugh—like a burst of sunshine. "No, I promise."

"Then I'll be happy to talk with her about it. Second question: when is it?"

"In a year, May twenty-eighth."

He raised his gaze to the ceiling as if his planning calendar was tacked up there. "I'm sure I have that date free. We could meet Monday morning at my grandmoth—my family's restaurant, Tapas." If he were to declare emancipation, he needed to start weaning Abuelita away, starting with his thoughts. "Around nine? We're not open for breakfast, so I take my catering clients in the morning. I hope *you'll* be there." Did that bold statement just come from him? "I mean. . .that is. . ."

"I can't come." Two different women argued in the background. Meranda told them both to settle it themselves. Then she came back on. "I have a tour, but my sister can make it. . .and apparently so will my mother."

After they said good-bye, Paul contemplated what a family of Merandas would look like.

"May I go home now?" Meranda had done her social duty and hooked her mother up with a respected caterer. At least she assumed so since he had the name of his business painted on his van.

"I still wish we could use Philippe. He was the best caterer I knew." What her mother really meant was that he was the most popular among her friends and therefore would stamp her social passport.

By the end of the planning party, Rose managed to keep her favorite color with a contrasting shade of pink that everyone agreed didn't look as "hideous" on Meranda. Except Meranda. The church was settled on, the flowers agreed upon, and the bridesmaids couldn't be happier with the design of their dresses.

Before Meranda left, she found Julianne on her knees searching through the cherrywood buffet, her strawberry curls jittering as she rooted inside.

"What are you looking for?" Meranda asked.

"The silver candlesticks. Doesn't Mom keep them in here?"

Their mother lingered over coffee in the parlor with Mrs. St. James.

"Mom!" Julianne called from the dining room.

"Julianne, don't bellow," Mom roared, breaking her own rule. "Come here to talk to me."

Julianne bounced into the parlor. Meranda stood near the entry and watched their exchange.

"Where are the silver candlesticks?"

"Why do you want them?"

"They probably need to be polished. Won't we use them for the shower or something?"

"I sold them. They weren't really my style." Mom waved her hand, dismissing the subject.

Irritation boiled in Meranda's stomach. The candlesticks were Nana Drake's. Mom should have passed them down. Meranda didn't care for them, but by Julianne's pout, they seemed important to her.

A thought hit Meranda, though. Did Mom need funds for the wedding? Didn't she receive a small inheritance from her father? Or had she squandered it while keeping up with her society friends? The way she spent money often alarmed Meranda. She pulled Julianne and Rose aside. They stood in the kitchen and kept their voices low.

"Julianne," Meranda started the brief parley. "Have you noticed anything else missing from the house?"

"Yes." The corners of her mouth dipped. "More of Nana's antiques, like her silver tea set, her jewelry, the vanity set with the matching brush and mirror."

"And some artwork," Rose contributed, "that had belonged to Grandma Muldoon."

"So, she's not only getting rid of things that remind her of Pop, but her own side of the family's as well."

They both nodded.

"Girls." Meranda placed her hands on both their shoulders. "Mom's in trouble."

"Should we confront her now?" The trepidation in Rose's eyes clearly suggested it wouldn't be she doing the confronting.

Meranda peeked out the kitchen door. Mrs. St. James continued to drone in the parlor. No telling when she would go home.

"Let's just monitor the situation for now, okay?" She doubted confronting Mom would do any good anyway.

She said good-bye to Mom and Mrs. St. James. As she headed for the door, Rose followed her.

"Thanks for coming, Mer." Rose hugged Meranda with the ferocity of a circus bear.

"I'm glad I could help. I may not be able to tell a lily from a dahlia, but I can manage a rowdy crew."

"That was the gift I needed." Rose's eyes went wide. "Gift! Meranda, tomorrow is your birthday."

A small dagger pricked her heart. She had hoped since no one mentioned it, they might have been planning to surprise her.

"I'm so sorry. We're so caught up in this wedding."

Meranda patted her sister's shoulder. "Don't worry about it."

"But Mom should have—"

"It's okay. She will also be dealing with another anniversary tomorrow. If she remembers me, fine. If not, I'm not worried about it."

"You, me, and Jules—and Mom if she feels up to it. Tomorrow for dinner. Okay?"

"Sure."

Meranda grabbed her jacket from the closet and picked up her duffel. Just as she was heading out, she noticed the mail sitting on the credenza by the door. The corner of a large manila envelope stuck out from under the bills. It was from the Crossroads Bay Maritime Museum and addressed to her father. She looked over her shoulder to see if her mother was watching, then slid it into her bag. Julianne had probably brought in the mail, and her mother hadn't seen it yet.

When she arrived home, she walked straight through the living room to Pop's metal desk that he'd bought at a navy surplus store. It sat under the back window over the balcony. The lighthouse greeted her beyond the window now that night had claimed the area.

"Look what we got, Pop." Taking a fish fillet knife, she slit the top of the envelope and spilled the contents onto the desk. The cover letter caught her eye, and she adjusted the desk lamp to read it better.

Dear Gilbert Drake,
   Your request for Augustus Drake's belongings only turned up the following:

*news clippings and old letters sent to his sister. The Crossroads Bay Museum may
have more information. I hope you find what you're searching for.*

Regards,
Richard Miller
Director of Marine Artifacts

The news clippings had yellowed and seemed to document the building of
the lighthouse, pictures that weren't much different from what she'd seen in the
Crossroads Bay Museum. But five smaller envelopes lay among the fragile papers.
They also appeared old. Her hands shook as she touched her own history. She
picked up the first one and carefully pinched the letter inside to draw it out. The
bold script proved difficult to read.

June 10, 1905

Dear Charlotte,
  I'm sure you have heard of the loss of the Victoria Jane *and feared I may
have met my end as well. I'm most happy to inform you that I am alive and
healthy. Many of us survived, for which I am grateful, but I grieve the loss of
the crew who valiantly braved the sea voyage from Hawaii.*

Meranda's upper lip began to sweat. This shipwreck had led to her father's
demise. She read further, hoping to gain some encouragement that he hadn't died
in vain.

  *I plan to build a lighthouse in dedication to those lost and to prevent
another such accident.*
  *I grieve not only for our brother, but also that you were not able to go with
me to officially say good-bye. All the villagers that he ministered to loved him.*

Your Faithful Brother,
Augustus

Well, so far she hadn't learned anything new. It was common knowledge that her
great-great-grandfather had lost a ship coming back from Hawaii. It was also known
that he had an older brother and that Charlotte was their sister living in San Francisco.
  She opened the other letters, all dated later and giving updates to Charlotte on
the lighthouse. The last letter would have to hold a clue, or nothing in this package
was worth anything to her.

July 2, 1907

Dear Charlotte,
  *As you know, with the untimely demise of our brother, I became the keeper
of The Inheritance.*

Meranda hopped out of the chair and let out a whoop. "Happy birthday to me!" Then she stood while she read the rest.

> *I brought it back from Hawaii with me and want you to know that it is safe, and I'm concretely sure it is where no one will find it.*

"This is it, Pop! Augustus says it's safe. That rules out the shipwreck, right?" The lighthouse winked.

The rest of the letter had to do with personal stuff. He'd met a woman, they were getting married. That union no doubt led to her grandfather's birth.

Meranda sat down to think. The lighthouse property was sold after Augustus's death. That owner had a falling out with Grandpa, who had moved out by then, and refused to let him back onto the property. No owner since would allow anyone past the gate that had been built to keep people out.

She needed to change that. Somehow.

Chapter 3

Paul's cousin Al poked his head in the kitchen doorway. "Is Abuelita here yet?"

"No, and a good thing, too." Paul grabbed some fresh parsley and scissors and began snipping the spicy-smelling greenery into the soup stock. "Sleep in?"

"Yeah. Baby kept us up all night."

"Now, Alberto." Paul squeezed into his falsetto voice and seasoned it with a Spanish accent. "Your *abuelo* and I raised seven children while working this restaurant. How can you let one tiny *bebé* keep you from doing your job?"

Al's gaze drifted past Paul and a look of terror laced his face.

Paul winced and whispered, "She's standing behind me, isn't she?"

"No, bro." Al slapped his shoulder and broke into an I-gotcha grin. "I'm just messing with you."

Paul grabbed his chest. "Don't do that!"

"Hey"—Al threw on his apron and chef's hat—"thanks for starting the base foods for me."

"Again."

"Again."

"Not a problem." Paul looked at his watch. "I have an appointment coming in about five minutes. After that I can help with lunch."

"Hey, isn't today your day off?"

Paul held his palms out and shrugged. "I've got nowhere to go. I'll help out here."

"Man, we've got to get you a girlfriend." Al waved him off with a disgusted frown.

Paul left the kitchen buoyed with thoughts of Meranda.

Mrs. Drake and Meranda's sister arrived on time. After introductions he led them to a table in the empty dining room.

"Let's sit near the window. It's dark in here."

Rose gazed around. "Yes, but I love the dark wood and the rich red walls. It all looks so. . .Spanish."

Paul chuckled. "Well, that's the look we're going for."

The two women sat in the wooden ladder-back chairs. Rose sniffed the air. "Smells like you're already cooking."

"We open at eleven for lunch. We only use homemade ingredients here, so what you smell is the soup stock."

140

He looked from mother to daughter trying to pick out a family resemblance to Meranda. Only a hint of the tall beauty showed on her mother's face—same nose and lips. Her sister had the same arched brows, and her eyes showed more green, but they didn't flash like Meranda's.

Before he stared too long, he opened his three-ring binder with menu choices. He focused on the bride, as he always tried to do. "At Tapas, we are known for the traditional Spanish appetizers that make a whole meal. Would you like to go that route, or would you rather stick with a three-course dinner?"

Rose began to answer, but her mother interrupted her. "We're very traditional in our family. Let's stick with three courses."

"Mothers often want to go with tradition, but we want this to be about the bride, right?" He made a point of addressing the bride-to-be. "Rose, is that your preference?"

Mrs. Drake slid her hand on the table in front of Rose and leaned forward. "Do you have anything French?"

"Mother! We're in a Spanish restaurant."

The older woman glanced around as if seeing her surroundings for the first time. "Yes, so we are."

"If I may. . ." Paul addressed Rose again. "I have a wide repertoire of dishes. My specialty is Spanish cuisine, but I can provide anything you'd like."

Rose glanced at her mother, her chin jutted forward. "I like the thought of several appetizers. Then the guests can mingle or sit if they wish."

"Mm." Paul tented his fingers and touched his lips. "Very European."

Mrs. Drake tilted her head slightly. "I think the Van de Horns had a similar party. But we can't do spicy. Remember your great-aunt Vera's gallbladder."

"I'd rather not think of Aunt Vera's gallbladder while I'm getting married, Mom."

The tension between these two women could be stabbed with a fork, run through a meat grinder, and still be indigestible. Paul leaned back in his chair. "Spanish food is not so much spicy as flavorful. I have plenty of nonspicy foods to choose from."

Rose's mother huffed and looked at Paul. "What do you suggest?"

"A mix of Spanish and other fare? Some with a kick, some not?"

She tipped her head. "If you will."

Paul raised his eyebrow at Rose, hoping she'd allow them to move on.

"Fine." She sighed. "Let's protect all of your friends' sensitive stomachs."

He led them through the menu, a mix of international foods. Everything Rose liked, Mrs. Drake hated, and vice versa.

"You know, Rose." Paul felt he needed to say something. "This is your wedding. You have the final say."

Mrs. Drake screwed up her face. "Cordon bleu!"

"Excuse me?"

"Cordon bleu is French. Can't you make that?" Her eyes challenged him.

"Yes, I can. Rose, what do you think?"

Rose looked from her mother to Paul. "I don't want to have anything French on the menu. That's all Mom and her friends have had at their gatherings. Let's do something fun. . .tacos!"

"Tacos?" Mrs. Drake's eyes bugged.

"I can do a taco bar." Paul caught Rose's eye and winked. She sent a small, conspiratorial smile back telegraphing her appreciation.

Mrs. Drake folded her arms. "We will not have *tacos* at my wedding."

"*My* wedding, Mother." The corners of Rose's mouth dipped.

"Of course, dear. I only meant that since I'm paying for it. . ." The excuse trailed off, but it was decidedly meant to thumbtack Rose to her place.

"You treat me like a child."

Okay. Time to check the soup. He stood. "I'll let you two talk in private for a moment."

They both ignored him.

"Of course I treat you like a child. Still living at home. Never married. Dolls on your bed." Mrs. Drake ticked each item off on her fingers. "Your new husband isn't going to put up with that, I can assure you."

Paul heard the smackdown with embarrassed interest as he retreated to the kitchen. No wonder Meranda took to the water.

Al stood at the block chopping green peppers. "What's going on in there?"

"A domestic dispute."

"Should I call someone? We don't need bloodshed. Abuelita does that enough here."

"Um. . .Al. . ." Paul pointed over Al's shoulder.

"Come on. I know she's not standing behind me." Al continued to chop.

"Alberto." Abuelita startled Al, and he nearly slit the end of his thumb.

Quickly choosing between battles, he left Al and Abuelita and joined the sparring in the dining room.

When he returned, the two women were still going at it.

He'd had enough. "I have a suggestion." Still standing, he leaned his knuckles on the table. "What if we have a contest? Invite friends here—we have a party room in the back—and vote for the dishes."

Rose recovered quickly from her verbal whipping and bounced in her chair. "I have a better idea. What if you come to our country club and put on a demonstration. I teach a cooking class there, and I'm sure they'd all love to see a professional at work."

Mrs. Drake rolled her eyes. Did she have a problem with a young socialite loving to cook? "No," she said with the guile of a fox. "Come to my house. I have a large kitchen."

Rose narrowed her eyes. "Home court advantage, Mother?"

"That sounds like a great idea." Paul quickly stepped in before another row began. He pulled out his chair and sat, then flipped through his day planner. "When?"

"This Wednesday." Again, Mrs. Drake challenged him. She probably didn't like the fact that he had been in Rose's corner throughout the meeting. Did she think he couldn't pull this off in two days?

"Wednesday is good for me." Paul penciled them in. "In fact, if you allow me to use this opportunity to let your friends know about me, I'll only charge for the food." Yep. This could be a great marketing tool. He jotted down prices for the proposal. "Make a party of it. Rose, bring your class and we'll prepare the food together. Mrs. Drake, you and your friends can relax or participate, but everyone will have a chance to vote."

Mrs. Drake stood. Conversation over. "This Wednesday. We'll have everybody there."

No doubt. Mrs. Drake and Meranda did have something in common. They could both bark orders.

⚬⚬⚬

Wednesday evening Paul and Jessie loaded the van and drove to the upscale neighborhood where Meranda's mother lived. Was this where Meranda grew up? How did she ever become a charter boat captain?

Rose greeted them and showed them the large kitchen and dining room where they would set up.

Jessie whistled. "I like this kitchen." She wandered around the room. Pointing at the cabinets she asked, "Cherry?"

Rose nodded while caressing the marble countertop. "This is the only room in the house that I care about."

Paul decided to watch this woman. If she were any good in the culinary arts, he might have to offer her a job.

The guests began to arrive, an eclectic mix of fifty-somethings and younger, about thirty women in all. How did they pull this party off so fast?

"This could be interesting," he said to Jessie as they laid out the appetizers.

Jessie cast her gaze around the dining room at the two factions squaring off in preparation for the tasting contest. "Reminds me of *West Side Story*."

"I don't think I want to get into the middle of a rumble." Paul ducked into the kitchen and laid out his knives near the cutting board—within quick reach—in case he had to use them on the crowd.

Mrs. Drake called for everyone's attention in the dining room. Showtime. He stepped to the doorway and waited for her to introduce him. Then he continued the announcement. "Thanks for coming out to help Rose decide what food would work for the wedding. I've already prepared a sampling of approved *tapas*—that's Spanish for appetizers—so you may help yourselves while I give a cooking demonstration in the kitchen."

Jessie had set out his business cards in strategic places throughout the house, and the pile on the table had already started to dwindle. Rumble or not, he felt this night would be a success for his business.

The women began milling about, nabbing bits of food for their plates—marinated olives, grilled eggplant, and red peppers stuffed with tuna, among a few others. Almost everyone followed him into the kitchen or watched from the pass-through as he began his demonstration. He'd laid down the rule that no one was to know which food Rose or Mrs. Drake preferred, but he suspected that each woman went to her friends privately. Hopefully his food would be so good, they wouldn't know which to pick.

"Our menu tonight, ladies, is red onion and orange salad, chicken and chorizo paella, and *empanadas.*"

Fifteen people in the large kitchen oohed appreciatively. Those in the dining room clapped their appreciation.

While setting up the vegetables for chopping, Paul glanced toward the other room and caught sight of a wild red ponytail somewhat contained in a skull and crossbones barrette. A song entered his heart. *Meranda, I just met a girl named Meranda.* "Rose, aren't your sisters going to join us? Or are you the only cook in the family?"

Rose had donned a pink pastel apron and was pouring rice into a cooker. "Julianne has decided she's going to marry rich and therefore won't have need of cooking knowledge."

"And Meranda?"

The lady in question entered the kitchen holding an olive-oil-soaked piece of rye bread.

Rose laughed. "Look at her."

Meranda frowned back.

I am.

He couldn't pull his gaze from her as she set the bread on the counter and rummaged through the cabinet until she found. . .oh horrors! Peanut butter. Surely she wasn't going to ruin his bread and alioli with. . . Oh yes, she did. Paul winced.

Rose shook her head. "Mer thinks the only cooking utensils she needs are an aluminum camping kit and a pocketknife."

Meranda speared her with a glare. "You don't think I can cook?"

"Not like this." Rose cracked an egg and separated the white from the yolk, all with one hand.

Impressive. Yes, Paul would have to take notes on this one.

Meranda joined them at the freestanding counter and set her partially eaten bread down. Paul thought of slipping a plate under it but didn't want to embarrass her. She grabbed an egg and slammed it against the bowl. It *splurched* all over her hand from the violent gash.

"See?" Rose snickered.

"I can crack an egg." Meranda grabbed another one. "You just had my adrenaline pumping." She tapped the egg on its side and transferred the yolk to a bowl with only a minute slimy drip.

Paul handed her a small whisk. "Since you're here, would you mind beating that?" With Rose's egg, he showed her how to do it.

She began slow and easy, but then truly proceeded to beat the poor thing.

"No." Rose stepped in. "Not like a jackhammer."

"Allow me." Paul parted the other chefs in the kitchen and stood next to Meranda. He placed his hand on her back and took her wrist. "Like this." Together they created egg art as the yellow yolk frothed in the bowl.

If he hadn't been standing so close to her, he would have missed the clean scent of her hair. He half-expected her to smell salty.

She turned her head and met his gaze, then pulled away abruptly. "I think I have it now."

"Of course." Paul attempted to recover from her nearness, but knew he failed miserably. Surely he'd turned red as the peppers marinating in the dining room. "Uh. . .now let's brush this egg onto our empanada dough for a finished shine."

Mrs. Drake stood at the doorway. "Meranda! Are you actually. . .?"

"Cooking," Meranda finished. "Yes, Mother, I'm cooking." She grabbed an onion and a very inappropriate cleaver and proceeded to rear it back as if she were a one-armed lumberjack.

"Use this." Paul caught her arm before she lost a finger, removed the weapon, and replaced it with his ten-inch. . .no. . .eight-inch chef's knife. Meranda Drake did not need a long knife in her hand. "It has a weighted blade so it does most of the work for you."

Mrs. Drake passed Meranda on her way to a drawer where she rummaged through and pulled out a business card. "Ah. Here it is. The man who does my hair. Mrs. St. James is asking." She paused at the doorway and glanced at Meranda. "Be careful, dear. Remember the Easter fiasco." The others in the kitchen tittered along with Meranda's condescending mother. "Fruit salad. She forgot to drain off the juice. We ended up with fruit soup."

Meranda seemed to take the jibing in quiet stride, but it ticked Paul off. "She's actually doing quite well. Tell me, Mrs. Drake. Have you ever captained a ship?"

Mrs. Drake puckered like a prune. "Certainly not."

"Well, I'm sure if you ever tried, it would be as equally difficult a task. However, since you and Meranda share the same genes, I'm sure you could pick it up very easily."

Mrs. Drake started to say something, hesitated, then said, "Thank you." Then she wandered out of the kitchen.

"That was amazing." Meranda's eyes glowed with what he hoped was admiration. "You put her in her place and complimented her at the same time. How did you do that?"

"Years of working with the public." And with women like Mrs. Drake.

A silent exchange passed between Meranda and Rose. Then the two smiled as if from the same joke.

Chapter 4

Meranda squelched the urge to pump the air and shout "Yes!" after her mother walked out of the kitchen in a confused stupor. Who was this guy, anyway?

For the next half hour, she chopped, mixed, and sautéed next to Paul. Even though Rose's students were there to learn, he used Meranda often to demonstrate. Finally everything was ready to put on the table. She couldn't wait to dig into the paella. The savory rice, chicken, and sausage dish lured her out to the dining room and was the first thing she put on her plate.

She rested her back against the arched entryway that led to the parlor. As she popped a piece of sausage in her mouth, Rose sidled up to her. "I'm sorry for the ribbing I gave you earlier. You're such an easy target when it comes to domestic stuff. I really appreciate you coming over."

"It's okay. Just gives me an excuse to exchange the ice ring at your reception with one I'll add spiders to." She offered a wicked smile.

"You wouldn't dare!" She laughed, but her eyes held that tiny bit of terror that Meranda had loved eliciting since they were kids. "By the way"—Rose discreetly slipped a note into Meranda's hand— "when you vote on the food, these are the ones I really liked."

Meranda deposited it into her pants pocket. "Got it."

"Paul is something, isn't he?" Rose took a bite of the empanada.

"He can cook." Meranda also bit into an empanada, the pastry crusting just right and the shredded pork loin tasting tender and succulent.

"He's also been watching you, with interest."

Warmth infused Meranda's cheeks. "Don't be silly."

"And you've been watching back."

"Have not!"

"Have so!"

"Girls!" Mom walked by, shaking her head. "Will you never grow up?"

Meranda bumped Rose's shoulder, and Rose bumped back as they left the entryway and passed Mom on their way to the kitchen. She rolled her eyes at them as she stopped to fill her plate again.

Paul stood at the sink washing the larger pans and empty serving dishes Jessie had brought to him. There was something intriguing about a man doing dishes. Meranda felt her cheeks warm again, as they did when she spent too long topside on her boat.

Meranda slid her plate and fork onto the counter near the sink. When Paul reached for them, he dripped suds onto her hand. "Oops. Sorry." He went to wipe them off, but only transferred more bubbles.

His touch cooled and burned at the same time. She grabbed a towel. "Maybe I'd better use this."

"Um. . .yeah." His shy smile created a pleasant sensation in her stomach.

Rose leaned against the counter, a knowing smirk on her face. Meranda gave her a warning look, hoping to signal her to drop the matchmaking.

"So," Rose began. Meranda feared she'd say something to embarrass her in front of Paul. "Any luck with the coins?"

"Coins?" Mom flew into the kitchen. Was there nowhere her ears couldn't reach? "Are you still looking for those things? After what they did to your father?"

Rose's hand flew to her mouth. "I'm sorry. I thought she knew."

"Answer me." Mom's nostrils flared.

Everyone in the kitchen and dining room froze. Even the soapy drip from Paul's hand waited to hear how this all played out.

Great, let's air our dirty laundry in front of the cute guy.

Paul hastily dried his hands and excused himself from the kitchen. Although he'd never be able to go far enough to escape her mother's shrill voice.

"The coins didn't kill Pop."

"No, but his obsession did. And now you're following in his footsteps?"

"Yes, Mother." The two women locked glares. "I'm looking for the coins. They were important to Pop, and they're important to me."

"They're a myth. He died over something that doesn't exist."

But they did exist, and Meranda had proof. But she wasn't about to share that with her mother, who'd only ruin her excitement over the discovery.

"What do you care?" Meranda knew she should swallow her rushing words, but they barreled through her teeth like a northeast wind. "You had kicked him out of the house months before that. You divorced him."

Mom jerked as if she'd just been slapped. "I loved him, but. . ."

"But what? He didn't fit in with your lifestyle? You were embarrassed by him? What?"

Mom's eyes narrowed to mere slits. In a low voice, she ground through her teeth, "I won't discuss this with you now. We have guests."

The house had become very quiet. Meranda's adrenaline continued to rush through her pounding heart even as her mother strode through the now-vacant dining room and disappeared into the parlor. Remorse hit her for her harsh words. When would she learn to think before acting?

"You may all stay and vote on the food," she heard her mother say, "but I'm going to lie down. I've suddenly acquired a headache."

Rose stroked Meranda's shoulder. "I'm so sorry. I didn't know you hadn't told her."

"Well, she knows now." Meranda willed her fists to relax. "Probably a good thing. I don't have to sneak behind her back anymore." She drew in a big breath. "I'm sorry. I didn't mean to spoil your party."

"You didn't. Mom was out of line. She should have waited to confront you about the coins until everyone had left."

Meranda still felt horrible and felt the need to be near the last vestige of Pop's memory in the house—his study.

But even that was no longer his. Disgusted, she walked into the redecorated room. How long had it been since she'd been in there? Pink and green paint had erased the nautical theme. Thankfully, Meranda had already snatched his models of tall ships or they might have landed in the Dumpster.

She sat in her father's favorite chair, reupholstered with a flowery eyesore. The marble-topped side table was still there but now sported a lacy doily and—what's this? A newspaper tossed casually onto the table caught her eye. Or rather, a picture of her lighthouse and an article about the owner. She picked it up and started to read.

"Judge Gordon Bernard will be giving his daughter in marriage at the Crossroads Bay lighthouse in a private ceremony." Yay. Great for them. Total strangers get onto the lighthouse property, but not the original owner's great-great-granddaughter. "Bernard recently presided over California's high-profile stalking trial of actress Trista Farentino." Meranda frowned. Leave it to the media to add a negative to a happy event.

Deciding to apologize to Paul for their fiasco, she tore the article out of the paper to explain why she and her mother had suddenly gone insane.

She left the study and searched for Paul, who stood in the dining room announcing the winners of the contest.

Blast. She had forgotten to vote. She fingered the note in her pocket, tempted to hand it to Paul. But by the glow on Rose's face, her dishes must have come out ahead anyway.

As the party broke up, she grabbed her jacket and helped Paul and Jessie load the van. "I'd like to apologize for our little drama in there."

"Believe me, that's not the first family squabble I've seen in my business."

"Maybe not, but it's the first time I've ever yelled at my mother in front of company. I don't know what got into me." Well, yes, she did. Ever since Pop's death, her animosity toward her mother had built until it finally blew at an unfortunate moment.

Changing the subject, she handed him the newspaper and pointed out the article. "This is what has me so hot under the collar. I'm frustrated that I can't get into the lighthouse my great-great-grandfather built."

"Seriously? The Crossroads Bay lighthouse?"

"Yep. And the coins you heard us arguing about? They're ancient coins, and I think he hid them in the lighthouse."

He perused the article while leaning against the van's sliding side door. "Wow. Hey, Jess, look at this."

Jessie deposited the bag of dirty towels and linens into the van and then read the article. "You should bid on this."

"You think? They might already have a caterer."

"Well, Philippe is out of the picture." Meranda reminded him of the popular caterer among her mother's friends. "They may be looking for someone at the last minute."

"And your grandmother would love it if you got the bid." Jessie looked at Meranda and raised her eyebrows. "May I keep this?"

"Sure." The wedding announcement was nothing but a slap in the face as far as Meranda was concerned.

Paul nodded. "I'll do it. Thanks, Meranda."

"Glad I could help." She slid her fingers into the front pockets of her slacks. "I wish I could go with you and look around at the lighthouse."

"Hey," Jessie said as she thumped the page with her index finger. "If we get it, we should snoop around for Meranda."

A tingling sensation hit the back of Meranda's neck as she thought of the possibility. But then her hopes were dashed when Paul backed away from both of them, his palms raised as if pushing that idea far away. "I'll put in a bid, but I'm not going to snoop."

Jessie plopped down on the van floor and dusted the concrete driveway with her shoes. "Come on, Paul. There will be a ton of people there. No one will know if we sneak into the lighthouse."

"We?" Paul shot her an incredulous glare.

Meranda's heart beat against her chest. She had an ally in Jessie. "I'm not going to ask you to do anything you're not comfortable with. But an extra set of eyes wouldn't hurt."

"Sure." Jessie's eyes danced. "We could knock on some walls to see if there are any hidden compartments."

His lips pinched in a dubious expression. "If I get the bid, there will be no snooping, by me or Jess. We will go where we're allowed, and we're not going to knock on any walls. It's *my* reputation at stake." He stabbed his thumb toward his chest and glared at his assistant. "This judge is not known for being a nice guy."

"I know." Meranda's gaze dropped to the driveway. "Even though my ancestor built the lighthouse, Judge Bernard refuses to let our family on his property."

Meranda had often thought of scaling the fortress since the judge was rarely there. But common sense prevailed.

"Look, I'd like to help you out, but I have to protect my business." He turned to go back into the house, and Jessie followed him.

Meranda hoped she hadn't upset Paul. She'd had fun cooking with him—okay, that's something she never thought she'd say—and wanted to get to know him better.

She'd have to figure out a way to get into the lighthouse herself.

Chapter 5

Meranda had piloted topside at the upper wheel on her boat while chartering a fishing tour. The afternoon had been relatively warm, with only one tiny squall to mar the trip. And now the near-cloudless sky promised a beautiful evening. With the days getting longer, she looked forward to spending more time on the water.

After she pulled into the dock, the family of seven, consisting of parents, grandparents, and three teenage sons—the oldest had developed a little crush on her—exuded their appreciation for the "highly enjoyable" tour. They insisted on taking pictures with Meranda and Ethan along with the mess of sturgeon they'd caught.

Once they left, Meranda grabbed some corn chips for her dinner and started cleaning the boat.

"Gotta run, Meranda." Ethan, who had night classes on Mondays, called to her.

"Go on." She waved him off. "I'll clean up."

He flipped on the water spigot from the dock and tossed her the hose. Then he raced to his car.

She filled a bucket with soapy water, deciding to swab the deck before rinsing off the salty sea. Not satisfied with the junk food she'd just offered her stomach, it grumbled as she thought of Paul's paella.

Her mind drifted to the tasting party last week. The guy had other good things going for him, too. She liked how he stood up to her mother. Not that she couldn't handle her mom, but it felt nice to have a man, an attractive man, do it for her. And that was the second thing he had going. Her first impression of Paul draped over her railing would not have led to her thinking about him day and night. But now she remembered his shy grin and the twinkle in his dark chocolate eyes.

As she mopped, the object of her musings sauntered toward her down the dock, hands in pockets, as if he didn't have a problem with boats. Her stomach did that funny thing again, like minnows swimming happy laps inside.

"Ahoy there." He raised his hand in greeting. "That is what you say, isn't it?"

She leaned on the mop handle and waved him on. "It'll do. Come aboard."

He stopped sauntering. "Um, no thanks. I just came to tell you something."

"Can it wait a moment? I need to finish this before the sun goes down." She dipped her mop into the bucket. "I took a family out fishing this afternoon, and the man landed a big one. It flopped around in the boat for a while. You should have seen it. That thing was this—whoops!" Her heel caught a slippery spot, and she went down hard on her hip.

Before she knew it, Paul suddenly stood above her with concern in his eyes. "Are you okay?"

"Yeah." How did he get there so fast? She allowed him to help her up. "That was just my evil plan to get you on my boat."

He looked around as if he just realized where he was. "Well, it worked." He must have noticed her rubbing her backside as she limped to a large white box on the deck and eased herself onto it. "Are you sure you're okay?"

"I think my pride is bruised. I've never fallen on this boat before."

"Maybe I distracted you."

A pleasant distraction. Yikes! She'd nearly voiced that thought.

Pain throbbed in her left hip. She shifted.

"Let me bring you some ice for your, uh, pride." He disappeared below, knowing where to go after catering, and came back a moment later with a plastic bag filled with ice. "Here, sit on this a moment. I'll finish mopping."

"I can't have you do my—ow." As she started to get up, blood rushed to what she suspected would be a glorious bruise on her backside. "Watch that spot there." She pointed, and he sidestepped the slimy spot, then ran the mop over it.

"So." She readjusted the ice pack. "You have something to tell me?"

"Oh, yeah." He stopped mopping and leaned on the handle. "I got the bid."

"To the lighthouse wedding?"

"Yep."

Excitement thrummed through her. "That was quick."

He sloshed the mop into the bucket and resumed the chore. "It turns out that Judge Bernard's daughter is marrying a Lopez. Apparently, I'm the only one in town who caters authentic Spanish food."

She chewed her lip. "Wish I could be there."

"I know." He wrung out the mop. "All I can promise is that I'll keep my eyes open, but I have no idea what I'm looking for. And I'll only have access to the kitchen and patio." Paul tossed a glance at her with a curious tilt to his head. "So, tell me about the coins."

❧

Paul found himself staring at the smile that blossomed on her face and, more directly, the tiny dimple that appeared on her cheek. He jerked his attention back to the dirty deck.

"My many-times great-uncle was Sir Francis Drake."

He paused his mopping. "Really?"

She nodded, seemingly pleased by his interest. "He looted from the Spanish for the queen." Her hand flew to her mouth. "Maybe I shouldn't have mentioned that, you being Spanish and all."

She sure looked cute flustered.

"I'm also a quarter English. Last name is Godfrey, remember."

"Oh, right." She adjusted the ice pack and went on. "There's a story of a bag of coins that *somehow* didn't make it to the queen. At first they were said to bring good luck to all who possessed them."

"Do you believe that?"

"No. I'm not superstitious."

He sent up a quick prayer of thanks.

"A couple of generations later," Meranda continued, "a member of the family traveled to Spain to return them. No doubt this was the result of some unfortunate incident where the coins were blamed. The king was so moved that he returned seven of the coins and blessed them. Forever afterward they were renamed The Inheritance, and each generation of my family would hide them for the next generation to find."

"So it became a game."

"Or a way to keep them safe. I don't know."

"And they're important to you now because. . ."

"They're mine." She pressed her fist to her chest and dropped her gaze to the deck. "And because my father died searching for them." When she looked back up at him, fire flashed from her gray eyes. "The town thinks he was crazy. I need to prove to them he wasn't."

And, he surmised, judging by the way she'd been treated at the tasting party, she needed to prove she wasn't crazy as well. But losing one's life for a material thing? He would reserve judgment on her father.

"Why did he think the coins are in Crossroads Bay?"

"Pop found documentation at the maritime museum chronicling the Drake family voyages. The coins were also mentioned in a few of the many journals he had found." Her passion translated to her cheeks as they flushed a pretty pink. "Looking for the code word *Inheritance,* he found several entries, some as simple as, 'I tucked The Inheritance in my belt and we set sail.' Once they made it to Hawaii in the eighteenth century, all mention of them ceased. We figured they stayed in one family, or at least in one place for another two hundred years."

"So do you mind me asking how your dad's death is tied to these coins?"

Meranda winced. "I'm sorry you had to hear about that at the party." She drew in a breath. "You know about the shipwreck off our coast."

"A little. We learned about it in school."

"My great-great-grandfather built that ship, and then later the lighthouse."

"Wait." He pressed his finger to his temple. "His name was. . ."

"Augustus Drake. He was on his way back from Hawaii after his older brother died, and he ran into a storm. The crippled boat never made it to shore."

"Older brother. So you believe the coins passed to Augustus after his brother died."

She nodded. "I have confirmation. He'd written some letters to a sister in San Francisco. In one he said The Inheritance was where no one would find it. And that's why we believed they were in the shipwreck." Her gaze drifted to the horizon.

His followed as well to see the gentle glow from the sun's rays give their final efforts before night swallowed them completely. Then, in a barely audible voice, Meranda spoke. "Pop had gotten trapped in the shipwreck and ran out of air."

Paul set the mop aside and knelt in front of Meranda, taking her hands in his own. "I'm so sorry for your loss."

She gripped his fingers and closed her eyes. He had the feeling she wasn't a crier, but a small tear slipped from the inside corner of her right eye. With a quick swipe of her hand, it was gone. When she focused on him once more, it was with clear eyes, and he knew the door into her grief had closed to him. But he thanked God for the brief glimpse he'd had inside. Now he knew better how to pray for her.

"Sun's down." She gingerly stood, testing her footing with her new injury. "I need to rinse the deck." She limped to where she'd draped the hose over the railing. "You might want to stand behind me."

Over the spraying water, Paul continued the discussion. He still wasn't clear on a few things. "Your father thought the coins were in the shipwreck. Why do you believe they're in the lighthouse?"

She spoke over her shoulder. "Pop and I dove the wreck several times. He hired a professional crew. To me it stands to reason that if we didn't find them after all our dives, they would be in the lighthouse. And recently I found a letter that confirms it—sort of."

"Sort of."

"It doesn't say where the coins are, just that they're safe."

"Could be they're safely buried deep in the hull of the sunken ship."

Meranda turned around, an exasperated expression on her face. Was she contemplating using the hose to rinse him off the boat? "Now you're confusing the issue. I just had my mind made up."

"Sorry." He tried his most charming smile, the one that kept him off the hook with Abuelita.

She shrugged. "It's okay. I'll concentrate on the lighthouse for now. Hopefully I'm on the right path."

"Sounds like a good plan."

Meranda grinned back, then quickly finished her chore. She excused herself to stow the cleaning supplies below and lock up. Paul stepped to the dock and coiled up the hose for her. While waiting, he allowed all he had learned about her to sink in. He had thought the beautiful captain a fascinating woman before learning her history. But now—oh, man, another thought hit him. When she returned from below with her canvas bag slung on her shoulder, he asked, "Were you with your dad on that last dive?"

"No." The light went out in her eyes.

Water gently slapped the boat. Screeching seagulls glided high in the sky. Voices from the other boaters drifted by.

But Meranda was silent.

The bruise on Meranda's hip throbbed like crazy, but it didn't hurt nearly as bad as her answer to Paul's question. No, she hadn't gone with her father.

She felt like a wimp as Paul helped her negotiate from the boat to the dock. Their footsteps played a wooden drumbeat as he came up beside her. Meranda cast a sidelong gaze at him. "Are you working tonight?"

"No. Monday is my day off from the restaurant, and I have no catering jobs this evening." He slipped his hands into his pockets. "You wouldn't want to get a bite to eat, would you?"

That's what she was going to ask. "I know a good place for paella, but I hear the chef is off on Mondays."

"Yeah. Too bad." He chuckled. "There's a little café not far from here, though. No Spanish foods, but the hamburgers are the best in town."

She pinched at her shirt. "I've been on a fishing trip. Even though Ethan did all the work, I'm not exactly fresh."

He gave her a brisk one-armed hug. "You're fine, and this place isn't fancy."

She may not have smelled great, but he smelled amazing. A girlie sense of enjoyment shot through her as she realized his mouth was about eye level. "Okay. I'll follow you."

Just a couple of blocks from the wharf, Paul pulled his hybrid into a small parking lot and Meranda parked her truck beside him. This was the touristy part of town, with gray-planked buildings and short timber posts with rope for fencing—all ambience to simulate Crossroads Bay a century ago. In a couple of months, the town would be teeming with visitors, but for now only a smattering of people wandered the boardwalks.

They entered the restaurant through a screen door and seated themselves at a wooden table shellacked to a waterproof shine. Paper placemats advertised the place—Capt. Tony's—and a peg-leg pirate logo greeted them with a salute.

"I've never eaten here before." Meranda's mouth watered as the smell of grilled meat drifted from the kitchen. With eager fingers, she pulled two vinyl menus from behind the salt and pepper shakers and handed one to Paul.

"They have good fish sandwiches, too, but I come here for the cheeseburgers."

"That's odd."

"Why?"

"You're a gourmet chef. Why would you come to a dive for hamburgers?"

The waitress came to take their drink orders, never indicating she'd heard Meranda say the word *dive,* then left with promises to return shortly after they'd looked at the menus.

Paul leaned in and with a conspiratorial whisper said, "I'm thinking of stealing the cook." He then placed his index finger to his lips.

Meranda put her forearm on the table and also leaned in. "Doing some pirating of your own?"

"You could put it that way." He winked. "This guy is a genius with food."

The waitress returned and took their orders of two cheeseburgers, coleslaw, and fries.

After an awkward silence, neither apparently knowing where to begin the conversation, Meranda finally opened a topic. "You know my story. What's yours?"

He tossed his head back and chuckled. "Ah. Where do I begin?"

"The beginning?" She took a sip of her soda.

"Okay. I was born here, in Crossroads Bay."

"Well, we have that in common."

"I was raised by a single mom and my grandparents. I never knew my dad. He died when I was a baby."

"Oh, I'm sorry."

"We managed okay." He shrugged. "We worked in the restaurant."

"Even you? As a little boy?"

"Well, no. As a little boy I played under the tables with my cousins and made Abuelita, my grandmother, angry." His smile told her he'd had a good childhood. "As I grew older, I took an interest in the kitchen. Then, a few years ago, I lost my mother." He tapped his fork on the table, a staccato rhythm that no doubt echoed his broken heart. "I was twenty-three."

So they both had endured loss. Meranda fiddled with her napkin. She ached for him. Losing a parent hurt like a harpoon to the chest. She wouldn't wish that on anybody, but especially not on a warm, gentle soul like Paul.

"My aunt and uncle needed someone to help on their alpaca ranch, so I moved there until a year ago. My grandmother called to tell me she wanted to retire from the restaurant, so I came back home."

"But you're a caterer. Do you run the restaurant, too?"

"No, when I got back here and discussed everything with Abuelita—"

"Excuse me, why do you call her Abuelita?"

He grinned. "It's Spanish for 'grandma' or 'granny.' Less formal than *abuela,* or 'grandmother.' "

"I look forward to meeting your abuelita."

Color leaped to his cheeks. Had she embarrassed him by suggesting she'd like to meet his family?

"Anyway," he continued, "I told her my real love is catering. I get pleasure out of helping people make their special day. . . well. . .special. I'm not confined to the restaurant, and I get to meet and interact with customers. My cousin Al also grew up working in the restaurant. So we comanage—he's responsible for the restaurant, and I do the catering."

"So that's something else we have in common."

He arched his eyebrow.

"We both went into the family business."

His smile came easily and reached deep into his eyes. "Yes, we did."

Their meal came, and Meranda had to agree that her cheeseburger was extraordinary. Juicy and full of flavor.

Paul rolled it around in his mouth, as if tasting fine wine. "Mm-hm." He nodded and pulled a small notebook from his pocket. "Sour cream."

"He puts sour cream in his hamburgers? How could you tell that with one bite?"

She bit into hers as he did, nabbing only the meat. As it rolled on her tongue, she tried to concentrate on the individual tastes of everything that went into the meat. She nodded. "Mm-hm." Then, "Uh-uh. All I taste is really good meat."

He laughed. "It takes practice."

As she munched, she searched her mind for something else to talk about. Naturally her mind settled on Paul's enigma. "Let's talk about your aversion to boats. I think I can help you overcome that."

The grin on his lips fell, and his face blanched. She hoped she hadn't ruined his meal.

"How?"

"Meet me at the dock next Monday morning, and I'll show you."

When he hesitated to agree, she reached out to still his fork playing staccato. "Trust me?"

His hand quieted, and he turned his deep brown eyes to her. "Yes."

Chapter 6

Monday morning Meranda hopped out of bed with more energy than she'd had in a long time. The plan she had hatched the other night to get him back on her boat spun in her mind. Would Paul go for it? Or would he back out at the last minute?

They had spoken on the phone nearly every night the past week. But no matter how much he begged, she wouldn't spill what she had in mind to help him get over his fear of boats.

As she dressed she opted for deck shoes instead of her tall rubber-soled black boots, which were reserved for work.

As she finger-combed her hair, it fought for control as always. She finally made it submit to a tight rubber band, but when she grabbed her scarf and started to tie it over her head, she stopped when she saw herself in the mirror. Shades of her sisters morphed from her image in a family resemblance, but she would never be as pretty as either of them. Rose resembled her name, soft pink features on a flawless face. Julianne's freshness was what made her special. Bright eyes, ready smile. Meranda's big bones and height kept her from feeling feminine.

The scarf still lay in her hand. She folded it into a thin strip, removed the rubber band, and shook out her hair, then used the scarf as a headband, allowing her hair to flow down her back. She turned her head from side to side to see the effect. The soft hair bordering her face helped to round out her features. She sucked in a breath. That was Mom staring back at her in the mirror. The mom she remembered as a child. When they were all happy.

She backed away from the mirror.

On the way through the house, she grabbed a jacket and a cooler full of food and drinks, then got into her pickup and drove to the dock.

When she arrived, Paul was waiting in his car for her. Butterflies warred with the minnows in her stomach as he got out and ambled to her pickup. She hopped out and reached for the cooler in the bed.

"Let me carry that." He grabbed the handle.

She found herself blushing—blushing!—as he seemed to notice her hair. He smiled, and her hand maddeningly reached up to finger a curl in an uncharacteristic flirty movement. *Blast!*

As they headed toward the dock, he asked, "How's your pride?"

"Huh?" Oh, the spill she took the other day. She rubbed her hip. "Much better, thank you. The ice kept the swelling down."

As they strolled, he stopped at the charter boat, but she kept going, ignoring his hesitation. His steps hustled behind her—a brisk clapping on the boards.

"Um. . .where are we going?"

She continued to walk on the pier until she reached the smaller boat slips. "Here." She swept her hand toward the twenty-five-foot cruiser. "This is my boat."

His brow furrowed, and his gaze swung back to the larger charter. "I thought that was your boat."

"They both are. My father gave this one to all of us girls. But my sisters never showed much interest, so it's virtually mine." In fact, the other two had been on the boat only a handful of times in the past year.

He glanced at the name painted on the side. "The *Romanda Jule.* I get it. Rose, Meranda, and Julianne." His gaze fell to the cooler at her feet. "Do you think I'm getting on that boat? It's a lot smaller than the other one."

"The way you leaped onto my boat the other day tells me you're trainable."

"Well, it's one thing to be brave when tied to a dock. Quite another out in the open ocean."

"So let's try the open ocean."

Paul didn't budge.

"I'm serious. The only way to get over your fear is to face it."

"I did face it, remember? I spent the entire cruise buckled over."

She refused to let that be his last experience on a boat. "So, are you afraid, or do you just get seasick?"

"I'm afraid of getting seasick."

"Okay." She rummaged in her bag. After drawing out the palm-sized plastic box, she handed it to him. "This will help the nausea."

He opened the box. "Wristbands? Am I going jogging?"

She lifted one and turned it inside out. "See the plastic bead? Situate this where it causes a pressure point on your vein. Like this." She helped him place both bands correctly. "It's the same thing I did to your wrists that first day when you catered on my boat. So," she slipped her hand around his elbow, "are you coming?"

The dock seemed to capture Paul's shoes, preventing him from moving forward.

She leaped from the dock to the boat and placed her fists on her hips. "Do I have to fall again to get you to come on board?"

"No." He gingerly moved from the dock to the back platform and finally made it on deck. "And don't fall while we're out in the middle of nowhere, either. I wouldn't know how to get us back."

"And that, my fine gentleman, is what I'm going to teach you today." She waved him to the helm.

"Seriously?"

"Yep. You're going to drive my boat."

"Cool."

Paul sat in the passenger seat, paying close attention to everything Meranda did as she motored the boat away from the dock—although her hair distracted him. His fingers ached to touch the soft curls.

"I've heard," she said as she grabbed the throttle and eased away from the dock, "that a good way to avoid seasickness is to steer the boat. I don't know if it's because you feel more in control or because you're concentrating on something other than nausea."

It didn't matter to Paul what the reasons were. He was willing to try anything to keep from looking like a fool again.

Once they were in open water, she slowed down and cut the engine. Then she stood, and he slipped into the captain's seat.

She patted his shoulder. "You okay there, skipper?"

"A little nervous still. But what man wouldn't want the chance to drive a boat on the open sea?" And have the chance to redeem himself in the eyes of the beautiful captain?

After she showed him the first thing he needed to know, how to radio the coast guard, she tutored him on how to start the boat, accelerate, and slow down. Paul eased into an enjoyable clip, pushing the speed slightly as he felt more comfortable. Invigorating chilly air wrapped around the vessel, but his adrenaline warmed him.

"What do you think?" Meranda asked him from the chair to his left.

"The wristbands are working. . . . Without the nausea, I think I like this." As he opened up the throttle, he didn't know what was more thrilling—the speed or this beautiful woman sitting in close proximity as she coached him. "It handles much easier than I expected."

"And how do you feel?"

"Great! It must have been a matter of control. The more I learn about the boat, the more confident I am on the water."

She checked the bearings and asked him to slow down. "Here—this is where I wanted to take you. See that buoy floating in the water? Head toward it."

He did so, and when they neared, she instructed him to kill the engine. She stood and motioned for him to follow her. They moved to the back of the boat into the warming sunlight where rays painted golds and reds in the strands of her hair. She pulled her jacket around her as the slight breeze blew moist air from the north. Should he rub her arms, warm her?

"This is where it happened." She pointed to the water below the boat.

He glanced around at the open sea, the shore several miles in the distance. "The shipwreck?"

She nodded. "This is where my dad died."

This time he couldn't stop himself from offering comfort by caressing her upper arms. She leaned back against him, and he prayed his presence would console her. "Do you know what happened?"

She shrugged. "All I know is what the report said. He was in Augustus's cabin. Pop had gotten a plan of the ship and a ledger, so we knew exactly where to look."

"You mean the ship is intact down there?" He looked at the water wishing he had special powers to see it without diving. "I figured it was in several pieces."

She pulled away and turned to rest against the rail. "Remember the *Titanic*, how she broke in two?"

He nodded.

"The part that had filled with water is still pretty much whole. That's how they've found so many artifacts. The other half had air still in most of the ship. When it hit bottom, it exploded from the pressure of releasing all that air. This ship," she pointed to the waves, "filled with water slowly. The crew tried their best to get her to shore, but she had nothing left to give. When she sank, she was like a waterlogged toy and drifted to the bottom."

Paul had to admit he knew nothing about shipwrecks. "I'm confused. If I knew about this shipwreck, I'm sure your dad did. Why did it take him so long to look for it?"

"For one, he didn't have the means." She held up her fingers. "For two, the *Victoria Jane* had been buried for almost a hundred years. He had scuba dived the area looking for a hint of his adult life, but it wasn't until the big earthquake a decade ago that her bell was unearthed. He found that and knew the ship was under the sand there someplace."

"Oh, so after that, he was finally able to get some funding to dig her out."

She nodded. "He hired a team to dive it before anyone else could get down there and claim the coins. The salvage crew sucked the sand off with an underwater vacuum cleaner called an air lift. They managed to get most of the deck and about a third of the bow cleared so they could go inside the ship. It took them several futile tries, but the *Victoria Jane* wouldn't give up her secrets easily."

"So they didn't find anything."

"Actually, they found plenty of things. The ship's bell, articles from the cabins, the dishes they used. These things are all in the museum now. But no coins. Pop obtained a sketch from the shipbuilding company and learned where Augustus's quarters were. It was tough figuring out the ship since part of it has been claimed by the ocean floor, but eventually he was able to find the cabin. He concentrated his efforts there, but died before he could finish."

"What happened that day?" Paul reached out and stroked her arm, letting her know he was there for support.

"Pop and Phil—did Jessie tell you about her dad's connection to mine?"

He nodded.

"They were in Augustus's cabin. They had tied off a nylon line so they could follow it out when they were ready. According to Phil, they were done, and he swam out of the cabin first when something fell off the ship that created a silt storm. Visibility zero." She held up her hand, creating an *O* with her fingers. "He continued on, thinking Pop was behind him. But when he surfaced, Pop didn't. Knowing Pop had little air left, he grabbed a couple of fresh tanks from the third man on the dive boat and told him to call the coast guard. By the time he got to Pop, it was too late. The line had broken and wrapped around Pop's legs. It looked like he'd tried to cut himself free, but he'd run out of air."

Her eyes grew even sadder, if that were possible. "I wish I'd been with him that day."

"What could you have done? You'd only have put yourself in danger."

She shrugged one shoulder. "At least he wouldn't have been alone."

They stood a few moments longer paying their silent respects. Finally she offered a brave smile. "Enough of that. I just wanted you to see why finding the coins is so important to me." She pushed away from the rail. "And now I'd like to show you something else."

Back in the captain's seat, Meranda urged Paul to hang on. She opened the throttle, and they bounced along at a thrilling clip. Paul gripped the railing near him. His fear barometer raised slightly, but nothing he couldn't handle. He concentrated on the exhilarating feel of the wind on his face, the g-force against his skin, and the amazing woman by his side.

After shooting across the surface for what must've been a couple dozen miles, Meranda slowed the boat to a putter. "Isn't the coast beautiful from out here?"

He tore his gaze from her and found the view breathtaking. Green hillsides huddled to the water's edge with occasional beaches in varying hues of dark and milk chocolate separating them. Large sea stacks rose from the water, rock formations that he'd seen shoreside but never from this angle. They drifted by Face Rock off Bandon Beach. It didn't look like a face on this side.

Within an hour, they'd made it all the way down to Gold Beach. Rogue Reef, a small island mound nearly three miles offshore, came into view.

Meranda cut the engine. "Listen. Do you hear it?"

Paul nodded. Two thousand harbor and steller seals barked a cacophonous concert as they sunbathed and played on the reef. He also smelled the banquet of rotting fish for two thousand guests. Thankfully, the seasick bands on his wrists were working to disable the trigger. "On shore this just looks like a big rock, but from here it looks alive." Hundreds of blubbery necks swayed and jerked, creating an eerie Medusa-like effect.

"We're about a quarter-mile from the reef." She opened a compartment under the console and brought out a set of binoculars. "Here, use these. This is a view you'd never get from shore, unless of course you've got some high-powered specs."

He placed the binoculars to his eyes and focused using the wheel on top. They immediately put him in the middle of the seal party. "Wow. I can see their faces."

She pointed to the north of the island where two seals were body surfing. "Now that looks like fun."

"Hey! Surf's up, dude! Wouldn't it be nice to be that carefree?" No grandmother looking over his shoulder, no catering dramas between mothers and daughters. Just a day of surfing. With Meranda. That would be like a three-course meal with crema catalana for dessert—very nice.

While they drifted, enjoying the remarkably serene chaos, Meranda stood. "I brought food. Are you hungry?"

Paul groaned. "You brought food? Did you cook it yourself?"

She cuffed his shoulder playfully. "I may not be a gourmet cook, but I know how to slap together a sandwich."

"Operative word: slap."

As she went below to the small galley, her voice drifted from the steps. "I think I'm very brave to fix you a meal. Especially after the fiasco at my mother's house the other night."

"What fiasco? You held your own with your sister's cooking class."

"Thanks. I just know that I'll never be as domestic as Mom or Rose." She brought out sandwich bags and cold sodas.

"And no one expects you to be. You have your own gifts."

She tilted her head. "Tell that to my mother."

As he opened the cellophane bag just enough so the ham and cheese sandwich peeked out, he continued. "I apologize for teasing you. Believe me, I'm appreciative that you thought of lunch. I'm starving." He took a bite, then pretended to choke and received another thump on his shoulder—an action negated by the smile on her face.

Although the nippy air tingled his skin, he found himself quite comfortable. It could have been the company. Or it could have been God smiling down on him. Whatever the case, he knew there was nowhere else in the world he'd rather be than floating in the Pacific Ocean with Meranda Drake.

While they ate, Meranda pulled a small envelope out of her bag. "I brought something to show you. Please be careful that the wind doesn't blow this away. It's the letter I told you about."

He opened it and saw it was from Augustus to his sister. He read aloud. " 'As you know, with the untimely demise of our brother, I became the keeper of The Inheritance.' " He stopped and raised his eyebrow. Seeing the word in a historic missive made it all the more real. He continued to read. " 'I brought it back from Hawaii with me and want you to know that it is safe, and I'm concretely sure it is where no one will find it.' " He whistled and handed it back to her. "This sure looks like The Inheritance is real and apparently somewhere close."

"Now I'm sure it's in the lighthouse. It would be a perfect place. Look at the word *concretely*. The lighthouse is a solid structure of brick and cement. I think that's a clue." She slipped the letter back in the bag. "You want to see what the coins look like?"

"Sure."

She unhooked a chain from around her neck and drew out a circular object from her shirt. When she placed it into his palm, he drew in a quick breath. "Wow."

"This pendant was my dad's, handed down from Augustus to Grandpa to Pop. We found pictures of the coins on the Internet and"—she pointed to the front of the pendant, a little larger than a minted half dollar—"this insignia is an exact replica of one side of the coins. Probably cast from the original. We think it had been made to tie the coins back to us if they were ever lost or stolen."

The image in the center was of two pillars with waves rising between them. On the back of the pendant he found an inscription, worn but readable. "JG.IG. What does it mean?"

"I don't know. The pendant wasn't mentioned in our research."

He shook his head. "I don't remember reading any of this in my history books."

"Which is why everyone thinks they're a myth. But my father found documentation. Captains' logs, letters to relatives. The coins do exist, and this pendant is proof." Her eyes flashed hot. "Pop was the last male Drake. I need to find them for him. Now do you see why your help is so important?"

"I do." He scratched his chin. "I can still only promise to keep my eyes open. Please understand that I can't risk angering a client by getting caught where I'm not supposed to be. They let us into their homes in full faith that we won't disturb anything. I have a code of honor that not only comes from my profession but also from my God."

Her mouth pulled to one side. "I understand."

But did she? And why did the passion in her eyes die when he mentioned God?

Chapter 7

As the lighthouse wedding drew near, Meranda decided she was asking too much of Paul. Maybe she should try to convince the owner to allow her in once more.

She drove up to the dreaded iron gate. If she ever got the land back, that would be the first thing to go. She left her truck and found an intercom box mounted to the fence made of solid black bars. Her trembling finger found the buzzer. The speaker grid on the intercom reminded her of an open O-shaped mouth—as in the word *no*.

"Hello. Who is it?" The male voice barked like a guard dog.

"Meranda Drake. May I speak to Judge Bernard?"

"This is he."

"I don't know if you remember me. I'm Gilbert Drake's daughter. Our ancestor built the lighthouse."

Silence. Had he hung up? Was he coming to the gate to talk to her in person? She continued on, hoping he could still hear her. "Since you're back in Crossroads Bay for your daughter's wedding, I was wondering if I might visit. I just want to see the lighthouse that my great-great-grandfather built."

The speaker crackled the judge's reply. "I'd like to indulge you, Miss Drake, but as you can imagine, there is a lot going on over here. Good day."

"Wait!" She gritted her teeth but tried to sound amiable. "I understand. I promise I won't bother anyone. You won't even know I'm there."

"Look. I'm sure you were able to play here with the previous owner's permission, but I don't have time for this. It's our lighthouse now, and we don't welcome strangers." A click ended the conversation.

Play? Is that what he thought she wanted to do? And no, she'd never been in the lighthouse because of jerks like this guy who wouldn't allow it. *Beelzebub himself could hardly desire better company.*

She stormed back to her truck and turned around. On the way to the main road, she turned right into Lighthouse View Park. Another car sat in the lot, and a family ate lunch at one of the two picnic tables. The viewing area, a knob of land above a cliff, beckoned her as it often did when she needed to feel close to the lighthouse. Pebbles on the short path crunched under her feet, and she stopped at the three-foot rock wall. A flat cement layer on top of the thick wall created a bench. She sat down, faced the lighthouse, and pulled her knees to her chin. The tall white structure stood proud on the point.

"I don't know what else to do, Pop. Other than scale the gate and trespass,

I think this door is closed to us."

A movement on the road caught her eye, and a black, decadent-looking sedan sped away from the property and past the park. The blue book value on the vehicle would probably feed a small country.

Was that the judge? Would there be someone else who might let her in? Meranda regarded the lighthouse and winked. There was more than one way to scale a fish.

She hustled back to her truck and rummaged around in her diver bag behind the seat. Among the accessories she used while diving, her hand grasped her underwater digital camera.

Back at the gate, she pressed the buzzer again. Perhaps she'd have better luck with the wife.

Thankfully, a female voice answered.

"Mrs. Bernard?"

"Mrs. Bernard passed away several years ago. I'm Glenys Bernard, one of the daughters. To whom am I speaking?"

"I'm sorry for your loss." If the judge had lost someone he loved, wouldn't he understand her situation? "This is. . .Judith Francis, reporter for the *Crossroads Bay Examiner*." Meranda had to squeeze the lie through her teeth. Pop had raised her to never deceive, but maybe just this once. . .

"How may I help you?"

Meranda quelled her excitement over the cordial greeting. "I understand your sister is getting married. May I interview her for our. . ." What was it called? "Oh, our society page." Smooth. Better keep the day job.

"Well. . .my sister isn't here yet. She and her fiancé will be arriving in a few days. But I'd be happy to grant an interview."

Meranda fought to maintain a professional tone. But she hopped on her toes as the anticipation gurgled inside her like a fountain. Hopefully there were no cameras.

Just as the gate began to slide open, the black sedan returned.

Blast! Had the judge forgotten something?

The car rolled to a stop behind her truck, and the driver's window lowered. A portly man with thinning gray-dappled hair stuck his head out the window. "May I help you?"

She cleared her throat. Time for Captain Ahab to confront Moby Dick. As she passed her truck's open driver door, she snatched the camera for effect and walked to the black car. "Judge Bernard?"

He nodded.

"I'm Judith Francis, reporter for the *Crossroads Bay Examiner*."

A pause. "Never heard of you."

"I've come to interview you on your daughter's wedding."

"No interviews." He backed up and positioned the car to go around Meranda's truck.

She couldn't let him go. "But I just spoke to your daughter about the wedding." The car stopped. "Alison?"

"No, sir. Your other daughter, Glenys. I told her I'd love to interview the family."

He sat back into his seat and rubbed his face. A frustrated father sigh escaped from his lips. "What did she tell you?"

"That she'd grant an interview. She seemed quite excited."

"She's an actress." The word sounded as if he'd said *cockroach*. "She was probably thrilled to get some publicity, even if it's through her sister."

"Since I'm here, may I talk to Glenys?"

The car started rolling again. "Glenys or Alison, it doesn't matter. We don't need reporters hanging around. Good day."

"Wait!" She was beginning to feel more like paparazzo than a reporter, of which she was neither.

He stopped again and thrust his head out the window. "You sound familiar. Are you that Drake person who was here not even an hour ago?"

Oh, why didn't she disguise her voice? The lie hovered on her lips, but try as she might, she could not deny she was a Drake.

He took her hesitancy as a confession. "I suggest you go home, Miss Drake, before I call the authorities." His head disappeared back into the car, and the window rose like a shield. After passing through the gate, it clanked shut, finalizing his answer.

Anger surged through her. She deserved to see that lighthouse.

⌘

The week of the lighthouse wedding, Paul had chosen staff from the restaurant to help. Now, the morning of, they bustled back and forth loading the two vans. He stood just outside the restaurant, the morning sun burning away the fog, as he checked off items.

"Pablo." His abuelita stood behind him, about elbow height.

"What do you think, Abuelita? This could be an important account. I hear the judge holds many social gatherings whenever he visits for the summer." And the judge had told him he, too, had been partial to Philippe, the deported French caterer. How great would it be to get all his disgruntled clients?

"It is good." Her wrinkled smile pleased Paul. "Would you like me to come?"

"No!" He squeezed his eyes shut and prayed for God to temper his tongue. "I mean, it's not necessary. You'd be on your feet all day."

"*Pshhh!*" Her way of saying tsk-tsk. "*¿De veras?*"

"Yes, really."

"Your abuelo and I built this restaurant."

"I know, Abuelita."

"From the ground up."

"I know, Abuelita."

"We bring our family's food to this country." She held out her palms, arthritic fingers like sticks trying to flex into sad little fists. "With these two hands."

"I know. And now it's time for you to rest and let Albert and me work for a change. Eh?" He kissed her forehead and pointed her toward the building. "I've got this under control."

"Pshhh!"

He shook his head at her retreating figure. The black and gray bun bobbed with the vitality of a teenager's ponytail.

Presently, he returned to the kitchen with his clipboard and checked off all the food they would be taking. Jessie had disappeared, and he needed her to supervise the equipment. Derrick, Jessie's boyfriend and a member of Paul's staff, walked into the kitchen for another load.

Paul pointed his pen at him. "Have you seen Jessie?"

"Uh, yeah. She's on her cell phone talking to Meranda, I think."

Meranda. Those two were getting thicker than his bouillabaisse. Were they up to something?

He hadn't initiated contact with Meranda since their day on the water. He sensed she wasn't a Christian, and he needed to pray about his growing affection for her. But she and Jessie had hit it off—their fathers and love of the ocean common denominators.

After the two vehicles were loaded, he gathered his team, including Jessie, for a pep talk.

"This is going to be a big party. Are you all up to the challenge?" They nodded. "Jessie, where is the sixth server?"

"She called in sick. I found a replacement and will pick her up on the way."

He'd have to be satisfied with that.

"You all know your stations, right?" he continued. "If you need anything, be sure to let either Jess or I know. And remember," he addressed Jessie more than the others, "the kitchen and back patio are the only places we're allowed to go. No wandering. We aren't guests."

He and three of the waitstaff piled into the larger van. He looked in the rear-view mirror as Jessie and Derrick pulled in line behind him. He lost them a few blocks later, and he assumed she had turned off to get the substitute server. Traffic thickened as they drove through town. Although tourist season didn't officially kick off for another month, the warm, dry weather this last week of April brought out the locals, who no doubt feared the sunshine wouldn't last.

The road he sought appeared, and he turned. Jessie hadn't caught up, but she knew the way. He meandered up the little paved road through grassy meadows until he came to a gate. He waited there for Jessie before alerting the house of their presence.

When she pulled up behind him, he got out and buzzed the intercom at the gate, then identified himself. The gate opened, and they both drove forward. The road broke into a *V*, the left heading toward the lighthouse and the right toward the dwelling. He took the right fork and after a quarter of a mile pulled toward the back of the house to unload the van.

Judge Bernard met him and started barking orders. This gave Paul no chance to breathe or meet the new member of the staff. He'd have to trust that Jessie oriented her.

Everyone bustled about, their white shirts and black slacks looking crisp and clean. He puffed with pride as he watched five people working like busy ants. He glanced around. Where was the sixth?

Finally, he spotted her behind the van gazing at the lighthouse. This wouldn't do. He walked up behind her and tapped her shoulder. She swung around and gasped. Gray eyes blinked at him from behind black-framed glasses, and she adjusted a dark wig.

"Meranda?" Why hadn't he recognized that leggy five-foot-nine stature? "What do you think you're doing?"

She peeked at him over the glasses but apparently had no excuse ready.

"Jessica!" His gaze searched the grounds for the commander of this operation.

Paul seized Meranda's elbow and led her to the patio. Her accomplice poked her head out the door. "Yes, boss?" When she saw Meranda standing next to him, she disappeared back into the kitchen.

Paul, not to be ignored, grabbed Meranda's hand and dragged her into the house. He prayed the whole way that the family was too busy to hear the conversation he was about to have.

"Jessie." He hissed at her back as she stood at the sink.

She turned innocent, round eyes on him. "Yes, boss?"

He thrust a pointing finger toward Meranda. "What is the meaning of this?"

Meranda stepped between them. "Don't blame Jessie. It was my idea."

⌘

Meranda stood her ground as Paul turned an angry glare on her. He had been her last hope to get into the lighthouse, and she wouldn't back down now.

"What part of 'no, it would hurt my business' did you not understand?"

"I'm sorry, Paul, but—"

He held up his hand. "Don't." He took a deep breath, no doubt calming himself to temper his words. "I should have someone drive you back, but they're all needed here." He looked at Jessie. "What happened to the sixth server?"

Jessie spoke without flinching. "She really did call in sick this morning." She glanced down at the ceramic floor tiles. "Meranda's protecting me. It was my idea to call her and give her the opportunity to come along. She didn't know I hadn't told you until we got here."

While this was the truth, Meranda's stomach felt queasy knowing she should have come clean with Paul. She dropped her gaze to his shoes. "I'm sorry."

"Are you?" He placed his hands on his hips. "You could have told me right away instead of sneaking around. I'm not happy, but I don't mind putting you to work."

She straightened and looked him in the eye. "I guess I handled the whole thing poorly. I'm sorry. It just felt great to get past the gate. I tried talking to the owner, but he flatly refused me after I told him who I was."

"He's a judge. He presided over some high-profile cases this last year. Of course he's cautious."

He was downright rude, actually. "I understand if you want to send me away. But if you let me stay, I'll pull my own weight. And you don't even have to pay me."

"I'm not condoning this at all, but. . .you can stay." Meranda's heart flipped in her chest. "However, you will not go into the lighthouse." He glowered at his assistant. "She's your responsibility. If she breaks, spills, or otherwise embarrasses this company, it's on your head."

"Yes, bo. . .sir."

"Thank you, Paul." Meranda vowed never to involve Paul against his wishes again. But she was grateful for his mercy.

Paul started to walk away, but threw one last parting shot. "And take off that ridiculous wig and glasses."

Her hands flew to the stiff wig that Jessie had lent her. "I can't. The judge will recognize me."

Paul pinched the bridge of his nose and left without another word.

∽∾

Less than an hour later, Paul looked out onto the lawn where his crew had dressed the tables with linens, sparkling china, and crystal goblets. Up the hill, two young men in suits, perhaps in their early twenties, directed elegantly dressed guests toward the 150 white chairs facing the ocean between the lighthouse and a pair of pillars.

He had a moment to breathe before the reception and a moment to say a brief prayer for Meranda. It wasn't fair that she had to resort to trickery just to see the lighthouse.

But Jessie! What had she been thinking? They were going to discuss this, and he had to think hard on whether he should fire her. He could only assume her fast friendship with Meranda had caused the lapse in judgment.

As the minister stepped into place and the music started, Paul positioned the waitstaff to be ready to serve. Judge Bernard had told him the ceremony would be brief. Meranda stood with Jessie. His neck tensed up, and he pulled his head to one side to crack it.

A flash near Meranda caught his eye. Fire leapt from her sleeve, and Jessie grabbed a towel to douse it. He ran over.

"What happened?" The smell of burning cotton invaded his nose.

"My fault," Meranda said. "I got too close to the Sterno can."

169

"Did you burn yourself?" His heart thumped hard in his chest at the thought she might be hurt. He inspected her arm where the flame had chewed a dark jagged hole into her white cuff.

"No, it just singed my blouse."

"And maybe some hair. Go to the kitchen and run some cool water on your hand."

"I'm fine."

He glared at her, and she obeyed. Where could he put her where she wouldn't hurt herself or others?

Finally, he stationed Meranda at the three-tiered wedding cake. "Don't cut any of it until the bride and groom get their first piece."

"I know how it works." She frowned, clearly miffed.

"Actually, don't touch anything. Derrick here will cut the cake. If you're good, I might let you serve the tables."

A swift breeze suddenly blew in from the ocean, catching a woman's hat in the back row of the ceremony. Paul ran to catch it as it tumbled on its wide brim like an errant tire on the highway. He snatched the sunny yellow hat before it found its way to the dirt road. With his heart palpitating from the exercise, he ran back to the grateful elderly woman.

He backed away from the guests and waited in the shadow of the lighthouse to catch his breath. He contemplated slipping inside, but after his lectures on the evils of sneaking around, he felt that might be inappropriate. Instead, he watched the end of the ceremony as his heart settled to a normal rhythm.

The minister and the couple stood between the two white pillars. He had thought the wedding planner had provided the seven-foot-tall posts—an intricate carving in the tops of each looked like castle rooks—and inwardly applauded her for finding some that were so realistic. But when the couple said "I do" and the wedding party moved, he could see the pillars were a permanent structure marking a path to the beach.

Wait a minute.

He hustled back to the patio, adrenaline now pumping his overtaxed heart. He told everyone to man their stations as the ceremony was over, and he grabbed Meranda's arm to pull her out of earshot from Derrick. "Do you have the necklace you showed me the other day?" His fingers formed a circle. "The big one." He wanted her to hurry before the guests started meandering toward the patio.

She pulled on the chain around her neck and drew it out.

"Look at the pendant and look at where the couple was standing."

Her gaze went from the pendant to the pillars and back. Her eyes widened as she focused on Paul. "It's them. The pillars on my pendant." She slapped her own forehead. "I thought they were just posts marking the stairs to the beach. Even in the pictures I've seen, they never seemed to resemble the pendant."

"From where I was standing directly behind the lighthouse, I saw this scene."

He tapped the insignia. "Are they there as a clue?"

All she seemed to be able to do was smile.

Paul wrapped his hand around hers as they clutched the necklace. "We have to get you into that lighthouse."

Chapter 8

Meranda would not have hurt Paul's business for the world. She'd been foolish to sneak onto the property.

But she was here now, and Paul finally seemed to have caught the vision.

Thankfully, they didn't have to scheme their way into the lighthouse. After the cutting of the cake, Judge Bernard made an announcement. "Anyone wishing to tour the lighthouse may do so now."

Paul's arm shot straight up. "Does that include the staff, sir?"

"Absolutely! The more the merrier I always say." Apparently social gatherings softened up the judge.

Meranda wanted to spring across the patio and lay a kiss on Paul. But she caught his eye and mouthed a thank-you instead. When he winked back, she felt as though her feet lifted off the ground. Jessie may have been her cohort in crime, but this man was stealthily stealing her heart.

Paul gathered his employees together. "Okay, it will be a little while yet. Once they get to the dessert, we won't be needed as heavily."

Jessie patted Meranda on the back and whispered, "We did it."

Yes, they did, but her conscience still niggled at her. Paul did it right and asked permission, although she had tried that and gotten shot down for her efforts. She heaved a huge sigh as she scraped dishes. However it happened, she was here now and about to touch a piece of her ancestors' history.

The house had belonged to Augustus, but the historic part of the structure was off limits. She glanced around the modern kitchen, probably still a part of the original house but updated considerably. Two doors led from the kitchen—one to the cellar and one to the rest of the house. If she wasn't afraid it would hurt Paul, she might have been tempted to take a peek—but no. The lighthouse was what drew her. The lighthouse held the secrets, she was sure of it. A beacon of light and hope. What other symbol would hold The Inheritance?

She silently saluted the still-sleeping beacon through the window. "We're close, Pop."

The father/daughter dance continued the celebration. Dessert appetizers had been laid out, and Paul shuffled across her line of sight, busy commanding his troops. The team cleaned up as pans of food emptied, and as each person finished his final chore, Paul sent him to the lighthouse. This was fair, but it also meant that Paul, Jessie, and Meranda had to wait.

Finally, as Meranda loaded the last of the dinner plates into the van, Paul touched her shoulder. "Let's go."

Jessie grinned behind him, and all three headed to the lighthouse. Meranda couldn't stop her feet from sprinting across the lawn.

Despite her excitement, she paused at the threshold, savoring every detail, allowing her senses to memorize the moment. The rough wooden door. The breeze as it whistled through the opening. In reverence she stepped through and into the small room built off the tower. Despite the cleanliness with not a cobweb in sight, there still lingered a musty smell. The smell of history. White walls inside the room mimicked the white stucco of the outside. The room couldn't have been bigger than a large camping tent and was very stark. No pictures. No curtains on the small leaded windows. But she didn't care. She walked where her great-great-grandfather had walked.

On the far side of the room, the entryway beckoned her. She stepped through and looked straight up. The cylinder was a geometric red-bricked marvel all the way up with a winding iron staircase creating visual art.

Paul and Jessie followed her up the steps as she ran her hands over the wall. "My great-great-grandfather touched every one of these bricks."

"Where do you suppose he would have hidden the coins?" Jessie's voice came from a few steps below.

Pulling herself from the awe of the moment, Meranda suddenly remembered why she was there. She glanced upward. "I don't know. Maybe up. The light draws people near. Perhaps it's a clue to draw us near the treasure."

They wound their way toward the top—Meranda, Paul, then Jessie. On the wall, small plaques had been mortared to the bricks. "Look! The pictures on these plaques are the same as on the coins."

"Pillars?"

"No, the other side. Where the crest is. See?" She pointed to one near his elbow. "A castle." Then one at her eye level. "A lion." She glanced up the tower and continued to climb. "They're staggered all the way up."

"No, Jessie." Paul admonished his assistant for something.

Meranda looked down through the waffle pattern of the metal steps but could only see a portion of Jessie's miffed expression.

"Well," her voice held an obstinate tone, "how will we know if we don't remove them?"

Meranda smiled at her enthusiasm. She had apparently tried to pry a plaque off the wall. Surely there must be a better option than demolishing the place.

Finally, the stairs reached a platform with a five-rung ladder leading through a square hole. Meranda began climbing, but her foot slipped on the second rung. She tumbled backward, and Paul caught her at the waist. His sudden, unexpected touch created the sensation of skittering minnows inside her stomach. She turned to look at his concerned face.

"You okay?"

"I'm fine, just a klutz." She continued to climb, torn between staying in the cradle of the gentle palms or continuing her quest. As her head cleared the hole, she encountered sneakered feet curtained by yellow gossamer silk. A feminine hand reached out and helped steady her as she climbed through the hole.

"Step to the side, please," the young woman said. Then she helped Paul and finally Jessie until they all stood on the platform with her, inches from the large lantern in the middle. Meranda reached out to touch it reverently. The heart of the lighthouse that symbolized family, heritage. . . Pop. Her chin trembled, but she willed it into submission.

"Please don't touch the light. I don't know why, but that's what I'm supposed to say." The woman offered an infectious smile. "My name is Glenys Bernard, sister and maid of honor to the bride." She curtsied, flouncing her frilly dress. The yellow did nothing for her coloring. Meranda could relate. They both had a red tinge to their hair, Glenys's lighter than Meranda's, but their skin tone was the same. *Blast.* She never would have had these thoughts if it weren't for her sister and mother.

They all introduced themselves. Meranda thought of sticking with her incognito name, Judith Francis, a blend of the first boat her ancestor commandeered and his name, but decided to honor Paul by using the honest approach. Thankfully, Glenys didn't seem to care that she had a dreaded Drake in her lighthouse.

"Nice shoes." Jessie pointed down at Glenys's feet.

"My dad asked me to play tour guide out here, so I kicked off the gold sandals and threw on the tennis shoes. These stairs are murder on heels." She cleared her throat, thrust her arm toward the light casing, and began to lecture. "This light is not the original light. That one resides in the Crossroads Bay Museum. A keeper who stayed in the house ran it. When automated lighthouses became popular, this light was installed. It has a sensor and turns on at dusk and off at dawn."

Jessie interrupted. "Do you know what the plaques represent?"

"Plaques?"

Jessie motioned down through the hole in the platform.

"Oh. The little pictures. I have no idea. They've always been there. My dad might know, though."

Meranda fingered her pendant from the chain. Should she share with this personable woman? Something about Glenys drew her in. Perhaps she could get to the judge through his daughter.

"I have this pendant that shows an image of the pillars on some of the plaques."

Glenys reached out and inspected the pendant. With wide eyes, she said, "This one looks like ours."

Meranda's neck tingled. "Two pendants?"

"Apparently, but ours has the image of the crest with the castles and the lions." She looked at the back. "And instead of this inscription, ours says IR1.345."

Meranda bounced on her toes, her excitement over this discovery about to ping her off the walls. Two pendants! That must mean something, but what? "How did you get it?"

"Believe it or not, it was hidden behind a brick in the kitchen, above the cellar door. When the kitchen was renovated a few years ago, the workers noticed the loose brick. Dad had the pendant appraised, but all they could tell us was that it was handmade. We keep it in a tin box on a shelf next to the cellar door."

"May I see it?"

"Sure, let's go back to the house." She motioned for them all to head back down the stairs.

On the way to the house, Jessie whispered to Meranda, "Do you think both pendants together would be considered valuable?"

"To me they would be, but if we found out they had been with the original coins, I wouldn't doubt some museum in England would pay a lot for Sir Francis Drake's property."

When they reached the house, Meranda hoped the judge would be distracted and not see her closely. But Glenys spotted him on the patio and asked him to join them in the kitchen when he got a chance.

They walked into the back of the house and into the kitchen, Meranda adjusting the wig to be sure she was still disguised. Glenys went to the cellar door and reached for a small box that sat with other knickknacks on a shelf to the left of the door. The lid had a tin top that showed a lighthouse in punch art. Meranda wondered how old the box was.

Glenys drew out a pendant with a leather cord and handed it to Meranda. "See? It's the same shape and style, but has a crest of lions and castles."

"This is the other side of the coins." Excitement surged through Meranda.

"Coins?" Glenys reached for the pendant and put it back in the box.

Meranda told her all she knew about The Inheritance.

"And you think they might be here somewhere?"

Meranda nodded. "More than likely in the lighthouse."

"Awesome!" Glenys's eyes sparkled like a child's on Christmas morning. "Oh, Daddy. . ."

Judge Bernard entered the room.

Meranda sidled behind Paul, using him as a shield. He shot a concerned glance over his shoulder, letting her know he understood her reticence.

Glenys hopped on her toes. "Daddy, I've just heard the coolest thing about the history of this place. But first, do you know anything about the plaques on the lighthouse walls?"

"I don't know." He scratched his nose. "A lot about this place is a mystery. The previous owner only bought it for an investment and didn't care about the history."

"And what about you?" Meranda clapped her hand over her loose lips, but too late. Her quick temper had just sunk her own ship, and now the judge glowered at her.

Chapter 9

"Excuse me?"

Meranda cleared her throat under his scrutiny. "I mean, the public hasn't been allowed in here for a long time. Don't you think it would be good for the community to be able to tour such an important artifact?"

"Oh, and Daddy, Meranda has a pendant just like ours." Glenys, oblivious to the tension that had just entered the room like a hungry shark, had unknowingly sliced and diced Meranda into a hearty meal for the judge.

He squinted at her. "You're that Drake woman." Meranda stood tall and removed the wig. But even through her bravado, her stomach held a tempest of emotion as she felt her dream capsizing.

The judge pointed at her. "Stay right there." He looked at Paul. "You, too." Jessie had disappeared. He stepped out a moment, leaving Meranda wondering what was in store for her. When he returned, he snapped at her. "I just called the police. I'm having you arrested for trespassing."

Paul stepped in front of her and confronted the judge. "Please, sir. Let me take the blame. She's part of my staff."

"Then I'll have you both hauled off."

Before long, Meranda and Paul were leaving in the backseat of a squad car, blinking their surprise at each other.

Paul stared out the window. Past him Meranda could see Jessie and the crew piling into the vans so they could follow them out.

Meranda wanted to read his face, but he continued to look out the window, even though it was now too dark to see anything. "I'm so sorry, Paul."

He turned pained eyes to her. "If my grandmother hears of this, all my hard work will be ruined."

She couldn't say it enough. "I'm sorry—"

"No." His voice still held venom. "I'm sorry for allowing you to do something that I knew was wrong. I compromised my integrity."

After a long silence, she spoke again, "You can't imagine how good it felt to finally stand in that lighthouse, to touch my family's history."

He shifted to further shut her out. "I'm happy for you then."

"I know I shouldn't have involved you, but I was blinded by the importance."

"And what is the importance?" He whipped his head around and glared at her. "Why are these coins worth losing your father's life and my career?"

"Because. . .I think my family is in financial trouble."

Her family needs the money? By the looks of her mother's house, that surprised Paul.

"How do you know?"

"Things are missing from the house. Artwork, antiques, jewelry, all gone with no explanation. Some of it was Pop's. It would stand to reason she'd get rid of his things. But the others. . ."

Her downturned mouth implied more to the story. Arguing in the home. Parents divorced. Daughters put in the middle.

"She loved my dad once."

Okay, Meranda needed to talk, and he was a captive listener. Might as well make the best of the situation. "Tell me about your dad."

The corners of her mouth curved upward into a tiny grin. "Believe it or not, Pop was a solid businessman. After he met my mom, her father, who was president at Crossroads Bank, offered him a job. Pop worked his way up to commercial loans and became the vice president."

"Hey, he probably helped my grandfather update the kitchen at our restaurant."

"I'm sure." She regarded her shoes. "He did very well. Moved us into the home you saw. But then the treasure called to him. He'd always been fascinated with the story of the coins and had contacted the maritime museum just for fun." Her grin turned into a full-blown smile. "He and I would go sailing, and he'd regale me with stories of the coins and the pirates that wanted them. All made up, of course. Pop was a dreamer."

"Sounds like he should have been a writer instead of a loan officer."

She tilted her head. "Interesting that you should say that. After he quit his job at the bank, he wrote down all of his pirate stories. He never did anything with them, but I've saved every one in notebooks."

"Why would he quit such a lucrative job?"

"So he could sail full-time. That's when he bought the charter boat."

"And that's when he left your mom?"

"Well, that's when she kicked him out."

It was becoming clearer now. The dreamer married the socialite who expected him to maintain her lifestyle.

"So, how did your dad get so caught up in the coins?"

Paul suddenly realized they had an audience. The patrolman in the front had become quiet. "We are allowed to talk to each other, right?"

He looked at them in the rearview mirror. "Please, go ahead. This is more entertaining than my dispatch radio."

Meranda frowned but continued. "Pop had known about the coins as a child, but it wasn't until the earthquake that he became obsessed. Remember, I told you the shipwreck was unearthed then. He knew the history behind the shipwreck and that Augustus built the lighthouse, but beyond that we just speculated. We contacted the Hawaiian Historical Society and learned through a journal that the last person known to have had the coins was Augustus's father, who had died before Augustus sailed to the mainland. So, it stood to reason that Augustus's older brother would have the coins. However, according to the museum records of Augustus's family tree, we knew his brother had died. We assumed Augustus ended up with the coins somehow, but it wasn't until I received the letter from the maritime museum that confirmed they had indeed been passed to him."

"Wow. You've done a lot of research to get to this point, haven't you?"

She nodded, suddenly looking very weary even while talking about her passion. "So, if the coins aren't in the lighthouse, does that take you back to the shipwreck?"

"I don't know." She closed her eyes.

They pulled into the station parking lot and were ushered inside. A deputy met them and informed the officer who had brought them in to take off their handcuffs. To Paul and Meranda he said, "You're both free to go."

Paul's heart stopped. Had his grandmother found out and put up bail? Would that even happen so soon? He knew nothing about being arrested.

The young deputy pulled them aside. "I'm sorry, folks. Seems Judge Bernard just wanted to put a scare into you."

Meranda's eyes flashed hot. "False arrest? Can he do that?"

He raised his palm. "According to the judge, he had told you to stay off his property. He was well within his rights to remove you. But he just called to drop the charges and said he hoped the squad car ride had been enough to let you know he was serious." He rubbed the back of his neck. "And frankly, I'm okay with it because it means less paperwork."

"I can't believe this! Seriously?" Meranda stomped her foot and looked ready to punch someone.

"Don't argue with the man," Paul whispered. "We're about to be set free."

She continued to fume as he steered her to a set of black plastic chairs along a far wall. He pulled out his cell phone and called Jessie, asking her to come pick them up. Jessie promised to be there in ten minutes.

When they walked out of the building and stepped into the night air, Paul took a deep breath.

Freedom. And Abuelita was none the wiser.

Chapter 10

P ablo, what is this?"

Abuelita waved the morning newspaper under his nose as he chopped onions in the restaurant kitchen. The heading of an article about the lighthouse wedding caused his eyes to sting—or was that the sudden pungency of his onion-saturated hands? He stabbed the knife into the cutting board, snatched the paper out of her fingers, and began reading.

BERNARD WEDDING MARRED BY CRASHER

Despite Judge Gordon Bernard's attempt to hold a private wedding, a party crasher still managed to get through his defenses. Soon after his daughter Alison Theresa Bernard said "I do" to Daniel Domingo Lopez this last Saturday, the judge discovered an uninvited guest. Meranda Drake, who owns a charter boat business out of the Crossroads Bay marina, had smuggled herself into the wedding using Tapas Mediterranean Delights Catering where she posed as an employee. Paul Godfrey, the owner of the catering company, admitted to helping the woman. He was also arrested, but charges for both people were later dropped.

Paul set the paper down, squeezed his eyes shut, and swallowed the dread creeping up his throat. When he opened them again, Abuelita stood there with her arms folded. "You did not tell me."

He grabbed the knife and began mincing the onion into tinier pieces than he had intended as he took his frustration out on the unsuspecting root. "It's no big deal. Meranda wanted to see the lighthouse, and she was willing to work for us to do that." He hoped his excuse didn't sound as lame as he knew it to be.

"The company's name is mentioned." She grabbed the paper and shook it in her tiny fist.

"But the article clears us."

"It is bad publicity." She smacked the paper against her hand. "People will remember that you were blamed. They won't remember that the charges were dropped." She pushed her lower lip into her upper. Paul felt a grin tug at his cheek despite the scolding and tried to remain respectful, even though Abuelita looked like a miniature bulldog.

"Who is Meranda?"

Paul cocked his head back and let out a groan. He didn't want to have to explain Meranda when he didn't understand her himself. "You remember. She's the one who recommended us for her sister's wedding. The Drakes?"

A smile played on her face, and he knew she was counting the dollar signs that account would pull in. "Ah. They ordered lots of food."

"Right. Lots of food, tons of it."

Her eyes suddenly twinkled. "Oh! Pablo, I get it." She walked out of the kitchen and into the empty dining room.

Paul followed. He should leave this one alone. Abuelita was happy, even though he had no idea why. "What? What do you get?"

"You have feelings for her, sí?" She waved her twiglike finger and chortled. "Your abuelo and I started out much the same."

"No, it's not like that. . . ." Well, okay, it was. But that's not why Meranda was at the lighthouse. Then again, maybe it was better Abuelita thought that.

She pivoted and faced him. "Oh. She has not returned your heart."

"No—I mean—"

"I will work on that." With a curt nod, she headed toward the front door and unlocked it for the lunch crowd.

Paul stood in the middle of the dining room, horror replacing the dread he'd felt earlier. Abuelita would stop at nothing to play matchmaker.

<hr>

Meranda arrived at her boat on Tuesday morning dressed in old jeans and a T-shirt. She had no charters that day, so she decided to do some painting on the *Golden Hind*. Her police scare three days prior had put her in the mood to make things new.

She thought about Paul, how he lived by honesty. Yet whenever she tried it, she got no reward. Only grief. Paul was a Christian, but so what?

When Pop died, God didn't care about her or her family. He took away a good man, leaving his loved ones to fend for themselves.

Her mind continued to ramble as she went back to the parking lot for supplies. It took her a couple of trips to lug paint, pans, brushes, and tarps to the boat from her truck. On the final trip, she happened to glance toward the *Romanda Jule*.

What? She dropped the paint trays with a clatter. Running to the slip—the empty slip—she looked around frantically for the boat. Had she not tied it after taking Paul out the other day? No, she remembered showing him how they did it.

No doubt about it. Someone had stolen her boat. Her stomach churned. How could she lose one more representation of Pop?

She pulled out her cell phone and called the coast guard. After stammering through the explanation, a bored voice told her someone would be arriving to file a report.

Her legs suddenly felt like limp seaweed. She lowered herself to the dock, sitting cross-legged with her head in her hands.

I'm sorry, Pop. I can't seem to do anything right. I've abandoned Mom to the point where she won't confide in me. I've lied for the sake of the coins. I've been hauled to jail. She wiped the tears off her cheeks. *I need you.*

Her cell phone rang. It was a woman from the sheriff's department.

"Miss Drake, I did a check on your boat, and it seems to have been repossessed."

Meranda's stomach no longer merely churned. It felt like an entire sea gale was crashing inside. "Excuse me? How can that be possible? My father bought this boat for my sisters and me." She had no idea there were still payments on it.

"I'm sorry." The woman's steady voice calmed her somewhat. "I suggest you contact your bank if you feel there's been an error. Is there anything else I can do for you?"

Meranda thought of Paul. What would he do? "Pray." She snorted the word, not really meaning to.

"I can certainly do that for you, as soon as we hang up."

A few minutes later Meranda held her phone and stared at it. Would that woman really pray for her? Sure sounded like she would.

Suddenly buoyed by the kindness of this stranger, she called the bank and made an appointment with the loan officer for later that morning.

After stowing away her paint and supplies, she went back home to change. On the way, she called Rose and apprised her of the situation.

"Oh, Mer, I'm so sorry."

"I wonder if Mom is paying any bills at all. Is anything else missing that she could have sold?"

"Not that I've found, but perhaps the bill paying would be next. You look into this, and I'll investigate here at home."

"Thanks, Ro. I'm glad we have each other."

"Always."

At home Meranda threw on a short-sleeved tailored shirt and tan slacks. May had arrived and with it warmer temperatures.

Once she walked into the bank, she knew exactly where to go. She passed the picture of her grandfather Muldoon, his stern eyes so like her mother's. Patrick Cooper stood and greeted her as she entered his office. She hadn't seen him in more than a year, and his dark hair seemed more speckled with gray.

"How are you doing, Meranda?" His honest blue eyes crinkled at the corners. She always liked Pat and his humble attitude.

"I'm not doing so well, Pat. My boat is gone."

"Well, let's see what happened." He started clicking keys on his computer. "Thirteen months ago there were several missed payments."

"Right after Pop died."

"Yes." The small word held a ton of compassion. "Looks like we sent out reminders, set up a partial payment plan. . ." He continued to search the screen. "Those were only sent for three months, then they stopped." He leaned back in his chair. "There were only six months of payments left."

She swallowed hard as she worked the math in her head.

"Meranda." He folded his hands on his desk. "I knew your father and respected him while he worked here. I wouldn't tell just any customer this, but I think you deserve to know."

Was that a disclaimer on his lips?

"He didn't manage his money very well. He took out several loans to fund his diving expeditions."

"How could he have worked at this bank and not managed his own money?"

"It happens more often than you realize. I fear that he overextended."

"Is that why my mother is selling her valuables? What happened to the insurance money?"

"It's possible that all went to pay for the expeditions, which would leave your family with only your incomes to stay afloat."

"My mother doesn't work outside the home. And Julianne still has student loans. Rose doesn't have a job, either." Meranda closed her eyes. She seemed to be the only one of the four with a career. "It's up to me to keep the house from meeting the same fate as my boat."

"Or"—Pat raised his brows, reminding her of Pop when he reprimanded his girls—"you could tell your mother and sisters that if they want to keep their home, they're going to have to get their own jobs. It won't hurt them to be responsible." Only Pat could get away with this kind of talk. "I'm sure your business does very well, but I doubt it's enough to support your family to the point of keeping them in their house."

She drew in a big breath. He was right. She couldn't shoulder this responsibility alone. But one thing she could do. "I want my boat back. How much is owed?"

Meranda paid the rest of the balance, which made a dent in her savings account, but once the title was switched over, the boat would be solely hers. Pat told her where to pick it up.

More than ever she needed to find those coins. Even though they had been in the family for generations, when it came to her own little family unit, she would sell the coins in a heartbeat to protect those she loved.

As she drove away from the bank, she realized how much she needed Paul's paella and perhaps his gentle smile. When she arrived at Tapas, the place buzzed with activity as patrons flocked for the noon meal.

An elderly Spanish woman greeted her. "How many?"

Meranda held up one finger. "Just me, unless Paul is here and can join me."

"He is here." The woman puckered her face. "But he is much too busy to take his lunch."

Meranda consulted her watch. She was starving, but despite her craving, she realized she was there to see Paul. "Perhaps I should come back another time."

A slow smile eased onto the old woman's face. "Ah. You are Meranda."

"Yes, I am." Heat flushed Meranda's cheeks. Had Paul been talking about her? Whatever could he have said?

"Oh, come with me then." The woman clapped her hands in two short bursts, and someone else took her place. "I have just the table for you."

She led her to a cozy alcove in the back where the lighting was dim. "Allow me." A match appeared in her hand, and a flame ignited from a candle resting in a red globe. "Ah, sí. I will go get Pablo."

How odd. A moment ago she had pictured Paul chained to the stove. Now this octogenarian, obviously his grandmother, seemed capable of freeing him.

He burst through a swinging door as if pushed, a bewildered look on his face. The sleeves of his white tailored shirt were rolled to his forearms, revealing brown skin. Then he saw her. His shy grin and the way he slipped his hands into his pockets made him look like a teenager on his first date.

Meranda felt a pleasant sensation in her stomach, and it wasn't from the anticipation of food. She felt like his prom date, for goodness' sake.

He slipped into the horseshoe-shaped booth but kept a respectable distance between them.

"Hi."

"Hi."

Scintillating conversation. But the way the candlelight warmed his mahogany-colored eyes—eyes that gazed at her appreciatively—it didn't matter if they used one-word sentences for a half hour. She realized at that moment that she liked this man. Really liked him.

"So, you came to eat by candlelight?" Both eyebrows rose as he swept his hand toward the globe.

"Not my idea." Meranda began playing with a curl that tickled the side of her face. "You have a very forceful hostess. She insisted I sit here."

His gaze traveled up and over the walls that cupped the table. "That was my grandmother. This is where she seats special guests."

"Am I special?"

"I believe you are."

Meranda grabbed her cloth napkin and started fanning herself.

"So, what can I do for you?" His lips curved in a pleasant smile.

"Um. . ." A waitress brought glasses of water, and Meranda gulped down a quarter of hers. Why was she acting this way? The candlelight? The romantic Spanish music—wasn't it fiesta-style when she first walked in? The gorgeous man across from her who could cook—which was every woman's dream? "Food!"

He arched his brow.

"I mean, of course, I'm here for food. But I don't have a menu."

The corners of his eyes crinkled. "Let me choose for you. It will only take a few minutes, and I'll prepare it with my own hands."

Yep. She was feeling better already.

He slipped back into the kitchen, and she leaned her cheek on her hand as the morning's disappointment ebbed away. She needed this oasis in the midst of her crazy life.

Her cell phone chirped with a text message. Rose managed to get across her angst with only the letters on her phone. *Mom is driving me crazy!*

Blast. Rose had impeccable timing. Meranda replied with, *I'll call you later. Can't talk now.* When Rose learned Meranda was about to have lunch with the attractive chef, the one she'd already picked out for Meranda, she'd understand.

Soon enough Paul returned, both arms laden with plates. It was one thing for a guy to cook for you, but quite another for him to serve you. Meranda fanned herself again.

She motioned toward the kitchen. "Who's minding the restaurant?"

"Albert. And my grandmother."

"She gets around, doesn't she?"

He grabbed his napkin and flicked it like a whip. "You have no idea."

Before they began eating, he reached for her hand. Her heart leaped in her chest, causing happy ripples. But he said, "Do you mind if we pray?"

Pray? She would have pulled back if his touch hadn't sent such enjoyable tingles up her arm. Now she didn't know how she should feel.

⟲⟳

". . .bless this food to nourish our bodies. In Jesus' name, amen." Paul looked up from the prayer, still not believing that this woman was in his restaurant and apparently enjoying his company. But she pulled her hand away quickly and avoided his eyes. Had he been too forward? With the commanding Captain Meranda Drake? Surely not.

To cover the awkward silence, Paul asked if she had her necklace with her. She removed it from her neck, and he flipped it over in his fingers, inspecting the engraving on the back. "JG.IG. Two initials?"

"That's what I thought at first, but Judge Bernard's pendant is different."

Paul pulled a small spiral notebook from his breast pocket and consulted it. "IR1.345. They can't be dates."

"Unless they're encrypted. But why? If you're going to create an artifact, why not put the date on there for generations later to know exactly when it was made?"

"And they can't be initials like you had thought because of the three-digit number on the judge's pendant." She rested her elbow on the table and placed her chin on her fist. "Unless mine holds the initials and his holds the date. But still, his doesn't look like a date."

Paul rubbed his thumb over the letters. "These weren't etched by a professional."

He handed the pendant back to her. "When Glenys revealed she had a second pendant, you seemed excited to hear that news. I would think you'd be disappointed you didn't have the only one of its kind."

She placed her elbow on the table and leaned forward. "Think about it. Two pendants. That tells me my shipwrecked ancestor had one that he wore and kept the other near the coins. Of course, that's just a guess."

"Ah." Paul nodded. "So two pendants was another clue."

"Exactly."

"What makes you think they're in the lighthouse and not in the judge's home?"

"Because the plaques are in the lighthouse."

"But what about the pendant behind the brick in the kitchen of the main house?"

"Good point. Either could be right."

"I've been praying that you'll get your answers soon."

She pursed her lips and began stabbing the chicken on her plate. Not to pick it up, but to torture it.

"That is okay, isn't it?" Hope suddenly fled out the door that this woman would at least be open to the gospel.

"Do what you want, but I'm wondering why God would care."

He reached out to touch her forearm. "God cares."

Paul vowed to lead her on the faith journey just as Ruthanne, his alpaca-loving friend, had done for him.

Chapter 11

Paul pushed his plate away knowing the food would settle like rocks in his stomach. "Why would you think God wouldn't care?"

"He didn't do much for my dad, did He?" Vehemence sparked from her words.

Paul winced as if the verbal blow had been meant for him personally. "I'm sorry about your father." What could he say to this hurting soul? He prayed for wisdom. "I've lost people close to me, too. After my mom died, anger wanted to eat me up from the inside out. And it probably would have if I hadn't trusted that God knew what He was doing."

He gauged whether he should go on, not wanting to push her further away from God. Even though she remained silent, he sensed the Lord pressing him to continue. "May I share a verse from the Bible that has held me together in my darkest times?" She tipped her head, and he went on. " 'I have been crucified with Christ and I no longer live, but Christ lives in me. The life I live in the body, I live by faith in the Son of God, who loved me and gave himself for me.' This verse from Galatians 2:20 tells me that no matter what my eyes see, I trust that God has my best interests at heart."

"It's a choice for you, then."

"Yes. Because I'm still in this old, sinful body." He pinched the skin on his shoulders. "I can so easily get caught up in the what-ifs of life. What if I could have made my mother's last days better for her? What if I hadn't run out on my grandmother to live with my aunt and uncle? What if I hadn't run back home after someone I thought I loved fell for someone else?" He smiled and reached for her hand again. "About that last one, perhaps it was God's will so we could meet." And so he could share his faith with her.

The brooding frown on her brow released its hold, and a small grin played on her face. "Perhaps you should hold that thought until you've gotten to know me better."

"Perhaps I won't be disappointed."

Continuing to hold onto his hand as if it were a lifeline, she closed her eyes and leaned her temple onto the knuckles of her other hand. He didn't know if she was praying or just trying to gain control.

Her cell phone rang. *Arrgh. . .Arrgh. . .*A happy pirate tone that contrasted with their conversation. "That's probably my sister." She released his hand—dare he think reluctantly?—and frowned at the ID. "No, maybe it's a charter client."

She answered, and her eyes registered surprise. "Oh hi, Glenys. . . . What?

Certainly you don't think I took it." Meranda wrapped her hand around the mouthpiece and whispered to Paul. "The other pendant is gone."

Paul's stomach dipped, but then he realized they couldn't blame them since they had an alibi involving handcuffs and a patrol car.

Meranda relaxed as she spoke to Glenys. Apparently she'd only called to inform her of the theft.

After Meranda hung up, she said, "Glenys wants to help look for the coins. She suggested meeting at the museum at two o'clock to inspect the original lighthouse lamp. Her dad is still angry with me, though, and would rather I stay away from the lighthouse."

"Does he understand that we couldn't have taken the other pendant?"

"Yes. There were still people milling about, but Glenys said she can't imagine any of them would have wanted it. There will be an investigation, but we're in the clear. As far as visiting the lighthouse again, she said she's working on him. I think I've made a friend."

"She seems like a good person and is probably sorry you got into so much trouble."

"Us." She pointed between her and him.

"True."

"I'd love to tag along to the museum if you don't mind. I don't have a catering job, and things are dead around here about that time of day."

Her slow smile made his heart beat faster. "I'd like to go to the library after lunch, but I'll come back here afterward to pick you up."

He could have sat there with her forever, but knew the little Spanish cupid in the kitchen would come after him if they became swamped. He stood and headed for the kitchen but turned back before pushing the kitchen door. "Two o'clock."

"I'll be here."

In the kitchen, Abuelita stood at the range, stirring the stew. "How did it go, Pablo?"

He grabbed his apron from the hook on the wall and tied the strings in back. "How did what go?" He knew what she was asking. Seriously. Candlelight? Soft music? The *love* alcove?

"Miss Drake. She return your affection now, sí?"

He kissed his abuelita's wiry hair. "It's in God's hands."

"Then I pray." With a satisfied smile on her face, she handed him the spoon and trotted out to the dining room.

He would pray also, that Meranda would soon choose the right path toward God.

⬡

Meranda finished her lunch and headed to the library just around the block. She decided to walk since the day had turned out beautiful. Spring azaleas and rhododendrons provided color in large cement pots along the sidewalk provided by the town.

While walking, she called her sister back. "What's up, sis?"

"Your mother has gone over the top." Rose's voice held all the frustration that Meranda felt.

"*My* mother? Have you disowned her now?" *Join the club.*

"She's taken over the wedding. Things have gotten out of control."

Meranda gripped the phone. "Is she continuing to pour money into this?"

"Yes. I no longer have a soloist. I have a choral ensemble." Disgust colored her sister's voice.

Would it be too much to ask that she'd found a volunteer group from her social status church? "What is she paying them?"

"She won't tell me, but it's a group one of her friends recommended. They tour the nation and just happened to be in town at that time."

Big bucks. "Rose, you've got to curtail her spending. She can't afford it."

"I know. But how can I stop her? She doesn't listen to a thing I say." A slight pause. "What am I going to do?"

Get a backbone and say no hovered on her lips, but she decided to temper her words. "Listen, only you can stop this madness. Be firm with her. You never wanted your wedding to be the event of the season."

"No, and it doesn't help that Mrs. St. James is helping to fuel the fire. My future mother-in-law seems to think that just because our name is on several businesses in town that we are higher on the social scale."

"Yeah, thanks to the founding Drake, Mom has had her head in the clouds for too long." She walked through the library, perusing the reference section. "What does Steven think of all this?"

"He's so clueless. 'Whatever you want, Mother.' I don't think he can stand up to his mom any more than I can to mine."

"Stay strong, Ro. This isn't her wedding, it's yours."

"Thanks. I just need to hear that once in a while."

Meranda hung up, furious with her mother. Would this be one of those times to *choose* to trust God? It made more sense to believe if man messes something up, man must fix it. But there was no fixing her mother. She was a barge with a full hull of ideas that didn't make a lick of sense to anyone else. There was no stopping her.

She decided to put God to the test. *Paul says I must choose to trust You.* She thrust her gaze heavenward. *How about it, God? Can You stop her from destroying herself and dragging us along with her?*

While she killed time at the library, she read about lighthouses and their various types of lamps. She didn't hold much hope that the coins would be in the old Crossroads Bay lantern. But, since Glenys suggested it, perhaps there would be more hope of Meranda visiting the lighthouse in the future.

Just before two o'clock, she dumped four books into her truck and headed back to the restaurant.

Paul's grandmother was now bussing tables. Was there nothing this woman couldn't do? By the looks of the dining room, they'd had quite a midday crowd.

"Abuelita." Paul walked out of the kitchen rolling down his shirtsleeves. "You don't have to do that."

When he spotted Meranda and smiled, warmth cascaded over her like the sun coming out on a drizzly day.

"I must keep busy, sí?" The mini senior citizen continued loading a square plastic container with dirty dishes and silverware. Fortunately it was sitting on a rolling cart, so she didn't have to lug it back to the kitchen.

He kissed her on top of her head. "I'll be back in time for the dinner rush."

She placed a tiny fist on her hip. With the corners of her lips drawn down and a scowl on her face, she asked, "Where are you going?"

He motioned toward Meranda. His grandmother shaded her eyes and peered at her. "Oh! Meranda? Come here, you are standing with the sun glaring behind you. I did not see you."

Meranda moved into the dining room. Only four tables were occupied now. With a firm grip, the woman grabbed Meranda's upper arm and peered up at her with snapping gray brown eyes. "What do you think of my Pablo?"

"Abuelita!" Paul's face went crimson. Even though Meranda was just as embarrassed by the question, his shocked look entertained her.

She patted the elderly hand on her arm. "I think he must be a wonderful grandson, and he obviously loves you very much."

The older woman looked at Paul. "I like her."

Paul finally recovered and gently freed Meranda from his grandmother's grip. "I'm glad she has your stamp of approval." He glanced at Meranda. "You two haven't been properly introduced. Meranda Drake, this is my grandmother, Carmen Espinoza."

She held out her hand and received a warm, but firm, handshake.

"You may call me Abuelita."

⚬⚬⚬

As they walked out a moment later, Paul shook his head. "Wow. I've never seen that happen before." He looked back at the door, befuddled at his ever-changing abuelita.

"What?"

"She has never told someone she's just met to address her so informally."

"Then I'm flattered."

"You should be, and maybe a little frightened. The next time you come to eat, she may put you to work."

Meranda laughed. "That would be fine with me."

That would be fine with him, too.

They decided to go in one car, his, and they drove across town to the museum. When they got there, Glenys was waiting outside the brick building.

Meranda marched in, leading the other two. "I've been here countless times with my father." As if to demonstrate, she nodded at a fortyish security guard sitting behind a counter. "Hi, Norm."

He saluted two-finger style from his eyebrow.

They entered the room that housed the light, along with other local artifacts, and gathered around the heavy lamp displayed on the floor. Paul felt dwarfed next to it. The polished brass and crystal lenses made this a true testament to man's achievements.

Glenys took her tour-guide stance and motioned toward the monstrosity. "This lamp used a five-wick kerosene burner and a fixed Fresnel lens, meaning it didn't move. Note the narrow panes of glass, creating the prism look."

Brass piping separated the panes of glass, and the whole assembly resembled a huge Christmas ornament. Paul remembered seeing something similar in a mini-version on Abuelita's tree every year.

Glenys continued. "The panes redirected the light so it could be seen farther, squeezing it, if you will, into beams that pierced the darkness. It was later replaced with a rotating lens that ran off of electricity, the one that's in the lighthouse now. A few years after that it went automatic, so a keeper was no longer needed."

Meranda gazed at Glenys. "I'm beginning to think you love the lighthouse as much as I do."

"When my dad bought it, I was eleven. I always loved coming here in the summers and playing." She regarded Meranda with a serious face. "I'm here often to retreat from my crazy life in Hollywood. My mom grounded us in good old-fashioned Christian values. I feel God's presence at the lighthouse every time I see the ocean crash over the rocks or watch a storm come in."

Now Paul definitely approved of this friendship. He watched Meranda carefully for her reaction, but her face held no animosity.

"As far as I'm concerned," Glenys continued, "you can visit me anytime."

Meranda pulled her into a hug. "Thank you."

Paul felt a glow in his heart as he watched this friendship form. He began pacing around the lamp. Meranda took over the tour guide role and led them to a wall, pointing to a print of a painted portrait. "This is Augustus Drake."

Paul noted the family resemblance despite the trim white beard on the mature face. Piercing eyes, gray, and full of adventure. This man knew how to live.

Meranda moved to another print, this one of a white ship with four masts. Multiple sails billowed from each mast. "This is the *Victoria Jane,* the ship that now lies off our coast. This clipper belonged to a fleet of sugar ships built for the sugar trade in Hawaii. Augustus had decided to travel to Hawaii to be with his family when his brother died." She moved down the wall to show them a series of printed-out facts under artist renderings of the ship in the storm.

"On the way back," Meranda summed up, "the ship encountered a storm and began taking on water. They tried to limp back here, but she didn't have it in her. After the shipwreck, Augustus and a few of the crew made it to shore. He decided to build the lighthouse in memory of the lives that were lost." That was the end of the facts, but Meranda continued. "Augustus never sold it, but when he died, the family must have decided not to keep it."

"That's why the coins have to be there." Paul drew his gaze from the articles and back to the lamp. "Or here." He paced around the lamp again, peering at it as though it were a huge diamond needing an appraisal.

Meranda joined him as he circled. "The only relatives Augustus had here were a wife and a teenage boy. His sister lived in San Francisco. I don't have any documentation of her trying to find the coins after Augustus's death." She stopped circling and frowned. "I don't think there's room for coins here." Disappointment colored her tone, but she continued to prowl around the object.

"The Drake family sold the property in the 1940s," Glenys continued the lineage.

"To the one who put the gate up," Meranda spoke with vehemence as she continued to pace the lamp.

Glenys nodded. "Instead of tearing it down, my dad mechanized it." She cast an apologetic glance to Meranda. "The guy we bought the property from sixteen years ago was never there. He just wanted it for an investment. We had a lot of fixing up to do, but my dad was determined to restore the two buildings as much as he could to their original states."

Meranda glanced up from her examination. "Tell your father thank you from me." Her gaze moved to Paul, who smiled his agreement. She grinned back, then went back to the lamp.

Glenys moved down the wall. "This is interesting." She stopped at a framed newspaper clipping.

"What have you got there? A clue?" Paul called to her.

"No," she answered while stroking the frame. "Just a picture of my property in a newspaper clipping from 1907."

He left Meranda at the lamp and joined Glenys.

The article heading under the picture stated, "AUGUSTUS DRAKE OPENS ARMS TO FAMILIES." In the picture an older Drake stood with his arms outstretched at the end of the forked road—the lighthouse in the distance to the left and the house to the right. "The article says," Glenys spoke with an emotional thickness in her voice, "Augustus held his first benefit for the families who lost their loved ones in the shipwreck during the dedication. He sold tours into the lighthouse to raise money for them, then invited them onto his property and fed them." She glanced at Meranda. "Your ancestor was a great man."

Meranda left the lamp to stand between Paul and Glenys. Paul felt her hand slip through his arm and noticed she did the same with Glenys. Silently, they paid homage to a man with an open-door policy and a heart of gold.

Chapter 12

For the next week Meranda kept busy with whale-watching excursions. The lighthouse continued to be her source of strength, a tall sentinel watching over her.

"We're close, Pop," she whispered as she stopped the boat in deep waters. While the fifteen passengers watched the western horizon for whale spouts, she turned in her seat topside and reached for her binoculars. She quickly found the lighthouse lamp in the lenses and followed the structure down to the twin pillars that marked the path to the beach. Odd that she hadn't noticed how they resembled the art on her pendant. But even now she had to strain to see them as they blended in with the white stucco of the lighthouse.

Now that she thought about it, the pillars were in an odd spot. Why not have the steps lead down from the house? The slope was gentler there. From where her boat sat in the water, the lighthouse was perfectly framed between the pillars. The back of her neck tingled. This had to be a clue.

Suddenly her mind's eye flickered to Paul. They had spoken on the phone nearly every day since their trip to the museum. She loved the way he had championed her in front of the judge when he called the police on her. Then the shy way he slipped his hands into his pockets when he saw her at the restaurant sitting in the alcove. Shyness and protectiveness. Two facets to this man whom she found herself eager to learn more about.

When she arrived home that evening, she called Paul's cell phone to invite him on the *Romanda Jule* for the next day, knowing it was his day off from the restaurant. She hoped he didn't have any catering jobs. She mostly wanted to get to know him, but also thought they could brainstorm the coins together while enjoying an outing.

"Do I get to drive?" His voice held a smile.

"Would that keep you from getting seasick?"

"Yes. It definitely would."

"I think you just pretend to get nauseous so you can drive my boat."

"You got me. My pasty white face? Makeup. The sweat on my upper lip? From a squirt bottle in my pocket."

"Okay! I get it." She laughed. "I think it's a control issue. Do you feel the same about airplanes?"

"Um. . .well. . ." He paused, and she took that as an admission, but then she heard him talking to someone in the background.

"I know you're still at work, so I'll let you go," Meranda said.

"No problem. I was just talking to Jessie. She overheard our conversation and wondered if she could come, too. And since we're brainstorming, what about Glenys?"

Okay, now her cozy twosome just turned into a foursome.

When she agreed, Paul said, "Great. Can you call Glenys?"

"Sure, I still have her number in my phone from when she called me."

The next morning, Glenys showed up first. Meranda waved to her from the *Romanda Jule* when she saw her standing at the dock entrance searching the boats and looking confused. Glenys smiled and waved back. With her hand still in the air, a seagull swooped her hand, apparently checking if she held a morsel he could steal. The young woman shrieked and ran in circles as if trying to escape a swarm of bees.

Meranda ran to her. She stopped the frenzy by grasping her shoulders. "Glenys, it's okay. It was just a seagull."

Glenys covered her hair with both hands but slowly lowered them as she seemed to focus on Meranda. "Yeah. Of course. Just a seagull."

Meranda escorted her to the boat, but Glenys continued to watch the sky with a wary eye. She relaxed once she settled herself into the boat and so did Meranda. One phobia at a time was all she could handle.

A few minutes later Paul arrived with Jessie and her boyfriend, Derrick, whom Meranda had only met the day she crashed the lighthouse wedding. But that was okay. With more people they would soon have a regular parley about the coins.

Paul still hesitated slightly as he stepped on deck.

"Still having qualms?" She placed her hand on his arm.

"Oh yeah, but at least I'm here of my own accord. Must be a breakthrough of some kind."

They went to the helm under the canopy as Derrick and Glenys made themselves comfortable on deck. Paul had brought snacks, and Jessie put them in the galley.

Meranda motioned for him to sit in the captain's chair. But before he did, he said, "I have a surprise for you." He reached into his back pocket and pulled out his wallet.

"Money?" She clapped her hands together in mock surprise.

"Better." He drew out a card and showed it to her.

"An Oregon Boater Education Card? How did you do this so fast?" Her heart raced when she realized she'd made a convert of a die-hard landlubber.

"Many nights on the Internet taking the course." He rubbed his eyes and fake yawned. "Made the day job a little risky, but I only lost one finger while dicing carrots." He held up his hand, back toward her, his ring finger crooked into his palm.

Ignoring his warped humor, she threw her arms wide and hugged him. "This is totally awesome!"

Meranda could have remained in the hug but, remembering the others, pulled away from Paul and waved his card. "Ladies and gentleman, I present your captain for the day."

Jessie moaned. But her smile belied her words. "Someone notify my family. I may not be going home."

Paul sat, and Meranda oriented him again on the controls. When she felt confident he knew what he was doing, she gave the go-ahead to start the engine.

He began to pull away from the dock, and Meranda placed her hand on his arm. "Um, Paul. Did you remember to untie us from the dock?"

"No!"

"Relax. I did it. But that's something the captain should always check."

Paul's face turned the same color as her maid-of-honor dress, dark pink. It looked better on him than on her. "Got it. No dragging dock behind us."

They headed out to sea, and he opened the throttle until they were skimming along at a fine clip. Once they were near the place she'd seen whales the day before, she asked him to slow the boat to a stop.

"Like a pro." Meranda patted his back, pleased he'd conquered his fear.

"And now," he said as he cut the engine, "I'm hungry. I brought some cold appetizers. Interested?"

"Race you!" She led him down into the galley while the other guests enjoyed the sunshine on deck. As he scooted in next to her to reach the tiny refrigerator, he knocked a book to the floor that had been sitting on a small two-person table.

"I'm sorry. Man, what a klutz." He bent over to pick it up.

"No harm. Look inside."

He did, and his eyes grew wide as he perused the pages. "What is this?"

"One of Augustus Drake's journals. I brought it today to search for clues again."

"How long have you had this?" He continued to flip pages.

"About a year and a half. My dad found it through the San Francisco Maritime Museum. They have an exhibition dedicated to shipbuilding. This was in their storeroom because they already had a similar item on display."

"Wow. It details parts bought, cargo loaded, times the ships left and arrived back at port. Hey look. Here's an entry from today's date, May 9, 1906." He read aloud. " 'Set out with beloved new bride to Hawaii. We passed over the grave of the *Victoria Jane* and said a prayer for those lost a year ago.' He also included scripture. 'So when this corruptible shall have put on incorruption, and this mortal shall have put on immortality, then shall be brought to pass the saying that is written, Death is swallowed up in victory.' 1 Corinthians 15:54."

Meranda looked over his shoulder at the entry. "I don't know much more about my great-great-grandmother. I'm assuming he was taking her to meet his brother's family."

He skimmed a few more pages. "No mention of The Inheritance?"

She shook her head. "At this point, the lighthouse would have been nearly finished. I'm sure the coins were safe and sound."

They stood together for a moment in the small space, him reading, her watching him read. His intensity as he turned the pages assured her that he truly was interested in Augustus. Finally he handed the journal back.

He placed his hand on her arm and squeezed gently. "What a legacy you have, Meranda." His gaze locked on hers, and he drew her closer. Just as she stepped into what promised to be a warm embrace and a very pleasant first kiss, joyful pandemonium broke out on deck.

"Hey, you two!" Jessie called to them. "There are whales out here."

"Cool!" Glenys's voice. "Spouts. . .no! I see whole backs of whales! Get out here before you miss them."

"Don't they realize"—Paul's breath tickled her ear—"that you see whales nearly every day?"

"It's a whole pod!" Jessie again.

"I guess we'd better join them before they come looking for us." Meranda reluctantly stepped away and opened the drawer where she kept her bag. She tossed the journal inside, closed the drawer, then headed up the steps, Paul trailing with a sliced fruit tray for their midmorning snack.

Sure enough, there were about six young whales migrating south. Meranda stood at the railing enjoying them with the others, but what she enjoyed more was Paul standing behind her, his hand on her waist.

As the whales moved away, the five in the boat seated themselves in a loose ring. Jessie turned and said, "Hey, great driving earlier, boss. You didn't throw us overboard once."

"I learned from the best." He winked at Meranda, who maddeningly felt her cheeks warm like a teenager's.

"We decided my fear is a control issue."

Jessie laughed. "Your control issue must be something you got from your grandmother."

The morning passed quickly with no more whales, but Meranda enjoyed the others' company. She found she had a lot in common with Jessie, beyond the fact that their fathers knew each other.

At one point Jessie asked, "Do you dive, Meranda?"

"Yes. I used to dive with my father all the time."

"Have you ever gone crabbing off the jetty?" Jessie's eyes danced.

"I've done that a few times. I love chasing them and trying to stick them into bags." Meranda laughed.

"I like bringing them home and cooking them."

"I'll bet you cook up a mean Dungeness crab, don't you?"

Jessie tipped her head. "I'd like to think so."

"How do you cook them, Jess?" The topic turned to recipes when Paul got involved.

And this made Meranda hungry. She brought out the lunch fare Paul had brought.

While they enjoyed spicy marinated mushrooms, vegetable sticks and artichoke dip, and hearty bread brushed with olive oil, Paul opened the topic about the coins. "Let's recap what we know. They can't be in the original lighthouse lamp."

"Right," Glenys said. "But we know the pendants are a clue."

"And," Meranda added, "I believe they are in the lighthouse because of the box your family's pendant was kept in. It had a tin punch-art top with a picture of the lighthouse."

"Well, actually." Glenys chewed on her thumbnail. "I made that box in sixth grade and gave it to my dad for Father's Day. It was the year we bought the lighthouse."

"Okay." Strike that one. "Great job, by the way."

"Thank you." Glenys preened at the tongue-in-cheek compliment.

Jessie asked, "What about the plaques in the brick wall of the tower?"

Meranda pointed to her. "That's right. There is no doubt they're connected to the coins. So the pillars and the plaques all lead to the lighthouse." Her brain whirred. "Maybe instead of the clues leading up to the light, they lead down to the floor."

"Yeah." Jessie turned to Glenys. "Could they be under the floor?"

"No. The lighthouse underwent a major renovation a few decades ago. The entire floor was replaced. If they'd been there, I'm sure someone would have found them."

Meranda feared she had hit another brick wall. How many clues would it take to unearth the mystery?

"May I see your necklace?" Paul held out his hand to Meranda. She unhooked the chain and passed it to him. He looked at the back again. "JG.IG." He squinted and looked at it again. "Wait a minute. . ."

Meranda, along with Glenys and Jessie, leaned forward. Derrick had disappeared. She assumed he'd gone below to use the latrine.

"What, Paul? What do you see?"

"Just a minute." He handed the necklace back, excused himself, and headed below.

A satisfying sensation prickled the back of Meranda's neck, signaling a breakthrough.

⟡

Paul jogged down the steps, but he nearly tripped over Derrick, who was bent over something near the refrigerator.

"I think we ate the last of the food. Are you getting another soda?"

"Um, yeah. Want one?"

As he stood, Paul saw him shove something into his pocket and try to shut the drawer that Meranda's purse was in, but the strap hung out, preventing him from doing so.

"Were you in Meranda's bag?" Then he noticed dollar bills sticking out of Derrick's pocket. "Are you stealing from her?"

"No way, dude." He shoved the money in deeper.

"Come on. Let's talk to Meranda." He propelled Derrick through the opening to the deck, but reached back for Meranda's bag before following.

Paul steered Derrick toward Meranda by pushing the back of his shoulder.

She looked up at both of them and squinted in the sun. Then her gaze dropped to the item in Paul's fist. "What are you doing with my bag?"

He handed it to her. "Check your money."

She hesitated a moment, but then complied. She pulled out her wallet, opened it, and frowned. "I had two hundred and fourteen dollars in here."

"I'll bet Derrick has two hundred and fourteen dollars in his left pocket."

"Derrick?" She held out her hand.

He rolled his eyes but reached in and pulled out the wad of bills. She counted them and glared at Derrick.

Jessie shot out of her chair. "Derrick, you idiot!"

Paul had never seen her so angry, her wrath making Derrick wither. Did he fear she might hit him? He shrank onto a seat on the deck.

Glenys joined Jessie in the verbal whipping. "Wait a minute. At my sister's wedding, you were the last one in the kitchen. I saw you go back in when the police arrived. Are you the one who took my dad's pendant?"

Derrick's gaze shot to Jessie.

Jessie stepped between them. "Of course he didn't. Why would he want your old pendant? He just went back into the kitchen to be sure we didn't leave anything." Was that the classic turnaround to protect her man when it looked like someone else might throttle him?

Paul held up his hand. "We'll turn him in when we get back and let the authorities figure out what happened."

Meranda nodded, and taking her bag with her, she stepped to the helm and grabbed her radio to report the incident.

Derrick sat with his arms crossed, scowling. "I didn't take the pendant."

"Maybe not," Paul said, "but you did take Meranda's money."

The boat engine roared to life, and before long they were underway.

Chapter 13

As Meranda chugged her boat to the dock, a patrol car and two men in uniform waited for them. Within the hour, she and the others had given their statements, with Glenys adamant the sheriff search Derrick's home for the pendant.

Blackhearted buzzard. There should be honor on a boat. Meranda had never felt the need to lock up her belongings before.

The sheriff cuffed Derrick and placed him in the patrol car. Jessie stood nearby, pacing the parking lot and flinging her small duffel bag around her body as if she wanted to hit someone with it. By the daggers shooting from her eyes at her boyfriend, Meranda assumed Derrick would be the one sporting bruises. Finally, as the car pulled away, Jessie seemed to gain control and glanced toward the trio.

"I'm sorry he ruined our trip, everyone."

"Has he ever done anything like this before?" Paul asked, not in an unkind way.

"Do you think I'd be with him if he did?" She scowled and moved toward her car. "Again, I'm really sorry."

"Jess, wait." Paul followed her. "Are you going to be okay?"

Meranda also wondered if Jessie could use some company. She called out to her. "Yeah, Jessie. You're welcome to hang out here."

An angry frown slashed across her forehead. "No. I'd rather be alone right now. Thanks." Then she stormed off to her car, gunned the engine, and peeled out of the lot.

Meranda stood with Glenys behind Paul as he watched Jessie's car until it disappeared around a corner. Tension had drawn his shoulders up to squeeze his neck. She thought of rubbing those shoulders, but reached out to touch his arm instead. "I'm so sorry for Jessie. What will happen to Derrick now?"

"Probably a slap on the wrist for the money if it was his first offense. If they find the pendant, depending on its worth, he'll be in a whole lot more trouble." He frowned. "In any event, he's fired."

All three stood silent for a moment longer. Meranda glanced up and down the dock. The other boaters had gone back to their regular activities after the squad car left. A cop dragging someone from the Drake boat in handcuffs? That had to have confirmed in her neighbors' minds that the family was someone to avoid.

Finally she returned to the boat. "Party's over. Guess I'll clean up."

Paul followed. "I'll do the galley. Too bad there aren't any leftovers. I could leave them for you. Next time I'll make extra."

"I've got the trash," Glenys announced. When she was through collecting soda cans and tossing them into a trash bag, she dropped onto the bench with the drama of a 1920s actress in a Rudolph Valentino movie. "I was having so much fun with you guys. Does it have to end? I'll be going back to California soon."

"When?" Paul asked as he reappeared on deck.

"I start shooting a small indie film in a couple of weeks. You'll probably never see it." She dragged herself to stand. "I have twelve lines. One scene. I'm a waitress." She grimaced and snatched her purse that she'd laid on the deck. "I hated waitressing before I became an actress. And now I'm playing one in a movie." She moved to the back of the boat and, with Paul's help, hopped to the dock from the dive platform. "I don't even get to die in this movie. Just take someone's order, make a wisecrack, and step offstage." With a huge dramatic sigh, she turned and made her exit.

She didn't get far, however. A large pelican stood on the dock blocking her way. "Shoo! Shoo! Go away!" She stood a good twenty feet from it and gesticulated wildly to no avail. When it started hopping toward her and clicking its bill, she shrieked as she did during the seagull attack and ran back to the boat, leaped on board, and hid behind Paul.

The look of terror in her eyes finally got Meranda's attention. "You really are afraid of big birds."

"And little ones. And all of them in between."

"I understand fear," Paul said. "Let me walk you to your car."

She accepted with a sigh and allowed him to go first. He waved his arms at the pelican, and it spread its wide wings and flew away.

When she was gone, Paul returned to Meranda. "That poor girl. I can so relate." He stroked his chin. "I just had a thought. I don't know anything about acting, but I remember meeting a producer at my stepcousin's wedding in Oakley. His uncle, I believe. I think I'll ring up Skye and see if he can do anything to help Glenys."

Meranda nodded her approval while sweeping the deck. What a sweet guy. Everyday she learned more about this unassuming man. And she loved every facet of this treasure.

With the boat back to its original spit shine, Meranda sank onto the bench seat.

"You really surprised me, Paul." Meranda propped her elbow onto the back of the seat and leaned her head into her hand.

He joined her, sitting close enough their knees touched. "Why?"

"Getting your boating card? Isn't that a huge step for you?"

"I think we had it right. Once my nausea was conquered and I learned how to drive a boat, I lost my anxiety. It was as you said—all about control. I've had to deal with out-of-control issues all my life. My dad dying when I was young. My single mom making difficult decisions that I had no say in. Then, of course, there's my grandmother—under her thumb until I moved inland just a few years ago. Since I've moved back, I realize how I really hate that."

"So you were projecting those control issues until they manifested under the guise of your fear."

He raised his eyebrow.

"College. Psych 101."

"Ah." He nodded. "I think so. And now that I've been through the online boating course, I feel that if something should happen to the captain, I'd be okay."

"So are you going to get your airplane pilot's license now?" Meranda cast a teasing glance his way.

A telltale sheen appeared on his upper lip. "No. I don't think so."

"Hey." She gently slapped his shoulder. "Not to change the subject, but you had a revelation before the Derrick thing but never got a chance to reveal it. What did you go below for?"

"Oh!" He hopped out of the chair and raced down the steps. When he returned, he had Augustus's journal. "Look at the inscription on your pendant."

She lifted the pendant from its chain around her neck, peering at the back. "JG. IG." What did the journal and the pendant have to do with each other?

He opened the journal to June 16. "Now, look at this date."

"Six, sixteen. So, what about it?"

"You don't see it?"

She studied the inscription and the date several times before the number six slapped her on the forehead. "It's the same."

"Right. Written in older script, the six resembles a *G*. And I think it's possible that's not an I, but a one. Not JG.IG, but J6.16."

She frowned. "It still couldn't be a date, could it?"

"What if it's scripture?"

"I suppose it could be."

Paul took the journal and began turning pages. "Augustus was a religious man. He quoted scripture often." He opened to a page where the author journaled about the numerous stars while on the same voyage with his bride. "Here he quotes Psalm 8:3–4. 'When I consider thy heavens, the work of thy fingers, the moon and the stars, which thou hast ordained; what is man, that thou art mindful of him? and the son of man, that thou visitest him?' Perhaps whoever scratched these letters and numbers was also a believer. Do you have a Bible?"

"Not on the boat, why?"

"How about your laptop? Do you have Internet while docked here? I can look up some verses to see if they hold any clues."

She always had her laptop with her, in case she might have a revelation and want to look something up. It was below in the same drawer as her bag. Could it really be scripture? That made sense. The journals and letters she'd read were written by people of faith. They often talked about God and quoted scripture. Then they signed off with *The Lord be with you* or something similar. When had her family stopped seeking the Lord?

Sitting down near Paul again, she handed him the computer. "Here you go."

He put it in his lap and turned it on. "I know of a Bible Web site that shows different versions. Your ancestors would have used the King James Version." He started clicking away, going through every book that began with a *J*, his face glowing as he read the verses aloud. Meranda thought about her ancestors and their faith. Faith had gotten them through some tough times according to what she'd read. Paul had faith in God, and it helped him through his mom's death. Glenys had faith also. If they all had gotten it right, did that make her wrong?

"This one looks interesting." Paul pulled her from her reverie. " 'Thus saith the Lord, Stand ye in the ways, and see, and ask for the old paths, where is the good way, and walk therein, and ye shall find rest for your souls.' It's from Jeremiah 6:16."

Meranda watched a rainstorm gathering several miles off the coast. She doubted they were in the path. It looked to be going southeast.

"What do you think?"

"I don't know. How would it apply to the coins?"

"This part about the old paths. These coins have been on an old path leading from generations past."

She leaned over and read the scripture on the screen. "Well, if I find them, I'll sure get rest for my soul."

He clicked on the keyboard some more, and another screen appeared. "Here it is in a different version. Hmm. That's interesting."

"What?" She almost felt as if a magnet were drawing her in to read what was on the screen.

"This one talks about crossroads and ancient paths." He bookmarked the page, then shut the laptop and looked at her. "Even if this isn't the verse on the pendant, would you be open to thinking that the Lord may be speaking to you through this one?"

Had that been the magnetic pull? She felt the skin prickle on her neck. "So what are you saying?"

He paused a moment as if he was thinking about his next words. "You may be at a crossroads right now. You can either continue on this path, which may or may not lead to the coins, or you can stop, pray, and let God lead you."

"But He may not want me to find the coins." She leaned back and crossed her arms.

"Then, if that's true, that's the path you should choose because God wants what's best for you." He placed his arm on the back of the seat behind her, his face just inches from hers. "And so do I." Mahogany eyes bored into hers so deeply she felt them prick her heart.

While still a breath apart, he said, "Good night, Meranda. Know that I pray for you every day and will say a special prayer tonight." Then he was gone. Her lips tingled as if he had kissed her, and she felt a little miffed that he hadn't.

That night, the sheets tangled her legs as she tossed in bed, wrestling with whether she should give up and hand her dream—Pop's dream—over to God or fate or whatever it was called. No. As long as she was in control, she knew she'd find them eventually.

Control.

Paul conquered his fear by learning how to run a boat, taking control over it. Yet his grandmother used control the wrong way. Meranda searched her own soul.

Am I a control freak?

Possibly, but she wasn't going to give control over to a God who allowed her father to die.

Realizing sleep had abandoned her, she got up, slid into her clog slippers, and padded out to the living room. Without turning on the lights, she stood at the back window and watched the lighthouse.

Wink. Wink.

"What should I do, Pop? Paul says I should give our dream to God." Mom needed the money. Meranda needed to validate Pop. The coins would not materialize out of nowhere; she didn't care how powerful God was.

She flipped on the desk lamp, finding the letter written by Augustus, and pored over it—again. It never stated the coins were in his possession, just that they were where no one would find them. Were they in the wreckage?

An hour later, light started to filter through the window and with it an idea. As she prepared for her day, weary from the lack of sleep yet charged with adrenaline, she called Jessie.

"Hey, you mentioned you're a certified diver?"

Chapter 14

The next morning Paul sat in the restaurant office with Derrick's employee chart. He had just finished up the paperwork to terminate the thief.

"Pablo." His grandmother poked her head in the door.

"Morning, Abuelita. Come in, I need to tell you something."

He stood and offered her the desk chair in the cramped space. As he pointed out the chart, he told her about Derrick and their adventure the day prior.

"I never liked him." She molded her face into the bulldog look. "His eyes are too close together." Sometimes Abuelita didn't like someone because of eyes that were too far apart. Or an offset nose. Or teeth that were too straight.

"We'll have to hire someone to take his place." An idea struck him. "What about Meranda's sister? She's been through culinary school, but I think she may be open to filling in as waitstaff to get her foot in the door."

"I would need to look at her very closely. Check her credentials. I will set up the interview."

He threw his shoulders back and shed the years of control she had heaped on him. "No, Abuela." He rarely called her *grandmother,* and this got her attention. Her head snapped up. "This is my business. Our agreement was that you would retire. What happened to that?"

Abuelita pierced him with a glare. "You are getting too cocky for your own good, Pablito."

Paul slipped his hand under her elbow and removed her from his chair. "I'm not 'little Pablo' anymore. I'm a grown man who needs to run my business as I see fit. You gave this restaurant to Albert and me. Now trust us." He tenderly, but forcefully, ushered her out of the office.

Closing the door behind her, he heaved a sigh. Man, that felt good.

Now back to filling the gap Derrick's absence had caused. He wanted to talk to Meranda before offering her sister the job. Considering Rose's social position, he wasn't sure how receptive she would be. He sat at the desk and called Meranda's cell phone, but her voice mail picked up. She was probably on a charter tour.

He checked his calendar. He could fill in until Thursday if he didn't connect with Meranda before then. He had no catering jobs on that day, so a surprise visit to her boat might be fun. He left the office for an appointment to talk about food choices for a birthday party and nearly tripped over Abuelita, who was standing in the corridor gazing with misty eyes at a picture of his grandfather.

"Abuelita?" He stroked the thin shoulder. Had he pushed her too far?

"Sevilla."

"Excuse me?"

She turned moist gray brown eyes to him. "Your abuelo and I had often talked about going back to our home in Sevilla, España."

His stomach dropped. "Spain. I didn't mean for you to go away. I just want you to rest now. You and Papa did a wonderful job with this restaurant. But it's time for you to pass the torch."

She nodded and wiped a tear, frightening him. Abuelita rarely cried. He pulled her into a hug. "Are you okay?"

"You have never spoken to me like that before, Pablo." She looked up at him with flashing eyes. *Here comes the backlash.* "And you are right."

"I'm right?" His head spun with this sudden turnaround.

"Don't back down now, Pablo." She stroked his cheek with bony fingers. "You are so like your mother. I had to push her out of the nest, too. Of course she came back, but she brought you."

Paul chuckled and hugged the tiny body. "I love you, Abuelita."

She hugged him back, fierce twig arms that nearly busted his rib. Then she pulled back, a mischievous grin playing on her face. "Then I stay."

He turned her by the shoulders and gently directed her toward the door. "No, you go. Take up painting."

Thursday morning when he arrived at the dock, Meranda wasn't on the charter boat. He searched the dock and spotted her on the smaller *Romanda Jule*. She was busy with her preparations and didn't see him right away as he walked toward her. She had on a black wet suit, the upper half hanging at her waist to reveal a navy blue swimsuit. Knowing she enjoyed diving, this didn't surprise him. Her reaction to him, however, did.

"What are you doing here?" Her eyes shifted like she seemed distracted. She'd just released the rope from the dock.

"I'd like to ask you something about your sister and decided to surprise you."

Jessie suddenly appeared from below holding a pair of goggles. She was also dressed in a wet suit. "Hey, Meranda. What do you use to keep your mask from fogging? I've heard a cut potato works." She stopped in her tracks when she saw Paul. "What are you doing here?"

He jerked his hands into the air. "Why are you both so shocked that I'm here?"

"Because you should be at work." Jessie's voice held more impatience than Meranda's had. What was going on with these two? She tossed the mask with the attached snorkel toward a pile of neon yellow vests and a couple of scuba tanks near the diving platform.

"Are you going to the jetty for Dungeness crabs?"

Meranda avoided his eyes as she tossed the rope into the boat and boarded.

Paul's heart dropped to his stomach. "You're *not* going to dive the wreckage."

With her characteristic captain stance—legs planted firmly on the deck and hands on hips—Meranda challenged him. "Is that an order or an observation?"

He leaped onto the boat and rushed to Meranda, grabbing her shoulders. "I thought you were going to let God guide you. Surely you don't believe He's telling you to put yourself in danger."

She shrugged his hands away. "I'll be fine. I have to do this." She removed the pendant from her neck and placed it in her bag sitting on the deck near the steps. Then she stormed past him and took the helm.

"This is crazy!" He followed her up the steps and into the small space.

She turned to face him. "I know this shipwreck." Meranda ground her teeth. "I dove it with my father. Maybe if I had gone with him that last time. . ."

"Is this a guilt thing? You know you had nothing to do with his death."

"I know I wasn't there to help. I know our last conversation was an argument." She sat in the captain's chair, turning her back on him, and with a voice barely above a whisper said, "I know I called him crazy."

"You what?" Paul couldn't believe what he heard. She hated others calling him that.

Her shoulders had been squared, but at her confession they drooped slightly. With her back still to him, she said, "His funds had run out, but he took the boat out one last time with a minimal crew to look for the coins—on my birthday." She turned to look at Paul and beat her chest. "And I wanted to spend it with my whole family. But that morning he grabbed me by the shoulders, right here on this dock. The look in his eyes scared me. He said, 'I'm close, Bonnie-girl. So close.' And he left me standing there. No promises of coming in early for the dinner Rose had prepared. I felt I lost him right then. As he pulled away, I called out to him. I told him he was as crazy as everyone said he was. He never looked back at me. I don't even know if he heard me. But if he did. . ." Her shoulders sagged even farther, but she placed her hand on the key and turned the engine over. "We had just lit the candles on my cake after waiting a couple of hours to see if he would show. That's when we got the phone call."

"And now you're acting just like him. How does that honor his memory?"

Without looking up, she snarled. "Either get off my boat or grab a vest and hang on because we're pulling out."

"I'll stay." Perhaps he could talk her out of it once they got there.

"No!" Jessie balled her fists. "Go home, Paul." When both he and Meranda turned shocked gazes toward her, she stammered, "I–I mean, this is ladies day out."

He looked back at Meranda, who shrugged. "Do what you want. But this boat is leaving in two seconds."

Should he leave? Something didn't feel right, and it was mostly a vibe he got from Jessie. But moreover, he hoped to talk Meranda out of diving the wreck. He sat and strapped himself in. Jessie slapped her chair before sitting in it.

He did have to hang on as the boat bounced on the water, bringing back his fear. *Lord, be with us. And be with Meranda if she attempts this stunt.*

Soon the boat spiraled to a stop like a teenager-driven car spinning a doughnut in a parking lot. The rumbling engine silenced, and the only sound was the water slapping at the hull.

Jessie had been sitting across from him during the rough ride, an ugly sneer on her face. She stood and grabbed one of the tanks, opened the valve, and sniffed it.

Paul removed his seat belt but had to sit a moment longer to quell his nauseous stomach. He wished he had his wristbands. Finally he stood and wobbled on land legs to try to confront her. "Jessie. You need to talk her out of this. Her father died down there. It can't be safe."

Jessie's glare shot venom. "I'm not at the restaurant right now. You can't order me here."

He staggered back from the verbal strike. "I know that. I'm asking as a friend."

"Move." She shoved him aside and grabbed a diving vest. "Meranda is a big girl. She's an experienced diver and knows this wreck. I'm certified with several shipwreck dives under my belt. Let her do this. Maybe she'll get some closure." She glanced down at Meranda's bag sitting near the steps, an almost yearning look passing across her face.

She then moved to the dive platform and dipped the vests into water while Meranda anchored the boat.

Paul watched helplessly as the two women slipped the vests over the tanks and helped each other put them on. He thought of calling the coast guard, but what could he tell them? His friends weren't doing anything illegal. He silently turned to the one Authority he knew he could count on, God, as Meranda's fins disappeared over the side.

When there was nothing left in the water but the bubbles from their tanks, he concentrated on the spot for an eternity, like a dog waiting for his owner to return. When his watch ticked by a slow half hour, another boat, a cabin cruiser like Meranda's, only smaller, was upon him before he knew it, startling him with its nearness. It came to a stop about twenty feet away. Derrick glowered at him from his place at the wheel.

"How did you get out of jail?" Paul clenched his fists, wishing he could get his hands on the twerp.

"Hey, dude. I didn't steal that pendant. The cops didn't find anything, so I got out on bail for the cash I stole. Just for the record, I've never done anything like that before."

Paul shook his head. So much failed to make sense. "Why are you here?"

"Jessie called this morning and told me to meet her out here. She didn't say *you'd* be here."

The two men held a staring standoff until a rubbery flopping sound on Derrick's boat caught their attention. Jessie had just tossed her fins onto the deck. She climbed up the ladder and stepped into the boat.

"Hey," Derrick spoke to her. "I couldn't do what you said with him there."

Not even looking at Paul, she ripped off her mask and shouted, "Shut up! Let's get out of here!" She tossed a book-sized object into a large canvas athletic bag. Then she proceeded to undo her gear, violently ripping the Velcro and shrugging out of the vest.

"Where's Meranda!" Cold fear iced Paul's nerve endings. He searched the water hoping to see her surface.

Jessie didn't answer him. While she sat with her back to Paul and slipped off her boots, he raced to the helm, radioed the coast guard, and managed to stammer that he thought his friend was hurt in a diving accident and that there could have been foul play.

"What's your location?"

"I don't know." He searched the console, hoping to see something with numbers. "Um. . ." He shook his head to clear it. "We're above the wreckage of the *Victoria Jane.*"

"Got it. We're on the way." Paul broke off before asking how long it would be. He ran back to the deck, nearly stumbling as the boat rocked beneath him. The engine of the other boat cranked a couple of times, but then nothing.

"Come on!" Jessie's voice graveled frustration.

"It won't start." Fear showed on Derrick's face as he struggled to start the boat. Whatever could he be afraid of?

Jessie reached into a compartment on board and pulled out a gun, pointing it at Paul. Now he understood. Derrick knew what Jessie was capable of.

"Jessie!" Panic seized his feet, but where could he run? "What are you doing? Don't be stupid."

She kept her eye on Paul but barked at Derrick. "Get on Meranda's boat. Bring it over here."

"But I don't have my swim trunks on."

She rolled her eyes. "Then you should have gotten closer. I don't care if you have to strip to your Skivvies. Just get over there." She flicked the end of the pistol toward him. "Remember who bailed you out."

Grumbling, he removed his tennis shoes and looked like he might consider throwing them into Meranda's boat, but must have thought better of it. He lowered himself, jeans and all, down the ladder while holding the shoes high and inhaled sharply as the cold water soaked into his clothes.

By the time he reached the *Romanda Jule,* his shoes had taken several dunkings. He struggled up the ladder in his heavy clothes and paused to rest on the dive platform.

"Hurry up!" Jessie stamped her foot. Derrick shot daggers with his glare but stood and walked to the helm, leaving large puddles of water on the deck.

With the gun trained on both of them, Paul knew he couldn't do anything to stop Derrick, so he let him pass. Derrick climbed the steps, started the boat, and swung it around to get close to the other vessel.

"Closer, you idiot!" Jessie stood at the side, her wet suit gone and wearing a two-piece swimsuit splashed with orange flowers. She flung her duffel bag over her shoulder.

"This is as close as I can get," Derrick roared loud enough for her to hear on the other boat. "You want me to bump into you?"

"Whatever. Just throw me the rope."

He rushed past Paul on his way to the dive platform. Derrick threw the rope to Jessie and she pulled until the boats bumped together. When Derrick held out his hand to help transfer her to Meranda's boat, a rogue wave rolled under both boats at that moment. Jessie yelped and ended up in the water.

Derrick, however, ended up with the gun. His wide eyes suggested he had no idea his day would include boat hijacking.

Paul's mind spun. These were real-life pirates! "Derrick, put the gun down. She's obviously insane." Derrick turned a stunned look toward him.

With Jessie still thrashing in the water, struggling to throw her bag on board, Paul rushed the larger man. He had to overpower him before Jessie made it on board. They wrestled, Derrick throwing Paul down onto the deck like a dockworker with a sack of potatoes. Paul kicked Derrick's ankles, sweeping his feet out from under him. He landed hard, and the gun went skittering. They both groped for it.

"Get it!" Jessie's voice sounded close, and Paul knew she was on board.

Paul's fingers claimed the weapon seconds before Jessie. He scrambled to stand, training it on her with trembling hands while keeping an eye on Derrick, still sitting on the deck and holding his head. Blood oozed from a gash in the back. He must have hit his head on the metal cleat in the deck where the rope had been moments before.

Jessie smirked, her lips an ugly slash. With her bag slung over her shoulder, she turned her back on him, snatched the pendant out of Meranda's bag, and ascended the steps to the helm.

"Stop, Jessie."

"Or what? You'll shoot?" She sat, again with her back to him, and turned over the engine easily. "We both know you won't do that."

"No, but *I* will."

Paul turned at the sound of the female voice. "Meranda?"

She stepped, finless, toward Paul and took the gun. With a steady hand, she held her arm straight in Jessie's direction. "Now, step away."

Chapter 15

Meranda aimed at her ex-friend's spine. Jessie raised her hands and moved slowly away from the wheel.

"What did you do with the slate, Jessie?"

When she didn't answer, Paul said, "She tossed some things into the bag she brought aboard. She took it with her up to the helm."

"Turn around, Jessie, and move down here to the deck."

She complied, her eyes two glowering orbs.

Paul raced up the steps. "I called the coast guard." He retrieved the bag. "What's in here?"

"Proof that my father was murdered." She glanced his way while still training the gun on Jessie. "Open it."

Paul unzipped the athletic bag. "What am I looking for?"

"An underwater writing slate, about the size of an address book."

"How could it have been there so long? Wouldn't the writing have faded?"

"No, we use a special pen that scratches the surface. It takes something abrasive to erase it."

Paul straightened, holding the slate over his head. "Got it!"

"Read what's inside."

He flipped open the cover and perused it briefly, then his eyes went wide. "What does this mean?"

"It means that Jessie's father murdered mine. Pop wrote that message on there." She motioned with the gun for Jessie to join Derrick on the deck floor. As she shrugged the tank off, she continued speaking to Paul. "It says, 'Kingston killing me.' How did he do it, Jess? Did he tamper with the guide string? Create a silt storm to disorient my father? Wait until his air ran out before he told anybody?"

"No! My dad tried to save yours. He returned to the boat for fresh tanks. He told the other member of the team to call the coast guard, then went back down. He acted heroically, but it was too late."

Paul still knelt by the bag and rubbed his neck. "Jessie could be right, Meranda. Maybe your dad just thought there was foul play."

"Then why did she just try to do the same thing to me? The acorn doesn't fall far from the tree, does it, Jessie?"

Meranda retrieved a rectangular object from a bag hanging from her belt. "I have a feeling the proof is in here. It's my dad's underwater digital camera. I've heard stories of divers losing their cameras for months and when they retrieved them, found the pictures as good as new. I'm sure my dad hid it from Kingston, knowing someone would find it eventually." She shot a look at Jessie. "I found it in the hole where the slate was, just before I was caught in a silt storm that she generated. Jessie took the spool of string with her so she could get out, but I couldn't see. Luckily, I had found his camera in the hole in the floor before all that happened."

Paul stood and joined Meranda. "Jess, how could you?" His voice held a hard edge. Meranda knew he was no doubt hurt and confused by the turn of events.

Jessie shot a defiant glare at Paul. "You don't believe her, do you? She's so obsessed over the coins she'd lie to cover her own insanity. You know me, Paul. Why would I hurt her?"

"For the same reason you would pull a gun on me, I suppose." He wrapped his arm around Meranda's waist. She leaned into him, grateful for both his physical and mental support. He could have believed his assistant whom he'd known much longer.

A coast guard ship approached from the distance. "We'll let the authorities sort it out. By the way, she has your pendant."

A half hour later, an officer loaded Jessie and Derrick onto the coast guard craft in handcuffs. Meranda turned the slate and the camera over as evidence and told them what Jessie had said about her father claiming to be a hero.

Derrick began singing his innocence, insisting that Jessie had told him to come and steal the pendant while the two were diving. "I'm not going down for another one, Jessie!"

"Another one?" Meranda looked at Paul.

He called out to the officer who handcuffed Jessie. "You might check her for an important artifact taken from Judge Bernard's house."

The officer gave him a thumbs-up as they sped away.

Meanwhile, another officer stayed on Meranda's boat and insisted on medically checking her.

"I'm fine."

Paul sat near enough that she could feel his support, but out of the way. "Sit down and let the nice man do his job."

She glanced his way, and while his eyes twinkled a teasing message, they also telegraphed that he'd help her sit if she didn't on her own.

With her seated, the officer checked her vitals. "How fast did you rise to the surface?"

"As fast as I could, but I tried to regulate it."

"Are you experiencing any fatigue, itching of the skin, stiffness in the joints, numbness, or shortness of breath?"

Blast! All she needed was the bends on top of nearly becoming fish food. She shook her head and wondered if they were checking Jessie for the same thing.

"Why are you rubbing your arm?"

"It's sore here." She indicated the fleshy part of her upper arm. "Probably from trying to get out. I had to squeeze through a hole."

"You want to tell me about that, ma'am?"

As she related her underwater adventure, she kept an eye on Paul. He seemed to suffer along with her.

She and Jessie had found the entrance into the skin of the ship. They tied off their line so they could make it back out. "I had been in there several times, so I knew where to go." They found the cabin, and Meranda saw the hole in the floor. It didn't go straight through to the lower compartment, but only to a subfloor. Meranda started moving debris from the hole, sure this was where Pop had left off before his death. Her hand felt the hard plastic casing of the camera, and she pulled it out and placed it in her bag.

"Divers lose things all the time," she told Paul. "It didn't surprise me that his camera would have fallen into the hole."

What did surprise her, however, was the slate.

"Pop's writing slate was also in the hole. Jessie was right there watching as I pulled it out. We both saw what he had written at the same time, and that's when we both knew. Her father had killed mine." She swallowed the new grief so she could go on. "Jessie grabbed the slate and moved to the guide string. She started kicking up silt until I became disoriented. Then Jessie followed the string out—taking the spool with her—leaving me to fend for myself. I couldn't find the door, so I dropped and searched the floor for the hole. I knew there was a way out from the compartment below. When I found the hole, I took off my tank and smashed through the subfloor. As I squeezed through, I strained my arm." She rubbed her upper arm, feeling like it might fall off. "Luckily, there was better visibility below. The jagged hole in the hull allowed light to filter in, so I headed toward it and out to safety."

The officer put away his equipment and smiled, perhaps for the first time since arriving. "You're one lucky lady. Let us know if you feel any of the symptoms I just mentioned. I'm concerned about the arm. We'll sling it, but I'm also putting you on oxygen and an IV just as a precaution. We don't want to mess with decompression sickness. We'll have an ambulance waiting for you at the dock."

"I don't need an ambulance."

"Yes, you do," Paul piped in. "I'll go with you."

Paul drove the boat back but needed some help from the officer to maneuver it into the slip.

In the ambulance, Paul sat next to her holding her hand. "You were awesome on the boat."

She smiled and lifted the oxygen mask just a little so she could talk. "By what I saw, you were holding your own with those two."

His chest puffed. "Yeah, well. . .you watch enough cop shows, you learn a few things. I didn't intimidate Jessie, though."

She patted his hand. "That's okay. We made a good team."

"That's right. We've got each others' backs." His eyes suddenly sparkled. "Oh, that reminds me why I showed up this morning. With Derrick fired"—he tilted his head—"and now with Jessie gone, I need some help at the restaurant."

Meranda pointed to her chest and raised her eyebrows.

"Good grief, no! I'm not asking you. If I ever need someone to make Twinkies and peanut butter sandwiches, though, you're my girl." He gently chucked her chin. "I was thinking of your sister."

"Rose?" She raised her thumb in approval. "You're her new role model."

"At first I was going to ask her to fill in for Derrick, but now I need a good sous chef. I didn't know if I should approach her about it, given your family's social status."

"Ask her. She'll be thrilled."

The tech inside the ambulance put a stop to her talking by putting the oxygen mask back in place, and they pulled into the emergency entrance of Crossroads Bay Medical Center.

She was wheeled into a room that had been partitioned off with curtains and transferred to a bed. Moans of several patients in various stages of distress reached her ears. As people came in and out, she tried to convince each one that she felt fine.

A woman doctor with spiky bleached hair finally came in and after an examination said, "I'd like to keep you here for just a few more hours."

"I don't have the bends." Meranda rolled her eyes, but then realized she had a dull headache. Probably from the stress of the day. Or too much oxygen.

The doctor regarded her with patience, as if she dealt with people all day long who knew their own bodies. "You don't seem to have DCS, but why take chances? I'm sure you'll be going home soon."

At least she didn't have to sit in a decompression chamber. She hated those things.

She asked if she could have visitors—Paul had been told to stay in the waiting room while they settled her in—and when she was told she could, she expected him to appear from behind the curtain. Instead her mother trotted in.

"Meranda! Are you okay? Are you hurting anywhere? I am so angry with you. Let me know if you need anything."

"Whoa, Mom. Lots of emotion there for me to weed through with my aching head."

"I'm sorry." She lowered her voice to just above a whisper. "I'll go tell them you're in pain."

"No, I can't have anything yet until they're sure I don't have the bends. An analgesic will just mask the symptoms." She patted the bed. "Come here. Sit with me."

Mom lowered herself to the bed, her shoulders slumped, tears threatening to spill from red-rimmed eyes that had probably already done their share of crying for the day. Meranda recognized this behavior. She'd seen plenty of it in the days after Pop's accident.

She reached out for her mother's hand. "I'm sorry."

Mom gripped the fingers in between her palms. "What were you thinking? What was your father thinking?"

"I know, Mom, you were right." This stopped her mother in midargument. "Dad was foolish to attempt to find the coins in such a dangerous place. When I thought I might join him in his watery grave, all I could think about was you, Rose, and Julianne. How losing one more to the coins would be devastating to you. Please forgive me for my selfishness."

Mom swept a curl from Meranda's brow. "You're so like your father." She spoke with a tenderness Meranda had never heard before.

"Is that a good thing, Mom?"

"I'm beginning to think it is." Her sigh bordered on exasperation. "My little adventurer. When Paul called to tell me they were bringing you to the hospital—and why—I was livid. But as I drove here, I realized this is who you are. You have your father's blood running hot in your veins. I can't change you. . .nor would I want to."

Meranda allowed the words to wash over her. She hadn't realized how much she needed her mother to understand her. "Thanks, Mom."

"And did you find the coins?"

"No, but I found Pop's camera." She shared what had happened between her and Jessie. "I turned it in to the coast guard. There will be an investigation."

Mom covered her face with one hand while holding onto Meranda's with the other. "I hate to live his death all over again, but I'll do what I have to do." The squeeze she gave to Meranda's fingers translated to a desperate clinging.

"We, Mom. We're in this together." She would not abandon her mother again.

"May we come in?" Rose and Julianne stood at the opening to the curtain.

"Of course." She opened her arms and both women flew into the cubicle, but only gently attacked her with hugs and kisses. "Where have you been?"

"In the waiting room with Paul." Julianne plopped into the only chair. "He suggested letting Mom come in first. Besides, she wanted to throttle you in private." After a glare from their mother, she added, "That's what you said."

"Well, the throttling is over." Mom patted Meranda's hip.

Meranda turned back to Rose. "Did you talk to Paul? He has a job offer."

Her sister's eyes lit up. "Yes, he told me about it."

"I know it will help pay for the wedding." She looked back at their mother. "I'm sorry, Mom. But we know you're in trouble."

Her mother nodded and dropped her gaze to her hands.

Meranda turned back to Rose. "I don't know how your fiancé will feel about you having a job, though."

"That isn't a concern anymore. We broke up."

"What? When?"

"This morning. I realized I didn't love him. Mom and I talked."

"She confronted me last night," Mom said. "She told me she didn't love him and that I was pushing the marriage. Honestly, I didn't know I was. He came from a good family, and I knew he would provide. But once she laid it out, I could see neither of them loved each other. Once he finds out we've lost our money, I'm sure he'll move on. Social climbers are like that."

It took one to know one. Meranda bit her tongue. None of that mattered now.

They stayed and chatted for a few more minutes. Finally Mom said, "Well, I know a young man who is probably pacing the floor out there. We'll go and let him sit with you."

She kissed Meranda on the forehead. Meranda couldn't remember when she'd done that last. Tears stung her eyes as she watched her family leave.

A nurse about ten years her senior poked her head in. "I have someone out here looking for you. If you don't want him, I'm sure someone out here will snatch him up."

"Send him in." Her heart began to flutter, and she hoped they wouldn't keep her for hypertension. "Oh, and by the way, I'm fine. I shouldn't even be here."

"Yes, you should." Paul stepped in as the nurse turned to leave, his arms folded and looking absolutely gorgeous in his protective mode.

Meranda felt that pleasant minnow sensation again, only this time it felt like they were chasing each other in a game of tag. She liked someone taking care of her. Who knew? He walked into the room and stood by the bed, taking her hand.

❧

Paul relished the feel of Meranda's hand in his. He tried to memorize every line, every knuckle as his fingers explored. Common sense continued to remind him to maintain only a friendship since he didn't want to be unequally yoked, but nearly losing this special friend had frightened him.

Meranda turned his wrist so she could see his watch. She gasped. "I had no idea it was almost evening. Do you have the dinner shift tonight?"

"No. I called Al, and he pulled someone in. Right now you're my priority." He settled into the chair near the bed.

"Paul, I need to tell you what happened down there."

He frowned, confused. "But I was listening when you told the coast guard."

"No, I need to tell you what happened in here." She pointed to her heart.

He leaned forward, eager to hear this story.

"After Jessie left, I was so alone. It was dark; I didn't know where the door was. . ." Her wide eyes reflected the terror she must have felt. "I was scared."

Shifting to the bed, he gathered her in his arms. Soft sobbing tore at his heart. He knew Meranda rarely, if ever, let people see this side of her. And he felt grateful that she chose him to show her vulnerability.

"Shh, it's okay now." He rocked her, letting her purge her emotions so she could talk.

Finally, she let go of his neck and sank back onto the pillow. "I thought I was going to join my dad. I wasn't ready to die."

"And I'm not ready to lose you." He smoothed her bedraggled hair from her wet face, thinking that even splotchy, she was the most beautiful woman he'd ever seen.

"While I was looking for the door, I prayed."

"You prayed?" *Thank You, Lord.*

"I thought about what you said. That I'm at a crossroads. When I chose to do this dive, I chose the path that leads to death. When I couldn't find the guide string, I thought about my dad and how he died the same way." Her sad eyes turned perplexed. "Then a strange thing happened. While I was thinking 'I've got to get out,' I heard in my head, 'Down.' It was then I remembered that the lower hold was accessible from the outside. Somehow I went right to the hole in the floor. I took off my tank and used it to smash through the subfloor. It wasn't hard to do, and I think Pop had the same idea. The wood splintered easily, as if it had only a few more good whacks to go. It's as if Pop saved my life." Her gaze turned back to Paul.

"Sounds like a miracle to me."

"I realized something else." She reached for his hand and gripped it tight. "I don't want to die not knowing Jesus as you and Augustus and Glenys know Him."

Paul's heart overflowed with praise. He cradled her hand with both of his and shared how all have fallen short of God's grace, how Christ died for her sins, and how all she had to do was accept God's free gift of salvation.

She closed her eyes and, gripping his hand, poured out her heart to the One who guided her out of the murky depths, both literally and spiritually.

When they were through, she seemed perplexed. "That's it?"

"That's it. The hardest thing is realizing you need a Savior. Asking Him into your heart is easy."

"Hm. I think I should work on my mom and sisters now."

Paul laughed and kissed the knuckles on her right hand. "So, you're back at that crossroads. What are you going to do now?"

"Give it to God. The coins aren't worth my life, and they weren't worth my dad's life. I'm through looking for the coins."

"I know that's what you're saying, and I know this latest search scared you, but are you sure you want to give up totally?"

She seemed to give his question some thought. A few seconds passed, and she thrust out her chin as if determined to live by her newfound faith. "If God wants me to find them, He'll show me the steps to take."

"What about your family?" One more test for her. It was one thing to trust God for one's own needs, but what about her loved ones?

"God will take care of my family."

"Yes, He will." He stood and leaned down to kiss her. "And we'll both take care of you."

Chapter 16

Pablo."

"Yes, Abuelita." Paul sat in the office finishing Rose's paperwork after hiring her and showing her around the kitchen that morning. With her scores at the culinary institute and the test dishes he had asked her to prepare, he knew she would make a good fit. She left with promises to be back early the next morning.

Abuelita smiled. "I like her."

Paul raised an eyebrow. "Really? Even though you didn't get to interrogate her?"

"Do not be smart with me." She pulled the bulldog face but left the twinkle in her eye. "I have my ticket. I will see my sister in Sevilla, España, next week."

This news sucker punched him in the belly. "I thought you were kidding about that!" He didn't want her to move to another country, just out of the restaurant business. "I'll miss you, my abuelita." He stood and hugged her close, a lump the size of Spain in his throat.

He felt her chuckling near his chest. She reared her head and looked at his face. "I'll only be gone a month. Maybe I'll find new recipes for us to use, sí?"

He pulled her close again and cuddled her stick body. "I love you, Abuelita. Thank you for giving me this chance."

"You have earned it, Pablito." Her hand flew to her mouth. "Oops! I mean *big* Pablo. Your abuelo would be so proud."

Al poked his head in. "Are you still here? I thought you had a date with a boat captain."

Paul checked his watch. "Gotta run."

He kissed Abuelita on her head.

"Pablo. Where are you going?"

"It's my day off. Tomorrow we'll plan your going-away party, sí?"

Her eyes twinkled. "Sí." Then she wandered toward the kitchen where he heard, "Alberto."

Paul shook his head. Not even an entire ocean between them could keep Abuelita from trying to run her kitchen.

He grabbed his keys off the desk and hustled out the door. Meranda waited on her front porch for him, and he drove her to the lighthouse property.

"I'm so happy that Glenys invited us before she goes back to California." It had been a few days since Meranda's scare. Paul thanked God that her injuries weren't more severe. A strained arm was all her adventure into the abyss had cost her. And it seemed fine now with her bouncing in her seat in anticipation of seeing the lighthouse again.

"And she said she had a surprise for you."

"Yes." Her eyes widened into gray green saucers. "Maybe she found the coins!"

"Well"—he turned onto the lighthouse road—"I wouldn't get my hopes up. She didn't sound that excited."

They stopped at the gate. Paul rang the buzzer, identified himself, and the gate slid open.

"I really like that!" Meranda said. "No more closed doors around here."

They parked in front of the house, and the judge met them there.

"Uh-oh." Meranda slowly opened her door. "I hope it's okay if we're here."

His wave and smile seemed friendly enough to Paul.

After shaking their hands, the judge opened the conversation. "I want to let you know how sorry I am. Glenys told me about your. . .uh. . .adventure, and I can see now how important finding your family's treasure is to you. You're welcome to the lighthouse anytime. I give you my permission to look around."

Meranda smiled and thanked him, but then said, "My father died looking for the coins. Why wouldn't you think they'd be important to me?"

"The lighthouse property is just my vacation home. I didn't know about your father. Glenys has been quick to inform me, however." He scratched his ear and chuckled.

Interesting. The judge had an Achilles' heel.

"Glenys is in the lighthouse if you'd like to join her."

Meranda bounded up the slope toward the lighthouse but stopped abruptly and turned. "Thank you for opening your home to us."

The judge laughed. "You're welcome. Now go." He waved her off.

She swiveled and sprinted up the path to the lighthouse, leaving Paul to scurry behind.

When they entered, a *chink, chink* sound greeted them. Meranda put a foot on the first step and called up the winding staircase. "Glenys? You here?"

"Come on up."

They found her about three-quarters of the way up the winding staircase, chiseling away at one of the plaques on the wall.

"Glenys!" Meranda grabbed the little hammer out of her hand. "Your dad will be furious."

"Relax." Glenys snatched it back. "Dad said I could pry off one plaque if I didn't make a mess and could put it back exactly the same way. If there's something behind here, it shouldn't be hard to remove it."

Meranda scooted past her to sit on the top step, and Paul stayed below Glenys, impressed by her precision with the hammer and chisel. "Where did you learn to do that so neatly?"

"I had a bit part in a movie about an archeological dig." She glanced down at him.

"I doubt if you saw it."

"You know, Glenys," Meranda said as she played with the pendant around her neck. "I don't feel the need to find the coins anymore."

Glenys continued to chisel.

"Paul showed me that before my dive I was at a crossroads with the coins. He shared a verse. 'Stand at the crossroads and look; ask for the ancient paths, ask where the good way is, and walk in it, and you will find rest for your souls.' "

Impressive that she could quote it without looking. She must have gone back to the bookmarked site on her laptop and thought a lot about their discussion.

"One path led to near destruction," she continued while twirling the pendant around the tip of her finger. "The other allows God to lead me if He thinks I should have the coins."

Chink. Chink. Glenys continued to work. Finally she said, "I'm happy you've found peace with the coins. I believe God will guide you, but now you've got me curious." *Chink. Chink.* "If you don't mind, I'll keep looking until I leave."

"I'm curious, too," Paul said. "From the first time I saw the pillars outside."

"May I see your pendant again, Meranda?" Glenys set aside the hammer and chisel. "I didn't get a good look at it the other day. Do the pillars outside really look like the image?"

"They do. Someone worked hard at crafting them." Meranda unclasped the chain, but as she handed it down, Glenys only grasped one side of the chain. The pendant slipped off the necklace and began rolling down the steps like an errant tire on the highway, creating a chorus of echoing clinks.

"Oh! I'm sorry!" Glenys started after it, but Paul stopped her.

"I'll get it." Paul grabbed the rail and hustled down the steps. The pendant didn't stop until it hit the solid floor and then rolled behind the open iron staircase. "Found it!" He squatted to pick it up and heard more chiseling above. "It's fine. Not a mark on it."

Glenys's chiseling stopped, and he heard her squeal. He called up to her. "Did you find something?"

A pause. "No, just brick behind here."

"Too bad." Before heading back up, a number etched on the back of one of the steps caught his eye. Upon further inspection, he saw other numbers, but not on every step. Each was a different number going up in succession with every higher step. He peered through the staircase and saw that within his vision the steps with numbers coincided with a plaque.

"Hey, ladies." He pulled out the notebook he kept in his pocket for recipe ideas and jotted down the numbers. "You might want to see this."

Their feet pattered on the metal staircase. Handing Meranda's pendant back to her, he pointed to a number, then to the plaque.

Meranda slipped the chain back through the hole in the pendant and put it back on. She looked at Glenys. "Do you understand what that means?"

Glenys shook her head.

Paul fingered the number on the seventh step up, about his eye level. "Could be the order of the stairs so they would be assembled correctly."

Meranda bent down to look at the first number on the second step. "Then why does this have the number one?" They all inspected further. The next step with a number was the fifth one, but it had a number three. And so on up the staircase.

"Do either of you have a compact?" Paul asked.

Meranda looked at him as if he'd lost his mind. "I don't even wear makeup."

"I have one," Glenys said. "It's in the house, though. I'll run and get it."

While she was gone, Paul and Meranda stood under the staircase looking at the numbers.

"They don't seem factory etched." Meranda rubbed her fingers across one of the numbers. "Wouldn't it look a little more professionally done even a hundred years ago?"

Paul reached out and touched the number, brushing Meranda's hand. He glanced around the small space and noted her nearness. He wove his fingers between hers, and she swung her gaze to meet his. He praised God silently that this woman to whom he was attracted from the first meeting now shared his faith.

"I'm very glad you picked this crossroad, Meranda. Because it brought us here." With his other arm, he reached around her and drew her close. She leaned into his kiss, her full lips soft and warm. When they parted, he searched her gray eyes. "I don't know what I'd have done if I'd lost you the other day. I wouldn't have gotten the chance to tell you how I feel."

She reached around his neck. "And how do you feel?"

"I love you." He captured her mouth once more. Never in his life had he felt this kind of emotion. He had never been truly in love before. He wanted to protect this powerful sea captain with all his might, but more than that, he wanted to spend the rest of his life with her.

When he allowed her to speak, her words did not disappoint. "I love you, too." She tickled the back of his neck as she played with the strands of his hair. At that moment his whole world came into alignment.

"You can thank your grandmother."

He pulled back. "My grandmother?" He didn't need that image at this moment.

"Remember? The alcove, the candle, the soft music?"

Ah, yes. The first day she visited the restaurant. When he came out of the kitchen that day, his legs nearly buckled when he saw her. Gone was the pirate scarf, allowing her hair to float in soft red curls around her face. Like now. He wound a ringlet around his finger. "I remember."

"Wow. I leave for a second. . ." Glenys stood inside the door with a mischievous grin playing on her face.

"You could have taken your time," Paul told her.

"You need to let me know these things. A signal or something would have been helpful."

Paul held out his hand. "You have the mirror?"

She placed an odd-looking contraption into his palm. "This is what my dad uses on his cars when he needs to see something buried under the hood. I ran into the house and told him what we've found. He suggested this."

Paul handed Meranda his notebook. "Please jot down the numbers as I call them out." He took the round mirror by the handle and adjusted the swivel, then headed up the stairs. At each plaque, he slipped the mirror between the corresponding steps. "Six," he called down, then moved to the next plaque and step. "Eight." And the next. "Nine."

The judge entered as Paul called down the last numbers. Glenys showed him what they'd found.

"Wish I could help," he said. "I didn't even know the numbers were there. Looks to me like a combination to something."

Paul bounced down the stairs to join them. "Like a safe?"

Meranda cocked her head. "Aren't there too many numbers for that?"

"Probably." The judge scratched his chin. "Could be the numbers add up to something. Why don't we go in the house and brainstorm."

Glenys led the way out. "I'll make sandwiches. It's almost noon."

⟨⟩

After lunch they all lingered around the kitchen table. Meranda wondered what Paul thought of Glenys's turkey sandwiches. They were good, but very plain.

Judge Bernard stood and cleared the plates. "Would you like to see some pictures of the property as they were building?"

"Are they the same ones as in the museum?" Meranda sipped her second cup of hot coffee, careful not to burn her tongue.

"Some are. These are the originals, the ones the photographer used to put in the paper. I found them in a box in the attic." He left to get them. When he came back, he laid a black photo album on the table.

"These are clearer." Meranda and Paul looked together. The album chronicled the building of the lighthouse from the groundbreaking to finished product. Besides the fascination of the process, Meranda paid close attention to Augustus in the photos. What a jovial man he seemed to be. The museum pictures didn't show this side of him. He was laughing in several of the pictures, shaking hands with the mason near a pile of bricks, showing a group of men in suits the partial product, beaming from ear to ear as he stood in front of the finished lighthouse.

She flipped the page. A large house-sized hole had been dug and boards formed somewhat of a structure. "Is this the construction of the house?"

"Yes," the judge said. "There aren't as many because it wasn't as interesting, I suppose."

The final picture in the album was of Augustus leaning against a sign and standing where the road split off. The right going to the house and the left to the lighthouse. Both structures showed in the background.

Meranda squinted. "Is this a homemade street sign?" She never noticed it in the museum pictures. An unobtrusive wooden two-by-four had been staked into the ground with two rustic planks nailed onto it. "Those look like ship planks."

The judge swiveled the album toward him. "I haven't looked too closely at this picture, but I believe you're right. Probably from the shipwreck."

Paul leaned in. "What's painted on them?"

Four heads pressed in on one another.

"Lighthouse Road and *something* Way," Meranda said. The first word was hard to see in the old photograph due to the angle.

"Starts with a *G*," Glenys contributed. "G–o–o—"

"Good!" Paul piped in.

Meranda frowned at him. "What's so good about it? We can't read it."

"No, that's the word. Good. Good Way." He tapped the table in his excitement. "What was the scripture you quoted to Glenys in the lighthouse?"

"Stand at the crossroads and look; ask for the ancient paths, ask where the good way is. . ." Her jaw dropped. "Good way! The coins are here in the house!"

Chapter 17

Okay, let's think about this." Meranda leaned her elbows on the table, squeezed her eyes shut, and went over all the clues. "Augustus's letter led me to the property. The pendant led me to the pillars and confirmed we were on the right track. The pillars led me to the lighthouse. Inside the lighthouse, the plaques led to the steps and their numbers. If I hadn't been clumsy and dropped my pendant, we might never have gotten this far."

"I think that was God," Paul said.

"What? He slid it off the chain?"

"You were telling Glenys about the scripture and what you'd learned. I think God honored your obedience to give the search to Him."

Meranda's heart warmed to this. Even though she was new at letting God captain her life, she felt peace that Paul was right.

"So," she continued. "The steps and the numbers are no doubt important."

"I just remembered something." The judge pointed to the photograph showing the homemade road sign. "This picture hung in the lighthouse until the renovation, just above the highest plaque."

"Cool!" Glenys stabbed the air with her finger, drawing an imaginary line upward. "The steps and their numbers were supposed to lead to the photo, which told us the treasure is in the house somewhere." She frowned. "But where? Alison and I have been all over this place. As kids we found every nook and cranny. If the coins are here, they must be inside a wall or under a floor."

Meranda cocked an eyebrow at the judge.

"Oh no," he said, waving his arms. "You aren't tearing this place apart."

"We shouldn't have to tear the *whole* place apart." She shut her eyes again. "The pillars led to the lighthouse. The lighthouse led to the plaques. The plaques led to the steps. The steps led to the photo. The photo led to the house." *Think.* She paused in her brainsqueezing to pray. *Lord, You led me this far. Please show me the rest of the way.* She went through the entire sequence again in her head.

As if God turned on a spotlight, she saw the steps and their numbers in her mind. Her eyes popped open. "Steps!"

Now everybody's eyes were wide. Together they repeated. "Steps!"

"Let me see your notebook." Meranda held her hand out to Paul.

She took it and raced to the staircase leading to the bedrooms on the second floor.

"The numbers are one, three, six, eight, and nine." She counted the steps in the narrow stairway. Ten.

With the judge's nodding approval, she took Glenys's hammer and chisel and pried the board away from the first step. As light flooded the dark three-foot by one-foot space, her heart thudded a drumming beat in her ears.

Nothing.

She pried the third step.

Still nothing.

What could she have missed? *God, why would You have brought me this far only to fail?*

She sat on the second step, one that didn't have a corresponding number, with her head drooped into her hands. Hot, unshed tears stung her closed eyelids. Rubbing her face and fingering her hair out of her eyes, she addressed the three silent members of the search party. "Is there any way they could have been here and someone found them?"

The judge shrugged. "I suppose that's possible. Although I was assured when I bought this place that everything was original to the house."

"Wait." Paul tapped his temples, obviously taxing his brain as much as Meranda was hers. "Do you have Augustus's letter with you?"

She felt gooseflesh on the back of her neck and quickly retrieved it from her bag. They both skimmed it, looking for another clue.

"Yes!" Paul removed the letter from her hand. "I doubt he would have put them in a wooden staircase. If the house burned down, surely someone would find them. Augustus writes that he feels 'concretely sure' that the coins were where no one would find them."

Adrenaline surged through Meranda as she reached for the letter. "Concrete!" She looked at the judge and Glenys, who by their furrowed brows seemed completely perplexed. "Are there steps in the house made of concrete? The cellar perhaps."

Glenys and her father looked at each other, then raced to the back of the house. Paul and Meranda followed on their heels as they headed into the kitchen. They stopped at the door with the shelf above it.

Meranda took note of the tin box that she knew was void of the second pendant. "You said your pendant had been found behind the wall above the door?"

Glenys and her father both nodded.

"Another clue! Your pendant pointed the way to the cellar."

Glenys threw open the door to the cellar. "There are ten steps down. And each one solid concrete."

Meranda looked at the hammer and chisel in her hands. "I'm going to need something bigger."

Soon she was pulling a sledgehammer over her shoulder and demolishing the first step. The concrete crumbled away easily, not the same quality as what modern-day builders used. At the bottom of the slab, a piece of leather began to emerge. Paul joined her, and together they clawed and chiseled at it until it was free. Meranda pulled the pouch out, opened it with shaky hands, and gasped at the two perfect gold coins with two pillars on one side and a crest on the other.

"Hello, welcome back to the family." She pressed them to her heart.

"Aren't there seven coins?" Glenys asked.

Meranda replaced the coins in the bag and tossed them to her, then leaned on the sledgehammer. "We found two of them. Augustus probably split them up in case someone found one batch. Anyone not knowing to look for seven would probably consider themselves lucky and not look anymore. So there could be one here"—she tapped the next step—"and two here"—she tapped another.

"Your Augustus was a smart cookie." Glenys sat on the kitchen floor and hugged her knees. "So let's see what's in the next step."

Meranda continued to pound the steps until she felt sweat trickling off her face. Paul offered to take over, but she held him off. "I need to do this."

He nodded, and she continued, finding two coins each in the next two steps and one coin in the eighth step. In the pouch holding the last coin, a note had been included. She carefully unfolded the ancient page, her heart pounding against her rib cage.

She read it aloud: " ' "Blessed be the God and Father of our Lord Jesus Christ, which according to his abundant mercy hath begotten us again unto a lively hope by the resurrection of Jesus Christ from the dead, to an inheritance incorruptible, and undefiled, and that fadeth not away, reserved in heaven for you, who are kept by the power of God through faith unto salvation ready to be revealed in the last time." First Peter 1:3–5. To all who find these coins, accept instead the perfect inheritance from our Lord and Savior Jesus Christ, who assures salvation and an eternal home where the treasure in your heart suffers not from moth nor rust, and where thieves do not break through nor steal. If the finder does not need these coins to survive, please hide them again for the next generation, and give them the opportunity to accept God's perfect incorruptible inheritance, Jesus Christ.' "

Meranda lowered the note, and while standing in the rubble of the stairs, leaned into Paul for support. He enfolded her in his arms and kissed her head with dusty lips. She was too stunned to think. This was bigger than she had ever imagined. Had she not accepted Christ in the hospital, she would have surely done so after reading her great-great-grandfather's words.

Glenys looked up at her father from her sitting position on the kitchen floor. He had been standing at the top of the stairs throughout the demolition. She spoke reverently, with a quiet tone one might use in church. "I wonder. We thought the inscription on our pendant was IR1.345, but what if the R was actually a P? IP.1.345—the verses in First Peter."

Judge Bernard sank to the floor. "Could be. The R always looked funny to me." He nodded and turned a dazed look toward his daughter. "I never put much stock in religious things. Your mother was in charge of that." He wiped his nose with a handkerchief and glanced toward Meranda. "This *game* has been going on for how long?"

Meranda carefully ascended the staircase, stepping only on those steps she hadn't destroyed. "Four centuries." She lowered herself to the kitchen floor, cuddling the coins to her chest, proud of her family for making the treasure hunt so much more than material blessing.

"Wow." The judge ran his fingers through his already disheveled hair. "I think I'd better look more into this God thing." He smiled at his daughter. "You think He'd take an old ambulance chaser like me?"

"Oh, Daddy." She threw herself into his arms and wept. "I wish Mom could know her prayers are being answered."

Paul looked up at them from the cellar floor. "She will know when all of you are reunited in heaven."

Glenys buried her face in her father's chest, where she managed a muffled, "Thank you, Paul."

"Um. . .wait a minute." Paul had out his notebook. "There's one more step."

"But we found all the coins." Meranda counted them in her hand again.

He picked up the sledgehammer and held it up to her. She leaned against the kitchen wall. "Would you? I feel as if my arms are coming out of their sockets."

His broad smile assured her that he was more than ready to play demolition. He spit on his hands, gripped the wooden handle, and swung at the step with all his might. The cement cracked. One more good whack. Then another. Finally he stopped to brush aside the chalky chips. "It's another pouch." He worked it from the cement and peeked inside, then drew out another note. A small grin spread across his face as he read silently.

Meranda's patience stretched as tight as the skin on a sun-baked mackerel. She stood with the other two at the top of the stairs, sure they must have felt the same. "Well? Is it another coin?"

"Nope. Read this note." He handed it up to her but kept the bag from her reach.

She read out loud, " 'The Lord has been very good to me. I pass my bounty on and pray that the finder will use it as needed. Augustus Drake, Crossroads Bay, 27th day of March, 1907.' "

"That's my birthday!" Meranda felt her neck tingle. Was God redeeming the day for her so she'd have something good to remember?

Paul climbed up the steps and stood with her. "Open your hands."

She held out her palms, and he poured a cup full of yellow nuggets into them. All four said in unison, "Gold."

☙

Two weeks later Paul joined a church group of about twenty people who had booked the *Golden Hind* for a deep-sea fishing charter. Meranda had called him the day before to see if he'd like to learn how to fish. Deep-sea fishing had never been something he considered doing, especially in view of his aversion to boats. But he found himself excited about the adventure.

He also felt it a good way to market himself. He boarded with enough food to keep everyone happy and had his business cards in his pocket ready to hand out. An idea began to hatch as he worked in the galley. If Meranda charged for the food, he could provide snacks and meals on a regular basis. Currently, she only provided fresh bottled water and informed her guests they'd have to bring their own food but could use the galley.

With everyone on board, Meranda tucked a disobedient curl under her scarf, gripped the throttle, and pulled away from the dock. Paul had joined her at the helm and stood behind the captain's chair. He praised God that he'd conquered his fear.

Glancing to the deck below, he saw that the passengers all seemed occupied looking out at sea. This gave him confidence to flirt a little. The warm sun kissed Meranda's cheeks, making them glow, and he did the same. "Okay, your kitchen is good to go. I brought plenty of tapas for your guests to enjoy."

Meranda smiled. "I saw you cart the appetizers in. We can't possibly eat all that food."

"No, but whatever is leftover can be yours to snack on. You know, something nutritious the next time you're out."

"Chips and cookies aren't in the major food groups? Not even the tiniest part of the food pyramid?"

"No. Those are convenient heart stoppers at best."

"I don't mind. Your food has changed my palate." She maneuvered the larger craft away from the dock and throttled up to head out to sea. "I loved Pop, but whenever we'd sail we would stop at the corner store and stock up on anything in a bag or a box."

Paul shuddered. "Plastic food. Yech."

*Arrgh. . . Arrgh. . .*The pirate ring tone came from Meranda's hip pocket. She drew it out and looked at the caller ID. "It's Glenys."

"I wonder if she started her movie project."

"I'll put it on speaker so we can both hear her." She did so and yelled at the phone. "Hi, Glenys. You're going to have to speak up and quickly. We're just heading out to sea, so we may lose you. Paul is listening in."

"Hi, guys!" Glenys's smiling voice sounded from the speaker.

Paul waved at the phone, then realized she couldn't see him. "Hi, Glenys. What's up?"

"The authorities found the other pendant in Jessie's house. The night of my sister's wedding, she must have slipped inside when the police arrived for you two."

"Ouch, don't remind me. We had talked about the pendants being valuable together. And the pendants with the coins would have made a handsome booty. Oh!" Meranda's sudden excitement made her bounce in her chair. "That makes the treasure complete then."

"What have you planned to do with the coins?"

"Right now I have them in a safety deposit box."

"Are you going to hide them for the next generation?"

She glanced back at the lighthouse. "No, I can't risk anybody else losing his life. I'm going to donate them to the museum. I'll include the research we found in the journals and the letters from Augustus."

"What about the pendants? They need to be on display, too."

Meranda fingered the pendant from the chain on her neck. Paul wondered if she would be able to part with it for the sake of history. She surprised him by agreeing enthusiastically.

"Maybe," she continued to talk to Glenys, "the curator will create a prominent display including the note we found with the coins. Do you know how many people will see that and be pointed to Jesus?" She rubbed her neck, and Paul knew she felt that tingle she always got when she solved a clue. He kissed her hair, proud of the shift she'd made from needing the coins at all costs to sharing the coins for Christ.

"I know you'll be blessed for that decision, Meranda." Glenys sighed. Was she remembering the tender moment with her father after the note was found with the coins?

Paul stood behind Meranda and massaged her shoulders, then kissed her hair.

"I'm blessed already, Glenys." She turned her head for a brief kiss. "Oh, and I have something to tell you."

"Go on, but hurry, you're breaking up."

"The camera I found in the wreckage proved to have evidence. Pop must have set it up in spy mode. It took several pictures in succession. Kingston never even realized it. It shows them pulling the boards from the cabin floor and Kingston finding a leather satchel under the boards. Kingston opened it. In the video, you could tell my dad was angry with him for doing so. You're not supposed to open items you find. They need to be processed slowly to keep the contents from deteriorating. He probably thought it was The Inheritance. Gold coins don't succumb to salt water. Thankfully, what was inside also doesn't corrode easily."

"Quickly! Tell me before I lose you. What was in the satchel?"

"Gold bars, ingots circa 1900. Augustus was probably going to use them to pay the crew. The video shows Kingston and my dad fighting over the bag. Kingston won. He must have then hidden it somewhere in the wreckage after he left Pop to. . ." Her throat caught just a little. "After he shut the door on Pop."

There was silence on the phone.

"Glenys?"

Nothing.

Meranda chuckled and put the phone back in her pocket. "If we went out of range before answering her, she's probably having a fit wondering what I said."

"I'm sure we'll hear from her later."

"Oh, no doubt."

Paul sat in the passenger seat. "I have a question. What about the third man on the shipwreck expedition with your father and Kingston? Was he in on it?"

"I didn't tell you? So much more going on, I suppose. The police questioned him. He seems to be in the clear. "

"I've been thinking about Jessie, too. I think she targeted you. It was her idea to bid on the anniversary party that chartered your boat, you know, the first time we met."

Meranda offered a wicked grin. "How could I forget? There was the man of my dreams, upchucking over the side of my boat."

Paul almost wished he still had the seasick bands since she mentioned it. "Anyway, she was pretty forceful. Went behind my back to my grandmother after I said no. The two of them ganged up on me. Somehow she knew about the coins early on."

"Probably from her father." Meranda's gaze dropped to the gauges on the console. Paul assumed they would arrive soon at the waters she wanted to fish in. "I'm sure he bragged about trying to save my dad. It's possible that Jessie learned about my chartering business and since she was already a caterer, thought that would be a good way to snoop on my boat."

"Could be. She turned out to be pretty resourceful."

Meranda slapped the wheel. "I didn't get to tell Glenys that the police found the satchel at Kingston's house and that the *Crossroads Examiner* reported that he was sitting on the bars looking for a buyer."

"I wonder what Jessie's reaction to that was." He scratched the side of his nose. "She must not have known about the bars, otherwise why would she bother looking for the coins?"

Meranda frowned. "I think she would have been greedy and wanted it all."

Paul hated to admit it, but she was probably right. It hurt to think that such a talented chef could stoop so low. "Do you think she knew your father died at her father's hands?" He asked the question with reverence and added a stroke to her arm to let her know he understood her grief.

She shrugged. "You know her better than me."

He chose to think there was some good in Jessie. But after deliberating with himself, he came to the conclusion that given her split personality, it was possible she knew. The Jessie that held a gun on him that day was a stranger. He had other questions about her. "I'm wondering why she needed you if she knew where the shipwreck was."

"She may have known the location, but why risk going down there if I could lead her to a different place? Remember how gung ho she was at wanting to demolish the lighthouse wall?"

Paul laughed. "And I thought that was cute. So what do you intend to do with the gold bars in the satchel?"

"It isn't mine, is it? Kingston found it. With him going to prison, it will probably be locked up in red tape."

"It doesn't matter that he found it. That was Augustus's property, and you are his heir. I did some research after we found The Inheritance and the gold nuggets. According to treasure trove law in Oregon, the money is only granted to the finder if the suitable heir can't be found. But here you are!"

Meranda smiled. "Here I am."

He stood behind her again and kneaded her shoulders with his palms. He could almost feel where the weight of the world had once pressed on her there. She'd worn her pirate scarf, no doubt to keep her hair from blowing in her face, but her ponytail cascaded between her shoulder blades, dancing to the rhythm of the wind. Her bare neck entreated him to draw near, and for the first time he noticed a small tattoo. A butterfly resting upon a dagger. The two sides of Meranda Drake. He leaned in and kissed it.

"You know, you shouldn't distract the captain."

"I'm trying to shiver your timbers. Is it working?"

"Oh yeah." She tilted her head to the side to give him more neck to shiver.

He checked below to see if they were being watched, but everyone was intent on listening to Ethan as he handed out fishing rods. They must be close to their destination. Paul pecked her neck again. "Isn't there such a thing as autopilot?"

Meranda throttled the engine to a stop. "How's this?" She stood and hugged him close. Then she kissed him thoroughly.

When they parted, a whale spout just a few yards from the boat created a distraction for the other passengers. Meranda pointed it out. "Look at that."

Paul turned in time to see the whale surface, then slap the water with its tail fluke. "God's creation. Who could see that and not believe?"

"Not me. Not anymore."

They stood together watching a pod swim by and said a prayer of praise together, for all God had done in their lives and for all He was about to do.

Chapter 18

This was a wonderful idea." Meranda snuggled with Paul on the deck of the *Romanda Jule* as they watched the water for whale pods migrating north. His arms warmed her while the autumn sun did not. A thin haze and a slight breeze enveloped them during their last excursion before Meranda would dry-dock the cruiser for the winter. "I've been so busy with charters lately, I've barely had time for you."

He kissed her ear. "I know. That's why I chartered my own tour."

"This isn't a charter boat, silly. I'm not going to charge you."

"Why not? I'm willing to pay."

"Then consider the food you brought aboard a catering job. How much do I owe you?"

He straightened and motioned toward the steps leading to the galley. "Those measly croissant sandwiches?"

"Yes, those and all the other times you've fed me."

"Fine." He settled back and pulled her close again. "We're even then."

She let the comment drift away on the seafoam and hugged his arm closer to her rib cage.

"I found a buyer for Augustus's gold ingots."

"That's great." His breath in her hair had an intoxicating effect. She could barely think straight, but she wasn't about to move.

"My sisters and I have agreed to open a foundation to help sailors and their families who struggle due to an accident at sea."

Paul squeezed her tight. "That is a very noble thing to do. I'm guessing you're naming it after your father."

She nodded and looked toward the lighthouse. "The Gilbert Drake Sailor's Fund. All those boaters who made fun of him because of his dream will whisper his name with respect."

"That honors Augustus, too. Sounds like something he would do."

Meranda let that sink in. She hadn't thought in terms of what Augustus would do, but what the Lord wanted her to do.

They drifted for a few more minutes, the boat gently rocking on the waves. Meranda thought about how, a mere five months ago, she was determined to find the coins at all costs. But after giving God the search, her priority changed. Even now, after finding The Inheritance, the coins weren't really what she was looking for at all.

"Thank you, Paul."

"For what?"

"For teaching me which path to take at the crossroads. Had I continued on the one where I was assured full control, I probably would have destroyed myself."

They sat in silence for a moment longer. Then Meranda continued. "I just realized it wasn't the coins I needed. They didn't validate my dad, nor give me peace. Truthfully, the one and only thing that makes me happy right now is that I've made peace with God. I was so angry with Him for taking my dad."

"And you're not angry now?"

"No, Pop made his own choices, chose his own crossroad. Just as I did when I decided to dive the wreck. God didn't kill him. If anything, God probably spoke to his conscience as He did mine and Pop ignored it—just like I did."

"However, you changed course, and that took more courage than your captain's heart ever imagined."

He scooted away from her, and she felt the whoosh of cool air where his body warmth had been. He stood and faced her, reached into his pocket, and took out a small box. As he lowered himself to one knee, Meranda felt the minnows inside her stomach beside themselves with loopy happiness.

"I'm not much of a sailor, and I learned a few months ago when you tried to teach me to fish that I really didn't enjoy it. . . ."

She giggled. He'd have to get over his fear of big fish before they tried that again.

"But what I do have is my love and respect for you. Captain Meranda Drake, will you marry me?"

She tapped her lip. "I don't know."

His smile fell, but he continued to hold the box out to her.

"Promise you'll make me paella whenever I want it?"

The grin returned. "Promise."

She pretended to think a moment longer, although she'd made up her mind before his knee ever hit the deck. Finally she let him off the hook. She threw her arms wide. "Yes, of course, yes." They embraced and kissed, neither willing to let the other go.

But Paul managed to slip the ring onto her finger with one hand while his other arm tucked her into his embrace. "I know it's not as impressive as your other jewelry."

"The pendant? It's not as heavy, either." She gazed at the diamond set in the simple gold band. She'd never been one for girlie jewelry, but this ring represented Paul's love for her, and that made her feel very feminine.

After several blissful minutes, Paul looked at his watch. "I hate to end this moment, but I have to work tonight."

"Blast! You'll have to take the helm because I want to keep looking at my ring."

He settled into the captain's chair with her by his side. As they neared

Crossroads Bay, he headed toward the lighthouse instead of the pier.

"Where are we going?"

"I just need to make a stop first."

He pulled up to the new dock connected to the lighthouse property. The judge had it built just for Meranda so she could visit anytime. Paul hopped out and offered his hand to Meranda. *Hm.* Something was up. But she allowed him to pull her up the steep wooden steps. When they passed between the pillars, he stopped.

He took both of her hands and gazed into her eyes. "This is where my crossroad led me. The pillars were what convinced me to help you look for the coins. That decision, I believe, led us to today." He took her left hand, turned her toward the lighthouse, and shouted, "She said yes!"

People flooded out of the lighthouse. Meranda's hand flew to her mouth. She recognized her family, his family, their friends, and among them Glenys and the judge. At the house, Paul's catering crew began setting out carts of food.

She started to speak but found herself breathless. She barely noticed he was pulling her toward the house. Finally she found words. "I thought you said you had to work."

"I do. I'm catering an engagement party. Ours."

"How did you know I'd say yes?"

He kissed her once more, then said, "Faith."

Author's Note

When I was doing my research in Oregon, I was told that Oregonians are very protective of their lighthouses—that I needed to get every detail correct. That had me shaking in my tall black boots because I knew I would have to use creative license.

So it is with much trembling that I must tell you this. I decided to create my own lighthouse as a tribute to those along the southern coast. The lighthouse in my story is loosely based on Cape Blanco near Port Orford, and my location is a mixture of Coos Bay and Bandon. The lighthouse in Coos Bay, Cape Arago, is not open to the public.

I asked myself, how can I research a lighthouse that I can't get into? Hm. That was Meranda's problem.

She also couldn't get into the lighthouse, but unlike me, she didn't have the advantage of writing herself out of the situation.

Meranda's problems intensified when she found herself at a crossroad while searching for the coins. She could follow her way, which led down a dangerous path, or God's way, which meant she had to wait on Him.

Have you ever had a crossroad moment, that one important life-altering decision to either go your own way or God's way? How long did you struggle—or are you still struggling?—before you realized that God's way was the best, or as the verse states, "the good way. . ." where "you will find rest for your soul"?

My prayer for you is when you find yourself standing at that crossroad, that even though your way is more familiar, you will trust God enough to turn from the path of destruction and let Him guide you.

And who knows? Perhaps that path will lead you to your treasure.

FINE, FEATHERED FRIEND

Dedication

To Jim, who, through his love, helps me spread my wings and soar.

I would like to thank my mother, Ruth Keal; my sister, Shari Warren; and my brother-in-law, Neil Warren, for all their help as they escorted me throughout Oregon and answered my incessant questions. To my awesome crit group who keeps me grounded—you all are the best. And to the Cascades Raptor Center in Eugene, Oregon, many thanks for the tour.

Chapter 1

I can't do this." Glenys gripped her cell phone with a sweaty palm while glancing back with longing at her rental car in the parking lot.

"Yes you can." Trista's voice reached her through the receiver and past the fear-induced buzzing in her ears. Her best friend spoke with a mixture of exasperation and encouragement.

"But there are birds in there. And not just birds. Big birds. Predators. Eagles." She swallowed hard. "Falcons."

The gate gaped before her, its teethlike spiked fence posts looking more like a fort than a bird sanctuary. She felt safer on the outside.

"I should have come with you." Trista sighed. "How badly do you want the movie role?"

Glenys squeezed her phone until she expected her friend on the other end to gasp for air. "Bad enough to fly here to Oregon and leave you in Los Angeles."

"That's not bad enough, although I do miss you."

"Okay, so badly that I've already written my Oscar acceptance speech."

"Well, I think Oscar is a little ambitious since this is a minor role. But I think you've proven you want it at all costs."

"The part is totally mine if I can just get over this fear." And moving past the sign that read SHADY PINE RAPTOR CENTER would be the first step to conquering that fear.

A crisp breeze signaling an early autumn whispered through the Douglas fir that hugged the hillside. Even so, Glenys broke into a nervous sweat under her rabbit fur–collared suede jacket.

"All you have to do is hold a falcon."

"I know." Why did the most promising movie role to come along ever in her career have to involve falcon handling? "By the way, have I thanked you for letting me stay at your cabin?"

"No, but I figured you were stressed." Trista laughed, and Glenys could imagine her tossing her dark waves with a flip of her hand. "I'm just happy I could suggest it. It's been in my family for years."

"Well, I'm grateful. The nearest raptor center to me was a seven-hour drive away. Kinda far for a day trip."

"No problem. Now, you can do this. Put one foot in front of the other. All the birds are in cages. And there are professionals in there who will be sure you're safe."

"You're right. I'm just being silly."

"No, not silly. Phobias are real—I know that. I'm still a little afraid of the dark."

Glenys closed her eyes and focused on her friend. She prayed that Trista would embrace the Lord and be redeemed from an eternity of darkness. Thinking of someone else loosened her feet to take one more step.

Trista sighed. "But we all have to make sacrifices in this business."

Here it comes. Trista had made it successfully in Hollywood with minimal sacrifice thanks to her daddy, Anthony Farentino, the successful producer who had helped launch a galaxy of movie stars. Yet she had no problem spouting advice to those who struggled with their craft.

"*Some* of us have had to make sacrifices, Little Miss Director's Daughter." Glenys and Trista often bantered on this subject. But Glenys made her tone light to make it known she was only kidding, although there was much truth in it.

"Hey, don't knock it. If it weren't for Dad, you wouldn't even be up for this role."

It was true. She had auditioned for Mr. Farentino in other projects, but for this one he had actually approached her, insisting she would be perfect for the role of falcon handler. How could she turn that down?

And now she stood outside a bird sanctuary that nursed injured and ill predatory birds—facing her largest fear.

"Have you moved yet?" Trista's voice held an impatient tone.

"No."

"I don't know what else to do for you then. I was hoping you could talk to someone with a passion for raptors. Maybe then you'd see they aren't so scary. And remember, there's only one scene in the movie where you have to actually hold one. Surely you can do that."

"I know. You've been a great friend through all of this. I'm just being a big baby."

A bubbling giggle in the receiver assured Glenys that Trista still loved her. "Hey, I'm just concerned you'll miss this opportunity. Consider my nudging a thank-you for holding my hand during the stalker scare. You and your dad really came through for me."

Another reason Glenys hated predators. Stalkers came with and without feathers.

"How is the judge, anyway?" Trista asked. "I haven't seen his name in the news lately."

Glenys laughed. "Laying low, thanks to you. I don't think he appreciates being labeled 'Judge to the Stars.' "

"Listen, I've got to go. Please promise me you'll give this a chance. I know it will work. You might pray to that God of yours. Doesn't He have a thing about fear?"

" 'Fear of man' "—*and birds*—" 'will prove to be a snare, but whoever trusts in the LORD is kept safe.' From Proverbs 29:25. I quoted it to you when you had to face your stalker."

"I remember."

Glenys sent a quick praise that the seed seemed to have burrowed somewhere in Trista's heart.

The two fell silent for a moment. Finally, to prove to Trista she practiced what she preached, Glenys took a step. "I'm moving."

"Forward?"

"Yes." Glenys allowed a tinge of irritation in the word, but knew the validity of Trista's question.

"Great! Keep those feet going, and report back to me this evening. I'm proud of you, Glen!"

Trista hung up, and Glenys's feet stopped with the silence. She continued to grip the phone—her only connection to sanity. No, that wasn't correct. God was her connection, and she repeated the verse on fear for herself and added, *I can do everything through Him who gives me strength.* Then she moved past the wooden sign and nearer to the sounds of screeching, cawing, and flapping feathers.

A school bus had pulled into the parking lot while Glenys was on the phone, and now four dozen seven-year-olds flocked by her, all doing their own squawking and twittering. The children and a handful of adults had smiles on their faces, as if they were actually happy to be near talons and sharp beaks.

She followed along, swept into their wake, more secure tagging behind the crowd. If something was going to attack, she had a solid human barrier.

No, Glenys, God does not condone sacrificing children. Well, maybe they'd make enough noise to keep any stray predators away.

They walked up a short hill to a log building. A rustic sign, basically a board nailed to a stake in the ground, pointed the way to the visitor center. She decided to duck in there while a member of the staff greeted the kids and laid out the game plan to the chaperones.

Gingerly opening the squeaky door, she entered a small room cluttered with brochures, promotional material, and children's educational pages to take home. There were also knickknacks, coloring books, small toys, and other items to buy. The inside reflected the rustic outside with its rough-hewn wood-plank walls. But those were hard to see for all the shelves of books and posters of birds on the walls.

"May I help you, sweetheart?"

The voice sounded like an elderly woman. She searched the room. No one was there. A slight flap of feathers to her left caught her eye. In the corner a large gray parrot sat on a perch and watched her intently with creepy yellow eyes.

Glenys froze. Why wasn't the creature in a cage?

The bird tilted its head and opened its beak. "May I help you, sweetheart?"

She clutched her chest where her heartbeat threatened to break through the skin. As she tore the door open with a vow on her lips to give up acting and take up snake charming, a male voice stopped her.

"May I help you?"

She turned slowly to see a man, probably in his thirties, tilting his head in the same way the parrot had. His sandy-brown shaggy hair fell into his eyes, and he swept it away with mild annoyance. By the eagle logo on his khaki shirt breast pocket, she gathered that he worked at the center.

As she leaned against the door, it closed with a click, but the doorknob became her symbolic safe place, and she curled the fingers of her left hand around it even tighter as she eyed the gray reaper in the corner.

"Um. . .I'm here to look at birds."

A smile tugged at his cheek, and she noticed his eyes for the first time. Brown with a twinkle of gold.

"Well, you've come to the right place."

"Right place, *awk!*"

Glenys jumped slightly. *Get a grip. It's just a silly parrot.*

"And here's your first opportunity." He walked over to the parrot and held out his hand. The bird hopped on and sidled upward to his shoulder. From there it scrutinized Glenys as if it were about to ask for her credentials. She shrank farther into the closed wooden door, her hand still on the doorknob behind her back. The man seemed to notice her consternation and kept his distance.

"This is Cyrano. Say hello, Cyrano."

"*Awk.* Come here, sweetheart."

The man rolled his eyes. "Sorry for his manners. He's influenced by too many people here." He fed Cyrano a sunflower seed he'd pulled from his pocket, then touched his chest. "I'm Tim Vogel, bird handler."

Glenys would have extended her hand, but didn't trust the parrot's sharp beak. "Glenys Bernard, actress. I'm here on a research mission."

Instead of the usual interest people would exhibit when she'd tell them her profession, Tim's eyes dulled noticeably. Then they shifted away as he placed Cyrano back on his perch.

Before she could ask why there was a tropical bird at a raptor center, someone opened the door, with difficulty since Glenys was still holding on to the doorknob. A woman poked her head in, bumping the door into Glenys's backside. "Oh, excuse me! Tim, they're ready for you."

"Okay, I'll be right there." He glanced at Glenys. "I'm giving a tour to those kids out there."

Glenys didn't want to be left alone with even a social bird like Cyrano. "May I tag along? I'll probably learn more in a group than by taking a self-guided tour."

His eyes darted to the doorknob. "Of course, but you're going to have to let go."

She released the knob quickly, as if it had turned into a hot charcoal briquette.

He motioned with his hand for her to go ahead, but the friendly smile had dissolved into a thin brooding line—and ice had entered the room.

⟨◈⟩

Tim followed the skittish woman to join Mandy and the students waiting for a day of raptor education. Ironic that an actress would walk into his sanctuary on the very day he received a cell phone text from his mother detailing why she couldn't visit—again. He couldn't decide if she was just in denial over Gramps's mental condition or if she simply didn't care about them anymore. It had been a couple of years since she tore herself from Hollywood and her stagnant career as an actress.

Mandy introduced him to the energetic group. He tried to forget about his mom, and actresses in general, because right now, at this moment, nothing mattered except sharing his passion with young bird enthusiasts.

"Hi, guys! You ready to learn about some awesome birds?"

"Yeah!" they shouted, which is what he knew they'd do.

"Then you'll have to do me a favor. This area here is the only place you can be noisy and run around, okay?" He leaned against one of the four picnic tables and gestured with his arms to show the craft area in which they were standing. "This is a bird hospital as well as a nature center, and some of our patients need their rest. So if it starts to get a little noisy, I'll just do this." He put his finger on his lips. "Then you all do the same, and when it's quiet I'll continue with the tour. Deal?"

"Deal!"

Tim laughed at their enthusiasm. At this impressionable age, he hoped most of them would come away with a new respect for the raptor. And maybe one or two would dedicate their lives to preserving the species. Which is what had happened to him during a field trip when he was ten.

He continued to address the group. "Okay, half of you are going to stay here for now and do a fun craft project with Miss Mandy, the center's director. The rest will follow me up the hill, and I'll introduce you to some of my friends."

The groups split off, and as he began the trek up the gentle slope to the large enclosures, he noticed the actress hanging behind. Was she contemplating doing crafts with the kids? However, she eventually trailed the group and was the last to join them as they gathered at the first enclosure. A little girl asked her if she was someone's mom.

"No, I came to see the birds, just like you. May I join you?"

The little girl in red pigtails nodded. "You can be my mom. She couldn't make it today."

The actress smiled, showing an intriguing dimple. "Thank you."

Tim waited until he had everyone's attention. "This first bird is a red-tailed hawk. Her name is Heidi." Heidi watched the children from a branch. "Who can tell me what hawks eat?"

Hands shot up, but they still called out their ideas.

"Bugs!"

"Lizards!"

"Dead stuff!"

"Actually, hawks hunt for live food. Farmers love hawks because they help rid them of grasshoppers, gophers, rabbits, and mice."

The actress went just a touch pale and reached out to hold the red-headed girl's hand.

Tim continued. "But Heidi can't do that right now because she was shot with a BB gun and has nerve damage to her wing."

"What do you do with birds who can't be released?" a teacher asked.

"We try to find a good home in a zoo or other place specifically designed for wildlife, but if there is none available, we keep them for educational purposes, which is what I'm doing right now." He left out the third option, euthanasia. "In any case, we must be very careful with our feathered friends and not shoot at them, right?"

"Right!"

"Now, since Heidi can't hunt for herself"—he rummaged in his sweatshirt pocket—"I need to feed her." He drew out a feathered carcass. "This is a our version of pizza delivery, only it's quail."

"Ew!" The kids spoke collectively, but the grins and mock-disgusted faces proved they weren't scarred for life.

He quickly replaced the dead bird into his sweatshirt pocket and turned to unlock the screened wooden door. "All of our enclosures have two doors. Double security to keep our birds in."

The actress raised her hand. "Excuse me. Have they ever gotten out?"

Tim shook his head. "Not since I've been here." He continued to walk into the enclosure and grabbed a gauntlet from the hook near the inner door. "Notice how I approach her. I never make her do anything she doesn't want to." He used his soft voice as he pulled on the glove. "Hey, you want to meet some kids?" He offered his arm, and Heidi stepped onto his hand. He held up a length of leather. "I use this leash to clip onto the leather straps attached to the anklets on her legs. These straps are called jesses." He demonstrated by clipping the leash into the ring at the joined jesses nine inches from her body. Then he wrapped the jesses and leash around his palm. "This helps me keep a tight rein on her so she won't fly away." When he brought Heidi out, he noticed that the actress had backed several yards away. Yep. Fear of birds.

The kids continued to ask questions while he tried to get the hawk to take the carcass from his hand, but she was too busy watching the crowd—specifically the actress, who, even though she'd backed away significantly, was still within Heidi's excellent field of vision.

Oh man! Why hadn't he noticed? She had a fur collar on her jacket. Heidi must have thought it was a rodent. Her gaze zoned in as if she were about to swoop onto her prey, and she flapped for all she was worth. Thankfully, Tim had a good hold on her, but he felt her strength.

"Shh. Settle down." Heidi tucked her wings back in as she lost interest in her target, who was now running down the hill, punching the numbers on her cell phone, and screaming as if she were in an Alfred Hitchcock movie.

Chapter 2

I can't do this!"

Glenys shrieked into her phone at Trista's voice mail. She snapped the cover closed as the hysteria threatened to collapse her chest.

"Miss!" The voice called to her from behind before she could reach the safety of her car. Glenys turned to see the short, stocky woman called Mandy chasing her down. When she caught up to her, she gathered her long brown-gray hair over one shoulder and wheezed, "Tim called me on the radio." She indicated the black box in her hand. "He was concerned something had upset you."

"That *something* was one of your birds. It lunged at me." A breeze flipped the fur collar on her jacket, tickling her chin.

Mandy's gaze honed in on Glenys's neck, and Glenys feared the woman would flap a feather and lunge, too.

"You might want to take off your jacket." Mandy pointed to the collar. "The hawk probably thought it was alive."

Glenys ripped the garment from her body and balled the collar inside while searching the sky for other predators. "That bird could have slashed an artery going for my clothing."

"You poor dear. How close were you to it?" Mandy's concern touched Glenys. She glanced around. "About as far as we are to my car."

Mandy took in the several yards of gravel, then looked perplexed. "That far away?"

"Well, it seemed much closer at the time."

Mandy touched her arm. "I recognize the signs. You have a fear of birds."

"Yes, especially predatory birds."

"Me, too."

Glenys couldn't believe that. "How can you work here?"

Mandy laughed while pulling Glenys to a park bench near the center's entrance. "Maybe I should have said that I'm a recovering ornithophobiac. It's why I initially wanted to volunteer here. Now I'm the director."

Glenys looked around at the rustic area. "You did this to yourself?"

She nodded. "Are you willing to come back in? I need to return to the school kids, but I'd love to tell you how I got over my fear."

Glenys hesitated. How much did she want the movie role? She'd been playing in indie films and obscure roles in commercials for too long. She not only wanted this role, but she also needed this role.

Mandy flashed a compassionate smile.

Everything inside Glenys said to run and not look back. But this woman's kindness drew her past the gaping teethlike spikes and back into her nightmare.

While walking, Glenys unbuttoned the collar from her jacket and jammed it into her purse. Then she pulled the sleeves back over her arms before the crisp air could produce goose bumps.

They entered the craft area where she sat at a picnic table with the kids, Mandy lowering herself next to her.

One of the boys passed her a fist-sized pinecone. "We're making owls."

"Okay." Apparently she had no choice but to craft. "So," she asked Mandy while sticking a piece of prepared poster board cut like a wing into the pinecone, "how did you overcome?"

"I met a guy I really liked. He was into hiking, camping, and outdoorsy stuff. I've been allergic to the outdoors all my life." She smiled. "I grew up in Seattle in an apartment. My family was artsy. We went to plays, art expos, operas." She passed the glue to a parent. "When I met Jason, our first date was an overnight biking trip with a group of friends at Mount Rainier. I knew I was skittish around anything with feathers, but when the camp robbers—beautiful but pesky blue jays—attacked the food on our picnic table, I freaked." She stopped to encourage a ponytailed girl across the table, then turned her attention back to Glenys. "Not only did I realize how afraid I was of birds, but I also learned that weekend I was afraid of bugs, flying campfire embers, and high places. Basically, I was afraid of nature."

"Maybe I should be calling *you* 'poor dear'!"

"Oh, I was afraid of the deer, too. I'd never seen one in the wild. It walked right into our camp."

"I'm guessing your guy is very patient."

"He must be because he married me twenty years ago." She laughed. "We both had to go through a patience phase early in our relationship. But I realized he was worth keeping, so I knew I had to get over some of my phobias if I wanted to keep him in my life. He's the one who suggested I volunteer here, and I'm not going to lie to you, it was hard at first. But once I got to know the birds and learned how to handle them, I started to feel comfortable. When the director position opened up, my past work experience met the criteria, so I snapped it up. And now I can't imagine doing anything else."

Glenys considered her words. "How are you at bugs and campfire embers?"

"I still hate bugs, but I'm getting better at campfires. On my next birthday, I'm tackling another phobia with my man—skydiving. Try that with a fear of heights!"

"Will you need prayer?"

"I'm sure I will!"

Glenys had just finished a wise old pinecone owl when a door opened on a building marked Clinic. A tall man sporting a thin black mustache sauntered toward them.

"Hey, sweetheart." He winked at Mandy. "How's it going?"

Mandy rolled her eyes. "Fine. You want to make an owl?"

Glenys lowered her voice. "Is that your man?"

Mandy belly-laughed. "No way. But Vic thinks he is, just as he thinks all the women who work here belong to him."

Glenys could tell Vic was a tad overconfident. After raking her with a glance, he strutted like a rooster in a henhouse as he showed off for the three mom chaperones. They giggled, which only fueled his flirting.

Then he looked back at Glenys and made an obvious note of her ringless finger.

He sauntered over to the picnic table and gently grasped the shoulders of the little boy who had been sitting next to her, sliding him aside.

The boy protested. "Hey!"

Plopping down onto the now-vacant space, Vic spoke out of the side of his mouth. "Great owl, kid."

"Thanks." That seemed to appease the child.

He turned his back on him and concentrated on Glenys. "Haven't I seen you somewhere before?"

Seriously? Did he get that pickup line from the book *Bad Clichés and When to Use Them*? Glenys wished she could slide in the opposite direction, but Mandy blocked her.

He continued to scrutinize her. "Are you a teacher?"

"No."

Clueless, Mandy introduced the two. "Vic, this is Glenys. Tim told me on the walkie-talkie that she's an actress. Just came here on her own and joined the kids."

He shook a pointed finger. "I know where I've seen you. That insurance commercial."

"Wow." Glenys was never recognized in her work. "You're right. I was an extra in the background talking to an agent while the spokesperson did his spiel. How did you identify me?"

"I never forget a pretty face."

Mandy fake-coughed and telegraphed a message with her eyes to Glenys that said, *See? God's gift to women.* Then she said, "It's pretty cool that you're an actress. I could never do that."

"Something else to overcome? You could join a community theater."

"One phobia at a time, thank you very much."

"So." Vic claimed her attention again. "What brings you here on your own?"

"I'm researching a movie role."

"Really?" His eyebrows shot up as he leaned in, clearly interested. She was suddenly drawn to this charismatic man, despite his flirting. But she knew to keep her distance. Hollywood was full of guys like Vic.

"The character I would be playing is a falcon handler. Since I have no experience with birds, I thought I would visit and get some, firsthand. But I'm slightly skittish of birds. So I have a challenge to overcome before the role is mine."

"Hey"—Mandy motioned toward the trail—"Tim could help with that. He's a falconer."

"He's busy." Vic dismissed the idea. "But I have some time. Let me show you around."

Glenys glanced at Mandy, who had stood to help the children tag their artwork so they could take their owls home after the tour. Mandy had conquered her fear by confronting the very thing she was frightened of, which is what Trista had drummed into Glenys's head. She sent up a quick prayer for guidance.

"Sure, you can give me a tour. But"—her bravado suddenly left as she thought of Heidi, the hawk, eyeing her as if she were a snack—"for now can we keep the birds in their cages? I'd rather do this slowly." She stood, and Vic joined her.

"Of course." He smiled, and she could tell it was genuine. But as they walked up the path together, he ruined it. "So, sweetheart. Wanna get married?"

✦

Tim finished with the first group of kids. He'd wondered about the actress throughout his tour. She was probably halfway to Hollywood by now.

However, as he led them back to the craft area, the subject of his thoughts came wandering down the owl path with Vic.

Well, that confirmed it. Two birds of a feather flocking together. Both could put on a good act.

He didn't know much about Vic, the new handler, but he'd seen his attitude around the women volunteers. Thankfully, none of them took him seriously.

After trading groups and leading the second up the path, he found himself distracted as he watched for Vic and the actress. The path consisted of a series of loops, and every once in a while he'd catch a glimpse of her hair, about the color of Heidi's red-brown tail.

A boy asked him a question, and he answered affirmatively, then realized he hadn't fully heard the question when one of the chaperones asked, "Are you sure? I'd never heard of owls having X-ray vision before."

"I mean, no, of course not. Sorry, I must have misunderstood."

Must pay more attention.

"Come meet Poe, our resident raven, kids." He entered the enclosure and brought out the large black bird. "Ravens aren't really raptors; they're corvids." Poe dutifully stepped onto the Astroturf-carpeted T-stand outside his enclosure. "We have other corvids here at the center, too. Magpies, crows, and jays. Ravens are the largest songbird and largest all-black bird that we know of in the world. They have been known to hunt very small prey, but mostly are scavengers."

He saw the confused looks on the audience's faces.

"Do you know what 'scavenger' means?"

They all shook their heads.

Just as he was about to define the word, Vic and the actress rounded the corner.

She took one look at Poe still on his wooden stand in front of the enclosure and froze.

"I thought they would all be in cages." As she backed away, Vic looked at Tim with eyebrows raised. Tim shrugged in answer, and then Vic followed her retreating figure.

Tim shook his head. He found himself torn between wanting to help this woman enjoy God's most fascinating creations and saying *hasta la vista* and have a good life.

Once the tour was over and the kids piled onto their bus with their pinecone birds, Tim noticed a car still in the parking lot. By the sticker on the back window, he could tell it was a rental. He scanned the area, but didn't see a redheaded shrieker anywhere. However, when he entered the visitor center to go to the back office, she stood there with Mandy, laughing at Cyrano performing flips in his play area.

"So"—he wandered over to them—"did you decide to stick it out?"

"Yes, even though the predatory birds out there disturb me a little."

A little?

"But I can relate to this guy. He's an entertainer like me."

"*Awk*. Stick it out, sweetheart."

"And he has wonderful advice." Her laugh created a glow on her cheeks, a pleasant change from the anxious expression she had during their first encounter. He noticed for the second time the dimple that punctuated the true beauty under her pretty actress face. But he shook that thought off right away. It was easier to wish her gone if he wasn't attracted to her.

"Glenys is thinking of volunteering." Mandy passed him on her way to the office. "I'll get the information packet."

Well, that wasn't good news. The last thing Tim needed was an actress hanging out in his workplace. Alone with her now, he walked over to Cyrano and offered his hand. Cyrano stepped onto it and said, "Treat." Tim gave him a sunflower seed.

"I assume you're like Mandy and want to get over a fear of birds."

Glenys cast down her eyes to the newspaper in the bottom of Cyrano's playpen. "Yes, I have a phobia. I've been offered a career-changing role playing a falconer. If I can get to the point of holding a falcon comfortably, I'll get the part."

"How long do you plan to be here?"

"The audition is in six weeks. Meanwhile, I'm staying at a friend's cabin."

Six weeks?

Gloom hung over his shoulders like a sweaty gym towel. An *actress* at his center.

"Of course, if things go well, I could leave earlier."

Mandy entered the room and handed her a volunteer packet. "Take this home and read through it. It lays out all the jobs you'd be doing."

Tim cleared his throat as the words he was about to say stuck in his craw. "If you decide to fill out the volunteer application, I'll be hap. . .I'll do what I can to help." If he could step up the training, he might be able to have her out of there in half that time.

She perused the stapled stack of printed paper. "Thank you. Vic offered, too."

That bothered him. Vic would no doubt do more flirting than actual training and stall the process.

"You should take Tim up on his offer," Mandy said, unwittingly helping his cause. "He's also a falconer, the best I've ever seen."

"Then you're my man." The actress flashed a brilliant smile.

Tim wanted to do his own running and screaming. What had he done?

Chapter 3

I might be able to do this." Glenys had the volunteer information spread out before her on the dining room table while talking to Trista on the phone.

"Well, that's a change in tune."

"It looks like I don't have to handle any birds until I get comfortable." Her overcooked frozen dinner sat untouched. She pushed it away and tapped on the application with her pen. "Looks like I'll mostly be cleaning cages."

"Ew. And you're okay with that?"

"I would work in a barn full of manure if it would get me this job. I'm not afraid of hard work."

"And. . .what do we have in common?"

"Not much." Glenys chuckled. "That's probably why we complement each other. So, is it okay if I stay here in your cabin a month longer? I promise I won't trash the place."

"As if I haven't ever done that before. Ah, memories." There was a short pause while Trista apparently rewound some of those memories to watch in her head. "Sure, stay as long as you like. Just don't miss the audition."

They said their good-byes, and just as Glenys was feeling good about her career, her phone rang. It was Daddy.

"Hi, Dad, what's up?"

"Oh, just wondering where you are."

She hadn't told Dad of this latest adventure. But she was twenty-eight and could make her own decisions, even if he didn't agree with them. "I'm in Oregon."

"At the lighthouse?"

"No, Shady Pine."

Controlled silence. "And what are you doing there?"

"Researching a role."

"I thought we agreed if you hadn't made your big break by August, you would go back to school." She could picture his brows dipped in a frown. The Daddy Look.

"But this opportunity came up, and I had to jump on it." She had hoped to stall him until the audition. By then she would know whether she was going to become a real actress or not. "I'm in a really cool place, Dad. It's just a few miles from Crater Lake, and it's educational. I'm learning about birds."

"Birds? You?"

"I know. But the part involves handling a falcon, and all I need to do is get past that fear and the role is mine. Trista's father said as much."

"Tony Farentino?" Skepticism colored his tone.

"Yes. He said I'm perfect for the part. Why do you sound doubtful?"

"I don't know much about show business, but I've heard things about Tony. He has a reputation for promising young women parts in his films just to. . .uh. . . date them."

"Dad! He's my best friend's father! He even told me he thought of me as a daughter."

"Just be careful."

She wouldn't let Dad put a damper on her excitement. "I'll be doing more acting in this movie than I ever did with the independent films and commercials. I have three whole scenes where I actually say something."

"Okay, but back to our agreement. A person's word is—"

"Law. I know, Dad. And law is what you do, and law is what my sister does and half our family. But it's not what I want to do."

She heard a heavyhearted sigh through her cell phone. "I'm just trying to guide you into a profession that will take care of you the rest of your life."

"I know, but do you really want me unhappy all my life?"

"You have an aptitude for this. I saw a glimmer during Trista's stalker trial. You found loopholes in my books her lawyer never picked up on."

"I had incentive. She's my friend, and I didn't want to see her hurt further." She flicked the hardened dry rice from her dinner with her fork. "Couldn't you support me? It will be my last chance to prove I'm an actress."

"Promise you'll consider dropping this crazy idea if you come against another wall?"

"Promise. But only if you promise not to push me into law if I decide that's not the place for me."

She actually heard him chuckle. "Your mother used to say you could negotiate the stripes off an alley cat. And that's why you'd make a great prosecuting attorney."

"Would she be proud of me, Daddy?" She wished she could remember more about her.

"She was proud of everything you did."

"Pray for me. Okay?"

"Sure."

After they hung up, Glenys decided not to be rattled by Dad's request, but rather rejoice because he promised to pray for her. Up until last year, he wasn't a believer. But thanks to her friends Paul and Meranda and a treasure of coins that included a note entreating the reader to believe, Dad gave his life to the Savior. Peace entered Glenys's soul and never left, knowing that should something happen to him, both he and Mom would be waiting for her in heaven.

She decided her meal was not fit for human consumption, so she threw it in the garbage and pulled out the pint of cookie-dough ice cream she had bought at

Thrifty Foods on the Rogue. While spooning the sweet therapy food onto her tongue, she got to thinking. Why did most of the businesses in town add "on the Rogue"? Was it just in case you missed the river flowing smack through the middle?

The next day she showed up at the center wearing her mucky boots from Mercantile on the Rogue. She walked through the gate with more confidence than she'd had yesterday, but that didn't negate the small pool of hysteria that simmered in the back of her throat. One errant feather and she knew it would boil over into a scream.

First order of business would have been an orientation session, but Mandy and Vic had covered everything the day before. Today, and for the next two weeks, she would shadow a volunteer. Following that, the probationary period was to last two months. But, since she wasn't a "long-term" volunteer, Mandy told her their main goal would be to work on her fear so she would eventually be comfortable holding a falcon.

Vic offered to watch her throughout the day—*I'm sure he will!*—and if she had any questions, he'd be available. She was grateful Tim had also made that offer. Even though she felt animosity from him, she preferred that to Vic, a predatory creature in his own right. She shuddered. One must suffer for their craft, right?

The door to the visitor center squeaked when she pushed on it.

"*Awk.* Hello, sweetheart."

"Hello, Cyrano. You seen Tim or Vic?"

"Vic *smahr-mee.*" Cyrano bent his neck into a ninety-degree angle.

Someone had been talking about Vic around the bird and called him smarmy. That cracked her up.

Vic walked in and raised a dark eyebrow. "Having fun already?"

Glenys felt her cheeks redden. Had he heard Cyrano? "Just enjoying the parrot."

"Well, we should take him with us if his presence keeps your eyes sparkling like that."

Oh brother. Any more false compliments and she'd walk straight into Heidi's cage and let her gnaw on her ears.

Mandy entered and greeted Glenys. "Do you have your application?"

"Right here." She handed it to her.

"Wonderful. The volunteer I wanted you to shadow isn't here right now."

"Is she sick with bird flu?" Glenys snickered at her own joke.

Mandy barely cracked a smile. "We've heard that one before. No, she just called and will be a little late. Dentist appointment."

"You want to hang out with me until she gets here?" Vic asked. He all but wiggled his eyebrows at her.

"*Awk.*" Cyrano had been chirping and making nonsensical sounds throughout their conversation. "Hang out." Apparently he also listened well.

Glenys had had enough of Vic's advances. "That's okay. You did enough yesterday. I'll just wait in here."

"It's no problem. I'm happy to do it."

He started to walk out and motioned for her to join him, but Tim entered, blocking their exit.

Tim brushed Glenys with a glance. "Oh, you're still here. Decided to volunteer after all?"

What kind of a greeting was that?

"Yes." She wasn't about to explain herself.

His lips pinched into a straight line, and he seemed resigned, like a man who had lost a bet. Shaggy hair fell over his forehead, and he swept it back into place. "Where are you starting?"

"The clinic," Mandy informed them. "That's where Camille will be working. Yesterday Glenys only saw the education side of the center. Today we're starting her on the rehab side."

"I'll take her over there, then." Vic's friendly attitude held undertones suggesting Tim had better keep his distance.

The two men locked glares. Finally, Tim broke away. "Fine. When you're ready to work with falcons, let me know." He stalked past them and into the administrator's office.

Glenys felt like a floppy piece of roadkill helplessly becoming the prize for the bigger bird.

⊂≈⊃

Tim forgot what he wanted in the office. What was it about the actress that got under his skin? He so wanted to dislike her, but his admiration for her tenacity continued to get in the way.

She's only here for a movie role. She doesn't have a passion for the center.

Back in the visitor center room, he wandered over to his parrot's play area and offered him an almond from the bag in his pocket. "I don't know, Cyrano. I think the pretty actress is going to be trouble. And I don't like the way Vic has latched onto her. But it's not my place to say anything."

"*Awk.* My place."

"I mean, if she wants to be associated with someone who so obviously doesn't respect women, that's her business. And more power to Vic."

"Vic *smahr-mee.*" Cyrano bent his neck.

A chuckle escaped Tim's chest. "Camille said she was going to teach you that. Good for her."

Tim suddenly remembered he needed to check on the patients in the clinic, even though he had already done that earlier.

When he walked in, Camille had arrived. She'd already retrieved a tray of dead quail and was showing Glenys how she cut into them to remove the eggs. Vic stood over Glenys, hovering like a vulture, watching the process.

"We do this," Camille was saying, "so we can feed them to the corvids."

Tim watched Glenys's face. She seemed to have no problem digging into the dead bird with a knife, despite the mess of feathers, blood, and crunching bones. "How can you be frightened of the caged birds, yet not even flinch over this chore?"

Glenys jumped at the sound of his voice, but smiled as she glanced his way. "I had a minuscule part in a soap opera. Just my hands. The star refused to touch anything that resembled blood, so they brought me in to perform surgery for her. I knew about it a week ahead, so I studied up and watched the Health channel. Never have been squeamish. I would have continued being her hand double, but they killed her off in that same episode." She sighed. "Story of my life."

Vic folded his arms and leaned against the counter. "So, Tim, I thought you were busy." His tone held a challenge.

"I am." Tim bristled. "I've come to see how Ingalls is doing." He shuffled into the tiny room, way too crowded at the moment, and lifted the sheet from the falcon's three-foot square cage.

"I didn't know there were live birds in here." Glenys's eyes went wide as she backed up to the door.

Tim replaced the sheet over the cage. "Whoa." He sought and held her frightened gaze while trying to make his voice tender. "This guy can't hurt you from in there. He has a broken wing."

Compassion replaced the fear on her face. "Oh. How did it happen?"

"May I?" He started to lift the sheet again. If she was going to work at the center, she needed to at least be comfortable with the birds in cages. She nodded, so he removed the sheet. "A Good Samaritan found him under a pile of leaves in a parking lot. Probably hit by a car. We pinned his wing near the wrist joint."

She took a step closer. "What kind of bird is it?"

"A prairie falcon."

"A falcon?" She reached behind her without taking her eyes from the bird and fumbled for the door handle.

"I'm praying he heals so we can release him, but the prognosis isn't good."

"You're praying?" A small grin dawned on her face.

He liked the positive response. "I pray over all the birds here." With an involuntary dart of his gaze to Vic, who was now preoccupied in a flirty chat with Camille, he added, "And some of the people." He shrugged. "Anyway, Ingalls is on the mend—"

"Ingalls? How do you people name these birds?"

Camille joined the conversation. "I named him after Charles Ingalls, you know, *Little House on the Prairie*? Pa?"

"Oh," Glenys nodded. "Because he's a—"

"Prairie falcon," they said together.

Vic leaned against the counter and folded his arms. "Because of Camille, we've had patients named Edwards, Garvey, Harriet, and. . ." He tapped his temple, apparently trying to remember.

Camille rolled her eyes. "Half-pint. The fledgling? How could you forget her?"

"Sorry. If they'd all been named after *The Terminator* movies, I might have remembered."

Camille slapped his forearm. "Men!" She looked at Glenys while Vic rubbed his arm. "I'm afraid I have a short day today. I could only come in long enough to prepare the food. Totally forgot about a kindergarten program at my son's school."

"I'll continue her training," Vic said. "And by the way, that hurt."

"Oh, you'll live, you big baby."

"No," Tim piped in. "She needs to be exposed to falcons." He turned his head to look at her. "Right? Do you mind if I take over your training?"

A wide, genuine smile blossomed on her face and rebirthed the dimple he'd enjoyed earlier. "Not at all. I think that's a wonderful idea."

Vic's steely gaze darted from Tim to Glenys and back again. Then with a sniff, he followed Camille out the door. "Hey, sweetheart," he called to her. "You can beat on me anyti—"

"Shut up!"

Glenys turned her attention back to Tim. "Are they always like that?"

"Worse sometimes."

Tim felt less claustrophobic near Glenys with the other two gone. "Now, where were we?" *Falcons? Names? Oh yeah.* "We'll wait until Ingalls heals to see if we can retrain him to live in the wild again."

"How do you do that?"

"With our flight cage. It's a long enclosure where they can spread their wings and fly back and forth. I'm sure you'll see it during your training."

Glenys moved a step closer to the small cage where Ingalls eyed her, but remained calm. "He doesn't seem to be a bad bird."

"None of them are. And once you learn how to handle them, I hope you'll gain a new respect."

"That's why I'm here."

He searched her face for sincerity. What he found there frightened him more than a false heart. He saw intelligence, determination, and two lovely pine green eyes staring back and causing his heart to beat faster.

I have to get her out of here—soon!

Chapter 4

Before Glenys left for the day, Mandy asked her to tidy the visitor center. "You can find a broom and glass cleaner in the closet back by the administrator's office."

Glenys had surprised herself by the way she dug in and learned. On her second official day, she'd been exposed to all kinds of menial jobs, from cleaning cages to bleaching out trash cans. She agreed to work the afternoon shift, from one o'clock to five. She'd be more exposed to the falcons during that time. Mornings were reserved for corvids. Evenings, they worked primarily with nocturnal birds. However, she discovered she could encounter any type of bird in there for rehab.

She quickly finished the sweeping, listening to Cyrano babble from the perch in his play area. While wiping off fingerprints from the glass case containing ceramic bird-related knickknacks, she glanced his way. "You're pretty chatty today, aren't you?"

He tilted his head. "Pretty."

"Yes. Pretty chatty. Can you say that?"

He bobbed his head. "Pretty. . .actress."

Glenys stopped wiping. "What did you say?" She walked over to him.

Apparently excited to have an audience, Cyrano danced on his perch. "Pretty actress."

She glanced around to be sure they were alone. "Are you talking about me?" She pressed a finger to her chest. Who else could he be talking about? She was the only actress there that she knew of. He could have heard someone talk about a movie or television show, she supposed. But she preferred to think Tim had said those words.

"Has Tim been talking to you?"

"Tim."

She leaned on the Plexiglas wall of his playpen. "Between you and me, he was watching me all day, especially when Vic was around. Is there a rivalry between those two?"

Cyrano's head bobbed up and down as if he understood every word.

"You're a smart aleck, aren't you?" She smiled and offered him a treat from the plastic container on a shelf near his playpen. Tim had shown her where it was and told her she was welcome to enjoy Cyrano anytime. "Who taught you how to talk?"

"Tim. . .smart aleck."

Glenys laughed. "Yes he is."

"Pretty actress. . .hang out my place."

"What?"

He cocked his head to the side. "Sweetheart."

Oh, now she understood. Vic must have been talking about her. Well, she would certainly not hang out at his place—ever.

Vic chose a wrong moment to saunter in. "Hi, Sweethe—"

"Ever!" She shoved the glass cleaner and rag into his hand and stalked out, leaving Vic with his mouth hanging open.

The next day Glenys walked into the clinic just as Tim was putting an injured crow into a cage. She watched from the adjacent room where the food was prepared, her heart hammering until the door clicked shut. Although she'd been told it was safe while the handlers had a grip on a bird, her brain disassociated that knowledge whenever they were in a confined space. Outside, she thought she was getting better. She could be within a car's length. . .well, okay, a Hummer limousine's length. . .of a tethered bird.

Tim joined her as she stood near the dry-erase chore board.

"Glenys." He nodded his greeting. "How was your day yesterday?" He slipped his hands into his back pockets while they both looked at the board.

"Wonderful. Everything on this property should be squeaky clean, thanks to me." She noted her initials on the board adjacent to each chore she had completed.

He chuckled. "The newbies always get the peon jobs at first." He walked to the door and glanced outside. She thought he might leave, but then he hesitated. "Are you working with Camille today?"

"I guess. She's the one who showed me how to clean the buildings. I'm assuming we'll work outside today."

"Would you like to follow me around until she gets here?"

Warmth spread throughout her chest. "Yes, that would be nice."

He opened the door wider and invited her through. "It might not be too nice. I'm headed to the breeder barn."

"Where the mice and chicks are?" She could think of nothing better.

With a perplexed look, he led the way down a narrow path.

"We use the mice and chicks for food, obviously. It's less expensive for us to breed them ourselves. The chicks are only fed to the permanent resident birds—those one week old going to smaller birds and the two-week-olds to the larger birds. This is so the released birds don't develop a search image for half-grown chickens as appropriate food. We can't have them getting the idea that they can hunt farm chickens."

"That makes sense."

"Day-old chicks are okay for short-term food," he added as he palmed the doorknob of the shed-sized building. "But we don't go long-term with them because of the yolk sac. It's not absorbed by the chick until it's three or four days old. That would be way too much cholesterol for our health-conscious residents."

"Will there be a quiz later? So much to learn."

He laughed. "You'll get it eventually. It's all pretty basic when you think about it."

"Sure, for you."

They entered, and Tim flipped on a fluorescent shop light that flickered to life, revealing various styles of cages and containers for the living creatures inside. They lined the walls with barely enough room for two people to pass. On the right, baby chicks peered out at Glenys from behind metal screens. On the left was a system of hanging plastic drawers, about four inches deep. They were stacked seven high and ten wide. Warming lights created a tropical atmosphere, despite the cool air outside.

"What's in here?" The labels all said BREEDING FAMILY.

Tim pulled open one of the drawers. A mouse nest with three adults and a mess of thumb-sized, furless babies seemed quite comfortable on wood pellets and strips of newspaper.

"Oh, this one looks like Jack." She pointed to a dark mouse with a pink nose. "He was a pet when I was little. My best friend until. . ." A lump formed in her throat. She hadn't cried over Jack in a long time. And she refused to do so now. But the tears stung the backs of her eyes nevertheless.

Tim dipped his head and looked at her with concern. "Until?"

Glenys gently shoved the drawer back in place. "Let's just say it's because of Jack I'm here."

She turned her back on the mice. "The chicks are cute."

"Would you like to hold one?"

"Sure."

He brought one out, and she cupped her hand. Its soft feathers tickled her palm.

"Um, Glenys."

She looked at him.

"You're holding a bird."

"Oh, chickens don't count."

"They don't count?"

"Well, not baby chicks anyway. My grandparents had a farm, and I'd help my grandmother gather eggs. I loved playing with the chicks." The pleasant memory was crowded out by the terrifying one. "It was on her farm when Jack. . .disappeared."

"I'm sorry." His sincerity touched her. Suddenly she didn't mind Tim knowing her tragic secret.

"Okay, here's why I'm afraid of birds. I was playing with Jack outside while staying with my grandparents. My mother had just died, and the family had gathered to pay their respects. I wasn't supposed to have him outside his cage, but I grabbed him and left because I needed someone to talk to. There was a field behind their house with large boulders that I could climb on. I sat there for a while telling him how sad I was. I started to feel better, and I left him on the rock while I got off. Before I could reach out to pick him up, a falcon attacked and snatched him away from me." She closed her eyes, forcing the hot tears back. "I lost my mother and my pet."

"It's no wonder you're afraid of birds with that imprinted on your mind."

"I didn't even realize it until we walked in here. I later learned it was a peregrine falcon. Which, of course, is what I need to work with for the movie role." A small spark of anxiety flashed in her chest, and she swallowed to keep it at ember level.

He took the chick from her hand and put it back in the cage. "Part of your job will be to come in here and take care of these guys. But now I'm concerned."

"Why?"

"You can't get too attached. All of these"—he motioned to the mice and chicks—"are food for the raptors. It hurts me, too, when we have to take a life to feed a life, but that's what we have to do to simulate the nature cycle. Are you okay with that?"

She glanced back at the drawer that had Jack's twin in it. She would have to be mature. With a straightened spine, she declared, "I'm okay."

But she may have to rescue Jack Jr.

⌘

Tim had dealt with volunteers who had problems with the live-food aspect, and he worried about Glenys now that he knew her story. But if she couldn't handle it, she would no doubt go home. Which would be a good thing. . .right?

While he showed her how they cleaned the cages and where they kept the supplies, an idea plopped itself into his head. Knowing the source of that idea, he still argued. *No, I can't do that, Lord. I can't bring this woman into my home.* But the thought refused to leave.

As they walked out, the words pushed past his teeth, loosening his tight lips. "I have an idea. You have no problem holding chicks. What if we started with smaller birds? Would you like to come over on Saturday to meet my two canaries? I could show you the basics of holding a bird, and maybe you can eventually work up to a falcon."

She seemed to think about it as she slowly nodded her head. "It might work. But only if you're sure. I don't want to intrude on your day off."

No, I'm not sure. "This weekend, about two o'clock?"

"You don't know how much I appreciate this." She sighed, as if just relieved of a huge weight.

⌘

By the time Saturday came, Tim had beaten himself to a pulp. He could think of a million reasons why he shouldn't bring an actress to the house. However, since she'd been traumatized as a child and it had ruined her experience with birds, he couldn't in good conscience let her remain where she was.

He glanced around his bachelor pad he shared with Gramps to be sure it was clean. She would be there any minute.

The doorbell rang shortly, and he expected to open the door to Miss Hollywood herself. But while her clothing wasn't as casual as when she worked at the center, her outfit hardly fit the stereotype. She wore a conservative pale pink sweater with a turtleneck, blue jeans, and black flats.

When she entered, her gaze swept the small living room. "This is a cool place. And right on the river. How did you score such a prime spot?"

"It belongs to my grandfather. He bought it with Grandma after retiring from the Air Force."

"It looks so rustic on the outside. I thought I'd see chinked log walls in here."

"It's just a façade on the outside. The home was built in 1965."

"*Awk.* Hello, sweetheart."

"Cyrano?" She followed the sound inside to where Cyrano's playpen sat in the corner of the living room. She put a fist on her hip, but her eyes twinkled—beautifully. "Tim. Bird theft?"

"Cyrano belongs to me. Well, me and my grandfather. We sort of have joint custody. I take him to work because the people who visit love him, especially the kids."

After she greeted Cyrano, Tim offered to show her around. "It's cozy. A total of eighteen hundred square feet comprise the first and second floors. Upstairs are three bedrooms." Realizing who he was talking to, he chuckled in embarrassment. "I'm sure this doesn't impress you. Hollywood mansions are probably more your style."

She laughed. "Hardly. But my dad is a judge. I grew up in an upscale neighborhood and spent summers at our lighthouse in Crossroads Bay here in Oregon."

"Really?" Was this woman never devoid of surprises?

"I'll tell you about it sometime." She continued to wander the living room, looking at pictures on the walls and seeming to enjoy them. "I live in an apartment right now. Burbank. Trying to make it on my own."

That impressed him. She had grown up with money, but chose to suffer for her dream. Was her passion any different than his? He decided to give her a glimpse of his life. "I moved in here after Grandma died because Gramps was lonely. Although now I hardly see him. He doesn't drive anymore, but he walks to town and hangs out with his buddies." Tim wondered how long that would last with Gramps's failing memory.

"Is that where he is now?"

He shook his head, then swept that annoying tuft of hair from his eyes. "He's out with my aunt. She had the day off, so she took him to the Dom to visit a friend of his."

"Dom?" She cocked an eyebrow as she turned from the photo of him and his grandfather salmon fishing.

"The Domiciliary. A veteran hospital. He had an appointment there yesterday and found out that his friend had been admitted."

"I'm sorry. Is your grandfather ill also?" Her brows knit with concern.

"We don't know. His short-term memory seems to be failing." Tim didn't want to talk about it. "But you didn't come here for the boring 'This Is Tim's Life' tour." He motioned to the hanging bird cage in the other corner of the living room. "Come meet your trainers, Hercules and Dragon Lady."

She stopped about three feet away and peered inside. "These two tiny puffs of feathers are named Hercules and Dragon Lady?"

"Gramps named them after aircraft—an MC-130 and a U-2. For short, I call them Herc and DL."

"I'd feel more comfortable if they were named Fred and Ginger."

"You'll do fine. They couldn't be gentler." He opened the door of the cage, and she took a step back. He'd started getting used to that, but with the canaries? Seriously? "When you go to hold a bird, always give her the option of coming to you. If she doesn't feel like it, don't force it."

"No problem." Her voice held a shaky tone.

This was going to be a long day.

DL stepped onto his finger and warbled a taunt to Herc to let him know she was Tim's favorite. At least, that's how Tim interpreted it.

"Now you try. Hold your hand sideways, keeping the four fingers together and the thumb tucked. Good. Now move it to just slightly above mine so she can step up."

With a trembling hand, Glenys held it out as Tim had shown her. "I've never been this close to a bird before."

"What about the chick in the breeder barn?"

"I told you—"

"I know, chickens don't count." What a quirky woman. "Just go slowly."

DL latched onto her finger with her tiny feet.

"Ew, the claws feel icky. Take her back."

The transfer happened too quickly for DL, and she decided to get herself out of the situation. Not unusual. He often let her out of the cage, and then she'd perch on the china cabinet in the dining room. However, when he looked back at Glenys, she stood there with her hands on her head and her gaze glued to the bird.

"What are you doing?"

"Trying not to panic."

DL didn't help matters when she decided to fly a reconnaissance mission around the room. Glenys shrieked and began dodging her.

"It's going to poop!"

Cyrano, who had been watching the lesson with interest, started bobbing in excitement. "*Awk!* Poop! Poop!"

Tim suddenly found the whole scenario hilarious. Between fits of laughter he said, "Yes, she might, especially if you scare her. Settle down."

That didn't help, and Glenys shot out the front door—with DL right behind her.

"No! Come back here." Tim didn't care if Glenys left, but DL had never been outside. Panic seized his gut as he searched the trees for the tiny yellow bird.

When he dared a glance at Glenys, she looked near to tears. "I'm so sorry. I don't know why I did that."

"Poop?" He turned on her. "That's what you're scared of?"

In a tiny voice, she answered, "To start. Then I was afraid it would land on my head and peck my eyes out."

He pinched the bridge of his nose. "Just help me find her."

For a half hour, they searched the area. Tim swallowed his dread. Anything could happen to her. There were cats in the neighborhood, cars, predatory birds. . . he had to find her. Finally he stood still and listened.

Glenys asked, "Do you see—"

"Shh. There, do you hear it?"

Glenys stood as still as a statue. Then her face lit up. "Yes! This way."

They both ran to the back of the house where DL was enjoying a refreshing splash in the birdbath. She allowed Tim to come near and hopped right onto his finger.

"You naughty girl. Now you have quite a story to tell Herc. Just don't give him any ideas."

He walked through the back door with Glenys trailing. "I'm so sorry, Tim. When the panic comes, I can't help myself."

With DL safely tucked away with her mate, Tim turned to Glenys. He'd cooled down somewhat and tempered his words. "You do realize this is irrational fear we're talking about?"

"With a canary, yes, but not with a falcon. It really could peck my eyes out."

"If you can't get near a canary, how do you expect to hold a falcon?"

She wandered to the couch and plopped herself down, looking as dejected as an orphan denied food. "Are you giving up on me?"

He dropped into the armchair. Seriously, he should send her packing. Right now. Helping her get a movie role wasn't worth his time and effort. But helping her get past her fear, and educating her about his misunderstood raptors, was worth it.

"No. You ready to try again? Or would you rather wait a few days?"

Her gaze searched his. "Really? I would love to continue. I know if I conquer this step, the next will be easier, and then the next."

He took a deep breath. "Okay. Let's try it again with Herc."

Tim put himself between Glenys and the door, and they went through the routine again. This time she managed to keep Herc on her finger. "Now that I know what to expect, it isn't so hard."

At that moment Gramps entered with Aunt Barb.

"Libby?" He offered a dentured smile.

Tim looked from his grandfather to Glenys, then back again. "No, Gramps. This isn't Mom."

His wrinkled face drooped like a hound dog's. "Oh."

That had never happened before. Glenys looked nothing like Tim's mom. But thinking back, Tim realized two years ago was the last time Gramps had seen his daughter. She'd stood in the same place as Glenys, holding Herc, and saying good-bye.

Chapter 5

Tim suddenly had Herc back as Glenys rushed to Gramps. With her hand held out, she shook his. "My name is Glenys Bernard. You must be Tim's grandfather."

Tim looked past both of them to Aunt Barb. She seemed in shock, her mouth lagging open and her eyes wide. She whispered to Tim as she sidled next to him. "I'm not sure what surprises me most. That Dad has mistaken your friend for Libby or that you were entertaining a woman."

Tim ignored her remark. She had played matchmaker too many times in the past, but he always forgave her because he knew she only wanted the best for him. But now she eyed Glenys as if sizing up a prize filly. He almost expected her to nod and say, "Good teeth."

As quickly as Gramps's confusion came, it left again and he was his old self. "Name's Walt, but you can call me Gramps. You're a pretty thing. Where did Timmy find you?"

Glenys raised an eyebrow. "Timmy? How cute."

"Yeah, yeah." Tim's face warmed. "Only family calls me that." He hunted for something to occupy himself, settling on plumping Gramps's back pillow in his chair.

"I found him, actually." Glenys walked with Gramps as he moved into the living room. "He's been kind enough to teach me how to handle birds. I'm an actress researching a role."

Gramps chuckled and lowered himself into his easy chair. "For some men, the way to their heart is through their stomach. Not Timmy. Just talk about birds, and he's your friend for life."

Tim intercepted any forthcoming embarrassing stories and introduced Glenys to his aunt.

"Pleased to meet you." Glenys shook her hand.

"Did Tim offer you anything to drink?" Aunt Barb turned toward the kitchen. "Or eat? I made apple cinnamon muffins for these guys yesterday. There should still be some if they haven't wolfed them down."

Tim groaned. "I'm sorry. It never occurred to me." He had the social skills of a barn owl.

"I'm fine. In fact, I was just about to leave."

Gramps reached for a bowl of butterscotch hard candy. "So soon? You just got here." He offered the bowl, and Glenys took one but slipped it into her pants pocket.

"Actually, Gramps"—Tim squeezed his grandfather's shoulder—"*you* just got here." He glanced at Glenys. "But you are welcome to stay."

Gramps pointed to the sofa, leaving no room to argue. "Sit. Tell me, do you know Doris Day? She's an actress, too."

Glenys chatted with Gramps for a good half hour, munching on muffins and laughing at his war stories. He had a few since he'd been a career military man spanning his tour of duty starting with the Berlin Airlift after World War II, then Korea and Vietnam.

When Glenys finally said her good-byes, Tim walked her to her car.

"Thanks, by the way," he said.

"Thanks for what?"

Tim motioned with his head to the house. "For helping Gramps not feel bad about mistaking you for my mother."

She waved the thought away. "I like your grandfather. Does he ever visit the center? Will I get to know him better?"

Tim wanted to tell her to stop it. Stop being charming. Stop being cute. Stop making his heart race, which meant she'd have to stop smiling. That dimple distracted him.

"Gramps visits occasionally, but not like he did when he had a car. Now he's dependent on others to get him around. He's not happy about it either."

Her brows furrowed. "Does he have a social life at all?"

"Oh yeah. He walks to town every morning to have coffee with a group of military veterans. My aunt calls them 'the boys.'"

The dimple reappeared. "Oh good. I'd hate to think of such a friendly guy wasting away."

She searched in her purse for her keys. "Well, thank you for today. This was a big help. And again, I'm sorry about your canary."

"It turned out fine, so don't worry about it anymore. I think on Monday we'll try the same thing on the smaller raptors. Maybe our American kestrel."

"Kestrel?"

"Yes. It's a very small falcon."

"Falcon?" The excitement of the day fizzled from her eyes.

"You have to do it sometime. Just think of the kestrel as a large canary."

She pressed the key fob to unlock the door with a *blip*. "A canary who can peck my eyes out."

As she slipped into her car, he smacked the roof. "No one is going to peck your eyes out. Get that out of your head."

She grimaced.

He also winced. "Okay, that was probably a poor choice of words."

As she drove off, Tim noticed the curtain in the living room move. The two conspirators were probably spying on him, wondering why he didn't kiss her, for goodness' sake. He squeezed his eyes shut. Now he would have that image to deal with.

That evening after supper, the phone rang. The male voice on the other end greeted Tim. "Hey, this is Chic."

"Hi, Chic. What's up?" Good news, he hoped. Chic volunteered his veterinary services and had been treating a Cooper's hawk for a broken tibia.

"She's ready to come home. I'll be at my clinic tomorrow around three o'clock if you'd like to get her."

"Sure. See you then. And thanks." He hung up and looked at Cyrano.

"*Awk.* Chic."

Tim grabbed an apple and cut off a small piece, handing it to Cyrano before he cut a piece for himself. "We like Chic, don't we, Cyrano?"

"Like Chic."

He liked someone else, too. But he hated to admit it to himself. "What about Glenys? What can I say? If she weren't an actress. . ."

"Pretty actress."

"Yes, she is. And she has pretty red hair."

"Pretty red hair."

Tim said good night to Cyrano and pulled the cover over his playpen. Then he went upstairs.

Gramps sat in his bedroom, reclining in his chair and watching television. He rarely hung out downstairs in the evening anymore. He seemed to stop doing that when Tim moved his stuff in several years ago. Gramps now only had his bedroom to remind him of Grandma. Her picture sat near his recliner, and Tim could sometimes hear Gramps talking to her, probably pretending they were watching TV together.

Tim poked his head in the door. " 'Night, Gramps. I'm going to read for a little while, then go to bed."

Gramps motioned him in, a confused look on his face.

Concerned, Tim entered the room. "You all right?"

"That wasn't Libby?"

"No, that was Glenys. She's an actress who is volunteering at the center."

"Libby's an actress, too."

"I know, but they don't look anything alike." Why was this so hard for him to grasp? Did he miss his daughter so much that his mind was playing tricks on him? Tim would call Mom tomorrow and once again try to talk her into visiting.

"I like Glenys. You two ought to get together."

And, we're back.

He patted Tim's ear. "She'd be good for you."

Tim kissed the balding head. "Don't worry about my love life."

As he walked out, Gramps called after him, "Well, somebody has to."

❦

The next day Tim and Gramps drove the winding tree-lined road to their church. In just a couple of weeks, the five-mile drive would pop with color. But for now the deciduous black oak and walnut blended in with the evergreen pine, spruce, and hemlock.

Tim rounded a corner and pulled into the parking lot of the white clapboard church with the steeple.

Inside, after greeting their friends, they sat in their usual seat near the front. Tim turned to talk to someone behind him, and in walked a red-headed vision. He swiveled back around, elation and dread warring in his body. *She's a Christian? What are You trying to do to me, God?*

He told himself to settle down. Just because someone walked into a church didn't automatically make them a Christian. She could be a stalker. He'd prefer that right now.

Get a grip! The bigger problem was that she was in his space, his world.

Tim sighed and turned to see if she'd found a place in the packed church. There was room on the other side of Gramps, so just before she seemed to consider an already overcrowded pew, he stood and caught her eye. Her genuine smile upon seeing him made his heart *tharump* in his chest.

He asked Gramps to scoot over, and she slid in next to Tim.

"I'm surprised to see you both here." Glenys smiled. "I pass this little church every day, so decided to give it a try."

Gramps leaned forward to see her better. "Libby?"

"No, Gramps, this is Glenys, not Mom. Remember, she visited yesterday?"

"Oh, the one we talked about last night?"

Now his memory has to be good?

Glenys raised an eyebrow. "You talked about me?"

Tim felt heat rise from his collar. "Uh, yeah. You know. The reason you came over. . .training."

"Oh." She seemed disappointed. "Well, thanks again. I hope DL wasn't too traumatized."

"You kidding? She keeps asking when she can go out again."

The music must have been uplifting. The sermon must have been deep. The time in God's house must have been refreshing. But Tim wouldn't know. A gentle wave of intoxicating perfume lapped relentlessly at his senses, numbing his brain. What was it? Some high-powered Hollywood stuff meant to keep your escort light-headed? Because if so, she'd gotten her money's worth.

Unfortunately, Gramps had noticed it, too. As they walked out of the church, he grabbed Glenys's hand and pulled it through his elbow. "You smell good."

"Gramps!" Tim stopped in his tracks, expecting his grandfather to at least look apologetic for being too bold.

However, they both ignored him as they walked into the sunshine.

"Thank you." Glenys's smile didn't indicate she was embarrassed. "It's lavender."

"I knew it!" Gramps held his index finger into the air. "Evie wore that when we first met. She was as sweet as she smelled."

Oh great. She just kept shooting down his preconceived notions of Hollywood types. She dressed conservatively, drove an economy rental car, and smelled like his grandmother.

Gramps continued charming the actress. "We always go out to eat on Sundays. Would you like to join us?"

The first thought that jumped into Tim's mind was, *No, please, no.* But the second thought pushed that one out. *Please say yes.*

Glenys glanced over her shoulder with a question in her eyes. Tim heard the words spill out of his lips, but had no idea where they came from. "Please join us. It would mean a lot to. . .Gramps."

"Okay, but only if you let me buy. It's the least I can do for all the help you gave me yesterday."

Tim agreed, but knew either he or Gramps would grab the check before she had the chance.

Chapter 6

That thing is bigger than a canary."

"Well, if I had a male kestrel it would have been no bigger than a robin. But this is a female, so she's a little larger."

Tim stood near the carpeted T-stand perch just outside the kestrel's cage.

Glenys, about twenty feet away down the dirt path, put her hand on her hip. "Do you have anything in between this one and a canary?"

Tim slapped his forehead and palmed his face all the way to his chin. "You're not picking out cars here. If you want to hold a falcon, you have to work with the birds we have."

"Maybe I should work with your canaries a little longer."

No. Definitely no. She'd already infiltrated his world by making his grandfather fall in love with her. Yesterday when they went to lunch after church, Glenys was cute and funny. Sweet and gracious. Great to look at and smelled out of this world.

Tim was miserable.

"Let me tell you a little about Kyla. It might help." She nodded, and he continued. "She was found in a cage in someone's backyard. They had illegally kept her as a pet and neglected her. As a result she didn't imprint with her own species. She's doing great now, but we can't release her into the wild." His blood still boiled over the insensitivity some humans exhibited. Criminal.

"Poor little thing." Glenys approached and nearly leaned into the wide circle he had drawn on the dirt around them. But a fear-induced force field kept her out.

"Now, I'm not expecting you to hold her. Just join me in the circle."

She looked down at the line and managed to scuff it with her toe.

"Okay." He nodded, happy for even a small victory. "Making a little progress. What is it about these birds, other than the fact that one took off with your pet, that scares you? Be specific."

Glenys scrutinized Kyla on his hand.

"Their eyes. Well, maybe not this one, she actually has a sweet face."

"Okay. We're talking falcons. What about them?"

"Well, maybe it's the eyebrows."

"Falcons don't have eyebrows."

"Then why do they always look like they're frowning?"

"So, basically, it's the look on their faces."

"Yes. They look mean, like they could—"

"I know, peck your eyes out."

Glenys gave him a *well, duh* look.

"Okay, I get it." *Not really.* He sent up a quick prayer. *Lord, please help this woman get over her fear. I'm running out of ideas here.* "If I find a raptor that is cute and fluffy, do you think you could work with it?"

She narrowed her eyes. "Maybe."

"Let me think, and I'll get back to you." He knew of no such bird. They were called predators for a reason. "But now I have to feed Heidi and her neighbors."

"And I still have some cleaning to do." She glanced at her watch. "I'll be leaving in about an hour anyway." Heading down the path toward the visitor center, she turned back around to face him. "Thanks again. I really am making progress. At least I didn't scream and run to my car when you brought Kyla out." With an endearing shrug and a smile, she flashed the dimple, blinding him, and headed on her way.

She was right; there had been tiny baby steps. But would she graduate from her fear in time? Tim entered the kestrel's enclosure and set her on the tree limb. He reached into his sweatshirt pocket and drew out a dead mouse. "This is for not making her freak out. . .and thank you for not frowning."

His radio squawked just then. "Tim, you there?"

He slipped the radio off his belt. "Yeah, Mandy. What's up?"

"Just got a call from the vet. He has a fledgling barn owl. Someone found him in the woods. Looked like he might have been attacked by a cat."

"Okay, I've got a feeding to do, but as soon as I'm finished, I'll set up a spot in the clinic and go get him."

A young barn owl. Cute and fluffy. *Thanks, Lord. This could provide the breakthrough we need.*

⟡

Glenys grabbed the broom and began sweeping the visitor center floor so furiously she coughed from the dust. They'd had several field trips come in that day, and the students trailed in everything but the flagstone steps leading to the craft area.

Cyrano aped her cough, then added, "Sweetheart."

She stopped and leaned against the broom handle. "Oh, Cyrano. I make myself so angry sometimes."

"Angry."

"Why can't I take the next step and just get close to a raptor? That's all we were trying to do today. Tim promised me I didn't even have to touch it, just step inside the circle. I keep giving in to my fear, so I certainly can't blame Tim."

"Blame Tim."

With the handle pressed into her cheek, she closed her eyes. *Lord, I know where this fear comes from, and it's not from You. I'm tired of it and want to be healed. And not only because of the movie role. It's been a thorn in my side for too long. Please give Tim fresh ideas, and help me to be strong. Amen.*

She opened her eyes to see Cyrano regarding her with an intelligence she'd never seen in anything nonhuman. She'd been using him as a sounding board; now she felt she could confide in him as a friend.

"Between you and me, I like Tim."

"*Awk*. Like."

"That's right. Despite the looks he gives me." She remembered her lunch with Tim and Gramps yesterday. She caught him several times rolling his eyes or looking at her as if she had two heads. "But we had fun together with Gramps. Tim even smiled once or twice."

"Like. . .Chic."

Glenys wasn't sure she'd heard Cyrano correctly. She dragged the broom across the floor, getting closer so she could listen.

"*Awk*. Like Chic. . .pretty red hair."

She pushed her fist into her hip. "Who likes the chick with the pretty red hair? And am I that chick?" Just when she was opening up about her feelings for Tim, Vic's words intruded. At least, she assumed they were Vic's. She couldn't imagine Tim calling anyone a chick.

Camille hustled into the building. "Put the broom down. You've got to come see something."

Glenys leaned the handle against a wall and hurried to catch up to Camille as she ran up the path. "Is something wrong?"

"No," Camille flung over her shoulder. "I just found out Vic is holding Mouse University with his eagle, Erland. You've got to see this."

Mouse University? She hadn't learned about that yet.

They ended their scurrying at the flight cage, which happened to be the last enclosure up the path. Glenys huffed for breath while scolding her treadmill for not doing its job.

Vic stood outside the enclosure holding a small plastic shoe box with holes punched in the top. He swept Glenys with a steamy glance. "Hi there, Green Eyes. Ready to marry me yet?"

Camille slugged his shoulder. "Get on with it. We're not here to listen to you be full of yourself."

Vic simply laughed, then entered the enclosure. Glenys stood with Camille and a half dozen other volunteers outside the broad length of the long flight cage. Erland perched on a sturdy tree limb watching Vic intently as he opened the small box and pulled out—oh no! A black mouse. Glenys looked from the mouse to Erland and dreaded what was about to happen. She slipped behind the gathering cluster of onlookers and peeked over their shoulders at the disturbing scene.

Vic held the squirming mouse by the tail and placed it in a space boarded off by wide planks perched on their sides. Located in the middle of the flight cage, Glenys assumed the plank-sided pen was to keep the victim from scampering away.

Then Vic hurried out of the cage and joined the group, rubbing his hands together. Glenys wanted to turn and run, but decided to try to stick it out. She needed to prove to Tim she could do this.

Erland spotted his target.

"So, that eye healed up nicely." Camille spoke matter-of-factly to Vic.

"We'll soon see. He's been soaring in there the last few weeks." Vic glanced at Glenys. "He had a nasty eye infection when he was brought to us. If it didn't heal, we'd either have to keep him in captivity or euthanize him." Vic's chin jutted out. "Those weren't options for me."

Despite her near hysteria, Glenys had the presence of mind to see there was more to Vic than she'd assumed.

"There he goes." It was a whisper, but held all of the excitement of a proud dad at a kid's baseball game.

Erland landed smack on the innocent mouse, then let out a victory screech.

"Got him!" Vic pumped the air.

Panicked squeaking emitted from the tiny, helpless rodent. Glenys fought the nausea, realizing that was the same sound Jack used when he cried to her for help.

I'm so sorry, Jack.

Sharp talons held the innocent victim to the ground. A menacing beak hovered inches above, then pecked in a lightning fast movement at the flesh.

Glenys felt the bile rise.

Must.

Get.

Out.

Now!

She turned to flee down the hill while the others were preoccupied with their celebration.

As she ran past the breeder barn, her feet slid to a stop. She had to know.

The wooden door squawked in protest. She pounced on the light switch, and the white fluorescent flickered on, almost as if blinking in surprise. Remembering exactly which drawer to go to, Glenys yanked it open.

"Oh, thank You, Lord." It hadn't been Jack Jr. who'd just met his fate. She snatched the rodent and sealed him safely inside her zippered jacket pocket.

"No one is going to make you into a meal."

As she hurried to her car before anyone could see her, she knew she'd just taken a step backward in her own rehab. How could she face another predator?

Chapter 7

Glenys stopped at Paws 'N Claws on the Rogue to pick up a small cage and food for her new pet. Then she headed straight back to the cabin knowing she was going to be in so much trouble. But she couldn't allow Jack Jr. to become a Happy Meal.

"There you go, little guy." She placed him into his new home, complete with pine shavings and food. "I promise you'll be safe."

She shook out the mouse droppings from her pocket into the trash. Good thing the mouse was used to living in a shallow drawer. That probably kept him from eating a hole through her jacket.

She heated up a bowl of soup and sat at the kitchen table with Jack Jr., then called Trista and related the whole sad tale. Her friend started laughing—uncontrollably.

"It's not funny, Trista."

"I know, and I'm sorry you had to witness the attack, but. . .mousenapping?" The giggles consumed her again.

"I really thought I could do it. I thought I could stand there as nonchalantly as the others. I tested myself, and I failed."

"Yes, well, consider it a quiz for the larger final exam. That one will cost you 100 percent of your grade, which translates to no movie role for you."

Glenys swirled the spoon in her tomato soup, bobbing the croutons until they could no longer float. "I just hate predators, feathered or standing tall on two legs. The guy I just told you about, Vic, thinks if he's in a room with a hundred women, they are lucky to be in his presence. So far he seems harmless, but he targets every woman he comes into contact with. The others just laugh it off, but what if your stalker started out the same way?" A wayward thought struck her. "What if someone starts to stalk me once I'm in the public eye?"

"Now, you listen here. You don't have to be famous to attract a stalker."

"Thanks. I feel much better now."

"What I mean is, if you sabotage your career because of this fear, it's like never driving again because you're afraid of getting into an accident. Don't you believe in that God of yours?"

Smack! Trista's words just hit her with a wet rag. "Of course I do."

"Then He must not be as strong as you keep telling me."

"Okay. Point taken. God is strong, Trista." She spoke with conviction, then trailed off with, "It's me that's failing."

"I don't mean to negate your fear. I know it's real. But if I can move on, so can you."

"You're right. And I will. I have to."

After hanging up, Glenys prayed for forgiveness. *Please don't let my lack of faith keep Trista from believing in You.*

☙

The next afternoon Tim had put in his day and entered the admin office as Vic wandered out.

Mandy, who was sitting at the desk, glared at Vic's back. He had no doubt ruffled her feathers with a sexist remark.

"You okay?" Tim asked as he flipped through the day-planner book to see what was on the agenda for the rest of the week.

"That man! If he wasn't so good with eagles, I'd toss him out on his behind."

Shaking off the encounter, she swiveled in her chair and rested her arm on the desk blotter. "So, how is Glenys's progress?"

"Slow." He continued to look at the calendar, even though he'd already gotten the information he wanted. No readings at the schools. Not even a field trip that week. "I've only managed to get her to hold a canary."

"Hey, that's a huge step for her. It's only been a week. It took longer than that for me."

He put the day planner down, turned to half sit on the desk, and folded his arms. "We tried a kestrel yesterday, but no-go. She couldn't even get close to it."

"Well, give her time. I'm very happy you've taken on this project. I can see how she trusts you." The phone rang just then, and she answered it.

Glenys trusted him. Why, he couldn't fathom. Of all the people at the center who could have helped the actress, he had been the one she'd gravitated to. Like a cat who jumps in the person's lap most frightened of it.

A heated female voice came from the gift shop. He moved to the door and trained his ear to hone in on who it might be. Glenys?

"Vic, you are the most insufferable—"

No, that was Camille.

"Hey, beautiful. You know you fear me."

Didn't Vic hear how he sounded to women?

Camille snorted. "Fear? No. Pity? Yes."

"*Awk.*" Cyrano naturally joined in. "Fear me, beautiful."

"See? Even the bird agrees."

The screen door slammed with a *whack.* Camille must have put an exclamation point on her exit.

Tim turned his attention back to Mandy. He assumed by her half of the conversation there was an injured bird somewhere.

"Okay," she said into the receiver. "I'll send someone out right away." She hung up the phone and glanced at Tim, then proceeded to scribble the name and conversation highlights in the log she kept for rescues. "That was someone from Cleetwood Cove at Crater Lake. Their boat captain just reported a downed falcon on Wizard Island."

"How badly is it hurt?" He thanked God for people who cared enough to report fallen birds.

"It's flailing around, probably something wrong with a wing. I told them how to approach it and to wrap it in whatever they have available. They're going to do that and get it back to the dock for their usual stop at four forty-five. Could you take a crate and meet them there?"

"I just finished the afternoon feeding." Tim consulted his watch. "Sure, I can run up there."

More voices sounded in the gift shop. "Hey, beautiful."

"Hi, Vic." Glenys's voice. "Have you seen Tim?"

Tim cringed. Proof positive that this cat sought him out.

"In the office," Vic said. "But you don't need him when I'm around."

"Thanks, I'll take my chances with Tim."

"Your loss."

Tim heard the door open and close again and assumed Vic had slithered out.

Glenys joined him and Mandy, no worse for wear after her conversation with Vic. After greeting them both, her gaze brushed his face but averted quickly. "I need to talk to you about something." She glanced at Mandy. "Privately."

"Can it wait until later? I'm about to run up to Crater Lake to get an injured bird."

"Oh." Her disappointment dragged her expression to a frown. "It can wait then."

"Would you like to come with me?" Wait. Who said that? He'd better have a stern talking to his mouth before it got him into trouble.

"I'd love to." There was that smile and the lethal dimple. "I have a fairly light workload this afternoon. I'll see if I can get away."

Mandy sealed his dumb idea. "You can go, Glenys. There's a person coming in today who is interested in volunteering, so I can have Camille show her your jobs. Then we can promote you to the clinic if you're comfortable with that."

A haunted look passed over her eyes. "But I haven't graduated to holding a bird yet."

"That's okay." Mandy leaned back in her chair. "You'll only be assisting when we're treating a patient, and the rest of the time you'll be cleaning, stocking supplies, and filing."

A tiny look of relief softened her demeanor. "Oh. . .well, I can do that."

"So, are you going with me?" Tim checked his watch. About an hour's drive up there and another half hour to hike to the boat dock. "We need to get going."

Glenys nodded, then followed him out. "I've never been to Crater Lake."

"Really? Do you have a camera?"

"In my car." Whatever had haunted her in the office had ebbed away. She now spoke with animation, as if excited to take this adventure.

"Why don't you get it and meet me out front? I have to get some equipment to take up there."

She rushed to the door, but turned before leaving. "We can talk on the way up then."

"Sure."

After she left, he slapped his forehead over just making himself a captive listener.

Mandy also passed him on her way to the door, leaving him alone with Cyrano. During a quick food and water check, knowing they wouldn't be going home soon, he said, "I'm having a hard time resisting those green eyes."

"Green eyes."

"But it's that dimple I fear most."

"Fear. . .me."

Tim shook his head. "I should put a restraining order on Vic to keep him away from you."

After loading his SUV, Tim and Glenys began the fifty-mile excursion up the mountain. He loved this drive, no matter the time of year. At this elevation the leaves were beginning to turn. Hints of gold and scarlet peeked at them through the Douglas fir as they snaked their way up the two-lane highway.

Glenys sat with her hand-sized digital camera out of the case, ready to snap away.

"So," Tim ventured. "What do you want to talk to me about?" Best to get it out of the way if it was something unpleasant, which he assumed it was by the concerned look on her face earlier.

She chewed her thumbnail. "Vic's eagle attacked a mouse yesterday."

"I heard—isn't that great? He's been working with Erland forever it seems."

"I was there. I watched it."

"Cool!" He glanced over to see her face—not excited by any stretch of the imagination. Then he remembered their conversation in the breeder barn about her pet mouse. "Not cool, huh?"

"No. I was back at my grandparents' ranch, and the little girl in me freaked out."

"But I know Vic and Camille were there. They didn't say anything about you running and screaming."

"Well, I didn't, exactly." She moved from thumb-chewing to finger-chomping, as if she were trying to hold in the words. "I left quietly. I doubt they even knew I was gone. They probably thought I'd just left out of disinterest."

"Okay, well, that sounds good. You're making progress."

"If I had just continued walking to my car, you could have called it progress."

"But. . .you stopped? What are you trying to not tell me?"

"Istoleamouse!" It all jumbled out of her mouth after, he assumed, being held behind her teeth for so long.

"What?" He whipped his head toward her just as they entered a curve. Bad move. They swerved slightly, and he had to jerk the wheel to get them back on the road.

"Jack Jr."

Now she was speaking in code. "Glenys, I don't understand."

She took a huge breath. "I stopped at the breeder barn and took the little black mouse that looked like Jack."

"Jack. . .the mouse you had as a kid that the falcon flew away with?"

She nodded her head, tears brewing.

"To save him, I'm guessing."

"Honestly, I've never done anything like that before. I never shoplifted as a kid, never took pens from businesses unless they were meant for that, never fudged on my taxes—"

"Whoa." A chuckle bounced in his chest. "You think I'm going to fault you for trying to save one of God's creatures? That's what we do at the center. You just decided to rescue the food used for the creatures we're trying to save."

"Then. . .I'm not in trouble?"

He shook his head. "Not as long as you stop at one. If I see all the mice on the lam tomorrow, I may have some concerns." He winked, hoping to relieve her anxiety.

Her shoulders straightened, as if she'd just released a huge weight from them.

"Um, Glenys, what was it you called the mouse?"

"Jack Jr."

He smiled. She was going to have an interesting surprise in a few days.

❧

Glenys glanced at the attractive man sitting next to her. At times he seemed distant, as if her very presence caused discomfort. At others, like today, he laughed with her, teased her, and, dare she say—flirted a little.

His smile came easily, and she enjoyed watching it spread to his eyes. Nice eyes. Brown with bursts of gold.

After a while they reached their destination north of the lake, the Cleetwood Cove trailhead parking area. Tim pulled in, but before opening the door said, "I forgot to tell you. The trail to the boat dock is about a mile with a steep grade. Would you like to wait here?"

She glanced down at her ugly work boots. Comfortable and durable. A far cry from the Manolo sandals she wore to a party Trista's dad threw for some Hollywood players last month. "No, I'm sure I can make it."

Before they got out, he pulled his cell phone from his shirt pocket and threw it into the glove compartment.

"What if you need that?" She pointed to the dash.

"I don't like taking it on a water rescue. I dropped it in the river once, and now

I guess I'm overly cautious."

She hopped out and, slipping her camera into her jacket pocket, watched him remove the plastic crate from his vehicle.

He held out a small backpack. "Think you can carry this? I have a few bottles of water, some protein bars, and the first-aid kit in here."

She weighed it in her hand and knew she'd have no trouble carrying it. She followed him down the neatly graded trail.

He wasn't kidding. At times she felt she was trudging the inside of a large cereal bowl. Tim's average size hid the fact that he was incredibly fit. Glenys puffed like the city girl she was, and she vowed to join a gym when she returned home.

He glanced back at her, grinning. "What do you think of the lake?"

She hadn't been able to enjoy the lake up to that point, but now took in the grandeur and beauty. She stopped briefly to take a picture. "It certainly is round."

"Yep, craters usually are."

She could see glimpses of cars along the rim drive in places where it neared the edge. From there pine trees softened the harsher landscape of sheer rock walls and ancient volcanic flows. But all of that paled against the star of the show, the lake, brilliant and pure. "I've never seen such clear, blue water."

"This isn't a stream-fed lake, so no silt or mud can trail into it. What you see is melted snow and rain. There are also no outlets, so the water just seeps down into the caldera. This is the deepest lake in America, which also accounts for its color."

They continued to walk, him easily carrying the crate by the handle and her struggling for breath.

Again, he looked back at her. "You okay?"

She nodded, but couldn't speak.

He glanced at his watch. "Let's rest a moment. We'll make it down there before they dock. You can take that backpack off, and we'll have a snack."

As she removed the extra weight, cooling sweat trickled between her shoulder blades. They sat on a fallen log and dug a couple of water bottles out. She resisted the urge to chug it. "I can't imagine taking this hike in the summer. The air is cool now, but the exertion is making me warm." She took another sip and held the liquid in her mouth while letting it trickle slowly down her throat.

"In the summer the mosquitoes are relentless. This is a good time of year to hike down." Tim dug out two chocolate–peanut butter protein bars and handed her one. "I know this is the whirlwind tour. Maybe we can come back sometime so you can enjoy it."

The fact that he said "we" did not go unnoticed.

"Here's the abridged tour." He pointed to a cone-shaped offset island. "That's Wizard Island, named by William Steel in the 1880s because it looks like a wizard's hat. It's the cone of an extinct volcano within a dormant one."

After taking a bite of the protein bar, he pointed to the far rim. "See that dark island near the wall?"

She squinted, but she could barely make out a rough, rocky, and unfriendly looking island.

"That's the Phantom Ship. If you drive the rim and look for it, it disappears and reappears as it blends into the wall depending on your location. The sun's position also contributes to its name."

"This place is amazing." Her eyes couldn't take in enough, and her brain couldn't process everything she saw.

"That's nothing. I don't have time to show you Pumice Castle, Vidae Falls, or Devil's Backbone." He put their empty water bottles and wrappers in the backpack and helped her put it back on. Then he grabbed the crate again. "Or The Pinnacles, Dutton Cliff, The Wineglass." He spread his free arm out. "It's advertised 'Like No Place Else on Earth.' "

"Okay." She laughed. "I get it. I need to come back."

He continued down the trail, and for the next fifteen minutes, she watched the back of his head. Out in the water, the small open tour boat with about seven passengers chugged back from the island, and by the time Tim and Glenys reached the dock, it was just pulling in.

Passengers filed out, talking with excitement about their unplanned passenger. They hung around, eager faces ready to see the bird guy work.

Tim set the crate down on the dock, opened it, and drew out his thick falconry gloves and a blanket. He tossed the blanket over the crate and slipped the gloves under his arm, and then he touched Glenys's shoulder. "You can wait on the dock."

She nodded, then pulled out her camera and began documenting the scene with stills. Standing at the edge of the dock looking down into the boat, she could clearly see everything.

The captain greeted Tim as he boarded. "We did what the lady at the center said." He motioned to a young man, about twenty years old, sitting in the back of the motorized skiff. He wore jeans and a white T-shirt. "This gentleman here found the bird and offered his overshirt to wrap it in." At the man's feet was blue chambray with an obvious lump in it.

Glenys felt her heart palpitate.

Tim knelt next to the bundle but looked at the man and extended his hand to introduce himself. "Tim."

"Ethan."

"Thanks for taking good care of this little guy, Ethan."

"No problem. I felt really bad. It was flopping around near the trail."

Tim cupped the blanket in his hands and spoke to Glenys. "I'm determining how he's facing. Don't want to get the beak end."

Visions of Tim losing a finger threatened to blot out rational thought. Glenys's perspiring face went cold.

Apparently satisfied, he donned the gloves and lifted the shirt just enough to peek inside. "I think we have a female peregrine here."

A peregrine! Please, God, no running and screaming in front of these people. Don't let me embarrass Tim.

After a little more inspection, he turned sad eyes to Ethan. "And she has a broken wing."

"How could that happen?" Glenys asked, trying to feel Tim's compassion.

Tim looked out at the island, then up in the air. "Oh, could have been an altercation. Maybe she was injured enough to fall and broke the wing upon landing. You never know."

He again cupped the shirt around the bird, which looked about twenty inches long. "I'm going to carry her to the dock. Then we'll transport her to the crate."

Once he passed Glenys, he motioned with his head. "Grab the blanket, please."

She did so and tried to hand it off to him as he knelt near the crate's open door.

"No." Tim looked up at her, still grasping the bird's middle. "I need you to drape the blanket over her and the crate, and then I can work to get the shirt off. Together, we'll transfer her into the crate."

"Together?" Hysteria began to climb up her throat.

Tim's look pierced through to her heart. "What I mean is, you'll hold the blanket so it doesn't slip while I scoot her inside."

Ethan approached. "May I do it? I kinda feel like she's mine."

Glenys jumped on the request. "Sure!" Relief flooded her, but as she looked back to Tim, she saw the disappointment in his eyes. The Shady Pine Raptor Center emblem on the polo shirt under her jacket burned accusingly through to her skin. She lifted her hand to pluck at it. The men proceeded, and she continued to take pictures, squelching the guilt.

Ethan did as Tim had asked and draped the blanket over the falcon and the open crate. Tim worked to free the bird of the shirt, while the blanket kept her calm.

His gentle voice also soothed the bird. "There, we'll get you fixed up. . .no worries. . .good job. . ." Then he placed her inside onto another blanket. Ethan let the first blanket fall over the crate.

The crowd of about twenty people now clapped, but Tim shushed them. "We don't want her nervous, do we?"

They all nodded and cheered in whispers.

Back on the steep path, this time going up, Ethan and his girlfriend joined them. Glenys tried not to hate the thin blond beauty wearing a purple hoodie and tan hiking shorts for her ability to keep up with the men. Glenys's legs ached after only five minutes, so she fell behind. Still, she could hear Ethan's incessant barrage of questions about the center.

By the time she caught up to them at the midway point, they had already rested for five minutes, but Tim patiently waited for her to get her second wind.

She pointed to the crate. "Isn't that heavier now with the bird inside?"

Tim glanced down at the blanket-covered carrier. "Not too bad. She probably only weighs two pounds."

Ethan spoke up. "I can carry her the rest of the way."

"You sure?"

"I kinda feel like she's my responsibility." Ethan stood and brushed off his jeans.

That signaled the end of the break to everyone else.

Glenys could barely feel her numb toes from the earlier hike down into the caldera. Now her upper leg muscles twitched in protest for having to climb. Knowing they had to get the patient back, though, gave her new resolve, and she joined the others—slowly.

At the top, Tim waited for her, the bird already safe in the back of the SUV.

Ethan was shaking his hand. "Thanks for the business card. I'll come by to check on her and maybe see how I can volunteer."

"We can always use help."

On the way back to the center, the thick silence in the car weighed on Glenys's chest. Finally, she rallied her courage. "I'm sorry."

"For what?" Tim's eyes never wavered from the road.

"For not helping back there. I hesitated for only a second when you asked me to work the blanket, but then Ethan stepped in. I know I would have been able to do it." She fidgeted with the digital camera in her lap, rubbing at the screen with her shirt to remove the fingerprints. "I should have refused his help and done my job. But the bird is a peregrine falcon."

Peregrine. Her enemy. The bird that had become her token for loss. For her mouse, Jack, yes. But symbolically for her mother. Why couldn't she step beyond that fear?

They came to a T intersection where the highways met, and he turned left.

Glenys chewed her thumbnail. "Aren't you going to say something?"

"What do you want me to say?" His voice was even, but a nerve jumped in his jaw.

"I don't know. Maybe forgive me for letting you down?"

Tim glanced her way briefly. "You let yourself down."

She turned her gaze out the window, where evening shadows had begun to gray the mountain road. "You're right."

Long breaks of silence were intermittently dotted with small talk for several miles. But the mood lightened, and by the time the road straightened out, they chatted comfortably once again.

Glenys turned on her camera to look at the pictures on the screen. She had snapped nearly fifty images in the short time between removing the bird from the boat and placing it in the carrier. Tim's professional determination to keep the bird safe showed clearly in the small screen, and she thought of her fear. Tim had taken authority over the falcon's fear just as God wanted to take authority over her fear. In the silence of the car, she heard a whispering in her soul. *I can do everything through him who gives me strength.*

Thank You, Lord, for sticking with me. She also thanked Him for Tim, a patient man who looked more attractive inside and out to Glenys every day.

Chapter 8

They arrived back at the center, and Glenys followed Tim as he carried the falcon to the clinic. Mandy had called him while they were on the road to say the vet would meet them there.

Glenys's shift officially over, she checked her watch as her stomach grumbled. The protein bar had worn off. "I guess I'll go home now, unless you need me for anything else."

"No, that's okay." His gaze swiveled to a different cage, one she knew had been empty yesterday. Now it had a sheet over it. "Before you go, though, come meet another patient." He lifted the sheet.

As she peered inside, two very large black eyes peered back, nestled inside a sweet heart-shaped face. "It's an owl!"

"A barn owl, to be exact."

"Have you named it yet?" Glenys could tell it was young by the downy white tufts sticking out from brown feathers, making it look like it had just lost a pillow fight.

"No. Haven't had time. He came as I was getting off yesterday; then we had the emergency today."

"He looks vaguely like my high school drama teacher, a very sweet, creative little man. We all loved him. His name was Mr. Dunkel, but we called him Dunk. Ooh!" She bounced as the idea hit her. "Can we name him Dunk?"

Tim's smile almost looked smug. "Dunk it is. Would you like to help take care of him?"

"Do I have to touch him?"

"Not until you're ready."

She looked back at Dunk, who regarded her with the wisdom of his species. Plus something else. Trust.

"Yes. I think I'm ready to get closer."

Before she left the grounds, she stopped at the visitor center to retrieve her purse. She'd forgotten to take it in her excitement.

Cyrano sat on his perch. "*Awk.* Hello, sweetheart."

She opened the plastic container and gave him a pine nut. "I had a wonderful day today. I think I'm about to conquer my fear."

"Fear."

"And don't tell anyone, but after spending the day uninterrupted with Tim, I'm really seeing the beautiful side of him."

"Beautiful."

"Maybe I shouldn't say that about a guy, but I don't mean his looks, which are great, too, but he's beautiful on the inside. He was so gentle with that falcon today. It barely ruffled its feathers. Whether Tim admits it or not, he's a beautiful person."

"Beautiful. . .green eyes."

"What? Who is talking to you, Cyrano?"

"Fear me, beautiful green eyes."

Alarm shot through her spine. Different than the other sexist remarks Cyrano repeated, this one could be dangerous. Was Vic plotting something? Was he more of a stalker than the women at the center gave him credit for? She shuddered.

After pulling her purse from the desk drawer in the admin office, she drew out her key chain–sized can of mace. Then she hurried to her car in the growing darkness.

When she pulled up to the cabin, a strange car was parked in her spot. And even more curious, the lights were on inside the cabin. She sat in her car for a few minutes, trying to decide whether or not to call 911. She quickly dismissed the thought. Certainly a robber, or stalker, wouldn't leave a car in plain sight and the lights blazing. Not even Vic. . .would he?

Get a grip, and see who has invaded your space.

Before she could step onto the porch, she heard a screech inside. A happy one. One she recognized. The front door burst open, and her robed and freshly showered friend swept her into her arms. "Trista?"

"Surprise!"

"Yes, it is."

Trista hugged her and pulled her inside. "You'll never guess what I did today."

"Um, fly to Medford, rent a car, and show up here? Unannounced?"

"Well, yes, but guess what I did between renting the car and showing up here." They plopped down on the sofa where Trista already had a glass of white wine on the coffee table. She must have seen Glenys glance at it. "You want one?"

"No, thank you. You know I don't drink." Glenys's mind spun in the gust of Trista's whirlwind.

"Anyway," Trista continued, as if her sudden appearance were as natural as a walk down the red carpet. "I stopped in at your raptor center to surprise you, but you weren't there."

"I went on a bird rescue." Those were six words she never thought she'd say. "I'm sorry I wasn't there for your surprise."

"Actually. . ." Her eyes twinkled.

What was she up to?

"The surprise wasn't me." She threw her arms wide. "It was that I decided to volunteer at the center, too."

"Excuse me? Why would Little Miss Director's Daughter don mucky boots and slave at a smelly bird center?"

Trista's arms dropped. "To support my friend, of course."

Glenys's insides went all mushy. "Were you the one Mandy said was coming to take over my duties?"

"That's me. Actually, besides supporting you, I want to learn about the place from the ground up and give a donation."

"That is so cool! When I become famous, I'll do stuff like that." Caught up in the excitement, Glenys had questions about the process. "So, is there a crew here filming your every move? Will it be documented on reality TV? Will you present them a check in a ceremony?"

Trista reached for her wine and quietly sipped during Glenys's inquisition. "Actually"—her subdued voice didn't sound like Trista at all—"I've asked the lady at the center—"

"Mandy?"

"Yes, Mandy. I've asked Mandy to keep it quiet that I'm here. I'd like this to be low-key."

"You? Low-key?"

"I know." She shrugged and ran her finger around the rim of the glass. "I'd just prefer it this way for now. Okay?"

Glenys narrowed her eyes. Trista's activities were always media magnets. She couldn't sneeze without it being reported in a gossip rag. Maybe she'd gotten tired of playing the game and just wanted some normalcy in life.

"Okay. I won't say a word."

"Thanks." Trista leaned forward and tilted her head in a conspiratorial position. "Now, what can you tell me about the tall guy I saw walking with an eagle. Dark hair, thin mustache?"

"Vic?" No! She couldn't have her sights set on Vic. She could hear Cyrano repeating, *Fear me, beautiful green eyes.*

Trista took a sip of her wine. "I was going to introduce myself, but the director suggested I should keep my distance. Does she have a thing for him or something?"

"Mandy? No. Vic is a womanizer, and she was warning you. I'm surprised you flew in under his radar."

"Me, too." Her face screwed into a miffed, I-can't-believe-someone-didn't-notice-me look. "He must have been preoccupied." She trailed her index finger around the rim of her glass. "Is he attached?"

"I just told you, he's a womanizer. You shouldn't want to have anything to do with him."

"Maybe." She dragged out the word and took another sip.

Perhaps it was a blessing that Trista decided to come. It would give Glenys the opportunity to present her Christian worldview in an up-close, personal kind of way.

Trista drained her glass and rose, no doubt to refill. From the kitchen Glenys heard a shriek. This time not in such a good way. She ran to see what happened.

Trista was pointing at the mouse cage.

Glenys frowned. "You knew about Jack Jr. Why are you freaking?"

"Because of those! What are they?"

Glenys leaned down to get a better look. Six tiny flesh-colored blobs cuddled together. "Hmm. I guess Jack Jr. is a Jacqueline."

Chapter 9

Wednesday afternoon Tim checked on his two new patients, Dunk, the barn owl, and the female peregrine falcon from Crater Lake. Chic had spent the night before working wonders with the broken wing. Now she just needed to recuperate.

"What should we call you?" He regarded the falcon. "Lady of the Lake. Yeah. Lady for short. How's that sound?"

Lady tilted her head as if trying on the name.

"Time for rest, okay? We'll have you up and out of here in no time."

As he replaced the sheet over the cage, Glenys entered the clinic with a woman in tow. By her expensive-looking gold-hoop earrings, leather jacket, and designer jeans, he wondered if she was an investor. "Tim, this is my friend, Trista Farentino. Mandy showed her around yesterday. She's going to take over my duties."

Wearing that?

"You look familiar." He searched his memory.

She tittered and struck a paparazzi pose. "Did you see my latest movie, *Love Stinks*? It was a romantic comedy."

Another actress. He shook his head. *Lord, what are You doing to me?*

She placed a manicured finger on her chin. "Hmm. You don't look like the romantic comedy type. I was also in several adventure movies, including *Danger Down Under*, the third in the spy-thriller franchise. I played Agent Risk. Did you see that one?"

"No. I don't have time to go to the movies." Two actresses. Two thorns in his side. Suddenly remembering where he saw her, he snapped his fingers. "You were on the news last night."

Her face fell. "The stalker." She nervously glanced toward Glenys.

"Wait." Glenys looked from Tim to her friend. "Last night?"

Trista turned to Glenys, looking smaller and more vulnerable than she had when she breezed in. "He's getting out today. Good behavior." She snorted a disgusted half laugh.

Glenys balled her fingers into fists. "Why didn't you tell me?"

"It's no big deal." Her gaze shifted to the ground.

"After what you went through? How are you feeling about this?"

"I have a restraining order." Trista lifted one shoulder and dropped it. "What am I supposed to feel?"

"Something. You're supposed to feel something."

Glenys followed Trista out the door. Tim didn't mean to eavesdrop, but they weren't exactly having a private conversation.

"Don't try to thrust your fear on me." Trista's voice bordered on shrill. "You're the one with a predator problem. How did my situation become yours?"

"I can't believe you're making this about me."

And these are best friends? Tim shook his head as he placed a chicken carcass in Lady's cage. She reached out and grabbed it with her sharp talons, then proceeded to rip at the feathers to get to the meat.

He'd take birds over women any day. At least they had a purpose for ripping each other apart.

After a few moments he hadn't heard anything from the two outside and assumed they'd left, but when he opened the door to attend to his other birds, both women were hugging and apologizing.

Oh brother. Two drama queens.

His radio squawked. "Tim, this is Mandy. Come to the office, please."

He left the clinic and slid past the two women still locked together.

When he reached the admin office, he pulled up short upon seeing Mandy's furrowed brow. "It's your grandfather."

"Gramps?" His heart thudded to his gut. "What happened?"

"He's missing. Your aunt just called and said she dropped in over there and he was gone."

"Thanks, I'll call her."

He slipped his cell phone from his pocket, noting the spotty service had missed five calls. He wasn't worried. Gramps probably just walked to town. But why would Aunt Barb call about that?

When she answered, her voice held a borderline panicked tone. She told him what Mandy had already related.

"Did you check his favorite places? The diner? The barber?"

"I called around, but no one has seen him."

Tim's alarm rose just a little, but he knew Gramps couldn't go far. Until she told him a neighbor saw him leave at eight o'clock that morning. Tim checked his watch, although he knew it was well after noon.

Aunt Barb continued. "I know he goes to breakfast with his friends, but isn't he usually back in a couple of hours?"

"I'll look for him in town. Don't worry, he probably just lost track of time."

As he headed to his car, she added, "Cyrano's missing, too. You did say you were leaving him home today, right?"

"Yes, Gramps said he wanted to spend the day with him." He hopped into his car and slipped the key into the ignition. "Nothing unusual about Gramps taking Cyrano to town, but you're right, he never stayed away this long."

"I'm worried, Tim. What if he never made it to town? What if someone picked him up thinking he was a hitchhiker? What if he fell in the river?"

"Hey." Tim knew his aunt was about to work herself into a frenzy. "Gramps has lived here a long time. Don't worry. I'll go to town, but you can pray he stays put wherever he is so I can find him."

"Okay." The small tenuous word tugged at his heartstrings. "I'll stay here in case he comes home."

"Don't you need to get back to work?"

"I called. My boss said it was slow at the restaurant, but he could pull in another cook if need be."

After a weak good-bye, she hung up.

He geared into reverse, unintentionally spinning his tires.

"Tim, wait!" Glenys ran to the passenger side, hooking her fingers over the door where the window was rolled down. "Mandy told me you had a family emergency. What's wrong?"

"Gramps is missing."

"I'm going with you."

Before he knew it, she yanked open the door and popped herself in. "What are you waiting for? Let's go."

"Yes, ma'am." He nearly floored it, and they spun down the dirt drive to the paved street. Realizing how grateful he was for her support, he said, "Thank you for coming."

"It's the least I could do for Gramps. What do you know so far?"

He related the scant information he had. "Driving up and down the streets may not help. We can cruise once, but if we don't see him, we may have to search on foot. You up for that?"

She smiled, and the dimple reassured him. "These boots took me up a hiking trail yesterday. Surely they can walk through town."

He thought of Trista's little spiked-heel boots trudging the dirt paths at the center. They would be ruined by evening.

After driving around with no sign of Gramps, they parked at The Grill on the Rogue. Only a family with two children sat inside the small restaurant enjoying burgers and fries. So Tim and Glenys set out on foot.

Every place they made inquiries, from the south side of town at Tools on the Rogue to the north side at the Bait Shop on the Rogue, brought the same answers. No one had seen him.

Tim pointed toward the river. "He may have crossed the bridge. But there's not much over there. He usually stays on this side."

"Isn't it possible that once he's done visiting, he'll go home?" Glenys pulled her hair off her neck and clipped it with a brown plastic barrette.

Tim shook his head. "He's never been out this long before. And he always goes to the same places. This town isn't that big. Where could he be?"

They headed for the bridge, and he noticed for the first time Glenys's bare neck had a freckle. A heart-shaped freckle. He averted his eyes. Now was not the time to be thinking of heart-shaped freckles.

They continued to ask people on the street, but no one had seen him. Finally, a couple dressed in hiking gear passed them, talking to each other. "What a crazy old guy!"

Tim stopped them. "Excuse me. You've seen an elderly gentleman?"

"Yeah." The woman pointed over her shoulder. "At the RV park. He's entertaining people over there, telling funny war stories."

"And his dancing parrot is a riot." The man chuckled.

Glenys looked at Tim and smiled. "That's our man. Let's go."

Jogging to where they could cross the street to get to Travel Ease RV Park on the Rogue, they maneuvered the two lanes across just north of the bridge. The river ambled past them on their right.

The entrance led them to a crushed-asphalt walkway that wandered along the green, glasslike river, cutting a path through trimmed turf. To the left, on the far side of the paved road, trailers and recreational vehicles of all sizes were parked in neat spaces. They passed a pleasant park bench overlooking the river while scanning the area.

"Up there." Glenys pointed straight ahead. "See those people gathered?"

Tim peered up the path, wishing he'd remembered his sunglasses. Light reflected off the water as the sun began its afternoon descent from its apex, nearly blinding him. But as they drew closer, he saw about fifteen people pressed together near the river. Bursts of laughter came from the small crowd.

Tim looked at Glenys. "You think?"

She nodded.

They jostled their way through the people to find the traveling comedy troupe they had sought. Gramps sat at a picnic table while Cyrano tumbled and clowned around.

"Gramps!" Tim couldn't decide whether to hug his grandfather or berate him for not letting Aunt Barb know where he was. So he did both. "What are you doing out here? You should have called."

Gramps never acknowledged him, but past Tim's shoulder, he spotted Glenys. "Libby?"

"No, Gramps—"

Glenys cut Tim off. "Yes, Dad. It's Libby. I've come to take you home."

The look in Gramps's eyes frightened Tim. It was as if he were looking at them through a telescope from the past. He didn't even seem to recognize his own grandson.

"This is my daughter, everyone. She's an actress."

The crowd clapped, clueless.

She placed both of her hands onto his shoulders. "And now we have to get Daddy home. Thank you all for making his time here memorable."

"We should thank *him*, miss." A man with a fisherman's vest reached out to shake Gramps's hand. "Your stories touched my heart, man. Thank you for serving and keeping my family safe."

Gramps gazed at him with tears in his eyes. "It was my privilege, son." He reached out to the table for Cyrano, who dutifully walked up his arm and perched on his shoulder. "Now, me and my old bird, we gotta go home."

He suddenly looked very worn. Tim whispered to Glenys, "Stay with him. I'll go get the car."

She nodded while sitting next to him, and then she hung onto his arm as if he'd take off again.

By the time they arrived back home, Gramps was back to the present, tired but coherent. They walked into the house where he collapsed in his easy chair. Aunt Barb was beside herself, waiting on his every need. "Here, drink this water. I'm sure you're dehydrated. Did you eat at the diner? Do you need a sandwich?" She suddenly teared up and turned away, pulling a tissue from her pants pocket.

Tim followed her into the kitchen where she sobbed on his shoulder.

"I'm so sorry. I should have checked on him sooner."

"Hey." He rocked her. "Don't beat yourself up. It didn't matter when you got here. He'd already been gone the whole morning. We didn't know he was capable of doing something like this, but now we know, so we'll take precautions."

She pulled away and blew her nose. "I wish your mother were here. I could wring her neck for staying away so long."

"I know. Stand in line." Aunt Barb often blamed everything on Tim's mom, but this was hardly her fault. "Gramps has you and me, though. We're enough. We'll call his doctor tomorrow."

"You turned out to be a fine man, you know." She looked up at him. "I'm very proud of you."

He chucked her chin. "Between you and my grandparents, how could I have gone wrong?"

With a swipe at her nose with a tissue, she set her jaw. "I'm going to make the old fool eat a sandwich, whether he wants one or not."

"Atta girl." A rumbling from his stomach prompted him to say, "Maybe make several?"

She smiled at him and marched into the kitchen.

He returned to the living room where Glenys sat on the floor at Gramps's feet chatting away. "My family owns a lighthouse."

"Really?" Gramps leaned in, his veined hands gripping the arms of his chair.

"Yep. Maybe you can visit it sometime. It's down by Crossroads Bay."

"I know the one. I seen it plenty of times in the distance."

"Well, we're going to open it to tourists starting next summer. We have a friend whose great-great-grandfather built it, and she's requested we allow people in."

"Oh, that's fine, fine." He leaned his head back and closed his eyes. "I'll get down there tomorrow."

"Gramps." Tim decided to catch him before he slipped into unreality again. "Aunt Barb is making you a sandwich. I want you to eat, then go to bed. Okay?"

Elderly eyes snapped open. "Why, you little squirt. If it weren't for them dragon fly wings on your shoulder, you'd still be in diapers. I ain't takin' orders from you lest you got a signed note from the captain."

So much for reality.

Glenys raised an eyebrow at Tim and mouthed, "Dragonfly wings?"

"Chevrons." He pointed two fingers and touched his arm. "The stripes on an airman's shoulders."

She nodded and mouthed, "Oh."

Gramps seemed oblivious to their quiet conversation as his quick flash of anger ebbed. He gazed lovingly in Glenys's direction. "Wanna dance, Evie?"

"Gramps, do you think this is Gram?"

"Shh." Glenys touched her lips. "What did she call him?"

Tim shrugged and searched his memory. He was only fifteen when she died. "She called him Walt most of the time."

Aunt Barb entered the room. "No, remember? Her pet name was Wally, but she was the only one he'd let call him that."

Glenys stood and helped Gramps to his feet. "They're playing our song, Wally."

Tim watched Glenys in wonder as she took on the roles needed to make his grandfather happy. As they swayed to an imaginary tune, he suddenly began to respect this actress.

Chapter 10

Trista proved to be a pain in the neck. How she thought she could do the menial jobs at the center when she'd never even scoured a toilet was beyond Glenys. Before the week was out, Trista had paid another volunteer to scrub the empty cages from the clinic, forgotten the laundry in the washer until it smelled, and nearly vomited when she walked in on Glenys slicing a quail for food. By Friday, Glenys didn't know how much more Trista could take.

Glenys had changed to the evening shift in order to work with the owls. Her first stop was the kitchen off the clinic where she picked up dead mice for the five owl residents. She made sure that each had the birds' names marked on them with a plastic card. Tim had told her all carcasses, whether they were bird, fish, or mouse, were tagged early in the day for the volunteers. Then as they came in and started their rounds, they knew who had been fed throughout the day. However, extra dead food could be used at any time for training or rewarding purposes.

She joined Tim on the owl path on her way to the enclosures.

As they started to walk together, Trista stormed past them, muttering, "I won't do it. It's bad enough Glenys is keeping a litter at my place. But I will not feed those rodents in the drawers."

Glenys giggled. "This is probably her last day."

Tim's mouth was still open but broadened into a smile. "You think?"

Glenys strolled to Trista's side after she had collapsed at a picnic table in the craft area holding her head in her hands. Glenys lowered herself to the bench. "Trouble in the breeder barn?"

"The smell. The wiggly little bodies. Baby mice are not cute, Glen."

"My baby mice are—you said so yourself."

"When they're safely enclosed in a hamster cage, yes. In a drawer, stacked on a drawer, stacked on a drawer—no." She started to whimper. "I can't do it, Glen, I just can't. I thought if you could do it, I could. But I can't. Don't make me go into that infested place again." She bounced her forehead off the redwood table.

Tim sat across from them. "You don't have to do anything you're not comfortable with."

Trista lifted her head, tiny shards of red paint clinging to her brow. "I know, but I admire Glenys for her dedication. And so does my dad." Her voice turned bitter. "We had a fight. He told me it was time to pay my own dues. Step out and get my own roles without his help. But I'm scared." She turned to Glenys. "I've never had to audition. I've never been in a cattle call. What if I can't do this on my own?

I have no other skills."

So, Trista's problems went deeper than drawer-dwelling mice.

Glenys felt for her. But if hard work and dedication were good enough for everyone else in the business, why should Trista be any different? "Wasn't it you who told me we all have to make sacrifices in this business? Was that the royal *we*? Translation, anyone who isn't you."

"You're making me eat my words? At a time like this?" Trista rose to leave.

"Wait. I meant that as encouragement." Although, it hadn't come off as encouragement when Trista said it to her the other day. "I'm sorry. We'll figure this out together."

Trista's gaze drifted to someone heading up the path to the eagles.

Vic.

Trista swiped her face to remove the last shed tear, leaving behind black streaks from her eyeliner that made her look like a distraught raccoon. "I'll figure it out with Vic." She shot a glare over her shoulder at Glenys. "He gets me." Then she stormed up the path to follow her target.

Glenys sighed. "I don't know who to feel sorry for most. That pair is truly two-of-a-kind." She didn't think Vic was right for Trista, but at least the women at the center seemed to have a reprieve from the chauvinistic remarks. She plopped back down at the picnic table across from Tim. "Did I handle that as badly as I think I did?"

He shrugged one shoulder and stood. "I don't know. I don't *get* her." He laughed and offered his hand. "Come on. Let's feed Dunk."

They wandered hand in hand to the clinic, and it surprised her when he didn't let go. She enjoyed his gentle fingers wrapped protectively around her own. Calluses spoke of long hours building enclosures.

What dedication. What a love he poured into these creatures. If only she could pour that much enthusiasm into her love, which used to be acting. But now she wasn't so sure. Could it be possible to have two passions?

She'd made a lot of progress after working with Dunk. That little owl stole her heart the minute he peered at her through the cage. And today, before the Trista meltdown, she and Tim had visited the other owls in the nature portion of the center. He gave her his spiel about them, teaching her their habits and showing her the pellets they regurgitated from the fur and bones their bodies couldn't process. They were fascinating animals, and Glenys couldn't wait to learn more about them.

That night, after doing all the jobs that her friend had left undone, Glenys headed home. She and Trista usually drove together, but the two worked different shifts now so they arrived home separately. Glenys assumed that Trista had caught up to Vic earlier that day and coerced him to take her out somewhere since she wasn't home.

Glenys fed Jackie and all the little Jack Juniors, then showered and went to bed. Her body ached from pulling double duty. No more of that. Trista would either have to buck up and do the job or quit.

She fell asleep moments after her head hit the pillow and dreamed of Tim, of dancing with him as she had Gramps, of his hand in hers. And just as he lowered his mouth to her lips. . .she jerked awake.

"Grrr!" She slammed her head back to the pillow, trying to recreate the dream. But it was no use. Whatever had awakened her had done a good job.

She sat up. The sun peered around the blinds in her bedroom, and the clock indicated she had slept in a little. It was Saturday, and after yesterday she afforded herself that luxury. But something was different in the house.

It was quiet.

Ever since her friend had joined her, quiet nights had become noisier than a construction site. Trista snored like a jackhammer. Glenys threw off the quilt and ran to Trista's room.

She searched the darkness of the room, the shades pulled down tight to keep the rays out. No Trista. Glenys couldn't tell if her bed had been slept in because she hadn't made it since she'd arrived. Had she even come home last night?

Probably not.

Glenys checked her cell phone for messages.

Nothing.

Why wouldn't she have called if she wasn't coming home?

A horrible thought struck Glenys. Had the stalker found her? Had he kidnapped her?

She punched Trista's phone number and waited for her to answer. All she got was the cheery, "Lucky you! You got my number. Unlucky you! I'm not here. Leave a message."

"Hey, Tris? Where are you, girl? Call me, 'kay?"

She sank into a kitchen chair. *Lord, please let her be all right. As much as I hate to think it, I pray she was with Vic all night and that this stalker hasn't found her.* But was Vic that much better? Again, she heard Cyrano's voice, "*Fear me, beautiful green eyes.*"

Her brain started to whir. What time did Vic work at the center on Saturdays? Wasn't it morning? She quickly dressed and drove to the center. If he was there, she wanted to see his face if he tried to lie about Trista.

When she arrived, she ran to the admin office. "Mandy," she puffed. "Is Vic here?"

Tim walked in. "Hey, it's your day off."

"Yours, too."

"Tim lives here." Mandy shrugged. "I guess we all do."

"I'm looking for Vic."

"He called in sick," Mandy informed her.

Tim grasped Glenys's shoulder. "What's wrong? You look upset."

"Trista never came home last night."

He dropped his hand. "Well, she did leave with Vic who called in"—he made quote marks—"sick."

"That's your answer? Do you just assume Trista sleeps around?"

"Hey, I'm sorry." He held his palms up in surrender. "That was out of line."

She leaned on the desk, aching for some kind of support. "Actually, you're right. It's very possible she spent the night with him."

"Did you try calling her?"

"Yes, but her voice mail picked up."

Tim nodded toward Mandy.

She picked up the hint. "I'll call his house." After punching the numbers on the desk phone and waiting a moment, she said, "Hi, Vic, I know I just talked to you, but would Trista be there by any chance?" She looked at Glenys and nodded.

Glenys held out her hand. "I want to talk to her."

"Vic? Can you put her on the phone? Thanks." She handed the receiver to Glenys, and then she and Tim left the office, giving her privacy.

Glenys pressed the handset to her ear. "Trista, what are you doing?"

After a slight pause, Trista answered, "You're not my mother. I'm not accountable to you."

Glenys heard her whisper to Vic, "I thought this was Mandy on the phone."

"A little common courtesy is all I ask." Glenys drummed the desk with agitated fingers. "Two seconds, and you could have let me know you were okay."

"And after those two seconds, you would have railed on me for doing something so stupid. You'd never have believed the truth. Right?"

Glenys gripped the phone so tight, her knuckles hurt. "When I woke up this morning and saw you hadn't come home, I thought the stalker had gotten you." She tried to hold in her sob, but it was all too much.

After a brief silence, Trista spoke softly. "Oh, Glen, I'm sorry. I didn't even think of that."

Glenys swiped away hot tears. "That's just it. You never think. What will it take for you to see that your actions affect others, including yourself?" She stopped for a moment, then backpedaled. "Wait a minute. You said I'd never believe the truth. What truth?"

"Vic really is sick. I followed him home and made him soup."

"*You* made soup?"

"I opened a can, okay? The point is, nothing happened here last night. He spent most of it in the bathroom, and I slept on his couch." She sighed. "I'm sorry I didn't call you. But I knew you wouldn't believe me. And I just couldn't take another upset."

"Yesterday was pretty emotional for you, huh?" Conviction hit Glenys in the heart.

"The whole week has been emotional. My favorite work boots are ruined. . . ."

"Those were work boots? Weren't they Prada?"

Trista clicked her tongue. "Last year's." She continued spilling her totally awful week. "I'll never get that mouse smell out of my nose. The breeder barn stinks, Glen. Then I got yelled at for leaving the inside door unlocked at a hawk cage. Really, isn't that overkill? Two doors?"

Vic hacked in the background and said something Glenys couldn't make out.

Trista spoke back. "I don't care if it's for safety. It's hard to remember both doors." She continued her tirade with Glenys. "And. . .I broke a nail."

"I'm sorry you've had an awful week, but it does get better—"

"No. I'm not cut out for the center." More background conversation, and then she came back on. "Vic just reminded me of something he suggested that maybe you and I could do together."

"I can only imagine."

"Stop it, Glen. He's not really the kind of person everyone thinks he is. He suggested we help with the reading program at schools. We could act out the dramatic parts. It could be fun."

Glenys had to process that. It did sound like a wonderful idea. Even if Vic had thought of it.

"Okay," she finally spoke. "I'll talk to Mandy."

"Great. Oh, I gotta go. Vic is shivering on the couch and needs a blanket. I love you."

"Love you, too, Tris." Even though she drove her nuts.

Glenys found Tim at the clinic, feeding Lady. She still wasn't comfortable with the bird, but managed to stand in the doorway, keeping her escape route in sight.

Tim glanced her way. "Everything okay?" He raised an eyebrow as he shut the cage door.

"Yes. She's playing nursemaid."

"Sounds like a noble thing to do."

"Mmm." She couldn't commit to thinking of Trista as noble. "So. . ." She needed to quickly change the subject in order to mull over the new development. "You're not usually here on Saturdays, are you?"

"Sometimes I pop in to help. Today I wanted to check on Lady." He peered in the cage and spoke soft words to the peregrine.

"How's she doing?"

"I don't know." Tim frowned. "After four days she should be eating better than she is. Might be an infection. The vet will see her Monday." He closed the cage and spoke quietly to the bird, then replaced the sheet over the cage

"I should call you the falcon whisperer. I've never seen her nervous around you."

"Well, we have an understanding. I work hard at not making her nervous, and she doesn't—"

"Gouge your eyes out."

"Exactly." He shoved three dead chicks into his sweatshirt pocket. "While I'm here, I thought I'd help with the feeding. Join me?"

While walking up the path to Heidi and the other birds, Glenys laughed. "Do you ever forget you have those things in your pocket?"

He chuckled. "Once in a while. A few months ago, I had gone to feed a bird, but there was still enough food leftover in her cage. So I pocketed the carcass thinking I'd put it back in the kitchen before I left, but forgot. Went to the grocery store afterward, pulled the dead, furry mouse out of my pocket looking for my keys, and freaked out the clerk."

"I can imagine."

They strolled a little farther, and as they stopped at Heidi's enclosure, Glenys approached the subject she'd been mulling over in her head since speaking to Trista.

"Vic told Trista that she and I might be able to help with the educational program. A reading thing you do at schools?"

"Vic suggested that?" He tilted his head. "Not a bad idea."

"And by the way, he wasn't lying about being sick. She slept on his couch last night while taking care of him. I believe her."

He pulled on his gloves and attached the jesses. "I'm glad you cleared that up. Sounds like Trista is blessed to have a friend like you to keep her accountable."

"It makes for some interesting arguments, though."

"Sounds like she's growing. Is it in her character to take care of the sick?"

Glenys cocked her head back and let the laugh tumble out. "No. Not even for a man." But then she sobered. "Do you think she really does have feelings for him?"

"I don't know." He unlocked the interior door and entered the enclosure. "Vic doesn't seem to be himself either. Could be because he wasn't feeling well, but yesterday he was very quiet, and I never once saw him flirt."

"Not once?"

"Not even with Camille."

"Wow. That does sound serious." He hadn't flirted with her either, but she'd been avoiding him as much as possible, especially after the "fear me" remark.

"Tim, do you think he might be capable of hurting a woman?"

He held his hand up, and Heidi stepped onto it. "Her heart? Oh yeah. Physically? No. I think he's just a jerk."

"How can you be so sure?"

Tim brought Heidi out of the enclosure and offered her the dead bird. She didn't take it. "Because I've seen him with the eagles, the injured ones. You think I'm gentle. You should see him with a fallen bird and how he nurses it back to health. He may be arrogant, but he'd never hurt anyone. Is that what you're worried about?" He looked into her eyes. "Trista is safe with him."

She relaxed. "Thanks. Coming from you, knowing how you feel about him, that means a lot."

"And do you realize something else?"

"What?"

"You are two feet from a hawk right now."

Chapter 11

Tim watched Glenys's face as she realized she'd made more progress. It was like a light had suddenly flicked on and shone in her happy eyes. He looked down at her feet. They never shuffled away, but stayed firm.

"Dare I ask if you'd like to try holding her?"

"No, not yet." Then the feet retreated.

"That's fine. You should be pleased with yourself."

"I am. No more screaming and running. Unless, of course, she got loose."

"That's a given." He cooed to Heidi as he returned her to the enclosure. She stepped back onto her tree limb and then snatched the food from his hand.

"I've been thinking." He locked both doors and started walking toward the next enclosure. "You've been working so hard here. Would you like a break? Heidi has a benefactor who gave me two tickets to see a play tomorrow at the Shakespeare theater. We could leave after church."

Please say yes. He marveled that he'd even asked her in the first place. A short time ago he was ready to rush her training to get her out of there faster. Now he dreaded the day she would leave.

"A benefactor?"

"Yes. Remember that first day of orientation? Mandy told you about the people who adopt birds and send money for their stay here."

"Oh, that's right. I'd love to go."

The next day Aunt Barb offered to take Gramps out to lunch after church so Tim and Glenys could make the matinee. He thought Gramps would be upset, but as he said good-bye, the sly old dog whispered in his ear, "It's about time you dated something without feathers."

As they drove away toward Oakley, Glenys asked, "Did you and your aunt come up with a solution for Gramps?"

"She's offered to stay with him while I'm at the center. She can jostle her schedule pretty easily." He reached over to turn down the radio, a habit of his whether he had a bird or a human passenger. "Gramps has a doctor appointment tomorrow. I'm thinking it's dementia. The other day at the campground, he wasn't just telling old stories, he was reliving them."

"I'm so sorry. I know you hate to see him age."

"Gramps and Gram were the only parents I knew." He hadn't meant for that to slip, but now that it was out, he decided he might as well open up to her. "My mother found herself pregnant shortly after she graduated high school. My grandparents insisted she go to college, so they agreed to babysit. I guess they hoped she would grow up, but she was never cut out to have a kid. I was. . .inconvenient. Instead of trying to make it work as a single mom, she left me with my grandparents after college and pursued her acting career."

"I'm so sorry. How old were you when she left?"

"Five. Old enough to know I had a mother one day, and the next I didn't." He paused, reliving every time she'd promised to come home. Sometimes she'd make it, but most of the time, she'd come up with an excuse. "You see Gramps as a silly old man—" Glenys started to protest, but he waved her off. "No, face it. He does silly things in his old age, but if you could have seen the man he was. . ." His heart swelled with love. "I'm sure it killed him to see his daughter, his baby, be so irresponsible. He never spoke angrily about her, always held out hope. Still does. I think that's why he wants you to be her so badly."

"I had no idea. Is she still around?"

He grunted a mirthless chuckle. "She's in Hollywood. Been trying to become an actress for thirty years."

She stirred next to him, her gaze darting out the window.

He glanced her way. "I'm sorry. I know you've been struggling, too. But you didn't have a kid at home that needed your love."

"No. And if I had, I'd have included him in all my successes and failures. There is no way I could leave a child with my father, even though he'd make a great substitute."

"Thanks. I think I needed to hear that from your own lips, you being of the same profession and all." He turned onto the interstate. "She's still irresponsible. My aunt and I have been trying to get her to come see us for a couple of years. And now that Gramps is going downhill fast, we think she'd better come soon before he forgets who she is."

"What's her name? I might know her."

"She goes by Liberty Elise."

"Is that what Libby stands for? Liberty?"

"No, her name is Elizabeth, so she took two variations of the name and came up with the conglomeration." He remembered hearing that name for the first time as a young kid and knowing it completed the severed relationship between her and the family. "She doesn't even acknowledge that she's a Vogel."

Glenys smiled, and he almost forgot what they were talking about when he saw the dimple.

"What? Why are you smiling?"

"Don't get me wrong. You have a lovely name—for a bird handler. But on an actress it doesn't roll off the tongue."

"I suppose not. Heard of her?"

"No, but I'll keep my ears open."

"Then you're still going back."

She jerked her head to look at him. "Of course. It's what I do."

"I know. I didn't mean anything by that." Actually he meant a lot by that. His brain was telling him that she would go back to her world and no doubt forget about him and the raptor center. But his heart insisted that she might stay. Gramps loved her. Tim. . .intensely liked her. Right now he couldn't bear the thought of her leaving. So he pushed it to the back of his mind. He would enjoy being with her right here, now.

The drive into the artsy town of Oakley always amused him. Various generations of hippies wandered the tree-lined streets: the young women wearing dresses with jeans, the older with braided leather bands or scarves around their heads. Multiple piercings for both sexes seemed the fashion.

They parked and entered the large theater, quickly finding their seats—good ones, three rows back in the middle. Tim would have to write a thank-you note to Heidi's benefactor for his generosity. Throughout the play, a modern romantic comedy of errors, Tim had trouble focusing. Glenys's perfume danced around his senses, making him wish they were alone. The blue dress she wore, while not Hollywood chic, still hugged her body in all the right places, yet had been discreet enough for church.

Then there was the dimple. Even in the darkened theater, he could see it all cute and kissable.

The play finally ended, and he hoped Glenys wouldn't question him about it. He'd have to admit that his favorite part was sitting in a lavender swirl next to a kissable dimple.

They left the theater, and the crisp late-afternoon air cooled his cheeks.

Glenys checked her watch. "We have a little daylight left. Before dinner, would you like to see an alpaca ranch?"

"Whoa. That's not something I had expected you to say. You know someone with an alpaca ranch?"

"Actually, I know someone who knows someone. That's how it's done in my circle, you know." Her eyes twinkled in their teasing.

He nodded. "Lead the way."

As he drove while she read the directions, she fessed up. "I have a good friend whose aunt owns this alpaca ranch. Apparently, Paul moved there when his uncle fell ill and ended up in a wheelchair. He became the office manager. Now he lives on the coast."

Tim cast a side-glance toward her. "How good a friend?"

She laughed. "He married my other good friend at the lighthouse my family owns."

"Oh, I like that kind of friend."

Her cheeks turned an attractive shade of pink, and she glanced down at her hands clutching the handwritten directions.

"Oh!" She thrust her finger at a side street. "Turn here."

He cranked the wheel hard. "A little more warning next time."

"No need. We're here."

They pulled into the drive, past a sign that read SINGING MOUNTAIN RANCH. A woman in her late sixties came out onto the front porch. She slowly made her way down the steps, clutching a knitted wrap around her shoulders.

She approached the car as they got out. "Are you Glenys?"

"Are you Hannie?" The woman nodded. "Then Paul says hello and to give you this." She leaned in and pecked the woman on the cheek.

She motioned for them to follow her around the back of the large house. "I apologize for moving slow. I was ill a couple of years ago and have never really bounced back."

"Paul told me you'd been in a coma. How awful."

"Not so awful. It brought my son and me together. I hadn't seen him since he was seven."

This got Tim's attention. Was she like his mother? "If you don't mind me asking, why not?"

She pierced him with her blue gaze that cut like a laser beam. "I don't mind. It's part of my testimony. But keep in mind, young man, that people have their faults. Only Jesus is perfect."

"Yes, ma'am." He must have put too much venom into his question.

She told them about her drug use, how she forgot her child in the park, left him in the foster system. "I'm not proud of what I did, but my disobedience eventually led me to Christ. He put the pieces back together, and the final puzzle piece fell into place when I got sick. Skye, my son, responded to my plea and through God's mercy forgave me."

"That is a strong testimony. Thank you for sharing that with us." Tim found himself, for the first time, praying for that kind of forgiveness in his own family. He cringed inwardly as God reminded him that it would have to start with him. He wasn't quite ready to forgive his mother.

The tour moved to the barn out back. Alpacas of various hues grazed in the pasture, and several were in pens near the barn. A large man with a faded red ponytail came out to greet them. Hannie's face broke into a wide grin. "Meet my new husband, Tom."

Glenys's hand disappeared between the man's paws. Ironically, so did Tim's.

"Paul told me about you two," Glenys said as the couple led them to a paddock where a white alpaca eyed them with intelligent curiosity.

Hannie linked her arm through Tom's elbow. "We've known each other forever. After my husband died, Tom became my anchor. But neither of us admitted to ourselves that we were falling in love."

Tom gazed down lovingly at his wife. "It took almost losing this woman forever to know that I couldn't keep my feelings to myself."

Glenys sighed. "How romantic."

Tim contemplated that statement. He was on the brink of losing Glenys, not to illness but to something even more diseased. Hollywood. If he didn't declare his feelings soon, she could walk out of his life.

He dared to take her hand in the guise of helping her walk the graveled path in her heels, but reveled in the fact that she didn't pull away when the ground was more stable.

Evening swallowed their short time at the ranch, and after the tour Tim and Glenys ate a steak dinner in Oakley, then headed back home. Tim continued to process what Hannie had told him about forgiveness. He would have shared that with Glenys, but she chatted nonstop about the play and about the alpacas.

By the time they pulled up to the cabin, night had fallen. Glenys looked as lovely in the moonlight as she had during the day. She wore a silver jacket over her blue dress, which made the whole outfit resemble a sparkling star. He walked her to the door where she lingered while looking for her keys in the small purse she carried.

"Thank you so much for this day. I didn't realize how much I needed to get away and relax," Glenys said.

"Thanks for accepting. When I received those tickets, I thought what better person to invite than an actress?" He paused for a second, wondering why it was taking her so long to find her keys. Surely there couldn't be much in that purse. "Oh, and thank you for the alpaca tour. I'd never seen one up close like that."

"It was a great day all the way around then." She slowly pulled out her keys, but held them instead of using them.

"Yes it was."

Small talk. All meant to stall the inevitable—the first kiss. They continued to chat aimlessly while he reminded himself, once again, that she would eventually leave.

Keys jangled in her hand, as if she were alerting him to the fact that she was about to use them. "Thanks again."

Lavender perfume grabbed his head and threatened to draw him near. "You're welcome. . .again."

A nanosecond before he succumbed to the urge to kiss her, another scent cut its way through the lavender. He jerked away and sniffed.

She frowned. "What's wrong?"

"I smell smoke."

Chapter 12

Is it the cabin?" Glenys drew in a breath while searching the roof with her gaze.
"No, it's out there somewhere." Tim tried to look past the trees, but the darkness prevented the ability to see smoke. The smell was faint, but stronger than a nearby campfire. Tim reluctantly walked away from Glenys. "Sorry. I have to go."

"Where?" Her expression filled with concern as she followed him to his car.

"The center. I need to listen to the emergency scanner."

"Please wait just a moment." She ran back to the house, unlocked the door, and came out a few seconds later with her boots on and pulling her work jacket over the blue dress. "I can't help in high heels, now can I?"

Before he could protest, she flung herself back into his car. He opened his door and sat, but couldn't stop staring at this conundrum of a woman.

Finally, she pointed at the steering wheel. "Drive!"

By the time they arrived at the center, the smoke had thickened. Tim threw the gear in park. "It must be near."

"What can I do?" She hopped out and raced after him as he headed for the visitor center and the admin office.

Once in the office, he dug in a drawer. "Here's a list of volunteers. Call them and put them on standby. Let them know there's a fire nearby and we may need their assistance."

While she sat at the desk and started pushing phone buttons, he turned on the scanner. Sure enough, fire crews had been called in. His heart pounded as he listened intently for the coordinates. Once he heard them, he wrote them down and looked at the large map taped to the wall. "It's only five miles to the northeast, but traveling straight south."

Glenys turned in her seat, still clutching the handset. "Then it could miss us, right?"

"Unless it turns. Either way, the smoke will only get worse." He rubbed the tension from his neck. How could a beautiful day go so wrong? "Call everyone back and bring them in. Ask them to bring pet carriers if they have them. I'll go gather what I can." He started to dart out the door, but turned. "And thanks."

By the time he'd pulled what empty crates he could from the clinic, Mandy arrived. Soon afterward Camille and three other volunteers showed up, all bearing pet carriers. They stood in the darkness awaiting orders.

"I didn't smell smoke at my house until Glenys called." Mandy spoke while adding two more cages to the growing collection. "I walked outside and caught a faint odor, but I would have thought it was a campfire. Were you outside when you caught the first whiff?"

"Um. . .yeah." He didn't want to admit that he was standing outside Glenys's door trying not to kiss her. He needed to change the subject, quick. "How many handlers have shown up?"

"You, me, and Camille."

"That's it? Where's Vic?"

"Still sick, I guess."

Tim glanced around at those assembled, which now included Glenys.

"I have an update on the fire," she said. "It's turning our way."

"Okay." Mandy took charge. "Everyone, grab a carrier. If you've never handled a bird, go with a handler and assist."

Tim stepped forward. "May I say a quick prayer?"

Mandy nodded.

"Lord of all living creatures, please have mercy on this little center. Move the fire away, but I also ask that no one else is in its path. Squelch the fire in the name of Jesus. And lift up our fellow handler, Vic. Heal him, and please don't let the smoke interfere with his recovery. Amen."

Amens echoed around the small circle, and then everyone dispersed to the four corners of the center. Glenys and another volunteer followed Tim.

"I can't have you squeamish, Glenys. You have to do what I say," he shot over his shoulder as they booked it up the path to the falcons.

"I can. . .handle it."

He couldn't see her face in the dark and the growing smoke, but could tell from the tiny response that she was frightened.

They made it to Heidi, who had retreated to the farthest corner of her enclosure to get out of the smoke. "It's okay, girl. We're here." He pulled on his glove. It took some coercing to get her on his hand. He managed to get her into the carrier, though, with minimal ruffling of feathers.

"Glenys, run her down and come back for the next one."

Glenys still stood outside the enclosure. Tears streamed down her face, mumbling part of a scripture verse over and over. "God did not give us a spirit of timidity."

"I'll do it," a female volunteer said.

"Wait." He held her off against his better judgment to hurry things along. "Glenys, you said you could handle it." He hated to bark at her, but she refused to move.

"I can, just give me a moment."

"We don't have a moment." He pulled out his radio. "Mandy."

The radio cracked. "Go ahead, Tim."

"I'm sending Glenys back down. She needs a different job." He glared at Glenys, whose shoulders slumped.

"I'm sorry, Tim."

"Yeah. So am I." He nodded to the volunteer who grabbed the carrier and followed Glenys down the path. Then he grabbed two of the four carriers they had brought with them.

He got to the next bird, still fuming. It was his own fault, really. He should have insisted Glenys find something nonthreatening to do. Over at the eagle cage, he saw Vic and Trista. She performed the same task as he'd asked of Glenys, and though she squealed while taking the cage down the hill, at least she did it.

He called over to Vic. "I thought you were sick."

"I am." Vic could hardly be heard for his borderline laryngitis. "But these guys will be dead. Which is more important?"

Well, he'd never doubted Vic's loyalty to his eagles. Just to women.

As Tim was closing the door on the peregrine, a man in his fifties ran up the hill, a blue handkerchief pressed to his mouth. He introduced himself as Chris Jenkins, and Tim recognized him as Heidi's financial supporter. "Hey, thanks for the tickets. And thanks for doing this. It goes beyond what we expect from a supporter."

"My pleasure. There's several of us here. We got a phone call about forty-five minutes ago."

As Chris hustled the cage down the hill, several other people swarmed the grounds. Tim ran to another enclosure to load another bird, shaking his head. The only list he'd given Glenys was of the volunteers. She must have seen the supporters list and called them, too. She may freeze around the birds, but her levelheaded thinking may have just saved some lives.

⟳

Glenys felt her fingernails prick her palms as she clenched her fists. Why couldn't she get past her fear? She'd let Tim and the center down. Forget about the stupid movie role. She needed to overcome her phobia right now, before her actions hurt others.

She noticed only one person working the owl path, Mandy. Without thinking, she grabbed a carrier and bolted to join her.

"Why are you alone down here?"

"I sent everyone to where the smoke was thickest. This is more protected, but we still have to get these guys out."

"Give me a glove."

Mandy jerked her head. "You sure?"

"I've handled Dunk in the clinic. He's only a little barn owl, but it can't be much different."

"Okay. You know what to do, right?"

Glenys nodded and entered the screech owl's enclosure. Without the heart-shaped face, this owl looked more sinister, but she kept telling herself it was Dunk's cousin. She took a huge breath, then hacked a little as the growing smoke filled her lungs. "Come on, big boy." She held her gloved hand out, and the owl stepped on. A rush of adrenaline flowed through her. She could do this. . .as long as he didn't try to fly. *Please, Lord. Keep his wings still.* She transferred him safely with only a small amount of flapping, and that, she knew, was more for balance than flight.

As she carried the cage out, Mandy congratulated her. "That's an important step you just took."

"Owls are less threatening, I guess. I know they can hurt me, but they don't scare me like the peregrines."

She nearly entered another cage when she stopped abruptly. "Um. . .Mandy? Can you get this one?"

"Can't handle the great horned owl, eh?" Mandy moved past her, chuckling.

"I think I'll work up to owls on steroids." She stayed to help Mandy with the cage, but then moved to another enclosure with a smaller, more manageable owl.

Glenys carted two of the owls back to the visitor center where she saw that the clinic patients were waiting near Tim's SUV. She loaded Dunk and another owl into the car and noted there was room for two more passengers. She spotted Heidi's cage on the ground next to Lady. She glanced around as the last remaining volunteers hustled to get out of there. She hadn't seen Tim for a while and wasn't sure she could face him.

As she stood by the cages, she chewed her thumbnail. Finally, after a quick prayer, she grabbed the hawk's cage. "Be nice to me, Heidi. I'm too big to be a snack." With her heart in her throat, and her fingers away from any holes, she slid it into the SUV. Coming back with all digits and eyeballs intact, she decided to try Lady, the dreaded peregrine. By the time all four cages were snuggled into the SUV, she turned to see Tim watching her.

Heat infused her cheeks. Despite her recent victory, she couldn't shake the shame of letting him down. Avoiding his eyes, she mumbled, "I told you I just needed some time."

"You ready to go home?" His smile broadened, melting her guilt.

"Oh yeah."

He loaded food for their guests, and they drove away from the center, barely able to see the road in front of them through the smoky beams from the headlights. But they drove out of it as they traveled up the hill to Trista's cabin.

"I called home a little while ago," he said as he turned onto the road leading to the cabin.

Glenys gasped. "Your grandfather! Is he safe?"

"Yes, but Aunt Barb moved him to her place. She said the smoke was extremely thick at my house. He's had breathing problems in the past."

"Oh, I hope he'll be okay." She bowed her head while Tim drove. "Lord, please be with Gramps tonight. Keep his breathing in check, and please keep him coherent so he won't be afraid. Also, please snuff out this fire so it does no property damage, and thank You in advance for keeping the center out of its path. In Jesus' name, amen." When she opened her eyes, Tim glanced at her with watery eyes. Had he been moved or was it the smoke?

"Thanks, that means a lot."

What could she say to that? It was the least she could do for letting him down earlier. "I'm sorry, for freezing up like I did. I really thought I could at least carry a cage. But knowing what was inside. . ."

"Hey, looks like you overcame that." He motioned to the back with his thumb. "Mandy told me you helped her load those owls. Plus you worked past your fear and picked up the carriers with Heidi and Lady inside. That's huge considering you couldn't even stand within five feet of them before."

"Well, there wasn't a piece of plastic between us then." She laughed, but her nerves made it come out as a twitter.

They pulled up her drive, and Tim cut the engine. "Looks like you ruined your dress."

She looked down at the tattered and soiled material. "Dresses can be replaced. Life can't."

His smile told her she'd given the right answer. He opened his car door and walked around to open hers. "Well, you go take a long soak and sleep well. You deserve it."

"Where are you taking the birds?" She slid out of the car, enjoying the fact that he didn't move much to get out of her way.

"I don't know yet. I can't take them home. It's still too smoky there, and Aunt Barb's place is too small."

"Leave them here."

"I'd have to stay with them. I'm fairly sure you're not at the point where you can feed them."

"We have a couch."

He glanced around nervously. "Uh, will Trista be here?"

"No, she told me she needed to go back with Vic. They'll be taking care of some eagles and vultures there. If you're worried about propriety, I'll be certain to bar my door."

That didn't seem to quench his nervousness. "I don't really have a choice, do I?"

"Not that I know of."

"Okay"—he wandered to the back of the SUV—"if you're sure your friend won't mind."

Glenys laughed. "Trista would be the last to mind."

They unloaded the birds and set the two from the outside enclosures in a protected part of the backyard. But Dunk and Lady earned places on the floor of the kitchen, where they could be kept warm. Glenys found some extra sheets and draped them over the carriers.

But when Dunk's peeps sounded unsure, Glenys lowered herself to the floor where he could see her. "So, what is the next step in his treatment?" She glanced at

Tim, who offered her a fresh cup of tea and squatted near her with his own.

"His puncture wounds are healing nicely, but he lost some key feathers in the cat attack. We've saved other owl feathers and will imp them in to see if they'll help him fly."

She raised a brow. "What does that mean?"

"Graft. We take a bamboo shoot and stick it inside the shaft of the donor feather and glue it in place. Then we stick the exposed half of the shoot into the damaged shaft, also gluing it in place."

"Wow, you go to all lengths to save these guys, don't you?"

He shrugged and moved to the table. "We try."

Satisfied that Dunk felt safe now, Glenys lowered the sheet over the cage door. "I can't believe it took a near disaster to get me to move forward in my progress."

"I'm sorry I snapped your head off. Gramps was right." He rubbed the back of his neck. "I do put more stock in birds than in people."

She stood and joined him at the round pine table. With a hand on his, she looked into his eyes. "There are times when that's appropriate, and tonight was one of those times."

He flipped his hand to hold hers, and a thrill shot through her arm and burst into a fireworks display somewhere behind her rib cage.

"I was proud of you tonight." The tone of his voice, as well as his words, soothed the need to prove herself to him.

He reached toward her cheek and stroked it with his thumb. "You're wearing battle paint."

"So are you." She knew they both proudly wore smudge and grime, evidence of their hard work.

"On you it looks becoming." He leaned in as his hand slipped behind her neck. Their lips touched in a salty mix that quickly turned sweet. When they parted, he touched her forehead with his. "I had hoped to do that tonight when we weren't both a sooty mess."

"Waylaid plans, huh?"

"Yeah. Leave it to a forest fire to—" Another spontaneous kiss drew them to stand where their arms could enfold each other.

After a moment Tim pulled away first. "Okay. This is nice, but I think I'd better go sleep in my car."

Warmth rushed to Glenys's cheeks. "I hate the thought of you out there in the cold. Let me do it. I've suffered worse while on location filming a training video on winter hiking in the High Sierra."

He cupped her chin and kissed the corner of her mouth. "What kind of a gentleman would I be if I let you do that?" Pulling away, he seemed reluctant to leave. "I'll check on the outside guests first."

As she watched his retreating figure, she praised God for this man of integrity. What a story to tell Trista.

Chapter 13

The next morning Tim's cell phone rang, and as he answered it, his left calf cramped. He tried to stretch, but the car door prevented it. It was then he remembered he'd spent the night in the back of his SUV.

"Hi. . .ow. . .Mandy," he said as he stumbled out of the car and stomped his foot on the ground.

"Are you okay? You sound funny."

"I'm fine, just a cramp." A baseball-sized knot, to be exact. He did a lunge stretch against the side of his car, and it slowly unknotted.

"Too much activity last night? That was a lot of going up and down those hills to evacuate."

"Yeah." And a night spent in his car afterward didn't help. "What do you need? Everything okay there?"

"The fire danger has passed. I'm calling everyone to let them know it's safe to return."

"Okay, I'll get my passengers loaded back up." He didn't feel the need to tell her he'd spent the night in Glenys's driveway.

When he closed his phone, he limped to the cabin. The back door was unlocked, so Tim went inside to get Dunk and Lady, then loaded up Heidi and Oliver, a screech owl that Glenys managed to get into a cage. He was so proud of her.

Since she was still in bed, no doubt exhausted from the day before, he left a note assuring her he could handle getting all the birds where they needed to be.

At the center, Tim removed Heidi from her cage and put her back into the enclosure. As he did so, he thought about the confusing events of yesterday.

Was it really just yesterday?

The outing to Oakley, where he'd convinced himself he'd only asked Glenys along as payback for her kindness to his grandfather; his conversation—and conviction—with alpaca-owner Hannie; a near-kiss with Glenys; a forest fire; and then a satisfying smooch that had him tossing and turning in the back of his uncomfortable SUV all night.

What had he done?

In daylight it all seemed clear. Glenys would leave and take his heart with him. Well, he couldn't let that happen. He'd have to resist her innocent seductiveness. Explain to her that he simply got caught up in the drama of the evening.

Then again, watching her meld into his world made him almost believe she might stay. But he couldn't ask her to give up her dream. Could he handle a long-distance relationship? With an actress?

As if on cue, he received a text from his mother.

Sorry to hear about Dad. I can't possibly get away. Important audition for margarine commercial. Give him hug from me.

"Yeah, Mom. Margarine is so much more important than your father's mental condition."

Heidi squawked from her limb as if in agreement.

He moved on to help deliver the other birds the volunteers had brought back to their homes, still mulling over his growing attraction to Glenys that overtook him nearly as fast as a forest fire. Would she leave and send back these kinds of texts? *Sorry, darling, but audition for greeting card company is more important than us being together. I'll mail you a hug, because I care enough to send the best. Please share it with Gramps.*

A shudder rattled his bones. Best to put their relationship back on a purely platonic level. If not for himself, then certainly for Gramps. He didn't need one more person letting him down.

Throughout the day, he worked at getting all the residents back into their enclosures as people brought them in, but his mind stayed on Glenys. He resolved to keep his distance emotionally, but when Glenys showed up to check on Dunk, her attention to the little bird endeared her to Tim all the more.

"I'm sorry I missed you this morning," she said as he joined her. "I would have made you breakfast."

Tim quickly looked around to be sure no one overheard their conversation. He didn't want anyone to get the wrong idea.

"I think the outing did him good." She peered at Dunk through the metal bars of the cage door. "His eyes are alert."

She replaced Dunk's sheet over the cage so he could rest, then turned to Tim. "About last night—"

Tim took a deep breath. "You're right. It was too fast. And you're leaving. So why pursue a relationship? Somebody will only get hurt."

The pain in her eyes stopped his runaway words. "I was going to say thank you for the wonderful evening—before *and* after the fire."

"I'm sorry." Tim pried his foot out of his mouth. "Can we start over? Things just happened kinda fast last night."

She pinched her lips, but appeared to think about it. Finally, she nodded. "That's a good idea. Let's maintain a professional relationship for now."

He caved to the lower lip that barely pouted. "No. Let's go back to a special friendship and see where that leads, okay?"

"Okay." Her dimple deepened. "Then back to the matters at hand. I love working with the owls, but I'm not getting much exposure to the falcons."

"I have an idea." He walked her out of the clinic into the chilly autumn air. She pulled her jacket closed, and he resisted the urge to put his arm around her.

"Would you be able to come earlier and catch me before I leave for the day? Follow me around during the feeding?"

The sparkle returned to her eyes. "I could definitely do that." She shivered slightly. "I'm glad I'll be going home before winter hits. I already miss my California sunshine."

Well, that nailed that dream inside the coffin.

As she left him to enter the visitor center, his cell phone chirped. It was Aunt Barb.

"Hi, Auntie. Are you on the way to Gramps's doctor appointment?"

"No, Tim. Listen. We're not at the clinic, we're at the hospital."

Tim's heart thudded with the rhythm of a sledgehammer. "What happened?"

"The smoke last night kicked off his emphysema. It started this morning and looked to be only a temporary attack, but he's really struggling to breathe. They'll probably admit him."

"I'll be there as soon as I can."

Glenys came out carrying her purse. She must have read the alarm on his face. "What's wrong?"

"Gramps is in the hospital. An emphysema attack."

"Let's go." She started to walk away from him.

"Wait." He grabbed her forearm and turned her away from the parking lot. "You don't need to put your life on hold again for my family problems."

Concern snuffed the sparkle from her eyes. "I love your grandfather. But if you'd rather I not go, I respect that. I guess I've been horning in on your personal life lately. I'll just go home and pray for him."

She started to walk away, a dejected slump to her shoulders. Tim couldn't leave her thinking she wasn't welcome. "Would it mean that much to you?"

She swiveled to face him, a smile blossoming on her face. "In and out. Just long enough to let him know I care. Then I'll sit in the waiting room and leave you two alone together."

He threw his arm over her shoulders, buddy style. "Come on, Sunshine. You'd probably do him a lot of good."

He offered to drive and bring her back to her car since they had to go into Medford. Once they were on their way, he regretted that decision. Lavender scent reached up his nostrils and dulled the common sense lobe of his brain.

To get his mind off the unpretentious, unactressy person sitting next to him, he asked her to pray aloud for his grandfather. "He brought this illness on himself from years of smoking, but he quit after Gram died."

She bowed her head and said a heartfelt, Spirit-led prayer that brought a lump to Tim's throat.

"Thank you."

This woman was nothing like his mother. Her actress friend was though, and Tim said a silent prayer of his own that Glenys wouldn't be influenced.

When they arrived at the hospital, Tim and Glenys walked into Gramps's room, where he lay on his back with a tube running oxygen into his nose. Aunt Barb rose from the one chair. "He's been sleeping off and on since they admitted him. Poor thing was probably worn out after our adventure yesterday."

Tim offered Glenys the chair and stood by his grandfather's bedside. "He looks so frail. When did he get so old?"

Aunt Barb stretched her back and looked as though she needed a break. "Seems all of a sudden, doesn't it?"

Gramps's eyes fluttered open, and his gaze rested on Glenys. "Libby?"

"No, Gramps, this isn't Mom." He wanted to shout at his grandfather, tell him to stop getting old.

Glenys pulled the elderly hand into hers, neither denying nor confirming. Just smiling.

"Oh. Timmy's girl." He smiled back and waggled her hand in his.

A pink blush bloomed on Glenys's face. "How are you feeling?"

"Oh"—he shook his head—"so much fuss over an old man with a cough. I'll be outta here tomorrow."

"You need to take care of yourself. I would be very sad if anything happened to you."

Gramps let go of her hand and brushed her cheek with a knuckle, her flawless skin contrasting with his age spots.

She started to rise, apparently to fulfill her "in and out" rule, but Tim suddenly couldn't bear the thought of her not being there. He placed a hand on her shoulder, and she relaxed back into the chair.

Gramps drifted off again. Tim looked at Glenys. "We'll be right back." He motioned to Aunt Barb, and she followed him out of the room. They wandered to a waiting area where they both sat on purple vinyl couches. The entire area had been decorated in bright, cheery colors.

"I didn't want to talk in front of Gramps. Mom texted me today."

"I know, she did me, too. I called her right away, but it went to voice mail. She's avoiding us."

Tim leaned on his elbows and rubbed his eyes. "You know, I'm at the point where I say cut her loose. She doesn't care about us. Why should we care about her?"

He felt his aunt's hand on his shoulder. "That's anger talking, not the Lord. I've had those thoughts plenty of times, but I'm always convicted. As long as we're able to connect with her, I feel we need to continue to reach out to her."

Tim suddenly remembered his conversation with the owner of the alpaca ranch. He told his aunt about her. "She hadn't been much different than Mom. Both went their own ways, leaving behind people who loved them. But God reached Hannie."

"God can reach your mother, too. I believe that with all my heart." Pain laced the faith he saw in her eyes. "I have to."

As they returned to the room, a sweet soprano voice drifted into the corridor, getting louder until Tim realized it was Glenys singing "I've Got a Crush on You." Gramps lay with his eyes closed, but a smile curved his lips. She stopped when they entered.

"How do you know the words to that song?" Tim marveled at this woman's versatility.

"Puh-lease. Everyone in the entertainment industry should know Gershwin. Gramps was telling me about his days spent with the Berlin Airlift back in the forties, and the conversation moved naturally to the hit parade."

A nurse came in and checked Gramps's vitals. Once she assured them he would rest comfortably for the night, Aunt Barb volunteered to stay at the hospital so Tim could take Glenys back.

He lost another piece of his heart to her when she bent and placed a kiss on the wrinkled forehead.

As they drove home, Tim's baffled emotions threatened to overcome him. His own mother couldn't give them the time of day, and the woman sitting next to him, whom he didn't want to become involved with, had apparently adopted his family.

I don't know what You're doing to me, Lord. Do You like me off-balance like this? He shouldn't have asked the question, because he felt that deep down, off-balance was exactly where God wanted him. Was God about to topple his world?

Glenys smiled at him from the passenger seat, the dimple acting as a pawn in God's master plan.

I'm in so much trouble.

Chapter 14

By Tuesday all was back to normal at the center. When Glenys showed up an hour early, as Tim had suggested, she looked for him in the visitor center.

"May I help you, sweetheart?"

"Hi, Cyrano. Tim around?"

"Around. . .Tim."

"Why do I bother asking you questions when your answers are never in the right order?"

"Order. . .Tim around."

Glenys chuckled. "Maybe you do know what you're saying."

"Dimple."

Her hand flew to her cheek. "Who is talking about my dimple?" Then again, there could be other people with dimples, or they could have been discussing dimples on a golf ball.

"Cute dimple."

Maybe not. She had no time to figure it out. She needed to find Tim. As she walked out, she found herself scrutinizing everybody's faces looking for dimples. From Mandy and Camille, who were cleaning up after a school talk, to a couple of women volunteers she barely knew. Of course, it didn't help if they weren't smiling. Maybe she should walk around with a funny face to see who she could get to laugh.

She lost interest in the dimple search when she saw Vic and Trista at the vulture cage. She shuddered. A vulture would be one bird she'd never handle.

She waved and joined them. "Feeling better, Vic?" He didn't have the pasty pallor he had the day before.

"Much. I had a great nurse." He winked at Trista.

"And is she still needed?" Glenys pinched her lips shut, but too late. The snide remark had already escaped.

"I'm sorry I haven't been home lately." At least Trista had the courtesy to look apologetic.

"Me, too. I was looking forward to some girl time." She pinned Vic with a look, hoping he'd get the hint and back off from pursuing her friend. The vultures looked down on them from their perch, leaving Glenys with an uneasy feeling. Were they waiting for her to kick the bucket?

"You're right." Trista laid a hand on Vic's arm, almost comforting him. "Vic's better now, so I'll be home tonight. Is that okay, hon?" She asked permission? What was happening between these two?

Vic slipped his fingers in his front pockets and drew his shoulders to his neck. "Am I going to live?"

Trista nodded and kissed his cheek.

He sighed heavily. "Then fine. I can suffer for the sake of friendship."

"Are you busy," Glenys asked Trista, "or can you walk with me while I look for Tim?"

"I'm done for the day." She brushed Vic's hand with the back of hers.

Yep. Glenys needed to nip that in the bud.

As they walked away, Glenys shoved her hands into her jacket pockets. "I thought you were going to quit volunteering here."

Trista glanced over her shoulder at Vic. "I was persuaded to stay."

"Do you know what you're doing, Tris?" She jerked her head in Vic's general direction.

Trista blushed. Glenys had never seen that before. "I like him, Glen. You've been wrong about him."

"I hope so. But I don't want you to get hurt."

"Don't worry. I know what I'm doing."

Tim came walking around the corner with Heidi on his hand. Glenys had made some progress, it was true, but the sudden appearance was still a shock. She put Trista between herself and Tim.

"I've been looking for you," both Tim and Glenys said together.

Trista pulled away. "Vic is taking me to dinner, but I promise I'll see you at home tonight."

When she was out of hearing range, Tim spoke in a near whisper.

"I've heard the other women talking. They said Vic hasn't been hitting on them lately. I thought it was because he was sick, but maybe it's because he has a girl now."

"Bite your tongue. Trista doesn't need someone like Vic. I'd rather she found a nice man with morals. A Christian man who will take care of her. Someone like—"

He raised an eyebrow, apparently waiting for her to continue.

"Never mind." She'd almost said someone like Tim.

"Okay. Staying out of that one. You know her better than I do. But it seems if someone is influencing Vic to behave himself, that might be a good thing."

She didn't want to get into it either. "So, are we working with Heidi?" She pointed to the bird on his hand.

"Yes. The center has been booked for a Raptor Reading on Friday. I thought we'd rehearse. We'll work in the visitor center since it's nippy out here."

"Do we need to cover Cyrano? Hawks and parrots don't mix, do they?"

"No, but these two have worked together a lot. Both are old hats at what they do in the bird theater world."

They entered the building, and Tim disappeared in a back room with Heidi. "I'll go find a T stand."

Glenys waited near Cyrano's playpen. He cocked his head in an impossible bend.

"Sweetheart? Dimple?"

Tim reentered, dragging a carpeted wooden perch behind him. He placed Heidi on it, then he pulled a children's book off a shelf.

"This is what we'll be reading."

She thumbed through it. "This is cute. I like the little old lady." She laughed at the stooped gray-haired woman who owned a bird.

"We usually just read, show the pictures, and have the bird sitting on the perch. Then we tell the kids some facts and go home. But it will be more interesting if you acted it out. It will only be effective if you're able to hold the bird. You want to try?"

"You're a sneaky man, Tim Vogel. Combining my passion with my fear."

An evil grin appeared on his face. "Hey, it was Vic's idea. We'll see if it works."

He handed her a stuffed toy bird so she could get down her part. "Pretend you're Mrs. Hawk. She loves her bird. And more than that, she trusts her bird."

"Well, look at her." Glenys pointed to the cover. "She doesn't have to worry about the bird gouging her eyes out."

Tim examined the artist's rendering. "Why not?"

"Because she has thick glasses."

He laughed, a hearty sound that made her want to make him laugh more often. "Then we'll get you glasses." As Tim read the story *Mrs. Hawk and Her Hawk*, Glenys pantomimed. It had been awhile since she performed, and she soaked in the movements, not realizing how thirsty she'd been for something familiar.

Tim's reading had her laughing, especially when his voice went falsetto to sound like the elderly Mrs. Hawk. Finally, after a particularly long giggling session, he asked, "Do you think I should let you say the lines?"

"Oh no, this will have the kids rolling on the floor."

He put down the book and stood, then grasped her shoulders and turned her toward Heidi. "Time to try this for real."

She donned a glove with a shaky hand, but relaxed as she concentrated on Tim standing behind her, protecting her if need be. With his hand on her left shoulder, he took her right elbow and straightened her arm. "Just like the canaries and the owls. You can do this."

Heidi glared at her, as if asking who she thought she was to approach her in such a manner.

"Heidi hates me."

"No she doesn't. She just needs to know that you won't drop her. You must appear more confident."

"Even if I'm not feeling it?"

"Yes. You'll become more comfortable the more you do this. Remember my canaries? You did great with them, eventually. And what about Dunk? Now you can not only handle him but all the other owls here."

"Not the great horned owl."

"I admit, his size is daunting, but I have no doubt you'll be able to work with him soon."

His confidence buoyed her resolve. "Okay, let's do this."

She held her hand near Heidi's feet. Listening to Mrs. Hawk's dialogue as Tim read, she took on her character and found the strength she needed. Heidi stepped onto her hand, and Glenys clipped the leash to the jesses and wound them in her palm. "I'm doing it." She whispered the words, afraid that by saying them out loud the whole experience would dissolve.

Tim interrupted his reading and also whispered, "Great job."

After finishing the rest of the piece, he said, "Now, take her back to the perch."

Glenys allowed Heidi to step onto the perch and unclipped the leash. "I did it." She wanted to shout, but certainly didn't want to spook Heidi. In her quiet exuberance, she swiveled right into Tim's arms.

He hugged her tight. "I'm so proud of you."

She leaned her head back to search his brown-gold eyes. "Thank you for your patience."

"Super-human patience," he corrected.

"It wasn't that bad."

"Yes it was. It was very bad."

As they stood holding each other and gazing into each other's eyes, Glenys felt the same magnetic pull as their first kiss just two days prior. Inches from his lips, she closed her eyes, anticipation zinging through her like love arrows.

But then his arms dropped, and he backed away. Confusion dissolved the arrows.

"I guess you'll be leaving soon then." A bitter tone laced his words.

This confused her even more. He knew she'd be leaving eventually, but it needn't be good-bye forever.

"I still have to handle the peregrine, but yes. Thanks to you."

"Yeah. Thanks to me."

"I still have a little time. I'd like to do something special for you and Gramps before I go."

He backed up, bumping Cyrano's playpen. "I don't know. We'll see."

They continued to rehearse the story, and this time she held Heidi with more confidence. But the fun had been sucked from the room.

"I think you have it now. You probably have work to do, and I need to get Heidi back to her enclosure." He left abruptly, leaving Glenys with Cyrano.

"Dimple. Green eyes. Pretty." The bird started in again with insistence.

"Okay, Cyrano. I'm getting that someone is talking about me."

"Tim. Around."

She gave him a treat, and he peered at it as if she'd given him a spider to eat. Finally, he nibbled at it.

"Birds." She shook her head. "What are you thinking?"

Chapter 15

What was I thinking? Falling for an actress?

Tim drove home with Cyrano chattering from his cage in the back-seat. With the cover muffling the sound, he could only make out certain words, like his name along with "order" and "around." He wondered if Glenys had said this and was tired of being ordered around.

Well, that would stop soon enough. She'd graduated to holding a hawk. Soon she'd be able to handle the peregrine falcon, and then she would leave. He couldn't bear a long-distance relationship, not after his mother had disappointed him so many times.

He pulled into his drive, then unloaded Cyrano and took him into the house.

Gramps sat in his easy chair looking weary after his latest adventure. Before being released from the hospital that morning, Gramps's doctor kept their appointment and paid him a visit. Tim told him about the trips down memory lane that seemed too real, and the doctor agreed Gramps should be evaluated. After learning that the lack of oxygen from emphysema could mask dementia symptoms, Tim promised to make another appointment after Gramps recovered.

Tim had brought him home afterward, but Aunt Barb had agreed to sit with him while Tim went to work. When he arrived home, she was just putting supper on the table.

"You don't have to cook for us." He pecked a kiss on his aunt's head.

"It's no trouble. I'm here anyway."

"Thanks for being here today." He noted her tired eyes. She wasn't used to watching an old man during her downtime.

She glanced into the living room where Gramps watched Cyrano on the side table entertaining him. "He's my father." Her eyes suddenly misted. "And I don't know how long he'll remember me."

Tim ushered her to the table and pulled out a chair for her, then sat next to her. "Let's wait and see what his doctor says. Could be a special diet might help. I've read they've done wonders through research in coming up with alternatives. And, of course, we'll pray."

She placed the palm of her hand on his cheek. "Why couldn't you have been mine? My sister doesn't deserve a son like you." Her bitterness created an ache in the pit of Tim's stomach. "She had you, and I was left childless."

"I had no idea you felt this way. I'm so sorry you and Uncle Mack didn't have children before he died. You've made a great surrogate mom through the years, though. Gramps and I could never have survived without you."

Love poured from her eyes, along with an errant tear. "Thank you, Timmy." She swiped the tear away with a finger. "I don't know what's wrong with me lately. I guess it just breaks my heart that your grandfather may never see his daughter again."

"I'll do what I can to get her to visit."

She sat with her arms folded, and her mouth turned down, looking very much like Gramps during his stubborn moments.

"Okay?" he prompted as he sat in her line of vision. If she would just look at him, she would come back from this mood she was in.

Finally, a small grin played in the corner of her mouth.

"That's my girl. Let's keep giving her updates as his condition changes. Maybe she'll come around." Well, probably not, but at least it made his aunt feel better.

"Hey"—she hopped up, once again the "mom" taking care of her boys—"this soup is getting cold. Call your grandfather in while I slice some bread." She stopped and looked at him in her bustling. "Did I ever tell you you're my favorite nephew?"

He chuckled. "I'm your only nephew."

Glenys finished her shift and left for the cabin, still confused over Tim's hasty departure earlier that evening. They had shared a kiss after the forest fire, but then he turned on her like a wild hawk.

When she arrived home, she was happy to see Trista's car in the drive, but disheartened to see Vic's there as well. When Glenys had said she wanted girl time, she thought Trista had gotten the hint.

Inside the house, Trista and Vic sat on the couch watching a movie. An innocent scene until Glenys took it in fully. The left side of Trista's blouse hung out sloppily, and Vic's shirt was buttoned crooked.

She mumbled a greeting to their hearty hellos, then headed straight for her room. After dragging her suitcase from the closet, she started pitching her clothes inside.

"What are you doing?" Trista stood at the bedroom door, her eyes wide.

"I think I should go to a hotel. I'm obviously a third wheel here."

"No you're not." Trista shouldered Glenys out of the way and proceeded to unpack the suitcase, tossing underwear and nightclothes back into the drawer. Then she whirled on Glenys. "Are you jealous?"

An inappropriate guffaw escaped Glenys's throat. "You can't be serious."

"Why else would you be upset?"

"Do you think I have feelings for that. . ."—she pointed to the now-closed door, but aimed at Vic on the other side—"predator out there?"

Trista's eyes went even wider than before. "No, I hadn't even thought of that."

"Then what do you mean?" Glenys, suddenly weary, plopped into the small armchair near her window.

"I'm talking about me. You're jealous that Vic is taking me away from you."

"Don't be absurd." But how close did that hit the mark? Was he a falcon come to scoop her dear friend away, and possibly away from the moral foundation Glenys had been trying to build? If so, then jealousy wasn't the right word. Anger summed it up better.

Glenys leaned on her knees and pressed her fists into her temples. "Can't you see him for who he is?"

Trista bristled. "Can't you?"

Glenys's head jerked up. "He's a womanizer, Trista. He doesn't care at all about anyone but himself."

"That's an act, Glen." Trista lowered her voice and glanced toward the closed door. "He's really very insecure around women. That's why he talks big."

"And you know this how?"

"He told me."

Glenys must have looked skeptical.

Trista continued to defend Vic. "Think about it. Why would a man as you portray him admit to that? He said he rarely lets people in because he's an introvert."

Glenys snorted. "Really? He used that word?"

"I'm serious. And if you weren't so busy judging him, you'd see that for yourself." After a long moment of silence, Trista said, "I have an idea. He wants to take me rafting this weekend. Why don't I ask if you can come along? You can invite Tim, and we'll make it a foursome. Then you can see Vic the way I see him."

Could Glenys handle a whole day of Vic's chauvinism? She nearly said no, but Trista's entreating eyes broke her down. "Fine. I'll call Tim, but after the way he acted today, I'm not sure he wants to go anywhere with me."

"Why? What happened?"

"I don't know. We were rehearsing a story that we're going to present to a school, I held a hawk—"

"You held a hawk?" Trista clapped her hands lightly. "Congratulations!"

"Thanks, but it seems a hollow victory. After our hug—"

"You hugged?" Now Trista's mouth lay open.

"Will you let me finish?"

Trista sat back and clamped her lips shut, but her eyes danced.

"After our hug and near-kiss—"

"What? Maybe you'd better start over."

Glenys left out the telling of their first kiss, choosing to relish it a little longer. But she related what had happened just an hour before without any interruptions.

"You know why Tim acted that way, don't you?" Trista put on a Lucy, the psychiatrist, U-shaped smile to Glenys's dim Charlie Brown.

"He hates me?"

"How can you be so smart, yet so dumb? Now that you're accomplishing the thing that brought you here, you'll be leaving."

"So he wants to drive me away?"

"In a sense, yes." Trista reached out and shook Glenys's wrist. "You goof. He's in love with you. But you're about to leave him, so he's pulling a protective shell around himself."

A warm, toasty feeling came over Glenys as if she'd just stepped into the light of a campfire on a chilly night. "Then I'll talk to Tim tomorrow. I think a day on the river would do him good."

∞∞

Saturday afternoon Tim drove up the highway and located the parking area near the reservoir dam where the Rogue River spilled out and continued on to the ocean. He almost stayed home. How did he get talked into rafting with the three people he most wanted to avoid?

The dimple.

If Glenys had called instead of accosting him with that beautiful smile, he might have been able to say no. Instead, here he was, dressed to get doused with chilly river water and waving at the two actresses and Vic.

"I'm so happy you decided to join us." Glenys bounced over to him, with a sparkle in her eyes that he hadn't seen before.

"Yeah. Well. . .thanks for inviting me."

Vic slapped him on the back. "I'm glad you're here, old man." He glanced at the women. "Not that I couldn't handle two girls."

Glenys rolled her eyes—Tim's sentiments exactly.

The raft had already been inflated.

"Is all this equipment yours?" Tim asked as Vic handed him a plastic helmet, orange life vest, and paddle.

"Yeah. I used to be a guide."

This guy was full of surprises—the first allowing two extra people to invade his date with Trista.

He proceeded to lay out the ground rules. "This will be a gentle thirteen-mile ride with twenty-three rapids. Don't worry, though, none is considered over a Class II. We still must maintain safety, though. Tim, you told me you've rafted before, right?"

"A couple of times."

"Then I'll sit in the back since I'm most experienced. You sit in front and help steer. We'll put the two ladies in the middle. Use your paddles the way I just showed you, but really, all you have to do is hang on and look pretty."

Trista blushed a rosy pink, but Glenys jutted out her chin, looking indignant. Her friend pulled her to the raft before the words piling up behind her pinched lips spilled out.

"So," Tim said as he stepped into the raft, "how are we getting back to get our cars?"

"I left my Excursion in Shady Pine. After we dock, we'll load the raft on it and

323

I'll drive us all back."

They each donned their helmets, gripped their yellow paddles by the blue handles, and shoved off. Tim felt Glenys's presence behind him. She and Trista sat side by side in the middle. He glanced over his left shoulder, and her smile made him look forward to the whole uncomfortable day.

The water soon buoyed them, and they floated away. Tim began to relax as he dipped his paddle into the current. There was something cathartic about rivers. Their gentle flow, the beautiful scenery. The giggles coming from the middle of the raft.

Concentrate, Vogel. It wouldn't do to capsize the vessel because of the tinkling laughter that relentlessly tickled his ear.

He also heard Vic talking to Trista and noted that he didn't speak to her the way he did the women at the center.

"You doing okay there, hon?"

"Yes, darling."

"Comfortable?"

"Very, knowing you're in control."

At times he wondered if someone had tossed Vic from the boat and replaced him with a kinder, gentler clone.

After an exhilarating ride, they reached a place mid-trip where Vic suggested they rest. He'd brought food, so they pulled the raft onto dry land and unstrapped the cooler. The edge of the raft served as a bench while they ate sandwiches and drank flavored sports water.

Glenys sat so near to Tim that their knees brushed. He wanted to shift away, but something anchored him to the spot. He realized after a moment it was her very presence that made him reluctant to move. No lingering lavender, no dimple, just Glenys.

This thought was disconcerting and exhilarating at the same time.

Vic's voice pulled him from his analyzing. He praised everyone for a fine job and warned them of white water ahead. That's exactly how Tim felt. His heart was headed into rough white water, and he didn't even have a paddle to steer clear.

Glenys finished her sandwich and took a sip of her water. She glanced at Trista, but directed her comment to Tim. "I'm looking forward to church tomorrow. Your pastor is so funny and entertaining."

Tim cocked a brow at her. Not only was her subject change abrupt, but he wouldn't call Pastor Rick entertaining. Sure, he knew how to tell a joke, but it was hardly nonstop as Glenys tried to make it sound. She motioned with her eyes to Trista. Perhaps signaling him? Was she trying to make the Sunday service sound exciting to the nonchurchgoer?

Vic was the one to pipe in. "You know, Tim, I've been thinking. After nearly losing the center to fire, you really kept your head." He toed a small pinecone that had fallen into the raft. "I heard about the prayer you said for me before everyone helped evacuate. Might be why I began to feel well enough to help. It touched me."

Tim marveled at the way God worked.

Glenys stared at Vic, her jaw dusting the ground. Tim checked his as well to see if it had also dropped. Now he was sure someone had replaced the real Vic.

Glenys recovered first. "Vic, would you like to come to church with us tomorrow? No obligation."

Vic glanced at Trista, who had been quiet during the conversation. She now glared at Glenys. Finally, after an awkward moment of silence, Vic spoke. "Yes. I'd like to go. My folks used to take me, and I'd attend Sunday school. I kinda liked it." He shrugged and glanced down at his feet. "But after they split up, that all stopped."

"How old were you?" Glenys asked.

"Eleven." He stood to collect their trash in a plastic bag and then shoved it into the cooler.

"How tragic."

"Yeah. I lived in two households until I moved out. Dad was always trying to make me macho and told me church was for weaklings."

Vic stood in silence for a moment longer than seemed comfortable. Tim sensed he needed to move on from that revealing statement. "You know, if you were a jock in school, we never would have gotten along. I was a science nerd."

Vic's mouth worked in a tense line. "That's the thing. I was a skinny geek myself." He pulled the strap tight around the cooler and grabbed his helmet. "Man, I don't know why I just confessed that." He began to drag the raft back to the water, and Tim grabbed a handle to help.

"Maybe we'd have gotten along after all," Tim said.

"I found out early on that I could get myself out of most any situation with a smile. The girls loved me." He wiggled his eyebrows as he helped the women step into the raft.

And there was Vic's defense mechanism. Having this brief glimpse into the man's past helped Tim know how to pray for him and how to interact with him at the center.

Tim and Glenys exchanged looks. He wondered if she felt as he had, that he'd misjudged Vic.

Despite Vic's flirting, Trista's face remained deadpan. A few strategic glares in Glenys's direction showed where Trista directed her anger. But as she settled into the raft, she lifted her paddle over her head and said, "Hey, we're getting too serious. I'm here to have fun. Let's go."

Vic glanced at his watch. "You're right. We don't want to be caught on the river after dark."

They finished the last leg of their trip, Vic and Glenys chatting during the slower flow of the river. But Trista's silence lay heavy in the raft. When he glanced over his shoulder, she sat straight, gripping the paddle as if fearing it would slip away.

Ice formed inside Vic's car on the ride back. Was Trista jealous that Vic and Glenys were hitting it off? No, if she were jealous, she'd probably be hanging on Vic, trying to gain back his attention. She was clearly angry with both Vic and Glenys over something.

After they arrived back at the parking area, Trista headed straight for her car without saying a word.

"There goes my ride," Glenys said while shaking her head at the retreating vehicle.

"I'll take you back." Tim turned to thank Vic for the day. "I had a great time. We should do it again."

Vic smiled back and shook Tim's hand. "Yeah, me, too. I guess we never got a chance to know each other at the center. This was a good thing."

Yes it was. Too good. Now Tim didn't have a nemesis, and he was more attracted to the actress than ever before.

Glenys told Vic when and where church was. When she joined Tim in his SUV, she grinned, then leaned her head back and sighed.

"Why are you smiling?" Tim pulled onto the road. "It looks like your friend has a beef with you."

"She's not happy that Vic is coming to church with us."

"Really? That's why?" He glanced again at Glenys's serene face in the evening glow. "And you're happy about that?"

She nodded. "If Vic comes, I'm certain he'll get her to go. I've invited her I don't know how many times."

She glanced his way. "Thanks for joining us today. I was afraid you'd turn me down."

He shifted in his seat. "Gramps asked about you today. I've been trying to let him know that you'll be leaving soon. He asked if I'd invite you to his birthday party this Monday. It's his eightieth, so my aunt and I want to make it special for him."

In the waning light as dusk settled in, a pink glow dusted her cheeks, rivaling the sunset. "I'd like that."

He'd like that, too. And after he dropped her off, he would go home and tell Cyrano that he would give her reasons to want to stay in Shady Pine with Gramps. . . and Aunt Barb. . .and with him.

Chapter 16

I can't believe you asked him to church." Trista whirled on Glenys before she could shut the front door.

"No, I'm sure you could believe that. What you can't believe is that he accepted. Why aren't you angry with Vic?"

"I am, but. . ."

Glenys waited, knowing Trista had no more excuses. She put down her purse and led Trista to the sofa. "Look, come with us or don't. I'll never stop hoping. But don't begrudge Vic for wanting to fill a need."

"He'll change." Trista pressed a fist into the arm of the couch.

"He'll grow. Why do you care if he goes to church? You never minded me going, and we've been friends for several years."

"Because I don't want to marry you."

"Marry?" Glenys picked her jaw up off the floor for the second time that day. "You barely know this guy."

"But we're soul mates. If he gets religion, we won't have anything in common."

"You have plenty in common that 'getting religion' won't change. And besides, it's just one day. You're acting like he'll come to church and then join a monastery."

Her eyes grew wide. "I hadn't even thought of that." She thrust her face into her hands.

Glenys chuckled and hugged her friend. "Relax. We don't have monasteries in our denomination."

Trista mumbled something behind her hands.

"What was that?" Glenys continued to rock and comfort her friend.

"I said, I'll go."

Glenys wanted to hop around the room and celebrate, but instead squeezed Trista a little harder.

The next day, Glenys sat in the kitchen reading her Bible while waiting on Trista. It had been tough to coax her friend out of bed that early. Glenys feared she might dig in and refuse to go, but she finally dragged herself to the shower. When she didn't show up for breakfast, Glenys checked on her.

Trista's bed had completely disappeared and was now covered with her entire wardrobe. "I don't have anything to wear," she wailed as she frantically held up one outfit after another.

Glenys looked at her watch. "If you don't choose something, it won't matter. We need to leave in twenty minutes."

She soon saw the dilemma. Trista's clothes were not appropriate for church. The skirts were too short, and the blouses too low cut.

"I have something you can wear." Glenys headed for her own room. She quickly found a navy blue shift dress. When she reentered the other bedroom, she held it out. "You're smaller than I am, but I think it will work with a belt."

Trista reached for the dress, then sank onto the bed. "What am I doing?"

Dread seized Glenys. She knelt in front of her. "I know you're not comfortable with this, but it's only one day, two hours tops. But"—she tried to swallow what she was about to say, but knew she had to say it—"if you truly are this miserable, maybe you shouldn't go."

Trista's eyes filled with tears. "Are you giving up on me?"

"Whoa! I will never give up on you." Now Glenys didn't know what to do. Should she continue to push and possibly alienate her best friend or back off and hurt her feelings? "I'm saying this is your decision. You know I love you. You know God loves you—I've told you that enough. He wants to have a relationship with you, but you must open yourself to that, just as you would with anybody else."

"That's just it. I've never had a 'relationship.' " She stressed the word, as if it were hard to say. "I've had flings. And that's what Vic started out to be. But when he got sick, something changed. Between us and inside of me." She shrugged one shoulder. "And that was startling enough, but then when he said he wanted to go to church. . .did you know he talked about it on the phone for an hour last night? It's like, after all he's gone through in the past, he's using it—"

"Like a lighthouse in a storm?"

"Yes." Trista twisted the bottom corner of her robe around her finger.

"I love that analogy. You know about my family's lighthouse in Crossroads Bay. It's been that to many people."

A frown took over Trista's face. "I guess I'm in a storm, too, but mine didn't start until just a few days ago."

"No. You've been in a storm for a long time, but you became so comfortable in it you hardly noticed. All those times you called me when you'd had too much to drink. . .all the times I had to talk you down after the tabloids tore you to shreds. . . all the times you felt lonely when no man was in your life and you called me for some girl time. . .that's when you were looking for a lighthouse in the storm, and you mistakenly thought it was me."

Trista lifted sad eyes. "And you kept trying to point me to God."

"The real Light. The only one who could save you."

Trista cast the dress aside and flung herself into Glenys's arms. They both stood and hugged while Trista poured out her heart. "You're right. I've been miserable. I only pretend to be having a great time. But with you I can be real. And I felt that with Vic, too."

Glenys pulled away to look into Trista's puffy, tear-stained eyes. "You can be real with God, too. He made you. He knows everything about you and loves you anyway."

Trista wiped her face with her fingers and sniffled. "I look a mess, but I don't care." She snatched the dress and went into her bathroom.

Glenys felt the first rays dawn onto Trista's new life.

Before long they drove to the church, and Glenys steered the car into the parking lot where she spotted Vic near the entrance with Tim. Relief flooded her. Trista wouldn't back out if Vic were there.

The blue dress trimmed Trista's already petite size. She wore a white floppy hat and large sunglasses, but without the wild party clothes or red carpet bling, she looked more beautiful than Glenys ever remembered.

Vic must have thought so, too. He didn't wait for her to walk across the graveled lot, but rushed to her side and offered a modest kiss.

Glenys caught Tim's eye and his subtle thumbs-up gesture. It felt great to share this moment with him.

Inside, they slid into a pew that Gramps was holding for them—Tim leading the way with Glenys beside him, then Trista, and on the end, Vic. Trista slipped her arm through Glenys's as if she were afraid she might be whisked off into a cult, but Glenys pressed the elbow to her side to reassure her.

Both Vic and Trista made it through the music, although it was apparent they didn't know the songs. However, Vic belted them once he learned the words. Barely a sound came from Trista's lips. Glenys knew this girl was not afraid to croon at the top of her lungs when the mood struck. But this was a different Trista standing beside her. No doubt the real Trista, sans the cloak of celebrity.

Ironically—or was it God?—the sermon that morning was on fear. The pastor spoke on allowing fear to rule instead of the Lord.

"Consider this verse from Psalm 34:4: 'I sought the Lord, and he answered me; he delivered me from all my fears.'"

It hit Glenys hard. She realized that by allowing fear to take precedence, she had shoved God aside. Suddenly she felt like a hypocrite.

After praying silently for forgiveness, peace drifted into Glenys's heart like a butterfly seeking a soft place to land. No more fear. No more running and screaming. The phobia had skittered away knowing there was no room for it.

Even if she'd been healed, Glenys realized she wanted to stay and learn more about the fascinating creatures she had so long avoided. Sadness overwhelmed her as she realized she didn't have much time left in Shady Pine.

The pastor quoted one last verse from his anointed arsenal, this time from Proverbs. "'Fear of man will prove to be a snare, but whoever trusts in the Lord is kept safe.'"

Glenys gasped. That was the verse she'd quoted to Trista during her stalker scare. Was she listening? Perhaps hearing it from someone else would make it sink in. She risked a glance in Trista's direction. Her eyes were closed.

Listen to the Lord, Trista. God, please get through to her.

When he was finished, the pastor gave an altar call to anyone who wanted to shed their past fears and grasp God's hand for the first time in their lives.

A stirring to her right caught her attention. Vic had stood and was heading down the aisle. Had he just shed a fear? His father perhaps? Glenys felt Tim's hand slip into hers, and together they raised their joined palms in tribute to their God of the impossible.

But there was one other soul in turmoil that needed her attention. Trista sat on her hands, watching Vic, the longing in her eyes evident.

Glenys put her arm around the slender shoulders. "God's grace is free, Trista. It can't be bought by your famous director father. It won't run away like the men in your life. It addresses the issue with your stalker. Just like the pastor quoted, fear of man is a snare, but if you trust the Lord, He will keep you safe."

Trista turned large, tear-filled eyes to her.

"I know you came here to run away." Glenys swept a hair from Trista's moist face. "All that talk about wanting to show your dedication because of me was transparent."

"But I do admire you."

Glenys smiled. "But that's not what drove you here. I wanted to believe you had blown off the released stalker, but deep down, you were hurting."

"I'm sorry." The dark tresses fell into her face as she bowed her head. "I used you."

Glenys pulled her into a fierce hug. "No, I was that lighthouse that we talked about. But now"—she pointed to the front where Vic was on his knees with several people gathered—"you know who the real lighthouse is. I can't do anything for you, but God can."

Trista watched the pastor go to each person and pray. Finally, she stood.

When Glenys started to join her, joy springing from her place of hope, Trista stopped her. "I have to do this on my own."

Through a mist of tears, Glenys watched her best friend join the last man she thought would accept Christ. Trista lowered herself next to Vic, humbling herself for the first time ever.

"God is good," Tim whispered in her ear.

"All the time," she whispered back.

He put his arm around her and kissed her head. Despite her joy of the moment, she suddenly felt sad. The days were soaring by, and she longed to stay in his embrace forever.

⸎

The next morning, Glenys woke to a new world. She lay in bed with her hands behind her head reliving the day before. She relished the joy she felt for Trista and Vic, and she delighted in the feel of brushing Tim's arm when she sat next to him at church.

Vowing to make the best of her time left, she rose to get ready for another fun day. Today was a presentation for some visiting schools. She'd been branded The Owl Lady and didn't mind the moniker a bit. Using her performing skills, she took on the role of an overenthusiastic bird-watcher. She'd pretend to have stumbled upon the center with her binoculars in tow and "discover" the owls. Then she'd flip open a book and read out loud about each one. Apparently the kids loved to learn right along with her.

Before she could leave the house, however, her cell phone rang. It was her agent. "Great news!" Sidney always started out that way, whether it was great news or not. She would just spin it to make it sound good. "They've moved the audition up to this afternoon. Tony Farentino is going out of the country unexpectedly and wanted to have this part of the process finished. Be there at three o'clock."

Glenys's heart thudded to her feet. First of all, she still hadn't held a peregrine falcon. She was going to work on that in the next couple of days. Secondly, she hadn't told Sidney where she was. She figured she'd beat her fear of birds and be back before anyone knew she'd been gone. "Um. . .I'm kind of not in LA right now."

"So? Mash that gas pedal and get here pronto."

"I'm in Oregon."

Total silence on the phone. Had Sidney fainted? Finally she heard a strangled groan. "What are you doing there? No. Don't explain. Just listen. I'm going to get you a ticket. Where will you be flying out of?"

"Medford, but—"

"Fine, get yourself to Medford and pick up your ticket. I'll get you here if I have to fly the plane myself." A click ended their one-sided conversation.

Glenys sank onto the couch with her keys still in her hand. She glanced over to Jackie Jr. and her babies, who were just beginning to look like mice. She warred within herself, one part telling her to grab her bags and go. The other, however, reminded her of Tim. Of their first kiss. Of his excitement over her breakthrough as she held Heidi for the first time. Of their holy victory as they watched two arrogant people humble themselves before Christ. She thought of Gramps and dancing with him to an imaginary tune. And she thought of Cyrano, the first bird she'd ever wanted to get to know.

But her life was in Hollywood. Her dream was to have a major cinematic role. She couldn't abandon her desire.

She ran to Trista's room, threw open the door, and pounced on the sleeping lump in the middle of the bed. "Wake up! I need to talk! Now!"

Trista's saggy eyes focused slowly. "Okay." She pulled herself up to lean on her pillow and rubbed her face. "What?"

Glenys recounted what had just happened. "And she wants me to get to Medford right away to catch the next plane back."

By the end of her tale, Trista was wide awake. She thrust the covers off the bed and started to head out the door. "What are you waiting for? Let's get you packed."

Glenys grabbed her arm. "But do I really want to go?"

This stopped Trista cold. "I know my dad, and if you blow this audition, he will never ask for you again."

"But I have obligations here. A school presentation today and Gramps's birthday this afternoon. I can't skip out on those."

Trista's demeanor changed. She patted Glenys's arm. "You know, the old me would pack for you, force you into the car, and toss you onto the plane. But I understand now that you need to pray." She smiled. "I can't be your lighthouse this time."

"Oh. That's just evil, throwing my own words back to me." But Glenys realized that it was true: Trista had become her career mentor and phobia therapist. Having a good friend to bounce things off of was never a bad thing, but she'd leaned too hard on Trista, sometimes choosing her over God. "You're right. This is too big a decision to make quickly."

"Then my advice is to go to the audition, and if nothing comes of it, you'll know that wasn't what God wanted."

"I can always come back, right?"

"Right."

Even while she packed, she knew she'd upset people in Shady Pine. But she told herself she'd make up for it later. She couldn't disappoint Tim over the phone, however. So on her way to Medford, she stopped at the center. She knew he'd be working in the morning since Gramps's birthday party was that afternoon.

Where was his car? Would she have to leave without the chance to say good-bye?

Mandy was just leaving the office in the visitor center as Glenys walked in. She stopped her to break the bad news. "They moved up my audition. I need to leave this morning, so I won't be able to be there for the kids."

The disappointment on Mandy's face tugged at Glenys's heart. "I'm so sorry to hear that. But we'll just give it the way we always have. Good luck. . .or break a leg."

She started to wander out the door when Glenys stopped her. "Where is Tim? I need to say good-bye."

"He's out picking up an injured osprey at Lost Creek Reservoir. You could try calling him."

Glenys sighed. If that was the only way she could talk to him, it would have to do. She punched in his number but only reached his voice mail. If he was doing a water rescue, he had probably thrown his cell phone into the glove compartment as he did at Crater Lake. She didn't leave a message, preferring to explain directly.

Glenys looked at her watch. No time to wait for him. Sidney had called while Glenys was on the way to the center to let her know the time and flight number. Maybe it was better to call Tim after all—from far away. Then she wouldn't have to see the disappointment on his face.

Alone for the last time with Cyrano, she walked over to his play area. He'd been unusually quiet, and she wondered if he was sick. "Hello?" She tried to coax him to talk. "Sweetheart?"

He lifted his wings in a quick flutter, then looked into her eyes. "Freckle."

"Honestly, Cyrano. You say the strangest things."

"Heart-shaped. . .freckle."

Her hand flew to her neck.

"Kiss. . .freckle."

Who knew about her freckle? She thought back. She rarely put her hair up because it never stayed. But she had pulled it off her neck the day she and Tim were looking for Gramps and she'd become overheated.

"Pretty. . .green eyes. . .dimple."

It was Tim saying those things about her.

"Oh, Cyrano. He does care." But she couldn't wait for him to let him know that she cared back. "If only I could be in two places at once. My home and career are calling me, but Tim has my heart."

All the way to Medford and the airport, she questioned herself. But once she boarded the plane, she'd reached the point of no return. Hollywood or bust, and she feared it was Tim's heart that would ultimately be busted.

⌘

Tim thanked the fisherman who had found the osprey flailing in the reservoir. They met at the marina where the man's boat floated near a dock. He was waiting for Tim in the parking area.

The leathery, timeworn fisherman introduced himself as Ron. He explained that he had spotted what he thought was an osprey and snatched it out of the lake. "I had a Mylar emergency blanket, so I covered it to keep it warm."

"Thanks for doing that. You're lucky he didn't fight back. You could have lost a finger." Tim followed him to his boat.

"I got steel-mesh fishing gloves. Gotta protect these dainty hands, ya know." He snickered at his own joke. " 'Sides, that little fellow was so spent, I don't think he coulda nipped at me."

They reached the small skiff, and Tim hopped in. He peered under a silver blanket on the floor to see a juvenile osprey blinking back at him. Once again, he was filled with awe at God's creation, even down to the black raccoon mask that served to reduce the sun's glare on the water so the osprey could hunt effectively.

With his thick falconry gloves on, Tim reached under the blanket and wrapped his fingers around the slender body and wings. "There you go, little guy. We'll get you fixed up." A spot of blood on the bottom of the boat told him they were dealing with something more traumatic than a broken wing. Upon further inspection, he noticed that the tip of one wing had been completely severed.

"Oh no." He looked into Ron's concerned face. "I'll take him in, but he'll never return to the wild."

Ron took off his hat and scratched his head. "How can the tip of his wing just come off like that?"

Tim's eyes scanned the area. "Did you hear a gunshot? That could have done it."

Ron shook his head.

"If you hadn't been out in your boat today, this little guy might have drowned." Ron dug a business card from his wallet. "Let me know if there's anything I can do."

The card indicated that Ron Fester was *The* Fishing Guy. Tours, instruction, and all things with a pole.

Tim pocketed the card and handed him one of his own. "Thanks. Feel free to call any time to check up on his progress. Just ask for the osprey named"—he peeked at the card—"Fester."

Ron's face lit up like a Fourth of July sparkler. "Thanks, man. I'll do that."

After loading the osprey into the back of his SUV, Tim waved at the man and started his vehicle, being sure to turn off the radio. His passenger didn't need rock and roll on top of a scary car ride.

He dropped Fester off at the vet, then fished his cell phone from the glove compartment and called Mandy to report. After relating what he learned about their new resident, he said, "Hey, remember I'm only doing a flyby to get Cyrano, and then I'm taking the afternoon off for my grandfather's birthday. You have people to do the feeding, right?"

"Yeah, no problem. And Tim?" Mandy's voice took on a concerned tone.

"What, Mandy? You have bad news, I can tell. Is it Lady?"

"No, it's Glenys."

"Glenys?" He nearly dropped his phone.

"She came by here looking for you. Just a minute." She paused to speak to someone who interrupted the extremely important and confusing phone conversation.

"What did she want? Come on, Mandy! This isn't the time to keep me hanging."

She had apparently taken the phone from her ear. After an eternity, she came back on. "Sorry, Tim. What was I saying?"

"Glenys? Came by to look for me?"

"Oh, right. Her agent called to say her audition had been moved up. She's probably already on a plane for LA."

"She left?" A huge hole appeared in his heart, as if someone had punched right through it.

"Yes, but she said she'd call after the audition."

"Nice."

"Excuse me? You're breaking up."

Truer words were never spoken. "Thanks, Mandy."

Breaking up. An already fragile relationship severed, like Fester's wing. Glenys was gone, and he didn't even ask her to stay.

⚬

After retrieving Cyrano from the center, Tim entered his house. Gramps had invited a handful of his breakfast buddies, and they sat in the living room swapping war stories. Would they never tire of that?

He placed Cyrano on his perch, wondering what was going on inside the bird brain. All the way home he had rattled on about a "heart."

"Did you remember the ice cream?" Aunt Barb greeted him from the kitchen.

"Rocky Road!" Gramps bellowed from his easy chair.

Tim kissed the balding head as he handed the plastic grocery sack to his aunt. "They don't make any other kind, do they, Gramps?"

Gramps chuckled and smoothed his thin patch of hair. "Not for me. Is that girl coming?"

The hope on Gramps's face broke Tim's heart. "No, I'm afraid not."

Aunt Barb poked her head out the kitchen door. "Why not? Timmy, what did you do?"

Tim took a defensive stance in the middle of the house, Aunt Barb standing there with her hands on her hips and Gramps glaring at him from his chair.

"Why do you think I did something? Believe me, she did this all on her own. Mandy told me that she's left to go back home. They moved up her audition."

"So"—Aunt Barb now folded her arms—"she didn't really have a choice."

"Oh, she had a choice. She could have told them she'd made a commitment here. But she just walked out on me." He kicked at the couch.

"You?" Aunt Barb raised an eyebrow.

Tim only just realized how that sounded. "I mean us. The center. Gramps and his party."

"Mm-hmm." She disappeared back into the kitchen.

Tim swiped at the hair near his eyes.

Cyrano flapped and danced in the corner, repeating unceasingly, "Tim. . .heart."

Yes. Tim had a heart, and he opened it for an actress. Stupid! And now he probably would never see her again.

Aunt Barb came out of the kitchen with paper plates and plasticware. "Are you just going to sit there pouting?"

"No. What still needs to be done?"

"Call the girl."

"I mean for the party."

"The party is taken care of. Go call the girl." Her drill sergeant demeanor didn't allow for discussion.

Tim suddenly felt twelve again. "What do I say? Thanks for the memories?"

"Thank her for volunteering at the center. Tell her how proud you are that she conquered her fear. Then explain how much she'll be missed and that she's welcome back anytime."

"Anything else?" He hadn't seen this side of his aunt in a long time.

"Yes, you might tell her that you love her."

"What? I don't—"

"*Awk!* Tim! Heart! Care!" Cyrano hadn't shut up since they'd come home. And now he was picking up on the heightened conversation between Tim and his aunt.

"Rocky Road!" And now Gramps.

"Fine!" Tim admitted defeat. "I'll do it outside where it's quiet."

He slammed open the back door and marched out to the river where he punched in Glenys's cell numbers. He prayed she was still on the plane and had her phone off, but when she answered, he suddenly couldn't remember any of the things Aunt Barb had told him to say, except the last one, which he wasn't about to admit.

"Um. . .so. . ." *Brilliant, Vogel.* He ought to follow that up with, "Der. . .Uh. . ."

"I'm so sorry, Tim. They called this morning, and you couldn't be reached. Mandy said it wasn't a huge deal about the presentation, but I still feel bad. And I wouldn't have missed Gramps's party if this wasn't important. Please tell him I'll bring him something extra special."

A knot formed in Tim's gut. "Then, you plan on visiting?"

"Of course, as often as I can. . .if you're okay with that."

"Oh, sure." He heard the bitterness in his voice. "We're used to revolving doors around here. But they get rusty after a while of nonuse."

"What are you talking about?"

"I know your kind." *Shut up, Vogel.* "You make an appearance, put on an award-winning performance, then leave. You may think you'll be back often, but you won't. We are just a stop on the tour and easily canceled."

"Tim, I am not your mother."

"No, but you're just like her, aren't you? Career over family?"

"Just wait a minute. Are you saying you consider yourself family to me?"

This immediately stopped his tirade. He wasn't family. He was just some guy she'd met while working at the center. But the way she had infused herself into his life, becoming the daughter to Gramps that he'd always wanted and making Tim look forward to working late at the center so they could be together. . .yes, she had become family to him. But what was he to her?

"Look," he finally said, "it was nice while it lasted. I knew you would have to leave someday; I guess it just came as a shock that it happened so soon."

"It shocked me, too. I wasn't ready to leave."

He rubbed the tension from his neck as his anger abated. "Really?"

"I was having so much fun. I almost didn't get on the plane."

"Then why did you?"

"I kept laying out fleeces. 'God, if You don't want me on that plane, make me late to the airport.' I was right on time. 'God, if You don't want me to audition, don't let there be taxis available at LAX.' My agent sent a car. 'God, tie up traffic.' I'm almost there now with plenty of time to spare."

"So you felt like I do right now."

"Which is. . .?"

He kicked a rock into the river. "Like I'm in a void. We didn't get to say good-bye." And—fine, he'll admit it—he didn't get to tell her how he felt about her. He didn't ask her to stay.

"A void, yes. Or a vacuum, like I've been sucked into the machinery of Hollywood without any care to my feelings. Before I left for Oregon, I wanted this audition so badly I could taste it. Nothing else would've gotten me into the bird sanctuary. But while there, I think I found another purpose. I'm very confused because working at the center is as important to me right now as winning this role. I'm praying that God will tip the balance because I obviously can't be in two places."

It meant a lot to hear that she was confused. He'd never gotten that with his mother. She clearly chose her career over her family, no looking back.

"Thank you, Glenys." Tim wandered along the bank.

"For what?"

"For helping at the center." No, those were his aunt's words. "I mean, for your courage, your passion. Not everybody knows what they want in life, and you worked past a major obstacle. I admire that."

"Thanks. I admire you for the work you do, too." Her voice sounded thick with emotion.

"I'll pray for you, Glenys. That God shows you clearly the desire of your heart and that he'll make the path smooth to attain it." And, if He chose to keep her in Hollywood, that He would dull Tim's pain.

Chapter 17

Glenys closed her phone and slipped it back into her purse. From the backseat of the sedan, she watched Los Angeles breeze by. Palm trees, storefronts, restaurants. All a part of her three weeks ago, but now seemed foreign. She glanced up at the sky hoping to see a proud eagle, but knew she'd never see anything like that in her hometown.

Hometown.

Where was that exactly? Could just a few short weeks totally alter her life, her dreams?

She arrived to her audition in time, but her heart wasn't in it anymore. However, she'd promised Mr. Farentino. And if he wanted her that badly, she certainly couldn't keep him waiting.

She walked to the room her agent had told her to go to, and when she opened the door, she was shocked to see other women waiting to try out. Mr. Farentino had told her that even though he wanted her in the role, she'd still have to audition. He'd led her to believe she'd be the only one. He'd probably told each of the twenty women the same thing. Was Dad right? Was Trista's father following his own agenda? But that was the biz. Half-truths, half-promises. She'd been disillusioned before, but the desire had always kept her going. Now she sat in the room full of people, wishing she were at the bird center. However, she knew herself well enough to realize that if she'd stayed at the center, she'd have longed to be here.

Someone handed her the usual form to fill out, and she sat next to a blond beauty who didn't look a thing like the character for which she was trying out.

"Excuse me." She pulled Blondie's attention from the fashion magazine she was reading. "Are we all trying out for the falconer?"

Blondie snapped her gum. "The what?"

"The role of the woman who raises falcons."

Seriously? Didn't she do her research?

"Oh, yeah. All of us. Plus I heard there was another session earlier today. There's probably a good fifty of us out for that part." She perused Glenys in her travel clothes and went back to her magazine.

After waiting a good half hour for her name to be called, Glenys's phone rang. Caller ID showed it was Tim. Her heart sang. Was he calling to wish her well on her audition?

"Hi, Tim. We only talked a little while ago."

"I know. I called to ask you to pray."

Jolts of alarm shot through her. "What's wrong?"

"It's Gramps. He went to blow out his candles and had a major emphysema attack. We're rushing him to the emergency room."

"Oh no!" Several of the women turned to look at her as she rose and left the room. "Do you need me there?"

A brief silence was followed with, "No. Just pray."

She was about to do just that aloud when he said good-bye and hung up. So she silently entreated God to watch over Gramps and heal him. When she reentered the room, she sat back down next to Blondie and listened to the gum snapping to the rhythm of the accusations in her own head.

You should have stayed. You shouldn't have skipped out on Gramps. You should show Tim that not everyone in the acting profession is like his mother.

Then again, a more familiar voice intruded. *This is what you've always dreamed of. Forget the fifty women—if God wants you in this role, it's yours. You've paid your dues, and now it's time to redeem them.*

She fidgeted in her seat. How long had she wanted to be an actress? She had never gotten this far in the process before. A director asking for you by name, even if you had to audition with fifty others, was better than a casting call of hundreds.

How long had she loved Tim? Not to mention Gramps, Shady Pine, and the center. When she worked with the owls, she never felt more fulfilled, like she was making a difference. She closed her eyes, and Dunk's sweet face appeared. And then Tim's face with his shaggy hair brushing his brow.

Tim said he'd pray for the desire of her heart.

Finally, she felt the balance tip.

∞

Tim stood near Gramps as he lay on the hospital bed. He had been admitted and was breathing easier now that he'd received treatment and oxygen. His paper-thin flesh draped over the skeleton of what was once a strong, capable man. But now he seemed to be disappearing before Tim's eyes.

Gramps swiped at the nasal prongs in his nose as he awoke, and Tim stilled his hands. A nurse with graying streaks in her brown hair walked in at that moment and checked the drip going into his IV. "How are you doing, Mr. Vogel?" She spoke in a loud voice, as if all elderly men were deaf. "Are you comfortable?"

"No." He glared at her. "I can't move while tied down. I'm not a prisoner of war, you know." He pointed at the clip on his finger. "And what is this?" He started to remove it, but the nurse gently but firmly clamped her fingers around his wrist and took his pulse, effectively taking his mind off the clip.

The pulmonologist who had admitted Gramps to the hospital also stepped in and checked the chart at the foot of the bed. Without looking at Gramps, he made a notation in the chart and said, "We're going to keep you overnight and discuss options for your COPD tomorrow. I'll consult with your doctor, but be prepared to be set up with oxygen at home."

"Why, you whippersnapper." Gramps frowned and pointed his clipped finger at the doctor. "I'm writing up a letter of reprimand and sending it pronto to your commanding officer."

The doctor's lips twitched, and he raised an eyebrow. "Check his oxygen again," he said to the nurse. "He seems to be hallucinating."

Tim rubbed the back of his neck. "Actually, he's been having problems with that lately. He had an appointment to be seen for dementia, but these bouts of emphysema keep stalling it."

The doctor checked the records again. "That should be noted here." He scribbled in the chart. As he turned to leave, he saluted Gramps with a weak Boy Scout gesture, his only attempt thus far at acknowledging his patient beyond the chart.

"Don't you salute me." Gramps craned his neck from the pillow, looking like an eaglet bobbing its head. "I'm a non-com and your sergeant. Save it for someone who gets paid enough to care."

"Yes, sir." Although the doctor received no brownie points for his actions upon entering, Tim's estimation of the man rose a little as he backed out apologizing.

"That's Sarge to you!" Gramps bellowed from the bed.

The nurse fisted her hips. "Now see here. You're in my hospital now, soldier. While you're here I pull the rank, understand?"

Gramps's eyelids flew open, and he seemed to sink farther into his pillow. "Yes, ma'am."

She winked at Tim as she left the room. A moment later he heard the door open again behind him and assumed she had returned. But Gramps's face brightened. "Libby?"

Tim closed his eyes and breathed a prayer of thanks. So Glenys had come after all. "No, Gramps, it's Gl—"

"Daddy!"

The woman swept into the room, her high-heeled open-toed shoes clicking on the floor and her chic purple scarf whipping him on her way by.

"Mom?"

"Oh, hi, Timmy." She air-kissed him on the cheek. "How is he? Barb called when they admitted him."

"How did you get here so fast? I just texted you an hour ago."

"I came in earlier today to see a friend perform at the Shakespeare Festival. He's starring in *Man of La Mancha* this evening. Since I was so close, it wasn't hard to hop in the rental and rush over."

It took less than a half hour to get from Oakley to Medford. Tim doubted she immediately rushed out.

She checked her watch. "I'll need to leave in a little while."

"Of course. We wouldn't want you to miss your 'friend.' "

Her shoulder raised in a defensive move. "This guy may be the one. Can't you be happy for me?"

"So you'd come to Oregon to see a guy, but not your family."

"Tim." Aunt Barb had just entered the room and gave him a warning look as she motioned with her eyes to Gramps. Okay, no confrontations right now. But later his mother, who frowned at his comment, would hear an earful.

She gazed at Gramps and plopped down on the bed, then swept her maroon nails through his thin white hair. "I'm so sorry I missed your birthday party, Daddy."

Tim controlled his gag reflex. What was her game?

Gramps sought Tim with his eyes. "Is this really Libby this time?"

"Yes, Gramps. It's Mom."

Pure joy beamed from his face. Tim had been wanting this moment for so long, but now that it was here, he couldn't keep the mixed emotions from overwhelming him. He left the room, bolting past his aunt.

⌘

Glenys landed in Medford. Two airplane rides in one day. Exhausted from the whirlwind she'd been caught in, she hopped into a cab and instructed the driver to take her to the Medford Medical Center, where Gramps had been last time.

Her heart thumped so hard she could barely hear, but once she arrived, she quickly found the room and entered.

Gramps turned his gaze to her, then frowned. "Libby?" He then looked at the woman sitting on the bed next to him.

Glenys stopped short when she saw her. Not because she looked out of place with her black and purple Dior dress, but because in an eerie Botox way, she had a familiar face.

Glenys peered more closely. "Aunt Barb?"

The woman regarded her as if she were a fly that had just entered the room. "She's my twin. Who are you?"

"Are you Tim's mom?" Glenys couldn't stop staring.

"Daddy, do you know this person?"

Gramps furrowed his brow as if in concentration. Clearly confused, he finally said, "I don't know."

Aunt Barb entered the room just then. "Glenys! You came."

Glenys turned and gratefully accepted the matronly hug. "You're a twin!" She waved her hands in excitement. "This reminds me of when I was an extra in a show from the science fiction channel, *Leave Me AClone*. It was horrible."

Aunt Barb chuckled and turned to the beautiful but hard-edged person guarding Gramps. "Libby, this is Glenys, Tim's friend. They met at the bird center."

Libby relaxed somewhat. "Well, if she's Timmy's friend. . ."

Glenys looked from one woman to the other. "I don't understand. If you two are twins, why does Gramps keep thinking I'm her?"

Libby bristled. "Oh please."

Aunt Barb continued to cradle Glenys's arm, offering comfort in this woman's wake. "I wondered that, too. He was never confused by me, and we're identical.

341

Maybe it wasn't the look as much as the attitude. Libby used to be a young, sparkling starlet."

"Oh, and what am I now?" Libby thrust out her chin.

"A middle-aged actress."

Libby folded her arms in a pout. "I'm not middle-aged."

"My dear, we're the same age. If it weren't for plastic surgery, you would sag in as many places as I do."

Libby huffed.

Able to breathe now that this startling revelation had come and gone, Glenys asked, "Where's Tim? He didn't know I was coming."

Aunt Barb glanced toward the door. "He's been very restless, hardly staying in this room for more than a few minutes. I imagine he's wandering around out there somewhere."

Despite the gatekeeper, Glenys approached and lifted Gramps's hand to her cheek. "I'm Glenys, remember? We've been to church together, ate some meals. I've hung out with you at the house?"

Clarity filtered into his red-rimmed eyes. "Oh. Timmy's girl."

She liked the sound of that. "I'm going to go find him, but I'll be right back. Okay?"

"Okay."

She kissed his hand and laid it back onto the sheets with care. Then, with much effort, she looked at Tim's mother. "Pleasure to meet you."

"Likewise." Tim's mom raised her nose in the air. Glenys suspected Libby didn't mean it any more than she.

Passing Aunt Barb, she reached for her hand and drew strength from her squeeze. Then she left the room in search of Tim.

Chapter 18

After leaving the hospital grounds entirely to get dinner for himself and Aunt Barb, Tim had cooled off somewhat. But he still wasn't sure he could handle his mother, regardless of the fact that he'd wanted her there. When he reentered the hospital room holding out the peace offering of a hamburger and lemon-lime soda, Aunt Barb accepted it gratefully.

"Thanks," she whispered. "The birthday cake wore off about an hour ago."

"For me, too. And I missed lunch when I picked up the osprey."

She glanced out the door, a weird grin on her face. "Did you happen to run into anybody on your way in?"

"No, why?"

"Oh, no reason. Someone was looking for you earlier, but I told them you'd be right back."

"Who?"

She waved away his question. "I'm sure it wasn't important. Let's eat this in the lounge so Dad won't want any." She darted out of the room. Perhaps the pressure of Gramps's illness was beginning to get to her.

His mom sat on the bed and had smiled at him when he came in. Guilt stabbed a bony finger into his chest. He hadn't thought to bring her anything.

"I'm sorry. Would you like me to run back out?"

She waved the offer away. "I'll be leaving soon."

He started to follow Aunt Barb out the door, but turned toward his mother. "Will you be coming back? After the play is over? How long will you be here?"

She stood and palmed his cheek and gazed into his eyes in the same way Aunt Barb always did, shocking him with the rare motherly moment. "You've grown to be an awesome person. Thank you for taking care of Gramps—my daddy." Were those genuine tears pooling in her eyes?

He noticed that she'd evaded his question, but what she did say began to heal the scar of her leaving. She'd never said thank you or acknowledged his dedication in any way.

All he could manage was a head nod. She kissed his cheek, then turned back to Gramps, who had been sleeping ever since Tim had gotten back. "He's so old."

Tim expected her to say something about her missing so much, but that never came.

She hugged herself and went back to her bedside vigil.

When Tim joined Aunt Barb in the visitors' lounge, he was shaking his head.

She raised an eyebrow, and he answered her unspoken question. "Mom is acting as if she's sorry she's been gone for so long."

Aunt Barb opened the white paper bag and drew out the burgers and fries, setting them on the white side table. "I think she is, but she doesn't know how to become a part of our lives."

Tim sat next to her and took a bite of a cold french fry but put the other half back in the paper envelope it came in. Hunger had fled, and in its stead came the same guilt that had attacked him earlier. "Do you think we've been making it hard for her to return?"

Again, the eyebrow raised as she considered his words. "Could be. Dad has always been welcoming, but you and I probably make her feel uncomfortable." She picked at the bun of her hamburger. "Maybe we should pray about how to love her instead of attacking her choices."

Tim had to let that marinate a moment. "One of the choices had been to leave her five-year-old child."

"You know," Aunt Barb continued, "Libby regretted getting pregnant when she was only eighteen, but the word *abortion* never crossed her lips. And giving you up, even for adoption, was out of the question."

"But—"

"Let me finish. I don't think anyone has ever explained this to you. Mom and Dad were supportive of her decision. She worked hard to get a performing arts degree, and by then the acting bug had bitten hard. She saw that she could do something she loved and still help support you. She sent home a portion of each paycheck for your care."

"I needed more than money, though. I needed a mom."

"I know, and if she'd been capable of those feelings, she would have stayed with you. But even she recognized that she hadn't been cut out to be a mother. The best thing she did for you was get out of the way so you could be raised properly."

Tim brooded about this information, training his eye on the pattern in the rug.

In his silence, Aunt Barb continued. "I want you to think about this," she said as she tapped the back of his hand. "She was an immature teenage mother, frightened to realize that she'd put herself in that position. The only way she could support you was to move away. She knew you were in excellent hands."

"Even so, I knew I was different growing up. On Mother's Day, I never knew what kind of card to buy. All of them gushed with sentiments like 'you were there for me' and 'my most wonderful memories were with you.' I watched my friends interact with their mothers and wanted so badly to be able to hug my mom instead of just telling her I loved her over the phone." He squeezed his fist so hard a knuckle cracked. "Being raised by two grandparents and an aunt and uncle was not the same as having a parent there."

"We did the best we could."

Tim glanced up. "I know. And I love you all for it."

She nodded, but her eyes suddenly shimmered with unshed moisture.

He suddenly felt an overwhelming love and appreciation for this woman and her own sacrifices and stood to draw her into a hug.

"You know how much I struggle with your mother, but don't be too hard on her," she said against his shoulder. "She will never be perfect. Your grandparents accepted that a long time ago. Instead they decided to concentrate their efforts into prayers for her salvation." She cleared her throat. "I think we need to do the same."

She will never be perfect. Those words jostled a recent memory. When he and Glenys went to Oakley for the play and then stopped at the alpaca ranch, the owner said something similar. *People have their faults. Only Jesus is perfect.* The woman— Hannie was it?—had done something even more horrendous than his mother. She had abandoned her child in a public park. Yet her son came to forgive her eventually.

His heart twisted at his own shortcoming. He'd always prayed that his mother would love him, want to be with him. But never had he prayed for God to help him love her, despite her actions—her imperfections.

Aunt Barb wrapped what was left of her hamburger and put it back in the bag. Then she patted his arm. "I'm going to go back to sit with Dad."

"I'll be there in a minute. I just need to be alone right now."

He leaned his elbows on his knees, his face in his palms. The room was empty now that night had fallen.

Lord, I can't forgive my mom on my own. As imperfect as she is, my shortcoming is in accepting who she is and loving her in spite of it. You have called us to love the unlovely. Help me to do that. Even if she never changes, never let me refuse to pray for her again. And remind me when needed that I'm not perfect either. I really blew it with Glenys, judging her before I got to know her. And please, give me a second chance with her. Amen.

When he looked up, feeling lighter than he had in ages, he saw a vision, an answer to his prayer. Glenys stood in the doorway, looking as though not sure if she should approach.

"Are you real?" The words were goofy, but he had to say them. The lightness from his prayer turned into giddiness from this woman's presence. He popped out of the chair and hugged her, relishing the feel of this flesh-and-blood woman after asking God for a second chance.

"I saw you and Aunt Barb in here, and I didn't want to intrude."

"I'm so glad you came." He pulled away abruptly. "What about your audition?"

With her arms still wrapped around his neck, she laughed. "I didn't stay for it. But it doesn't matter. I'm where I belong now."

"Did they have a falcon there? You didn't leave running and screaming, did you? Not after all your progress?"

Her dimple deepened, and she waved the thought away. "No. I could have handled any bird they might have thrown at me. Except a vulture." She shuddered. "I left because I have a new passion. And a new reason to live it." She pointed at his chest. "You."

He stroked her red-brown hair. "I've loved you from the moment you ran away screaming that first day."

"I know."

"You know?"

"A little bird told me." Then she whispered, "Cyrano has loose lips."

"Well, he's a fine, feathered friend."

"Good thing, too, because you weren't talking." She tilted her head, and he lowered his for her kiss. When they parted, she chuckled while nuzzling his cheek. "Who knew I'd fall for a bird guy?"

He swallowed the lump in his throat. "Who knew I'd fall for an actress?"

She narrowed her eyes. "Hmm, let's say actress on hiatus. I've put my career on hold until I figure out what I really want to do. And right now, I like performing little bird books at the center."

"Then you're here to stay?"

She nodded, and he claimed her lips once more.

Epilogue

Y ou've been here eleven months. It's time to go."

Tim's words created a sweet pain in Glenys's heart. If she could trust her sorrow-filled throat, she also felt the need to say something. "It's been life-changing getting to know you." A half-sob escaped her throat. "If it weren't for you, I'd never have gotten over my fear."

They both stood on the Cleetwood Cove dock at Crater Lake saying good-bye to Lady, the once-feared but now much-loved peregrine falcon.

Mandy and Camille, along with Ethan and a slew of people from the community, pressed in. All of them had been more than willing to brave the steep hike down to Crater Lake.

"We have to do it, Tim." Mandy placed a hand on Tim's arm. "It's always hard releasing a bird we've come to love." She glanced at Glenys. "And I know it's especially hard for you."

Yes, Lady of the Lake had frightened her. But now she stood with Lady on her fist, confident of her falconer skills.

Tim faced the crowd. "Thanks for coming everyone."

They all, about twenty-five people, whisper-clapped as they had been taught, enthusiastically showing their support for Lady, but making little noise so as not to spook her.

"You have all been important supporters for Lady's success," he continued. "From the monetary to the hands-on, it was all needed to put this magnificent creature back where she belongs."

Everyone grinned back, Ethan's smile especially broad. He had eagerly volunteered his time, taking care of Lady and learning all the ins and outs of the center. And now he wore the Shady Pine Raptor Center emblem on his shirt.

"Lady had a tough go of it. Several infections and that scare when we thought she might lose a part of her wing." Tim's voice cracked. "But through your love and prayers, she rallied. She became the star attraction at the flight enclosure as she made breakthrough after breakthrough, learning to fly again and to hunt."

Glenys remembered fighting not to scream and run as she watched the predator stalk an innocent mouse. But she had hung in there, gripping Tim's hand until he winced. That part of the process still stirred emotion, but she knew it was an important part of the raptor rehab process.

Tim glanced at her. "Ready?"

She nodded, feeling like a mother watching her daughter walk down the aisle and away from the nest. "Let's do it."

Lady of the Lake tilted her head as her sharp eyes caught every movement beyond her grasp. She had been banded so they could keep tabs on her, but other than that, she looked like the free bird God had intended when He created her.

Glenys breathed a prayer. "Lord, please keep Lady safe out there. Fly with her."

She cast her arm upward. Lady thrust her wings out and leaped, soaring overhead as if saluting with her wings one last good-bye.

Her victory screech as she disappeared across the lake and out to the island finalized not only her rehab, but Glenys's as well. Lady's freedom had become Glenys's freedom, and her heart soared with the falcon in thanks to a loving God who would not leave her, nor forsake her.

⊂⊚⊃

"I can do this." Glenys spoke to Trista on her cell phone a month after Lady of the Lake's release. She was in the car, meeting Tim at a middle school for a presentation. She had settled into her own rented home in Shady Pine, but once in a while still needed to connect with her friend. "I've spent one winter here and am looking forward to the next. This California girl is where she belongs."

In fact, Glenys had endured winter at the center surprisingly well. Despite the cold and snow, her heart warmed at working side by side with Tim.

"So, you're fitting in there. Who knew you'd become a bird person?"

"They've given me a title. I'm their first ever Production Manager. I get to work with the education department to write, direct, and usually star in plays featuring a cast of predatory birds. And Cyrano gets into the act often, hamming it up."

"I'm so happy that you're happy." Trista sighed. "Is your dad still bugging you about becoming a lawyer?"

"No, he knows that will never happen. After he visited me at Christmas, he could see my contentment. And miracle of all miracles, he got along with Tim."

"What about Tim's mom? She on board with you two as a couple?"

"She's the same. All about her career. She doesn't care who Tim dates. But she's making more of an effort to stay in touch."

"I'm sure you're praying for her."

"Every day."

"Keep the faith. If God can save me, he can save anybody."

Glenys took a moment to thank God for His faithfulness. "So, how are you?"

"I'm veh-rry happy." She dragged out *very* until she almost purred.

"I never thought I'd miss Vic. How is he doing in his new job?"

"Great. The LA Zoo is a good fit for him. He's really enjoying working in the California Condor Rescue Zone."

Glenys shuddered. Condors were too close to vultures.

"Hey, Tris, I'm looking forward to visiting next spring for the wedding. Have you decided on my maid of honor dress?"

"I'm thinking something with tons of ruffles. . .maybe orangé."

348

Glenys laughed. "I know you better than that." She remembered the sweet time when Vic and Trista both accepted Christ into their lives. They would be starting their new life with a firm foundation, and this brought tears of joy to Glenys's eyes.

The school came into view, and she pulled into the parking lot. "I'm here. Gotta go. Give Vic a hug from me, okay?"

Tim met her at his SUV, and after a quick kiss, she helped carry the birds needed for the presentation into the middle school.

She had written the near-autobiographical story "Miss Hoot Learns to Love." After donning a dowdy costume, Glenys threw herself into character for the role of Miss Hoot, a person frightened of birds until a little owl named Dunk stole her heart. Throughout the play, her costume changed from colorless to colorful with clever tricks. A gray hat turned inside out became bright yellow with a red ribbon. Her plain sweater became orange dotted with daisies in the same manner. The ankle-length skirt converted when she pulled up one corner and buttoned it to the side, revealing feminine purple petticoat ruffles. In the end, Miss Hoot's gray, fearful world became full of happy colors.

As she delivered her last line in the small assembly, thanking Dunk on his perch for helping her see that all birds have a place and need not be feared, a gray feathered flurry caught her eye. Cyrano flew in and landed on her hand.

Surprised to see him there when he wasn't in this story, she asked, "What's this?" Something shiny hung from his beak. She held out her palm, and he dropped a gold ring with a solitary diamond into it.

"*Awk.* Marry us."

On cue, Tim walked across the stage, plucked the ring from her hand, and bent on one knee. Then, holding the ring out to her, he said, "Please."

Joy like she'd never known bubbled from her like the headwaters of the Rogue River. "Yes. Of course!"

He slipped the ring onto her finger, then stood and glanced into the audience of kids where Gramps and Aunt Barb stood at the back, smiling. "She said yes!"

While the kids all groaned their corporate *E-e-e-w*, Glenys suddenly found herself swept into his hug, happy kisses preempting her breathing. Cyrano had moved to Tim's shoulder and became the official announcer.

"*Awk!* Pretty green eyes. . .dimples. . .heart-shaped freckle. . .care. . . Yes! Yes! Of course!"

Author's Note

This story was about fear. A subject I'm sure we can all identify with. Glenys had a severe case of ornithophobia, a fear of birds. It debilitated her to the point of getting in the way of her dream.

Fear comes in all degrees. I used to fear the dark when I was a child. But that fear slowly diminished over the years. Now I have no trouble walking through the house at night. However, I've developed a fear of stepping on something the cat left behind. Perhaps that fear isn't as irrational as others.

When I was researching this book, Brian, the bird handler at Cascades Raptor Center in Eugene, Oregon, showed me the Breeder Barn. I have a thing about mice. Not a "jump on the chair and scream" type of fear (well, maybe a little), but a sickening, "I remember the smell from when my house was infested that one year" type of fear. As he spoke, his words sounded as though they came from deep inside a cavern. I don't know what he told me in that cramped shed. I just knew I had to get out in the fresh air.

Do you have a fear that is ruining your life? Is it something you can face head-on as Glenys did, or is it more subtle, such as a fear of a memory—as was my mouse experience?

Whatever your fear, God wants to replace it with a "spirit of power, of love and of self-discipline" (2 Timothy 1:7). Glenys repeated to herself, "I can do everything through him who gives me strength" (Philippians 4:13). That verse may often be said in a flippant manner, but look deep into its truth. Only through Christ can you find strength. If you are fighting a fear, don't look within yourself, but look to the Lord. He is the only one who can give you the power to overcome.

A Letter to Our Readers

Dear Readers:

In order that we might better contribute to your reading enjoyment, we would appreciate you taking a few minutes to respond to the following questions. When completed, please return to the following: Fiction Editor, Barbour Publishing, Inc., P.O. Box 719, Uhrichsville, OH 44683.

1. Did you enjoy reading *Oregon Weddings* by Kathleen E. Kovach?
    ❑ Very much. I would like to see more books like this.
    ❑ Moderately—I would have enjoyed it more if _____
    _____
    _____

2. What influenced your decision to purchase this book?
    (Check those that apply.)
    ❑ Cover   ❑ Back cover copy   ❑ Title   ❑ Price
    ❑ Friends   ❑ Publicity   ❑ Other

3. Which story was your favorite?
    ❑ *God Gave the Song*   ❑ *Fine, Feathered Friend*
    ❑ *Crossroads Bay*

4. Please check your age range:
    ❑ Under 18   ❑ 18–24   ❑ 25–34
    ❑ 35–45   ❑ 46–55   ❑ Over 55

5. How many hours per week do you read? _____

Name _____

Occupation _____

Address _____

City_____ State_____ Zip_____

E-mail _____